THE TAKEN

Book 1 of The Taken Saga

AVERY BLAKE

NINIE HAMMON

STERLING & STONE

THE TAKEN

Day One

Chapter One

SAWYER MATHESON SAT in the quiet of his office while life as he had always known it came apart on the other side of his door.

He imagined he could hear the ugly growl of incipient chaos rumbling louder and louder outside the walls of the building.

He'd instructed his deputies to hold all calls, told them not to disturb him for anything less than the end of the world. He'd meant that last part as a joke, but who knew? Who knew anything anymore?

He was seated in his well-worn office chair at his desk, a tall man with broad shoulders, a rugged face with strong features that just missed handsome somehow, and gray eyes, the color of a winter sky before a snowstorm. In the right light, his hair looked red — a least a chestnut shade of brown. In the summertime, the sun bleached the red out of his hair and turned his skin a deep brown, creating a meshwork of fine white lines around his eyes when he wasn't smiling.

Shoving the flotsam and jetsam of accident reports,

incident reports, logs, time sheets and personnel evaluations off in a heap on the floor, Sawyer just sat, aware of the overloud ticking of the wall clock. He looked at his hands, turned them over, examined them. He was impressed that they were steady. His insides sure weren't. They felt like that dessert he'd begged his grandmother to make to go with the hot gingersnap cookies that scented her whole kitchen a lifetime ago. The dessert had been called Jell-O. You hit it with a fork and it vibrated, like his guts were vibrating now.

But the hands that held his phone weren't shaking. The Astral app was clearly visible and he stared at what it revealed, willing the tiny dots visible there to disappear, to vanish as instantaneously as they'd appeared. Or to break formation so it was clear they were only meteors after all and the whole world could take a deep breath, heave a global sigh of relief, laugh self-consciously and claim they never had believed it anyway.

The sheriff of McClintock County, Kentucky, believed it. He'd give his pension and his bass boat and his collection of Beatles albums — *vinyl!* — and everything else he owned for the sweet blessing of disbelief.

Not hapnin.'

What was it his brother Taylor always said? *Even a blind cave fish could see it.* Those spots Sawyer could see on his phone were—

"Alien spaceships."

He forced himself to say the words out loud to make them real.

"Aliens!"

He burped out a sound as the word left his lips, a mangled laugh or a bleat of denial. One or the other. Likely both.

The spots were an invading armada.

4

Invading?

Did anybody know that for sure?

They were definitely on their way to Earth, but *invade* had major implications of war and battle and subjugation. How did humanity know this wasn't the best thing that'd ever happened in all the long millennia of its history, that maybe the aliens were coming to bring technological advancement, spiritual enlightenment and—

"Riiiiiiight."

He said that out loud, too, but not to make it real. It just popped out, though it centered him as much as the other had. The aliens hadn't traveled untold light years across galaxies, through black holes and worm holes and whatever-other-holes to hang out with seven billion humans who were right proud of themselves, thank you very much, for reaching out into space as far as their own moon. They weren't toting a welcome basket from the Universal Brotherhood of Celestial Beings, complete with a magic decoder ring and a secret handshake.

Not likely.

Bottom line: you come this far, it's to kick ass.

That realization shooed the rest of the cobwebs out of his brain and left behind what he needed to function.

Training. Logic. Common sense.

And what those told him was nothing he wanted to hear.

What happened when the aliens actually arrived might very well be anti-climactic compared to what was going to happen in the six days the world held its breath waiting for them to show up.

What would people do in the face of an invading armada of *aliens*?

Duh. They'd panic. They'd do stupid things. If Sawyer had learned anything in his decade in law enforcement, it was that panicked people never ... *ever* made good decisions. The six days between now and when the aliens actually went boots-down ... or tentacles down or whatever down would be fueled by panic, society devolving into anarchy. The world the aliens finally landed on would not be the one that'd been humming along on autopilot this time yesterday, when the most burning question on anybody's mind was what was going to happen on the last episode of the remake of *LOST*.

In the next six days, the world would shed its very thin veneer of civilization. Sadly, he suspected it wouldn't even take the whole six days. Humanity was what it was and Sawyer had no illusions about what it was. And he had very little time between now and when it did to put a lid on his little corner of the world.

If he chose to.

And did he? He could walk away. Nowhere in the fine print of his job description did it list protecting the citizenry against invading aliens as one of his responsibilities. He could take Noah and hole up in Matheson Caverns, the cave system that had been in Sawyer's family for generations. Nobody'd ever find them in 250 miles of tunnels. Or he could ...

He took a breath, let it out slowly. Listened to the clock tick, tick, tick.

Aliens. Seriously?

Oh, who did he think he was kidding? He might not technically be *obligated* to play in these reindeer games but it was his job alright. And even if it wasn't his job ... well, it was still his job. End of discussion.

Did he actually sit up straighter in the chair? He supposed he did, probably had his "game face" on, too.

What was the game? It boiled down to the allocation of resources.

What did he have to work with and where could he position what he had that would make the biggest difference to the greatest number of people?

It was all about triage. In any disaster, you couldn't save everybody. Fact of life. You had to determine who you could reasonably rescue and concentrate on them. The rest ... well, you couldn't let that be your problem or you'd be lost before you started. He was in charge of a lifeboat and there were only so many seats on it. It wouldn't hold every one of the passengers and the entire crew of the *Titanic*. Try to load them all and the boat would sink and *everybody* would drown. But it would hold *some* and without the lifeboat, *no one would survive*.

He had to accept the limitations of the situation.

So, given the resources he had, who could he reasonably be expected to save?

And by save, he meant keep them from killing each other and protect them from whoever threatened them from the outside, and there would be dangerous outsiders — *human* outsiders. It might take a while, but they'd come. It was the nature of the beast. And the aliens, when they showed up, if they ever did actually show up in flyover country? Well, it would be what it would be. That was then. This was now.

His job now was to maintain civilization, *the rule of law* over ... whom?

McClintock County?

Again, not hapnin'.

He had to bow to the superiority of geography. The county was too big, too sprawling and isolated. He didn't have the manpower to hold it together over an area thirty-five miles wide and forty-two miles long.

He had to think smaller.

Jessup, then, a town five miles by seven miles snuggled

into a hollow offering protection on two sides. Could he police that? He could. And any county resident who wanted to move into town — they'd be welcome. Some would do that, but not many. Kentuckians were a hardy, independent lot. They'd hunker down, stay where they were, take care of their own and protect what was theirs. And rural families had the firearms to do that.

The people he could reasonably be expected to protect and defend were the four thousand residents of Jessup, Kentucky. And it wasn't like he'd decided to gather up four thousand strangers at a bus station. This was a community as close knit as steel wool where lifetimes of shared experiences had so marked people's faces Sawyer sometimes thought everybody looked like family. Civility would hold with them longer than in the world at large. Out there, anarchy's decree would reign supreme: *every man for himself!*

So ... what was item number one on his Save Jessup To-Do list?

First, he needed to secure the most vital resources, post officers at the supermarkets and filling stations before—

There was a knock on his door. Deputy Barnhouse didn't wait for Sawyer to reply, just shouted through the door.

"Sheriff, we just got a call that there's a fire at—"

Fire. Sawyer missed the location, shaken to the core as he'd been for the past three years by that single four-letter word. His hands trembled then until he grabbed hold of his emotions, walled off the tangle of grief/anger/fear working its way through his belly. Fire. Yeah, that was appropriate.

And so it begins.

"Sir, it's the Cricket Bottom Visitor's Center at Matheson Caverns."

Matheson Caverns was out in the county, not in the

8

city limits of Jessup. His brother, Taylor, was the manager of the attraction that hosted more than a hundred thousand visitors a year, and he'd seen Taylor in town only fifteen minutes ago taking the boys to school. Taylor's wife, Kelly Jo, was at work as a legal secretary. They were safe. But Noah! He'd signed a permission slip for his son to go on a field trip to Matheson Caverns with his class today ... which meant he was somewhere down in the guts of the cave by now. Safest possible place to be in a fire. Noah was not in the visitor's center. *Not.*

Sawyer picked up the receiver off his desk phone and punched one of the four pre-programmed red icons on the phone's lighted display, certain the call wouldn't go — it rang once and then he heard the voice of McClintock County Volunteer Fire Department's Chief Anderson Black.

"Yo, Sawyer, we just got a call that somebody drove a tour bus into the visitor center—"

"Send the trucks and crews, Andy. I need you here."

"What—?"

"Meet me at City Hall in ten minutes."

He ended the call, got up from his desk and walked with purpose through the office and out into the parking lot. His deputies followed him out of the building and then stood motionless, arms at their sides. Waiting.

He pointed to Joe Thurman.

"Joe, I want you to go to Castor's Supermarket. Shut it down. Lock the doors. And don't let anybody inside. Do you understand me?"

Thurman looked surprised, but replied "Yes, sir," and raced off toward his cruiser.

"Tyler, you and Hawkins do the same thing at Phillips's Foodtown, Buy Low and the Minute Mart." He turned to the remaining deputies. "Watson, get to the elementary school. Help out with traffic control. There will be a mob there. Morrison—" He looked around for Deputy Morrison.

"He's not here, sir," Betty Hawthorne, the dispatcher, said. She had come outside with the deputies and was fluttering around them. "He … he just left, said his wife and the little ones needed him."

Betty mother-henned any officer she feared might have run afoul of the sheriff. "But he just wanted to check on them, said he'd be right back. He will. You know he will. Besides, I saw Franky Hardesty heading out toward his house — driving his cruiser." Hardesty was a Jessup City Police officer, and city police cruisers were supposed to remain within the city limits of Jessup. "And—"

"Make me a list," Sawyer said. "Who's here, who's not. Call in all the off-duty."

And so it really begins.

Chapter Two

STAR COULD SMELL her next customer through the door.

The woman's cheap perfume reminded her of … something damp, like a rainy day at the petting zoo.

What was it *supposed* to smell like, Star wondered? She didn't hazard a guess, though that's how the eleven-year-old passed her time between customers — playing guessing games in her head.

Or composing nonsense rhymes — *Phoebe B. Beebee nuked her new canoe canal.*

Or making up dumb knock-knock jokes.

Knock knock.

Who's there?

Alien.

Alien who?

How many aliens do you know?

She even practiced the stupid multiplication tables Aunt Mary Ellen insisted she memorize, even though they weren't listed on Star's home school study guide.

"What if something happened and you couldn't access

the net with your binary calculator?" she'd said. "You always need a fallback."

Star didn't even know what that meant.

Twelve times twelve was the hard one. She never got that right, but she didn't let it go this time — concentrated, aware even as she did so that she was frantically doing mental acrobatics, flitting from one thing to the next in her mind like a water spider to keep herself from dwelling on the images that for weeks had been greeting her every night as soon as she closed her eyes.

The dream.

She would *not* think about the dream! Not now. It creeped her out in a way she didn't have words to describe, not that she had anyone to describe it to if she had known how. Certainly not any of her "siblings" — the four foster kids. She already creeped *them* out. She couldn't admit to being any weirder than they already thought she was. Her adopted parents had enough problems — especially Uncle Clyde. She smiled at the thought of the man who was more father to her than her own had ever been. She'd overheard him once describe her as his "regala preciosa" and Star *did* know what that meant. Precious gift.

If only Papa Eagle Feather ...

But her grandfather wasn't here. She never knew where he was or when he'd be back. Uncle Clyde had his phone number — well, not his number, but the number of somebody who lived down the road from the little house where he lived when he wasn't out ... doing whatever he did ... wherever he was. They would get a message to him if it was important. She didn't think bad dreams were important enough.

Brushing aside images of shiny silver balls hanging above the mountaintops, she pretended to have X-ray vision so she could see through the concrete block wall to the line of people waiting outside. Except there was no line now, it being a weekday and not yet so hot the tourists were looking for something to do inside where it was air conditioned.

It'd been half an hour since the two fat ladies had sat across from her, clothed in gaudy upholstery-fabric dresses. They could actually have been wearing bikinis or burkas for all Star knew, but she always drew pictures in her head of the people she met and she imagined these two in floral dresses, looking like a sofa and matching loveseat. They'd both had pudgy hands with sweaty palms, the rings on their fingers sunk in flesh as deep as that piece of barbed wire in the trunk of the tree that was twelve steps, facing the sun, from the back porch of the trailer house.

The buzzer near Star's foot vibrated, Uncle Clyde's signal that he'd reeled in the customer she'd smelled through the door, hooked out of the small stream of humanity flowing by, mostly families with kids not yet in school on their way to RetroRides — the nostalgic antique amusement park with a Ferris wheel, Tilt-a-Whirl and merry-go-round out by the petting zoo. They still had human operators, nothing computerized, no robots, used rusty chains and pulleys, manual off-on switches and machinery that made a grinding nose loud enough to drown out the digitalized calliope music blasting out the speakers.

"Some kid's gonna get killed on one of them rides," Aunt Mary Ellen predicted in dire tones at least once a week. "It's only a matter of time."

Uncle Clyde called her Chicken Little. When Star asked who that was, he just said "the sky's always falling," which made no sense at all.

Pumpkin had felt the vibration from the buzzer even more acutely than Star had, but still she gave him the "down" hand signal and the golden retriever obediently dropped to the floor in front of her and put his head on her feet. She pulled the tablecloth out over him so he couldn't be seen.

"Aw, come on, Mildred," said a man's voice just beyond the door. "It's all a con. This whole thing is. This whole *town* is. You know that well as I do."

"You think ever'body in the world's trying to get their hands in your wallet."

"Little green men painted on the walls of the bus shelters is bad enough … but did you see the Arby's sign? 'Aliens welcome.' On an Arby's sign for crying out loud!"

"I *missed* that. Why didn't you say something? I woulda took a picture."

The man made some kind of groaning sound.

"We already had this discussion, Earl. You agreed to spend—"

"To *waste*—"

"It's my vacation, too, you know."

"I'm the one operated them robots cleaning out just about every gutter in the city of St. Louis—"

"It's just one day."

"Right. One day. One *whole* day in scenic Roswell, New Mexico, a town full of wack jobs who think every funny-looking cloud is a flying—"

"We *agreed*—"

"*Fine*! Fine. Whatever you say, Mildred. Get your fortune told by alien rocks. I'll be in the car."

He must have walked away, then turned for a parting shot.

"If she can see the future, get her to tell you if them bean tacos you had for lunch are gonna give you gas tonight. If they are, I'm getting us separate rooms."

The door to Star's "seance room" opened for Earl's

wife Mildred. Uncle Clyde's boots clomped on the plank floor. Mildred's flip-flops flopped.

"This is Mildred Peabody," Uncle Clyde said, "and this here's Falling Star Yellowhorse, a full blood Mescalero Apache princess."

That statement brushed up next to the truth in a couple of places. Star was full-blood Apache, alright — at least as much as any Native American could lay claim to being "full-blood" these days. She looked it, with high cheekbones and shiny black hair parted in the middle, lying in fat braids on her shoulders. And she was the daughter of a chief, too — the fire chief of the Chaves County Volunteer Fire Department. At least he had been until he ran off with the red-haired waitress at Bob's Diner. Star had never been told that's why her father'd bailed, of course, but she had learned early on that because she was blind people tended to forget she was there. If she kept her mouth shut — what Uncle Clyde called "doing her cigar store Indian imitation" — there wasn't much people wouldn't say right there in front of her.

Nobody used her whole Indian name, including Uncle Clyde, but he said Falling Star sounded more mysterious that plain old Star.

"This child has a sight that goes beyond the view of mere human eyes." Clyde Baker's voice had the rounded, modulated tones of a juke newscaster. "She can see inside your soul. She can see what lies hidden behind the veil of tomorrow. She can tap into the power of the 'Alien stones.'"

Uncle Clyde always warmed to this part of the story, and Star had long suspected that it brushed up next to the truth in places, too. All about the alien spaceship that'd landed out in the desert, the one the government claimed didn't exist after they carted it off to study at Area 51.

"When that ship touched down it was so hot it melted the sand beneath it into glass," Uncle Clyde said. "My daddy seen it all. Then he went out there to the landing site later, after they'd hauled everything away, when wasn't nobody around, and picked up these rocks."

At which point Uncle Clyde indicated a collection of broken pieces of volcanic obsidian he'd bought at a souvenir shop at the foot of Mount St. Helens twenty years ago. They were arranged on a piece of red velvet on the table in front of Star, sparkling in the flickering light of the candles that provided the only illumination in the room.

"We didn't realize there was anything special about them rocks. We'd all picked them up and examined them, everybody in the family, strangers too, dozens of people, for years." He paused. "But then Star come along and there was something different, something special about her. She was just a little bitty thing when we adopted her—"

Not adopted. Not at first. Just foster care while her mother went through detox and her father played bump-and-tickle with everything in a skirt for fifty miles in every direction. About the time her mother'd overdosed on oxycontin, Clyde Baker had discovered that the little Indian girl had stolen his heart and he couldn't give her up like the other wards of the state he and Mary Ellen had been looking after. The adoption papers had already been filed before Uncle Clyde discovered something else about the child. She had a knack, a talent, a gift. Once he spotted it, he realized she could help out the floundering family business, and Lord knows it needed help, as one of the attractions in the collection of garish, orange, concrete-block buildings that sat beneath the last and biggest of the equally garish signs on roadsides all across New Mexico.

Along Interstate 40 on the stretch between Amarillo, Texas through Albuquerque to Flagstaff, Arizona.

Around the Mescalero Reservation Casino in Ruidoso in the Sierra Blancas.

And spaced at ten-mile intervals on US 285, hoping to seine road-weary tourists swimming north out of the nowhere-land outside Carlsbad Caverns.

The signs proclaimed in thirty-foot letters, "See the wonders of *ALIEN WORLD*!

Marvel at what the aliens left behind in the MARTIAN MUSEUM.

Find out your future in ALIEN ROCKS ASTRAL READINGS.

Keep the kids entertained at the RETRO-RIDES AMUSEMENT PARK, the LITTLE GREEN MEN MINIATURE GOLF COURSE and the ever-popular EARTH ANIMALS PETTING ZOO."

Tourists were also invited to "eat a family-style meal" at the Moon Glow Restaurant, and stock up on camping supplies, power bars and bottled water at the Greater Crater General Store.

"Falling Star musta been about three years old the first time she picked up one of these rocks out of the bowl on the coffee table."

Dramatic pause, during which Star could hear the woman breathing. Through her mouth. Clogged sinuses, maybe. No, it was something else. The smell of taco sauce mingled with the wet animal stink of the woman's perfume. Pumpkin must have smelled it, too, and he whined, a sound so soft only Star could hear him and she reached under the table and scratched him behind his ears.

"She just stood there, holding the rock, staring off into space."

Another dramatic pause.

"And this rock is the last thing her pretty brown eyes

ever seen. At that moment, Falling Star Yellowhorse *was struck blind*."

The woman gasped.

That certainly made a more entertaining story than the truth, that the closed-head injury from a car accident on the day after Halloween four years ago had taken her sight. Stoned on metha-trexadone, the designer drug that made users see the world as a series of multi-colored cartoon images — her mother had pulled out in front of an eighteen-wheeler. Star watched in horror as the big truck roared down the interstate at them, and that really had been the last sight her "pretty brown eyes" had ever seen.

Star was more fortunate than people who had been born blind, though. She could see blobs of dark, light and color, but more importantly, she remembered what things had looked like, could *picture* a cactus or an armadillo — Uncle Clyde called them rats in body armor. She could "see" in her mind — cars and people's faces, horned toads and the purple-and-yellow striped grananas that grew on the hybrid tree in the front yard. She could recall every detail of the face of her ratty old Barbie Doll, too. It couldn't even walk by itself. There was no way to program it to carry on even the simplest conversation with the other dolls. But it was precious beyond measure to Star because it had been Grandma Morning Dove's doll when she was a little girl.

Star put the doll on her pillow at bedtime, cuddled up with Pumpkin, and then drifted off to sleep to greet the comforting, familiar images that always appeared in her dreams: the red bluffs of Sedona, the boy about her age with pale blond hair and eyes a startling bright blue, and the sun-bleached skull with a spider crawling out one eye socket and a snake out the other. The skull should have been frightening, but it wasn't and she didn't know why not. The boy talked to her and she always strained to hear him but could never catch his words. Both images had appeared in the background of her dreams every night since the car accident that blinded her and killed her mother.

Until the night a month ago when her dreams had been … *hijacked.* Other images had appeared as if they'd been piped into her head from somewhere, like music so loud it drowned out every other sound. Bug-like monsters with needle teeth. Bald giants as white as chalk. Gigantic silver balls, shiny marbles hanging weightless in the sky. Star shivered at the thought of them, shook the images away and focused on Uncle Clyde's fairy tale.

"That poor little girl never seen another thing. We hauled her off to first one doctor and then another for years and they couldn't find nothing wrong with her eyes. They said that something real powerful had caused her optic nerves to shut down, like flicking off a light switch. Couldn't none of them figure out where a power like that'd come from."

He lowered his voice to a whisper.

"But *we* knew. It come from … *them.*" He likely lifted his eyes and looked knowingly at the ceiling at this point. "You ask me, I don't think they ever intended to hurt Star." *Them* and *they.* Uncle Clyde carefully avoided referring to the beings as "aliens." He'd discovered quickly that it made normal people uncomfortable, everyone except the wild-eyed loonies. The whole thing was easier for curious-but-unconvinced tourists to swallow if he didn't spell out exactly who/what he was talking about. "Wasn't their fault. That much power zapping all at once into a little bitty girl. Just … blew a fuse, like."

He usually patted Star's shoulder sympathetically at this point, but he didn't this time.

"They took her sight — accidental — but they give her back way more than they took away. From that moment on, ever time Star touched one of them rocks ... *they* talked to her. Told her things she couldn't possibly know. Showed her things *that hadn't even happened yet.* She'd get that thousand-yard stare, looked kinda like she was straining to hear something, and then her face'd light up and she'd start babbling about what she could see, when there wasn't nothing to see, except inside her head."

Uncle Clyde could have made up stories about Star's strange power in the same way he'd invented her connection to the rocks. But the truth was, he had lots of real stories to pick from. Star *did* know things she couldn't know, sometimes saw things before they happened, had been like that long before she lost her sight, before she ever touched a piece of volcanic glass from Mount St. Helens.

She was in first grade before she figured out other people couldn't do what she could do. Uncle Clyde had been the first grownup to spot the ability and he never questioned it, never tried to define or understand it. He just came up with the alien-rock cock-and-bull story to explain it and made Falling Star Yellowhorse a celebrity of sorts in Chaves County with a growing statewide reputation that drew hundreds of tourists a year to Alien World.

There was a down side to that, though. Even in a town like Roswell, whose residents had made lemonade out of its bizarre notoriety, the hustler/huckster Clyde Baker's alien-psychic Apache daughter was a bridge too far for most people. Particularly after the Easter Sunday tornado that Star "saw" during a psychic reading a week before it touched down. The SWSS (Satellite Weather Surveillance Service) showed clear skies that day, not even a thunderstorm — which the MMC (Meteorological Management Center) strictly controlled. When it got out that Star'd seen a twister in that woman's future, some folks were spooked. They knew about the little girl's "strange power." And when the skies began to darken, a few residents of the community of Slidell decided there wasn't any harm in heading down into the old storm cellars, you know, just in case.

Star should have been a hero when eighteen people climbed back up into the sunlight that afternoon to a town reduced to toothpicks. That's not what happened. More than a hundred people had been injured, maimed, crippled. Fourteen people were *killed.* Irrational as it was, their friends and family members didn't blame a malfunctioning SWSS. Somehow, it became Star's fault. That's when the mothers in the trailer park where the Bakers and their brood lived refused to allow their children to play with her anymore. The Bakers stopped going to church because when they sat down in a pew, everyone else got up and moved.

Uncle Clyde didn't tell Mildred Peabody that story, though. He picked another one, more tame. How Star had described the new manager at Hologram Theaters, down to his funny little bow tie, a week before he showed up in town. Then told how she'd seen Aunt Mary Ellen's garnet ring that'd been lost for years, said it was stuck in the baseboard behind the chifforobe and it was right where she said it'd be.

After that, he must have changed his mind and decided to go for broke.

"She seen a tornado comin' before it ever touched down and a whole bunch of people was safe in hidey holes in the ground when it hit. Town of Slidell. You can ask anybody."

Another pause, timed to sound spontaneous.

"Here I am running off at the mouth." He chuckled.

"How about I stop telling you what she seen in my life and you find out your own self what she can see in yours."

The woman giggled, nervous.

"Put your hands on the table so she can touch you. Then just sit for a bit, quiet, let her focus."

"She's not deaf, too, is she?" Mildred asked.

Star bit down hard on the inside of her cheek to keep from responding, "Why, yes, ma'am. Deaf as a fire hydrant. Didn't hear a thing you just said." But Uncle Clyde didn't get paid his twenty dollars until after the session was done.

Besides, this woman needed to know that she had bigger physical problems than taco farts. Something was wrong, *bad* wrong with her heart.

Chapter Three

THE LIMITLESS BLACK expanse of space was no darker, no emptier than the endless night of the gigantic cave deep in the guts of Joppa Ridge where the little boy sat on cold stone.

Noah Matheson liked to imagine he could hear the cave darkness, though, that it whispered to him sometimes. In reality, the twelve-year-old couldn't hear anything at all. He and the other dozen or so students seated around him were deaf.

Noah didn't need to hear to know what the man in the green guide uniform was saying. He could recite the spiel by heart. Still, he concentrated with his whole body, his bright blue eyes fixed, his blond hair, so pale it was almost white, falling unnoticed across his forehead. He wished he could hear the excitement he knew would be in Howard Thomas's voice.

Unlike some of the other guides, Thomas had never lost his sense of awe and wonder at the marvel of the caverns or his joy in sharing the dark tunnels, chambers, underground rivers, blind cave fish and bats with the visitors.

Noah had grown pretty good at reading lips in the past four years, not that lip reading was the primary focus of study at Zion Academy. Rich, famous parents from all over the world hadn't sent their children to a nowhere little town in the Kentucky mountains to learn how to "cope with their deafness." They'd sent them to learn how to *hear*, using the cutting-edge technology of the Weiss-tech implants, micro-magic devices that converted sound into brain waves in the hearer's head. The implants were only located in the ear because that was a convenient place to put them and they granted normal hearing even to those born profoundly deaf who had never heard a single sound.

Noah still relied on lip reading and sign language, however, because the implant didn't work on him. Every one of the other 120 deaf students had opened their eyes in surprise when the implant was activated, able to *hear* — some of them for the first time. Of course, what they heard was "raw sound" that their brains had to learn to interpret. That's what Zion Academy was for.

But today, all of the fifteen students on this field trip had been struck deaf again, returned to whatever level of hearing they'd had when they first stepped through Dr. Weiss's door. Signals from Dr. Weiss's lab that operated the devices wouldn't penetrate a thousand feet of solid rock.

Noah had not been born deaf so he could still remember what it was like to be able to hear. If the implant had worked, he would have required little brain retraining. When Noah spoke, which was seldom because he knew, even though he couldn't hear it, that he sounded funny, he could call on fading memories of how words sounded and how you formed them in your mouth.

The girl sitting next to Noah on the paved pathway was

restless. She kept wiggling, bumping him, making it hard for him to focus on the lips of the guide. Mandy Harrington was one of the students who had never heard before Dr. Weiss's miracle implant and she was having a hard time adjusting to the intrusiveness of sound. She turned Nicole Broadbent's face toward hers and spoke slowly, so Nicole could follow. Noah could see what she was saying, too.

"Booooooring! It's just a dirty hole in the ground. What's the big deal?"

Mandy rolled her eyes in agreement.

Boring? That proved it — girls were stupid! How on earth could this be boring? They were sitting inside one of the great wonders of the world — a cave system more than 250 miles long! Of course, the "long" part made it sound like the caverns were just one cave that stretched out from here to Tennessee or Virginia or something, when in reality the caves were more like a pile of spaghetti, six different levels of tangled tunnels all beneath the family's property that was seven miles long and eight wide on Joppa Ridge.

Oh, Matheson Caverns wasn't as big as Mammoth Cave, the national park a few miles away that was the *world's longest cave system* — with 450 miles that'd been explored and who knew how many more that hadn't. But in his heart, Noah was certain his family's caverns were even bigger, that as they continued to explore the labyrinth of tunnels, they'd map hundreds more miles of passageways. Noah's uncle Taylor, who managed the cavern family business, was convinced that the tunnels connected somewhere to Mammoth Cave, which would make the whole cave system unbelievably ginormous!

Though Noah had been in the caverns almost daily his whole life, he never tired of feeling the cool air settle around him as he walked down the long line of steps that'd been carved into the rock at the Historic Entrance, the one people had used to get into the cave for thousands of years. There were cave paintings deep inside that the archaeologist guy from the University of Kentucky said were five thousand years old.

Noah liked the smell of cool dirt mingled with other smells he couldn't identify but liked to think were exotic. Like maybe he could smell bat guano. He knew the bats weren't in the part of the cave where the guides took visitors, but still … Mostly the caverns were just dark and shadowy and mysterious beyond reason and the most special place in Noah's life.

He turned from Nicole back toward the guide, reading his lips.

"… more than a hundred thousand visitors tour the cave every year. Five generations of the Matheson family have explored and mapped and surveyed the cave, which formed inside a mesa called Joppa Ridge fifteen hundred feet above sea level. Six levels of caverns extend all the way down to the Twin Forks River, which flows through the floor of the cave thirteen hundred feet below."

Those magnificent caverns were the canvas on which Noah's whole life had been painted. They formed the backdrop of his dreams, too, along with the dark-eyed girl with long black braids. And the skull with a spider crawling out one empty eye socket and a snake out the other, which should have been creepy but wasn't. After the … bad thing … stole his hearing on the night after Halloween four years ago, the girl and the skull had hovered in the shadows of every dream, every night.

Until a month ago, that is. That's when silver balls, razor-toothed monsters and white giants had invaded his dreams and had elbowed out everything else. Now, nightmares woke him, tangled in sweaty sheets, so frightened his heart hammered in his chest. At the thought of the dreams, a sudden shiver like ice water trickled down his spine, dripping from one vertebra to the next.

Noah couldn't fathom why he'd suddenly started having the nightmares, why they were the same night after night. It was almost like they were piped into his head from somewhere ...

Dr. Weiss flipped the switch on the blinker light he carried in his pocket. The light shot out multicolored beams of bright light, almost like a supercharged prism strobing harsh shadows that were hard to miss. That's what he used to get the attention of his students since he couldn't call out to them.

The students turned to face Dr. Weiss when they saw his light. They were seated on the pathway on the rock floor in the lighted walkway that ran the length of the cavern called Broadway. Noah marveled at how his grandfather, father and uncle — or whoever it was who'd done it — had placed lighting behind rocks so you never actually saw the lights, just the glow from them that lit up the cavern walls all around. As the tour progressed, the guides stopped at mounted switches, turned off the lights in the cavern they'd just passed through and turned on the ones in the cavern ahead.

The four-mile stretch of Broadway that was shown to visitors was the main artery on Level One, with smaller tunnels branching out in tentacles from it in all directions. It wasn't the longest or the biggest or even the coolest cavern, though. There was a cavern called Wiggle Room on Level Two so broad and tall you could have played football in it and even an NFL punter couldn't have kicked a ball high enough to hit the ceiling. On Level Four, the petting zoo, at least that's what the Mathesons called it, had dozens of rock formations that looked like things, mostly animals. There was a gigantic cricket right by the cavern opening, which was why the entrance to Level Four was called Cricket Bottom. And the Twin Forks River that ran right through Level Five of the caverns had blind cave fish in it.

"Class, I want you to pay particular attention as Ranger Thomas explains how the cave was formed." He wasn't really a ranger, not like the ones who worked for the National Parks Service in Mammoth Cave, but the visitors didn't know the difference and called the green-uniformed guides rangers anyway, so everybody else did, too.

Dr. Weiss spoke slowly, signing as he spoke. He was a small, round-shouldered old man with a soft wrinkled face and wispy white hair that was always a little shaggy so it fell onto his forehead and he had to brush it away. He insisted on wearing Ben Franklin glasses, had refused to have the routine retinal surgery that would have returned his vision to normal.

Noah had never heard him speak, but he imagined his voice was soft and gentle, kind and grandfatherly.

Some of the other kids, the rich-snob kids who had grown up with everything money could buy and nothing that it couldn't, the ones who had placed themselves on some level above the rest of humanity by virtue of the size of their fathers' stock portfolios, made fun of Dr. Weiss behind his back. Called him old and senile, mimicked his slightly gimpy walk and his habit of pushing his glasses down his nose so he could look out over the top of them and fix you with a stare from eyes as clear blue as a mountain stream.

"The cave was created in limestone, a rock that dissolves readily in water," Ranger Thomas said. "That's how most caves are formed, by the dissolving action of underground water as it seeps through cracks in limestone.

Does anybody know why the water didn't just dissolve all the limestone away, why it formed caves instead?"

"There's a rock on top of it that is kinda like a lid that protects it," replied Derek Roberts, in feigned roll-your-eyes boredom. He had been profoundly deaf until the Weiss implant and Noah was sure his speech had that nasal quality common to those who had yet to master the art of sound resonance through the sinuses.

"Very good, Derek," Dr. Weiss said/signed. "Above the limestone is an impervious layer of sandstone that doesn't dissolve in water. So caves formed around where water managed to leak through the sandstone. Imagine the water dripping, drip, dripping though a crack in the sandstone, for thousands of years, slowly dissolving the limestone around the crack, making the crack bigger and bigger and bigger — an underground cavern."

Noah glanced up at the ceiling, wishing there were bats in this portion of the cave. He loved to watch the bats rush out in a flock at sunset to go hunting bugs in the nearby woods. There were so many they blackened the whole sky. He'd begged his father to let him have a bat for a pet, but his father had said his mother thought bats were nothing but rats with wings.

That had been in … Shiny.

Noah's childhood was divided into two parts, sundered from each other with the accuracy and precision of a scalpel cutting through flesh in surgery. On one side, in what he thought of as *Shiny*, was everything that had happened before his mother and sister had … died. And he'd gone deaf. *Shadow* was now, and all the time that would follow it forever until he died and went to hell.

Sometimes, he thought hell was right now, though, was every moment walking around feeling the sunshine on his face, smelling the flowers when he had taken all that away from his mother and Rosileigh—Rosie-Posie.

When he returned his eyes from the ceiling to Dr. Weiss, the old man had stopped talking, suddenly distracted by something back down the walkway. Noah turned in the direction Dr. Weiss was looking and saw a cave guide, Reece Brown, sprinting toward them. Running. In the cave! Without his hat.

The hat was the flat-brimmed kind with the pointy top that was totally dorky-looking. Noah was determined to change the hats to caps, like baseball hats, or even cowboy hats, when he grew up and took over running the family tourist business. But even if the hats were dorky, the guides were supposed to wear them all the time. Ranger Brown was shouting as he ran, clearly upset about something.

The students nearest Dr. Weiss could read the ranger's lips, and reacted to what he was shouting with a mixture of emotions that ran the gamut from fear to ridicule.

Ethan Taylor turned around and announced to the group. "… says there are aliens coming," a broad grin splitting his freckled face. "This must be some new thing in the tour program."

That couldn't be. If they'd added something to the tour, Noah would have heard about it.

Suddenly, the lights in the cavern went out, plunging the cave into an inky blackness it was impossible to imagine without experiencing it. The guide who had run toward them appeared a moment later holding up his phone flashlight, still managing to run even though he could only see an area eight or nine feet in front of him.

Nicole Broadbent reached out and touched Noah and he instantly felt her terror well up in his chest. He pushed the emotion away and ignored it, as he'd ignored the ache of sadness he'd felt when the school nurse patted his shoulder this morning, and he *knew* she'd had a miscarriage, though he didn't know what a miscarriage was. And the bus driver's hand-up that had shown Noah the man was scared some spots he'd found on his arm meant he had a bad disease. Over time, Noah had taught himself how to wall off the emotions of other people he felt sometimes when he touched them, mostly managed to pretend it wasn't happening.

The sprinting guide reached them and stopped in front of Dr. Weiss and the other guide, too winded to speak. When he caught his breath, he began talking fast. Noah could tell because he was gesturing with the hand holding the light of his flashlight and it cast dancing shadows on the cave walls and roof. But with no light on his face, Noah had no idea what he was saying.

Dr. Weiss produced his cell phone then, as did the other guide. Every kid on the trip could have pulled out theirs, too, if they had not been required to leave "all electronic devices" in lockers at the visitor's center before they entered the cave.

Even with the lights of the three men bouncing around as they spoke, there was enough light for Noah to see Reece Brown's face and catch most of what he was saying.

"… can see them, right there on the Astral app."

Noah had an Astral app on his phone, almost everybody had one. The website selling it crashed from the volume of traffic when they first released it because it was so popular. Noah loved his, looked at it all the time.

The Astral app showed the view from high-resolution telescopes on the far side of the moon — black space, in real time. It captured meteors crashing into the moon's surface and sunspots and all sorts of other cool stuff.

"… true! On the news."

Ranger Thomas, whose face wasn't lit, must have asked a question.

"Because they're in formation," Ranger Brown said. "Meteors don't travel in precise rows. It's not a meteor shower. It's an armada."

Noah wasn't precisely sure what an armada was but he thought it was a bunch of ships in the ocean, which made no sense at all.

The lights flickered once and then came back on. The news that had come in the darkness had been something staggering. The guide who'd been conducting their tour stood rooted to the spot. Dr. Weiss looked surprised and something else … frightened. Dr. Weiss was scared.

Sophie Sunderland, whose mother was a senator from Vermont, turned to Gretchen Hampton and Astrid Kirkpatrick. Astrid's father owned a shipping company — he'd know about armadas. She looked too shocked or frightened to form words.

He signed to her, asked what was going on. Noah read Gretchen's lips. Her eyes were huge and rimmed with tears.

"Aliens are coming!" she said. "In spaceships. On the Astral app, you can see them, little white dots that just appeared out of nowhere. Not there and then there. Near Jupiter. A whole fleet of them."

Noah's first reaction was to laugh. Spaceships with aliens. Riiiiiight. But from the reactions of Dr. Weiss and the rangers it was clear that this was no joke.

Then Gretchen signed to him, "They'll reach Earth in six days."

"And then what?" he signed back but she just stared at him.

He turned back toward Dr. Weiss, in a gesticulating conversation with the two rangers. All Noah caught was:

"… can't go out by the visitor's center. It's on fire. That's why the electricity—"

On fire? How could …?

"… the children out of here!"

The lights went back out, plunging the cave into the darkness that was its natural state. This time, they didn't come back on.

… *out of here* …

Noah knew exactly where they were, could picture the spaghetti-like map of passages in his mind. They had entered the cave through the Cricket Bottom entrance, which opened into Level Four about two hundred feet above the river. A second visitor's center had been built there years ago in addition to the one beside the Historic Entrance on Joppa Ridge because what the weird rock formations the tourists wanted to see — the petting zoo — was on Level Four.

The students had spent the whole morning winding their way up through the caverns to Level One at the top of fifteen-hundred-foot Joppa Ridge. Even if they went for the *nearest* "out," didn't stay on the tour route but cut through connecting passages and left through the Historic Entrance, that was still at least three miles away. Miles of shadowed passages, narrow canyons, steep underground hills and bottomless cracks in the cave floor. Even to Noah, the caverns would be creepy, maybe even … *scary* … in the dark.

Chapter Four

NOTHING SCARED A SHARK.

That's why the big kid wasn't concerned, or was strutting around acting like he wasn't.

"They gonna try to scare the shit out of us, but I am Tiburón" — Spanish for shark — "and sharks fear náda."

This particular land shark stood six-five, had full-sleeve tattoos and wore the Bloods colors. He'd been raising hell from the beginning, swaggering around the holding cell and then the Corrections Department transport van, chest out, daring anybody to cross him.

In reality, he was Júan Cervantes, a drug-dealer wannabe who'd murdered his step-father when he was nine and harbored a psychotic fear of rats. Paco knew that about him, like he knew the pimply-faced white kid had crabs and the fat van driver was cheating on his wife. Paco could "push" people like that, too, some of them. He could get inside their heads, get them to do what he wanted or see things his way, though he seldom did because sometimes it gave him a headache.

Grandma Rosa had pointed out guys like Tiburón to

Paco almost every day when he was a little boy as she'd walked him, his personal old-lady guard dog, through his east Los Angeles neighborhood — stepping over needles on the sidewalk and around prostitutes on the street corners — to the St. Francis of the Fields Catholic School.

"With those híjos, is no *there* there," she'd said. "Comprendes? All icing and no cake, those ones are. You be better than that, Paquito."

She'd told him that there was strength in silence, that he should keep his mouth shut.

And she'd warned him — "tenga cuidado" — to be careful not to let the devil know what he was thinking.

It seemed that God could listen in on your thoughts but Satan couldn't. Which made no sense because the voice in Paco's head sure as shit wasn't God! The nuns at St. Francis had provided Paco a clear understanding of the three fundamentals of the Christian faith: right, wrong and guilt. Along the way, he'd figured out for himself that the devil was a whole lot more interested in what he was thinking than God ever seemed to be.

He never told Grandma Rosa that, of course. There was a lot he never told Grandma Rosa. If he had, she'd have shipped him off to some program like this a long time ago.

Paco had gotten a look at the Scared Straight permission form she'd signed as the "legal guardian of Ricardo Luís Sálazar, a sixteen-year-old minor." Which he wasn't. "Through prison tours, youth get to observe the consequences of criminal behavior and the harsh realities of life in prison. Presentations by inmates rely on intimidation, fear, and hostility, and use a confrontational approach to describe the detrimental and destructive effects of committing crimes."

Then there'd been boxes to check indicating the level

of "physical contact" she'd allow, and of course she'd checked every damn box!

All the way from handcuffing him to throwing him into a cell with real inmates and letting them have at him "in a limited fashion."

Right. Limited fashion. What the fuck did *that* mean?

She'd given them permission to do a "cavity search," hose him down, dress him in prison orange and lock him up overnight.

A disclaimer at the bottom assured her that he would be in no real danger, that minimum, medium and maximum security prisoners were rigidly segregated, with the maximum security prisoners locked safely away in Cell Block C. He'd only encounter minimum security inmates who'd earned the right to be there through good behavior.

Ricardo Sálazar, Paco to his friends — though he'd only ever had one of those — was the youngest of the boys hauled off to prison on that morning in mid-May to get "scared straight." Not yet sixteen, he looked fourteen but had become a man the summer he turned twelve. On the night after Halloween four years ago, he had been hurled out of childhood, forever different. Hardened. He had evidence of that change. Scars all the way from his chin to his navel would testify to it, as would the "watchers," a blond boy and a little girl in braids who'd hovered in the background of his every dream since that night. He had become so used to their presence that he somehow saw them as friends. Until a few weeks ago, that is, when silver balls, razor-toothed monsters and white giants began to appear to him as soon as he closed his eyes. He never spoke of them, of course, refused to admit even to himself how much the images frightened him.

Paco was handsome, with almost movie-star good

looks, black hair and eyes so dark they looked black, too. There was a coldness in those eyes, though, a *knowing* that put people off, so they edged away from him, their smiles of greeting draining off their lips.

Smarter than most people, Paco "got there" faster than others, was always calculating his moves — like playing chess, he supposed. He'd never had any use for the Anglo game, but he understood the principle that the way to win was to stay two or three moves ahead, with a goal in mind and a plan to get there. He had both of those for his life, had already ditched his accent and was shedding his Latino culture like a snake wriggling out of its skin.

When he "played chess" with his current situation, he calculated what he had to do to survive — keep his head down, his eyes averted and his mouth shut! He hadn't yet laid down a sheath of muscles around his slender frame, which left him half the size of some of the other boys. In fact, at three months shy of sixteen, he was technically too young for Scared Straight, but they'd made an exception in his case. The court had hoped to nip his criminal career in the bud by adding him to the list of juveniles from all over the state who'd been sentenced to the program for their "petty crimes." Petty crimes were all Paco had been busted for, all they'd caught him doing. What he'd gotten away with — the things he had done in the dark when nobody was around — those had required some stones.

While Tiburón had been strutting his stuff, Paco had been weighing the odds of escaping, blowing this pop stand and leaving the others to take the fall for it. He'd seen cracks he might slip through when the van returned them to the city jail from their overnighter at Radcliffe Correctional Facility, out in the middle of nowhere a mile beyond the little town of Clarksburg.

If he nudged a couple of "pawns" into place, he wouldn't be serving the remainder of his four-month juvie-jail sentence. Still, he had to negotiate the next twenty-four hours in custody *unharmed*, and the best way to do that was to fade into the paint on the wall, there but not there, so nondescript and unremarkable the eye flitted over him and came to rest on something more interesting and colorful. He could make that happen, knew how to *push* others so they didn't notice him.

There were no windows in the van but Paco had seen pictures of the prison, gray stone buildings, stone walls, razor wire, guard towers, attack dogs. It wasn't the largest prison in the California Department of Corrections system, but there were more riots here, more guards injured, more inmate deaths. It was designed for 750 medium to maximum security inmates, but it had been jammed full of more than a thousand. It was by reputation the state's worst hell-hole, which, of course, was the reason it'd been selected for the Scared Straight Program.

Paco and the others were unloaded in a stone court-yard, then ushered into a holding cell, a birdcage, all bars. The van guards handed off paperwork to the prison guards, then the fat one who was having an affair — what woman would willingly fuck *him*? — smiled a crooked-tooth smile.

"You boys have fun now, hear," he said. "When I come get you tomorrow, you ain't gonna have no piss and vinegar left."

The prison guard who'd taken the paperwork spoke into some kind of intercom and two guards showed up, along with three sumo-wrestler inmates — a white guy, a black guy and a Latino, each one bigger and meaner-looking than the last. The five of them escorted the teenagers down hallways, through locked doors and past guard stations to a big room that smelled of disinfectant and bleach. There were piles of towels and sheets on shelves and dozens of different orange prison jumpsuits hanging on bars beneath designations — Small, Medium, Large, 1X, 2X, 3X, 4X, even 5X — which even on a hanger looked big enough to house a family of illegals.

"Strip!" said one of the guards, a short Asian man. "Buck naked."

Paco watched to make sure he wasn't the first to reach up and start unbuttoning his shirt — not too eager, but neither did he hesitate — no reluctance that could be construed as disrespectful. He watched the eyes of the inmates crawl over the boys as they took off their clothes, saw the hunger there and felt a cold dread settle in his belly. He was way too good-looking for this situation, too slender. His black hair fell in his eyes, and constantly brushing it off his brow could be interpreted as a come-on gesture. Most damning of all was the fact that the other boys strutted carpets of coarse chest hair, except the fat white kid who looked like a beached whale. Tiburón's whole body was as hairy as an ape. Paco's back and buttocks were covered in a light down of soft black hair, broken only by the bristly mat of pubic hair on his crotch. His chest was totally hairless, though, covered with a gigantic tattoo — a skull, with a spider crawling out one eye socket and a snake out the other.

Instructed to fold their clothes and put them on a shelf, the boys were to select a jumpsuit they thought would fit, then line up on the side of the room where the overflow of towels and other linens were in chest-high stacks on the floor.

Then it started.

"Fold your hands in front of you over your junk," yelled the biggest convict, a black man who had to have played professional football — arms the size of sides of beef, legs like tree trunks. The other inmates called him Spade. "Hold hands witch yo'self and don't you let go for no reason, you hear me."

The two guards who had accompanied them from the holding cell opened big double doors on the opposite wall that lead to a hallway. On the other side of the hallway was a birdcage like the one they'd been in when they arrived. This one was filled with inmates, who immediately rushed the bars on the hallway side and began to yell and taunt.

The guards leaned casually up against the wall by the door to watch the show. The three inmates started down the line, gratefully at the other end, going from one boy to the next, yelling in their faces, shoving them, baiting them.

Standing in front of the fat white kid with blond hair and a face full of pimples, a white inmate with a nightstick got nose to nose with him, slapping the nightstick rhythmically into his palm as he spoke.

"You gonna get 'xactly what you asking for. Whatever you're afraid's gonna happen to you, we're gonna oblige. You scared now, huh?"

Then all three inmates lunged at the boy at the same time, their faces inches from his, all yelling.

"You want to cry?"

"You want your mommy? Want your teddy bear?"

"Suck your thumb, do you, need your blankie?"

The prisoners in the birdcage across the hallway were shouting, too.

"He mine. Look at them pretty brown eyes, just look at them pretty brown eyes."

"No sir, I get him first. I'll break him in for you."

Another inmate mediated. "First night he stays w'chew, next night he stays w'chew, next night—"

"He won't be able to walk after he stays with me!"

The group roared with laughter.

Paco was one from the end, with a trembling Latino kid on his left and Tiburón on his right. Suddenly, Tiburón turned and darted behind a pile of stacked towels and Paco heard a sound he couldn't place at first. A squirting, splattering sound that — then the stench hit him and he knew. Well, how about that. For all his tough-guy attitude, Tiburón was so scared he'd gotten the shits.

Before anybody noticed he was gone, Tiburón stepped back into place, daring Paco with his eyes to say a word.

The inmates came down the line, screaming obscenities, poking and prodding the boys.

"Nobody told you to take your hands off your junk," said Spade and he grabbed the offending boy and literally threw him across the room, where he crashed into the wall and slid down it to the floor. Then all three of the inmates were on him, yanking him to his feet, shoving him back against the wall. The inmate with the nightstick using it like a cattle prod.

When they got to the terrified Latino kid on Paco's left, the big inmate started his routine. Then he paused.

"You smell somethin'?" he asked. The two other inmates shrugged. "I do. I smell shit. Where is it?" He looked around, then followed his nose to the back side of the stack of towels and returned like a charging rhino.

"One of you so scared you shit your pants!" he bellowed. "I bet you wet the bed, too. Who is it? Which one of you did this?"

No one moved. Paco concentrated on keeping his eyes forward, unfocused, not making eye contact with anybody.

When no one responded, the white inmate stepped

forward, slamming his nightstick into his palm to punctuate every word.

"If you done this, you better own it," he said. "I ain't cleaning up that mess. If don't nobody admit they done it, I'm gonna take all of you, one at a time, and make you lick it off the floor."

Chapter Five

DR. WEISS GOT the ranger to hold his cell phone light on him so the students could see. Then he spoke and signed at the same time.

"We're going to have to leave the cave now and I don't know if the lights will come back on or not."

Someone asked a question.

"We'll save talking about the aliens until we get on the bus, right now—"

Someone else must have interrupted him.

"I don't know," he said. "We'll be leaving through a different entrance than the Cricket Bottom entrance where we came in, so we won't be going back past the lockers."

That must have ignited a storm of protest.

"Hold it down, I know you need your belongings, and we will get them. Right now, I need you to listen to me and do exactly as I tell you."

Dr. Weiss turned on his flashing colored lights. Noah watched the colors splash on the brown cave walls, red, then blue, then green, creating harsh shadows like a strobe light.

Dr. Weiss signed that each child was to take the hand of the one next to him. Well, Noah was *not* going to hold hands with Astrid Kirkpatrick! It would take more than an alien invasion to get him to do *that*. He scooted over next to Derek and took his hand on the left, then took Kareem Jabari's hand on his right.

"Does everyone have hold of someone's hand? On both sides? The ranger will be at the end of the line and he'll take Jonathan's hand."

If they'd been anywhere else but the cave, there would have been conversations going on all around Noah that he could see. But now, the other students were as deaf as he was, sealed in a silent bubble, in the dark — literally — with no idea what was going on.

Dr. Weiss had come back down the line of children and hugged some of the girls, who were crying. Noah wouldn't have cried even if he'd felt like it, which he didn't. He didn't know how he felt, as a matter of fact. He certainly wasn't frightened by being in the cave in the dark. He *liked* that part of it, liked the shadows the lights cast on the rocks, liked how the darkness rushed in to take the light's place when the ranger turned the flashlight on his phone in another direction.

It occurred to Noah to wonder why neither of the guides had flashlights. There was a loop on the uniform pants for flashlights. They were standard equipment, like Noah's father carried both his service revolver and another gun strapped to his ankle.

Thinking of his father put a feeling in Noah's stomach he couldn't define. It seemed to be equal parts fear and longing. He suddenly wanted so badly for his father to be here beside him. He had gone on so many trips into the cave with his father and uncle, places not on any tour. Their house had been on Joppa Ridge, so close to the cave that when the days grew long in the summer, they'd come after his father got home from work, getting in a few hours of exploring before dinner.

Noah's father was the McClintock County sheriff and got to set his own hours, which didn't mean he worked less than his deputies, it meant he worked more.

But after …

In After, his father had tried to be home more. Not *home*, but the rental house they moved into where everything was either new or borrowed or somebody's cast-off junk and nothing looked familiar and Noah hated every inch of it. Were it not for having to live in the rental, he might have been reluctant to move into the dormitory at Zion Academy. He might have been homesick, wanted his …

But there was nothing to be homesick for and living at the academy meant he didn't have to put up with Mrs. Bailey, who looked after him after school until his father came home. Mrs. Bailey couldn't sign and though his father had explained it to her over and over, Noah could tell she still thought if she just talked loud enough, he could hear her.

He was at the academy as a "scholarship student." That was code for poor kid who could never in a million years have afforded the tuition. He wasn't the only scholarship student, but he was the only one who actually lived in McClintock County. The rental house was in town, Jessup, not out in the country near the cave so they almost never went there anymore.

After he moved into the dormitory, his father came by to hang out with him every day, sometimes twice, and had dinner with him almost every night. The other kids were impressed with his badge and gun, the younger ones anyway. The teenagers weren't impressed with anything

45

except a new Porsche or vacationing in Montenegro — and Noah didn't even know where that was.

Thinking of his father upset him because he knew his father would be worried about him. And he *never* wanted to cause his father emotional pain. He would do anything not to, because, of course, he had been the source of the greatest pain in his father's …

He didn't go there, concentrated on trying to see the shadowy figure of Dr. Weiss, signing instructions to the students.

Ethan Taylor let go his hold on Kareem's other hand and signed to them both, his movements barely visible in the pale ambient light. "You think maybe the aliens will just pass by the Earth, not even stop?"

Kareem signed back, "You think they came all the way across the universe to wave at us?"

Then Dr. Weiss's attention light flashed again. He and Ranger Thomas had gotten into a rhythm, and the ranger knew to light him up when he used that light so the students could see what he was signing. Ranger Brown had taken up a position at the rear of the line of students.

It was amazing how little light the flashlight on a cell phone actually put out, gobbled up as it was by the black hole of cave darkness. Noah had trouble seeing Dr. Weiss's hands well enough to know what he was saying and he couldn't see his face and lips at all.

It was something like, "Stay together" and "go slowly in the dark" and "take a long time."

How long would they be able to use the flashlights on their cell phones before they ran out of charge? Then what? It would be a long way to go in absolute darkness. And absolute silence. Noah felt the first little tingle of fear deep in his belly.

Chapter Six

THE LIGHT from the flashlight on Dr. Weiss's cell phone reached out into the cave darkness and broke like foaming surf over the rocks. In the shifting shadows cast on the cave walls, Dr. David Weiss fancied he could see the walls of Masada.

The ancient fortress. Stark. Bare.

He had to concentrate on the path before him, not lit up by lights strategically placed behind rock formations all around the cave as it had been when he led the children into the cave hours ago, before a tour bus slammed into the Cricket Bottom Visitor's Center and exploded. The ranger had whispered that information to Dr. Weiss so as not to upset the children. They wouldn't be going back there to get their phones and whatever else they'd left in the lockers because the visitor's center was in flames.

A tour bus!

The ranger had said the driver lost control when he swerved to miss the cars pulling frantically out of the lot, families who'd just heard the news of the—

Alien invasion.

A first, he couldn't make himself believe it. There had to be some colossal mistake, some miscalculation … dust particles on the lens of the telescope — *something*. Had to be.

But the reality slowly began to sink in, like cold water going down through him.

They were coming.

They *who*?

Aliens.

Aliens were coming!

His heart began to pound, each beat throbbing his vision, pulsing in the illumination from his cell phone flashlight — a pitiful, paltry glow, no match for the massive blackness of Matheson Caverns.

Just like the Jewish resistance fighters had been no match for the Romans.

Dr. Weiss looked out over his glasses at the pathway trying to shake the images out of his head, that out there in the darkness loomed the rock stronghold called Masada.

The ancient fortress had hijacked his thoughts the moment it became clear that the world had only six days until the invading armada of aliens arrived. The world would watch as they got closer and closer, day by day. There was nowhere to run, nowhere to hide. The humans would be no match for alien beings capable of the technology that allowed intergalactic flight, could never stand up against the might the aliens could bring to bear on this tiny green planet. Just like the Jews had watched the Roman soldiers, day after day, building a ramp up to the fortress door. Knowing that when the ramp was complete …

Masada.

David's father, Jakob Weiss, had been smuggled out of the Warsaw ghetto in a laundry basket as an infant after the Nazis marched on Poland in 1939. Both Jakob's parents were Jewish resistance fighters who died heroically in the ghetto, where Jews armed themselves and fought back, holding out against the German army longer than the entire country of Poland. Jakob grew up in Israel, ran a tourism business, and his only child, his son, David, often accompanied him with the busloads of tourists shepherded around the country to Israel's most famous historic sites. Little David's favorite place of them all was Masada, the stone fortress in the Judean desert overlooking the Dead Sea where the Sicarii, a sect of Jewish rebels, fighting the Roman occupation had made their last stand.

The mighty rock stronghold, built on a mountain precipice, was invincible, unreachable, unassailable. But in 73 BC, the Roman governor of Judaea, Lucius Flavius Silva, headed the Roman legion and laid siege to Masada, surrounded the fortress. And then the Romans, fifteen thousand strong, built a ramp, 375 feet tall against the western face of the plateau. A giant siege tower with a battering ram was constructed and moved laboriously up the completed ramp. And all the while the 960 Jews, men, women and children in Masada watched them coming. Day after day, closer and closer.

As the world now watched the approaching alien armada.

The ranger who walked in front of Dr. Weiss was agitated, anxious. Kept wanting to hurry the children along. But the class was moving as fast as they could. They had to take care to ensure there were no obstacles in the children's path because there was no way to shout out to them to look out.

"It will take hours at this rate to get out of here," the ranger said.

"You got an appointment, a date with some hottie, maybe?" Dr. Weiss asked.

"I got a *family*, a wife and three kids sitting alone in a house on a hillside. They need me."

"These children need you, too. They're your responsibility. I fear it won't be long before people start shirking their responsibilities, abandoning their jobs, dismissing such un-useful concepts as duty and honor. But not quite yet, I don't think — do you?"

"I'm not going to bail on you, if that's what you're thinking. But I got to get home, same as everybody else, got to take care of my family." He paused as reality reared its head in his mind. "How do I do that now? I just became unemployed."

The man was right, of course. It didn't seem likely there would be tourists lined up tomorrow to tour a natural wonder of the world when the greatest wonder the world had ever seen was out there just six — no, tomorrow it would be five. Five days away.

Now that the man had started talking, he poured his thoughts and fears out into the darkness to the old man in front with a cell phone lighting their way. The deaf children couldn't hear a word.

"I mean, will the electricity go off? It will, won't it? The power grids will go down, whatever the hell a power grid is." He stopped, started to apologize for cursing in front of the children and then realized they hadn't heard him. "Without electricity—"

Dr. Weiss had stopped listening as a new horror of realization settled on him. Between now and when the ships arrived, the world would be in such turmoil there was no way to predict what would and wouldn't continue to function. And after the ships arrived... Well, there might not *be* an after. The world might be living through its last six days of existence. But if there was an "after" it would be a very different world.

And in that *very different world*, what would happen to the communications satellites? Would they remain aloft and functioning? Because if they didn't, thousands of people all over the world, and 120 children right here at Zion Academy, would plunge back into a world of total silence.

Chapter Seven

STAR REACHED out and took the hands of the woman seated across from her. She was wearing red, Star could tell that much. She could see blobs of light, too blurry to see any detail, but she could sometimes see bright colors if they were close.

The woman's hands were cool, her fingers long and boney, like the wings of a baby bird. Mildred must have been as skinny as a string bean. Star struggled to get past the rancid perfume smell, had to concentrate, focus on sensing something from the woman with bird-wing hands.

Star had no idea how she could know the things she knew, what exactly the process was. All Star knew was that when she touched other people, images about them appeared in her mind. It happened whenever she touched anybody, but she had taught herself long ago to ignore the images unless she decided to attend to them, concentrated, cleared her mind of extraneous thoughts.

Very often they were images of something that hadn't happened yet, a "vision of the future." But not always. Sometimes it was an image from the past. Sometimes the images were what the person was thinking about at the time. Or what they were trying *not* to think about. Maybe it was something they didn't even remember.

She knew that her last two customers had been to the Grand Canyon before they got to Roswell. Images from it flooded their minds. She also knew that the big one had a little white dog, one of those yappy dogs that never stopped barking. She'd named the dog Salt because she already had another dog named Pepper who had died. But there was no image of Pepper along with the image of Salt in her mind ... maybe because it was too painful to remember.

Sometimes Star thought of her gift as a drain pipe.

A drain pipe didn't get to pick what flowed through it. It was just a conduit. That's the way images came to Star. It wasn't like she got to decide what to see about a person, like she could concentrate and see the house the person lived in or the car they drove. She touched a person, and random images appeared in her head. She had to examine the images like photographs and try to figure out what they might mean.

Didn't do any good for a girl to ask her, "Is Joe going to propose?" Star might see the image of a wedding when she touched the girl, but it could be that the girl had been the maid of honor in her sister's wedding last week. Or maybe she was sitting in the back row of a church a year from now crying as Joe married somebody else.

She couldn't have explained to anybody how she knew this woman had something really bad wrong with her heart. It just came to her, flowed down through her pipe. Along with other images. A big punchbowl with little gobs of sherbet floating round. A banquet maybe? She could see a boy, the woman's grandson whom she loved way more than her husband thought she should. The woman sent the boy gifts and called him every day while her Earl was at work.

"Your name is Mildred, right?"

"Yes, oh, my goodness it is, it's Mildred!" She giggled with excitement as if Star had performed some incomprehensible psychic magic trick. Uncle Clyde had introduced her, for crying out loud.

"Mildred, I see a curly-haired little boy with big brown eyes playing with something, it looks like a juke of some kind."

"Yes." She squealed. "That's Danny. I got him a kiddie juke and sent it to him last week." She leaned over and said conspiratorially, "Earl don't know I did it, though."

As if on cue, someone burst through the door and the woman said, "Earl, what are you doing—?"

He didn't let her finish.

"Gimme your phone! Where is it?"

"In my purse. You got your own phone."

"Let me see it."

"What for?"

"'Cause you got one of them apps … never mind, just give me the phone."

Star heard the woman dig around in her purse and then there was silence.

"It's true," Earl said. He wasn't excited or upset, said it almost like he was speaking from a dream, a sleepwalker.

"What's true?" Mildred asked. Either Earl gave her the phone or she snatched it out of his hand.

"What is this? What are these little dots?"

"Aliens."

Mildred burst out laughing, but her laughter trailed off when nobody joined her.

"What are you talking about?" That was Uncle Clyde.

"You got a Astral app on your phone?" Earl asked.

"Uh huh."

"Well, look at it."

Silence, then, "Yeah, I see little spots. What—"

"They said on the news in my Vellum that it's an armada. The dots are spaceships."

"That's ridiculous," said Uncle Clyde, a man who made his living trying to convince people that aliens weren't ridiculous at all.

"It's all over the news, the *only thing on the news*. CNN, NBC, FOX — all of them. Go watch yourself if you don't believe me. This ain't no joke." The man must have gestured at Uncle Clyde's phone. "Look at 'em. Them neat rows. Couldn't be no meteors because they don't line up like blackbirds on a clothesline."

"Are you saying …?" Mildred's voice was high-pitched, rising at the end.

"I'm saying, well not me, all the newscasters, too. There are spaceships, out by Jupiter. A whole fleet of them and they're headed this way. I bet the government woulda hushed it up if people couldn't see them for themselves on their own phones."

"What are we going to … Earl?" Her voice had gotten squeaker, and it was shaking.

"How would I know," he snapped. "But we got less than a week to figure it out. They said them ships'd be here in six days."

Mildred didn't say another word, she just crashed down on the table and almost landed in Star's lap.

"Mildred, what the—?"

Star was tangled up with the woman and poor Pumpkin had almost gotten squashed by the collapsing table.

There was pandemonium then. Someone, Uncle Clyde probably, pulled the woman off Star and must have laid her out on the floor. Earl was calling out, "Mildred. Mildred. Open your eyes, look at me."

"She's had a heart attack," Star said.

"There ain't nothing wrong with her heart. How would you know a thing like that?"

"Listen, you need to believe Star. If she says this woman's had a heart attack—"

"Her heart's fine."

Star heard the sound of a slap, and not a gentle one.

"Mildred, wake up."

Now Earl's voice rose in volume.

"Do you hear me? Mildred. *Mildred*!"

"I'm calling 911," Uncle Clyde said as the man kept calling his wife's name, his voice changing, shifting from irritated through concerned all the way to frantic and near desperate.

"She ain't breathing!" He suddenly cried. "Oh my god, she ain't breathing." Now Earl was near hysteria. "Do you know CPR?"

"No." A pause, then, "Nobody's answering 911. It just rings and rings. How can there be nobody home at 911?"

"Somebody's got to know CPR! Is there somebody here—?"

"Nobody who works here, not that I know of. But the ambulance will ... I'll keep trying 911."

"We can't wait for no ambulance. We got to do CPR *now*!"

The man must have jumped up because Star heard the door open and Earl's voice calling to the people outside.

"Anybody know CPR? Please, help. Somebody ... please!"

Now that the door was open, Star could hear the crowd sound, the murmuring of voices. It sounded like all the people at the various attractions in Alien World — the petting zoo, the amusement park, miniature golf, restaurant, the general store — were rushing past her door at the same time. Were … *leaving*.

Were they leaving because they'd heard, too? Or looked at their Astral apps?

Could it possibly be … *true*?

"I'm a paramedic," said a man's voice outside the door and there was scuffling feet as he came in and must have knelt beside Mildred. It was a small room. Star had merely scooted on her butt with Pumpkin to the corner of the room to get out of the way when the woman fell, taking out the table. Star didn't know where the table was. But with Uncle Clyde, who was a big man, Earl, the stranger, and a woman sprawled out on the floor, Star supposed somebody — probably Uncle Clyde — had stepped outside and was standing in the open doorway.

"Tilt her head back," said the man's voice. It was deep and gravelly. "I'm going to do four compressions, then you breathe into her mouth. Keep her head tilted back and pinch her nose shut. Then I'll do four more."

Star heard the man counting, grunting with each count.

"One. Two. Three. Four. Now a breath," he said.

There was silence as Earl did his part, then the man started again.

"One. Two. Three. Four."

And so it went, for how long Star couldn't tell. It seemed like hours but it might only have been minutes. Time had unhooked, wasn't pulling the world along with it at a speed you could sense. Huddled in the corner, forgotten, Star had time to think about what Earl had said.

Aliens. Aliens? Seriously? That was absurd.

But Earl didn't think it was absurd. And after Uncle Clyde looked at the app, he hadn't thought it was absurd, either. And the people rushing by outside. She could sense them, sense the fear and confusion wafting up off them like heat off the pot-bellied stove Papa Eagle Feather used to heat his cabin.

"Six days," Uncle Clyde said from the doorway. "The ships, they'll be here in six days."

"How could they know a thing like that?" the gravel-voiced man said between counts and grunts.

"One." Grunt. "Musta calculated their speed … two …" Grunt. "Three." Grunt.

"Mildred." Earl's voice didn't sound hysterical anymore. It was plaintive. Pleading. "Mildred, wake up, please, wake up."

Aliens on Earth in six days. Star couldn't get her mind around that at all but she was sure nobody else could either. Why had they come? Were they the same ones that had come …? If there really had been aliens here before and she had never believed that. Until now.

Pumpkin whimpered and Star realized she'd been squeezing him to her chest so hard he couldn't breathe.

"Three." Grunt. "Four."

Then the man stopped counting.

"Why are you stopping? She's still not breathing."

"I'm sorry, buddy. But we could pump here all day and it wouldn't do any good. I've worked on dozens of heart attacks. She's … gone."

"No! That's not true. If we keep—"

"I can't stay here. My family's out there waiting for me. We got to get out of here, run."

"Run where?" Uncle Clyde asked.

"Away," the man said. "I don't know, hide somewhere."

"Mildred." Earl's voice was tear-clotted now. "Mildred, honey …"

"I'm sorry," said the gravel-voiced man again. Then

Star heard him get to his feet, footsteps and then he was gone.

Uncle Clyde came back into the room but he didn't bother to shut the door behind him.

"Baby, you got to talk to me," Earl said. He was not trying to hold back the tears anymore. "Please don't leave me. I need you, you can't go."

"911 still doesn't answer," Uncle Clyde said, probably just for something to say. Then nobody said anything. The only sound was Earl's sobbing. After a time he stopped and coughed. She heard Earl get to his feet. "Help me get her up," he said.

"What are you going—?"

"We're leaving. Me and Mildred, we're gettin' out of here."

"Where are you—?"

"We're leaving!"

Uncle Clyde didn't argue. There were scuffling feet, then a sound, a stifled sob.

"Do you need help?"

"I got her now," Earl said and Star heard heavy footsteps cross the floor and out the door. Had he lifted her up into his arms like a sleeping child? Yeah, probably. Her hands had been so boney she probably didn't weigh much. And Star couldn't imagine that he'd tossed her over his shoulder in a fireman's carry, but maybe. Star didn't know.

The man said nothing to Uncle Clyde. He was just gone.

She tried to picture it. Earl, carrying his dead wife out to the car in the parking lot. Putting her … where? The backseat. But maybe the front seat, slumped against the door, as he drove away. And he'd have to drive manually until he got out of the mass of cars leaving the parking lot. To where? Where do you go with your dead wife in the front seat? They lived in St. Louis. They were on vacation, Mildred had said. Mildred, who was dead now. Shocked into a heart attack by learning there was about to be an alien invasion.

"Uncle Clyde …?" Star said into the stillness. She wanted to ask what it all meant, what was going to happen in six days when the—

"Aliens," he said, as if he was the one who could read minds. Then he barked out a laugh, mirthless and hollow. "Can you beat that." He let out a deep sigh. She could hear him righting the table Mildred had fallen into, putting the chair back in place. "Guess it's poetic justice."

"What's *poetic justice*?"

"It's when real aliens put fake aliens out of business."

Chapter Eight

NOAH HAD TO GO. Had to. No way around it. He shouldn't have drunk that whole thirty-two-ounce Big Gulp cola right before the tour left. But he'd known at the time that he could make it back to the visitor's center in plenty of time, and he would have, too, if they'd gotten back there when they were supposed to. But now they weren't even going back to the Cricket Bottom Visitor's Center. It was on fire! The historic entrance was closer, and more importantly didn't involve climbing down through the steep columns they'd climbed on their way in — which would be treacherous indeed in the dark. But without the cave lights to illuminate the way they were moving as slow as slugs. It would be hours before they made it out. And Noah couldn't wait hours.

When he looked away from the glow of Dr. Weiss's cell phone flashlight far ahead, it was as dark as the inside of a chocolate drop. Nobody would see him. Nobody *could* see him. He hated to do it, though. It was like sacrilege. He and his father ruthlessly removed all traces of their presence when they went into the caves. Candy wrappers, soft drink cans, even wiped away their footprints. And here he was considering urinating right there beside the path!

Well, it was either beside the path or in his pants. One or the other. And soon. As in *now*!

Noah released Derek's hand in front of him and then quickly reconnected it, not to his own but to Kareem, the boy behind him. Then he took two quick steps back away from the trail, out of the glow of the cell phone flashlight of Ranger Thomas who was bringing up the rear of the caravan. Noah knew where they were. They were in Carver's Dome Hall. The trail ran straight ahead, no twists or turns before angling off to the left to enter the narrow Fat Man's Misery Cavern. He had plenty of time to do his business and then catch up to the group before they passed through the hall.

As soon as the ranger passed him, Noah turned away, took another couple of steps and unzipped his pants. As quickly and inconspicuously as he could, he relieved himself, staring out into the black void in front of him. Then he quickly zipped up.

Or tried.

In his haste, he caught the cloth of his underwear in his zipper. It stuck, not even an inch up. He yanked at it furiously, trying to get it back down so he could get it up without the offending piece of cloth in it. But it was frozen, would go neither up nor down. He was frantic. He could sneak past the ranger and get back in line with his pants unzipped, but as he turned and looked over his shoulder, he saw the light of Dr. Weiss's cell phone disappear as the group turned the corner into the next chamber. He had to go *now* to catch up.

With his pants *unzipped*? He couldn't work to free his zipper as he walked along if he had to hold onto Derek's and Kareem's hands. And as soon as they got into the light, the girls would see.

Astrid would see!

No way.

Wait a minute. Noah knew where they were. He could see the cavern in his mind's eye even with the lights off. The Fat Man's Misery Cavern the group was entering was a switchback cavern that ran alongside this one for about seventy-five yards and then passed over a bridge that spanned a little three-foot-wide rift in the rock. The rock split started in this cavern, where it was only a few inches deep across the trail, they'd stepped right over it. He'd noticed the big, flat rock beside the beginning of the crack next to the path when Ranger Thomas's light had flicked over it. He could go to that rock, locate the rift in the floor. He could feel the crack even if he couldn't see it. He could follow that rift straight across and catch up with the group on the other side at the bridge.

Should he——?

The decision was taken out of his hands when the light on Ranger Thomas's cell phone in the rear blinked out and the room fell into total darkness. Absolute black. Like Noah had always imagined it must be like to be blind. At least he had until he'd met the blind man at the zoo. He'd been blind all his life and he'd laughed when Noah asked what it was like to see nothing but darkness.

The old man said he didn't see black because he didn't know what black was. He had no concept of sight of any kind, black or light.

"Does your foot see blackness inside your shoe?" the man had asked him.

Then waited for Noah to get it.

"My foot can't see——"

"Neither can my eyes. It's not black. It's just … nothing."

So this wasn't what a blind person saw. It was what a sighted person saw when all light, every last trace of it, was gone. This was how Helen Keller must have felt, he thought, and his heart kicked into a gallop. She couldn't see or hear. She walked around unable to hear her own footsteps or see where she was going.

Being deaf was not frightening. But Noah discovered to his great dismay that being blind was *scary*. He quickly dropped to his knees and began to crawl back down the trail to the far side to find the rock and the crack beside it that he would follow through the wall separating the caverns and into Fat Man's Misery by the bridge. He crawled, his hands out, feeling for the rock.

He crawled. And crawled.

He knew it was here. Knew it. He had seen it when he looked back at the ranger, in the glow of his cell light.

Sudden realization stunned him. He'd been looking *back* at the ranger. Now, he was facing in the same direction the ranger had been facing. So the rock was on the *other side* of the path! His heart started pounding like a kettle drum in his ears, making it hard to think. He slowly backed up, crawled down the trail to where the ranger had been standing. He could feel the trail, could tell when he left it and crawled the few feet from it to the flat rock that marked the beginning of the crack. But when he got to where the rock should be, the rock wasn't there.

He turned his head slowly from side to side, his eyes stupidly straining to see. He'd just have to go back to the trail … which way was the trail?

Noah wasn't sure. It couldn't possibly be more than a few feet away. But which way?

The dark was so disorienting. The blackness so …

empty. As empty as the blackness of space, except space wasn't empty now. An armada of alien ships was streaking across the black "emptiness," bearing down on Earth. They'd be here, *the aliens would be here in just six days.*

And right now Noah Matheson didn't care. He didn't care about anything except getting out of here.

Chapter Nine

ELLIE HAMPTON TURNED off the shower and stood dripping in the stall. She'd been belting out a husky-voiced imitation of an old country singer her father listened to. Bonnie Taylor, no Tyler. The song was "Total Eclipse of the Heart" and she was getting into it when …

She felt around, sure she had been mistaken. When she was soaping her breast, she thought she felt—

Then her finger tripped over it. On the lower left side of her left breast, there was … a lump.

No, it couldn't be. It must be …

She felt of it, gently fingered it with her right hand. The lump was bigger than a pea, smaller than a marble. The size of a gumball.

It was solid. It didn't hurt, even when she pinched it a little. But she didn't pinch it hard.

The lump hadn't been there yesterday when she took a shower. She was sure of it.

Was she, really? She had been in such a hurry, late for her appointment with her attorney who was prepping her, yet again, for today's court appearance.

She shivered, standing there wet in the stall, her soaked hair sending rivulets of water down her forehead into her eyes.

A lump. In her breast.

Sweet Jesus.

Terror grabbed her by the throat so suddenly the intensity made her nauseous. Bile rose up in the back of her throat and she had to scramble to get out of the shower stall and lean over the toilet before it spilled out over her lips. Nothing but coffee mixed with acid and bile.

When the reflexive heaving was over, she dropped to her knees on the soft bath mat in front of the toilet, closed the lid, flushed it and then knelt there leaning against the bowl, her head in the crook of her arm.

A lump. *A breast lump!*

She tried to cry to make the knot in her belly go away, but no tears came.

Well, it wasn't like she didn't know what she should do. She wasn't some wack job in denial. She had to get to a doctor, her gynecologist. She had to call him *now.*

She got to her feet, a little unsteady, stepped wet and naked into the bedroom and grabbed her phone up off the cradle where it was charging.

Contacts.

Dr. Lebronski.

She touched *call.*

It didn't ring. Instead, a recording played in her ear.

"I'm sorry. All circuits are busy. Your call cannot be completed as dialed. Please hang up and try again."

She hit the red cancel button, then the green call button. No ring, just the recording.

She tried again. Same result. And again.

Over and over. Finally, she threw the phone across the

room in a fit of rage. She saw her face in the mirror over the dresser when she did that and didn't like what she saw.

She was a beautiful woman. She knew that, not in some arrogant, showoff way but simply acknowledging an obvious fact. Her face was the color of whipped cream, her features formed out of a cloud of it — chin a bit pointed, high cheekbones, pouty lips, feathered brows. All of it beneath a mane of thick chestnut hair she had just yesterday paid her hairdresser three hundred dollars to cut in a carefree style that looked casual, natural. Three hundred dollars could buy a lot of natural.

Now, her face in the mirror was drawn. Apprehensive. Fearful.

A lump in her breast.

The thought hit her in the belly and she almost groaned from the blow.

Dear holy God, what did that mean?

"Cancer?"

She whispered the word out loud, her voice soft and awed.

Did Ellie Hampton have cancer?

No. She couldn't. She didn't. She had no time or space in her life for something like that. Chemo. Would all her hair fall out?

She burped out a sob, went to the other side of the room to retrieve her phone and called the doctor again. She would demand he see her now, today, *this morning.* Get that … thing out of her breast and send it off to wherever they tested such things. She wanted results — tomorrow! How long could a test like that take?

"I'm sorry. All circuits are busy. Your call cannot be completed as dialed. Please hang up and try again."

She tried to call her attorney then and got the same message. Something major had gone wrong with the phone system and she did NOT have time for that today. She was supposed to be in court at ten o'clock for the hearing and now she'd have to get her attorney to get a continuance. She had to get to a doctor. Today. *Now.*

And some little part of her mind was grateful to have an indisputable excuse to put the hearing off. It wasn't the final one — this one was about motions and stuff. She didn't even know why she had to be there. The result was a foregone conclusion. Of course, she'd be granted custody of Gretchen. She was Elliot Thurgood Hampton, for crying out loud. Any judge on the planet would give her her little girl. Her husband was a philandering loser who was just using Gretchen as a bargaining chip to get Ellie to void the prenuptial agreement he'd signed so he could get his greedy fingers on her father's fortune.

Her fortune now.

Daddy was gone.

The thought didn't stagger her this time. It had been six months since his heart attack and she still wanted to burst into tears at the realization he was gone.

Court would wait. The whole world would wait until she could get to a doctor because she had a lump in her breast!

She picked up the phone and called again.

Same response she'd gotten every other time she'd tried. She wanted to throw the phone across the room, but instead, she went into the living room of the apartment, with its exquisite view of Lake Michigan, dripping shower water on the white Moroccan tiles, and switched on the full-wall juke.

If there was some city-wide phone outage, it would be on the news. She had to know when there'd be service again—

A pretty blonde anchorwoman on CNN was standing

in front of a display that looked like a picture of the solar system. She wasn't interested in a *National Geographic* space lesson now.

She switched stations. Another news anchor, this time a man, was pointing at a display similar to the one the first woman had been describing. She punched the button on the mute switch, turning on the sound.

"… not a hoax," he was saying. "The president is expected to address the nation later this afternoon, asking for calm, urging Americans—"

She switched to another channel, uninterested in some political crisis.

The third channel showed the same picture that had been on the first two stations. It was a shot of dark, black space, a huge planet in the foreground.

"… a few hours ago by NASA." The voice speaking was not some news announcer.

"Explain again, if you will, Dr. Stanley, why it is not possible that these spots are merely natural phenomena."

The view on the screen switched to a studio where two news anchors, a man and a woman, were interviewing a third man. The type under his face identified him as Dr. Sterling Stanley, the chairman of the Astrophysics Department at UCLA.

"It's not rocket science," the professor said. Maybe he intended to be funny but nobody was laughing. "Examine the spots." The screen filled with the view of space again. "Even from this distance, all the way out by Jupiter, it is clear that this is not a random assortment of objects. Meteors, asteroids, don't come in standard sizes. These are all identical."

"Isn't it possible that at this distance they *look* identical but on closer observation—"

"The signal from the astral telescope on the far side of

the moon has to be relayed via satellites, so there is a slight delay, but for our purposes, what you're seeing is a real-time image."

Then the image switched and the light specks were replaced by a much clearer image showing a cluster of small round objects.

The anchorwoman was clearly struggling to remain professionally objective, but her voice shook a little.

"Will you please explain again why these spots aren't meteors or asteroids or—"

"Random space debris — meteors and their larger cousins, asteroids, don't travel in formation. And they don't decelerate."

"They're slowing down?"

"Imagine an airliner coming into O'Hare. It starts slowing down thirty miles out as it begins its approach."

"So let me make sure I understand you, professor," said the male anchor. "You're saying—"

The professor lost patience.

"I am saying," he said, enunciating each word slowly and clearly, "that these spots are alien spacecraft. There is no other determination you could make, given the evidence at hand."

"Coming … *here* …?" The anchorwoman sounded like the breath had been knocked out of her.

"Yes, here! Based on current estimates of their speed and trajectory, they'll reach Earth in six days."

Ellie flicked the button and the screen went blank.

The only sound was the hammering beat of her heart, each beat explosively forcing blood through her veins.

Alien spacecrafts.

She bleated out a little laugh, then put her hand over her mouth to seal in any other sound like it.

This is real, sports fans. Not a hoax. The aliens are invading. Have a nice day.

A sudden wave of emotion washed over her, an aching fearful longing. The court appearance didn't matter anymore. Neither did a doctor's appointment. Only one thing mattered now. *Gretchen.*

Her trembling hands picked up her phone and she touched the little green telephone receiver icon — when was the last time anybody'd talked on a phone with a hand-held receiver that looked like that icon?

Expecting the same message again, she was about to disconnect when the Universe granted her one.

"Whittaker Aeronautics, this is Joe." She was so startled by the voice that for a moment she couldn't speak.

"Hello?"

"Joe, this is Elliot. Dispatch a chopper to the heliport on the top of my building immediately."

"Have you heard the news, Miss Hampton?"

"Of course I've heard the news."

"Then you know—"

"I know I want a chopper on my roof in fifteen minutes. Clear? *Fifteen minutes.* I'm going to Kentucky to pick up Gretchen."

She hung up before he could argue. Then dropped the phone and raced back into the bedroom to dress. The trip from the small airport to her building was short. The chopper could easily make it in fifteen minutes. If it came. If Joe dispatched it. Well, he damned well better have dispatched it. He worked for her. This was her company now. That chopper was her property! And there was no shortage of qualified chopper pilots and if he wanted to keep his job …

Job? Now?

Would he care now?

Would anybody care about anything now?

She shoved her feet into her shoes and grabbed her purse. He *would* be here in fifteen minutes! And she would be on the roof waiting for him.

Chapter Ten

NOAH TRIED the best he could to grab hold of his emotions, to get a grip on his rising panic. But he couldn't manage it. The panic drove him. He had to get back to the trail. He'd just crawl down the trail if he had to, they would miss him eventually, they would when Dr. Weiss did a head count after they left the cavern. Dr. Weiss was always doing head counts. The whole school hadn't come on the field trip, only the children in Noah's class, but it seemed like every time Noah looked at Dr. Weiss, he was mouthing thirteen, fourteen, as his eyes went from child to child.

The trail couldn't be more than a few feet away, ten feet at the most. Noah had to find it, and then just stay on it and crawl down it until somebody came back to get him. It would be embarrassing to be left like that, maybe even to have to own up to having pissed right here in the cavern, but that wasn't as bad as this.

He crawled frantically now, scuttling along the ground like a sand crab. But only for a few feet. Ten. Well, maybe it had been more like twenty.

There was no trail. He was crawling across the rocks out in the cave, not on the visitor's pathway. He had to backtrack, get back to where he'd started crawling and go a different direction. If he kept doing that, he'd hit the trail eventually. He stopped, his heart pounding in his ears, the terror making it hard to breathe, turned and crawled back the way he'd come.

Halfway there, rocks appeared in front of him and he had to go over them, rough rocks, and then a shallow indention, not the crack he'd been looking for, but he was sure he had not crawled across the indention before. So he wasn't going back toward the trail after all.

That thought sent him over the edge and he began crawling off in another direction, scrambling along, his breath hitching in his throat, tears streaming down his face. He crawled and crawled. And then he hit the crack. The crack. He struck his hand down into it and he actually started sobbing but this time in relief. The crack. He could do what he had intended to do all along before he got so turned around. He could follow the crack out through the side of the cavern and catch up to the group on the other side when the trail they were on switched back. He might even get there before they did. No, he had taken so long crawling around in the dark that surely they had passed beyond the bridge over the crack now.

Well, that didn't matter. It would be better to be there than here. Once there, he could turn and crawl along the trail in the direction the class had gone so he wouldn't be so far behind them when they missed him and came looking.

He began to crawl along the crack, kept his left hand trailing along the crack's edge as he moved forward. Then he began to crawl upward and the fear returned. There wasn't a rise between this cavern and the next. There was a hill in the cavern they had been in when he stopped to go to the bathroom, but it was in the other direction, the exact opposite direction this crack was leading. But this was a crack and it would take him to …

He refused to think about the hill. Just crawled up the side of it and back down the other side. He hadn't noticed, that's all, or maybe there was a hill right before the crack crossed the trail in the other cavern.

But there wasn't. He knew there wasn't. And he should have come to a tight space by now. He would have to crawl through a tight space where the crack neared the side of the cave wall. It should have been so small it would barely have room for him. But he came to no such crack. He kept reaching out his hand, feeling for a cave wall.

He stopped, took a breath. Peering again into the darkness as if the act of looking itself would reveal light to show him the way.

Nothing. Then he started crawling again. Panic suddenly seized him, like a dog with a rag in its teeth, shaking its head from side to side and he crawled in abject terror, crawled and crawled and crawled, the absolute darkness black tar that flowed into his body through his mouth and nose and ears. He finally had to stop to get his breath, his chest heaving, his hands raw from scuffing over the rocks, both knees torn out of his school uniform pants.

He should have cried out. As Noah sat trembling in the darkness he realized he should have called out to the group. Made some kind of noise. He could yell help, it wasn't like he couldn't *talk*. He might not have heard his own voice but the rangers and Dr. Weiss would have.

Except now it was too late for that. They were far down the tunnel by now. Oh, they might hear him, the guides anyway, but with the sound echoing in the cave, they would have no idea where he was. They'd go back down the trail looking for him but he wasn't on the trail anymore. He was somewhere else, some dark place the dim lights of their cell phones wouldn't reach.

He realized he was sobbing so hard his chest hurt and he made himself stop. He was on all fours and he could feel his nose dripping and he reached up and wiped his face, his breathing hitching in and out, like he was a little kid bawling. He hadn't cried this hard since—

No, he wouldn't think about *that* now. If he let himself think about Mama and Rosie-Posie now he would lose his mind. He would stand up and run as fast as he could until he hit a wall or fell and broke a leg or tripped and tumbled down into some crevice. The Mole Hole at the end of the tunnel called End of the Line was three hundred feet deep!

He could be anywhere now, down any of the side passages that led off from the main cavern called Broadway where they had been. There were, after all, 250 miles of cave here! *Explored* cave. There were untold hundreds of miles of unexplored passageways and he might have wandered into one of those. The image of his father filled his mind and that calmed him a little. What would Dad do? If Dad were here, what would he tell Noah to do? He imagined his father, big and tall and solid, his brown uniform starched and pressed, his gold sheriff's badge shiny. What would his father say?

His father'd never talked about getting lost in a cave, but he remembered what he'd said once what Noah should do if he ever got lost in the woods. Which was never going to happen, of course, because there were only three or four large stands of virgin woods on the whole Matheson property, the six-mile by eight-mile parcel of land on Joppa Ridge beneath which the tangled caves Matheson Caverns wound in a heap of tunnels like a pile of spaghetti. Those stands of woods weren't big enough to get lost in for long, and besides he knew every inch of them.

But his father had said that if he ever got lost, he should hug a tree. Hug a tree until somebody came and found him. In other words. Stay still. Stay in one place. Don't move around or the search party would be trying to find a moving target.

He should do that now. He should stop. Stay still. They would miss him eventually. They would.

But when? Would it be so chaotic up there now, with everybody upset about the aliens — *aliens!* — that Dr. Weiss would just load up the kids and drive as fast as he could back to Zion Academy?

They'd miss him then, though. They would. They might not before, but somebody would see he wasn't there when they unloaded the bus. Then they'd have to call Uncle Taylor, the manager of Matheson Caverns, so he could get the guides to start searching. But … did the phones work? Noah didn't know why the electricity had gone out but whatever happened to it might have knocked the phones out, too.

Well, then Dr. Weiss would just have to drive into town and get his father. Dad would come! He'd bring all his deputies and get all the other guides to help look for Noah. But that would be hours from now. That thought kicked him so hard he actually gasped. It might take them the rest of the day. Might take them all night and the next morning. And afternoon. Because it would be *very hard to find* Noah. When you were looking for someone, you called out to them. He wouldn't hear searchers calling.

He should call out now. Start calling out for help every two or three minutes until somebody came. He tried that, but once he started crying for help, he couldn't seem to stop.

"Help, I'm here! Come get me. Somebody, anybody, *help me!*"

He called and called until his throat was so raw it hurt to talk.

Then he just sat in the dark, sat still, his breathing about back to normal, no longer hitching in and out as it had been. He pulled his knees up to his chest and wrapped his arms around them and found himself crying softly now, his terror so great it had blown up in his chest like that Navy dinghy he'd seen once that inflated when you pulled on a strap.

Breathing normally calmed him, left him just as terrified as before but no longer hysterical and he tried to be logical. If he stayed still, searchers would not be looking for a moving target. But there were no searchers yet. The others hadn't even had time to get out of the cavern, didn't even know that he was gone. Sitting still now accomplished nothing. But if he continued forward, he had at least a chance of crossing the trail, or a bridge … shoot, he might even bump into one of the visitor handrails. Dad said once they'd installed almost three miles of railing in the four levels of the cavern.

He would move forward carefully, try to go in a straight line until he reached a cavern wall, then feel his way along it.

And so he began to crawl again, aware now of his raw hands and knees. He tried counting, so maybe he could judge the passage of time. But he lost track. Time was meaningless in the black nothingness around him. He could have been lost here for hours, believed that he had been. Maybe it'd only been half an hour, though. Or maybe it was midnight.

He crawled over rocks, up inclines, down the other sides, found cave walls, followed them as they opened into other chambers. He was tired and thirsty, was thinking about a big drink of water when he realized that he'd climbed up a rocky incline and his way forward seemed blocked. He felt around, figured out that a large slab of rock, like the size of a pool table, had fallen from the roof and was leaned up against a cavern wall. Rather than turning around and retracing his steps, he crawled behind the rock, felt along the cavern wall and found an opening there. It wasn't a very big opening, but it occurred to him that there were dozens or maybe hundreds of small openings in the cave walls of the caverns, openings that lead into other caverns. So he crawled through the opening, a small tunnel that soon opened into another cavern. He could sense it was a big cavern, would have called out to make an echo if he could have heard it. He didn't. His throat hurt too bad for that. He merely crawled into the cavern and reached out to the cave wall so he could crawl along it.

The cave wall was smooth.

He crawled along the wall with his hand out, feeling it. It was as smooth as a plate, as a granite countertop.

And that was impossible. Cave walls were never that smooth. They were rough, bumpy, had holes in them and ridges on them, chunks missing — they were rocks and that was the nature of rocks. He slowly stood, keeping his hand on the cave wall, felt around as high as he could reach. He could find no imperfection of any kind in the surface.

This was no cavern he had ever been in, had ever seen, had ever even heard of. Instead of getting back on his hands and knees, he inched forward standing up, shuffled his feet along the floor to be sure he didn't trip over something or fall into something. The floor of the cave was as smooth and flat as the floor of his garage, and flawless as the walls.

That was certifiably crazy.

Was that it? Had he lost his mind? He began to walk forward instead of scooting his feet, trailing his right hand along the glassy surface of the rock and feeling around at the empty air in front of him with his left. He walked on and on and on, counted his steps until he lost track, stepping on a smooth floor, his hand trailing along a smooth wall. It was like being inside a glass globe; he would bet the ceiling, too, if he could reach it, was shined up as slick as a marble, too.

He was certain he was going crazy, that was the only explanation, so when he felt it, at first he dismissed it. Couldn't be. He stopped. Concentrated. It felt real. The barest breeze, hardly more than a breath, tugged at the hair stuck down to his sweaty brow. He could smell …

It was fresh air.

And maybe he was imagining that, too, but he continued forward walking slowly, feeling along the wall until his fingers stumbled over a crack in it. No, not a crack. A crack was jagged where something had broken. The edges of this opening were about three inches apart and as smooth as the wall itself. The fresh-air smell seemed to be coming through the crack. He stood there, feeling around in the absolute blackness, stretching his arm as far into the crack as he could, trying to picture what his fingers touched. He felt up the crack on tiptoes as high as he could feel, then felt down the crack, going to one knee.

The crack ended about two feet off the floor. Between the crack and the floor was an opening, an ordinary hole in the rock. He felt around inside the opening — just ordinary lumpy, bumpy rock. Fresh air was coming through it, he was certain.

This opening wasn't nearly as large as the one he'd come through to get into this cavern, and that one had been snug. Could he squeeze through this opening? What if he tried and it got smaller and smaller and he got stuck in there? He'd gone with his father, uncle and cousins into unexplored caverns, shoved himself into some small openings. He knew that it was difficult to push yourself with your toes through a tight space. More importantly, he also knew it was all but impossible to *pull* yourself with your toes back out of one. Nobody would be holding onto his ankles here. If he got stuck …

He leaned back against the cave wall, trying not to think about the story his mother'd read to him about a boy named Tom Sawyer who got lost with his girlfriend in a cave. They got out because they saw a light. But if it had been night instead of day, they'd have missed it. Noah knew he'd been in the cavern a long time, but it was still daylight outside. If he just sat, waited, did nothing, the sun would go down and he could pass right by an opening without seeing it.

"Please…" he croaked out loud, to God. Or the Universe. Or his father who wasn't there.

Then he lay down on his belly and scooted himself into the opening.

Chapter Eleven

NOBODY MOVED. The had-to-be-a-football-player inmate called Spade was eyeing Paco, a murderous look on his ugly face. In a millisecond, Paco assessed the situation and reached a conclusion he didn't like. As the youngest and smallest, he'd be blamed for the pile of shit. He couldn't rat out Tiburon; that was a guaranteed death sentence. The other boys would think he did it — and when he didn't admit it, they'd all be punished. Then he wouldn't be facing just the hostility of the guards and the inmates, but the wrath of the other boys, too. He'd have to watch his back all the time, stay constantly on guard.

There were too many people here, too much going on for Paco to exert any control over the situation. It was what it was.

"I'm gonna count to three. One. Two."

"It was me," Paco said. "I ate something that made me sick. I couldn't help it."

They were on him then like flies on shit, yelling at him, their breath rancid, inches from his face, their spit on his cheeks and in his eyes. Spade grabbed him and hauled him across the hall where the cage bars kept the inmates in the courtyard.

"You want him?" he asked them.

Their cries of greedy yearning made Paco want to shit his own pants. The eyes that looked at him froze his heart. He couldn't catch his breath. These were human animals. There was *nothing* they wouldn't do to him.

The inmate hurled Paco up against the bars, and hands reached through to grab and grope him. Faces pressed through the bars next to his.

"I'll rip you a new one, boy."

Someone groped his leg with a hand missing a thumb, but when he grabbed Paco's genitals and squeezed, he had strength enough in his fingers alone to make Paco shriek in pain. The inmate pulled him free of the hands holding him, dragged him away from the bars and he collapsed in a heap.

"Now, you get down there and clean up your shit."

Paco was doubled over, pain washing his body like waves against the shore.

"If you can't walk, *crawl.* I'm gonna make you lick it up, gonna—"

There was a commotion outside the room. It sounded like it was coming from the receiving room down the hall where they'd been unloaded out of the van. Shouting voices, not menacing like inmates or intimidating guards. The voices were excited. No, not excited … scared.

A guard burst into the room and ran up to the Asian guard leaned against the wall, like maybe they were friends.

"You seen this?"

He thrust his phone out and the guard took it.

Paco had been trying to get to his feet, but his knees buckled and he toppled to the floor, bumping Spade's leg.

The inmate kicked out, absently, like you'd flick a fly off your sleeve. His foot caught Paco in the chest and knocked him flat on his back just out of reach of the prisoners, who were no longer clawing at him, but shouting at the guard, wanting to know what was up.

The world grayed out then. Paco couldn't seem to draw back in the air the inmate had knocked out of him. His diaphragm wouldn't cooperate, screaming in pain that rivaled the agony swimming up from his groin into his belly like a school of piranhas. The room throbbed in and out of focus in rhythm with his heartbeats.

Then it filled with people, guards who seemed upset about something. Very upset, almost panicked. The prisoners were screaming now, yelling, "Let us out of here! You gotta let us out of here now."

Paco felt somebody grab the back of his shirt collar and drag him across the room away from the prisoners and the door and lean him up against a pile of towels.

It was Tiburón.

"What's—?" Paco didn't have enough air to finish the question. Tiburón responded, but it sounded like he said, "aliens."

"What—?" Again he got no further.

Tiburón squatted down beside him.

"I told you. Aliens! They seen 'em. Ships coming this way. They'll be here in six days."

It was no time for joking, but Tiburón seemed to be completely serious. Which was absurd.

Then one of the guards who'd taken their paperwork from the van driver left the room and quickly returned. He didn't seem all macho now, mean and confrontational. He seemed distracted. Shaken. Rattled.

"Warden said to send you back to the city," he said, but before relief and joy had a chance to set in, he continued, "but there ain't nobody to take you. Tried to call the DOC to get the van back, but nobody answered the phone."

"How can that be?" the pimply-faced white kid popped off. "You saying there ain't nobody home at the Department of Corrections?"

The guard didn't reply. All he said was, "Get comfortable. You ain't going nowhere. The prison's on lockdown."

With that, he walked out of the room and slammed the door. They heard him engage a heavy bolt lock on the other side.

Could it possibly be…?

"Aliens?" Paco croaked, but Tiburón was no longer kneeling beside him. He had joined the other boys at the door, banging on it, demanding to be set free.

But nobody came.

THE TUNNEL WALLS squeezed the air out of Noah. There wasn't room enough to hold his head up to look where he was going, but in the absolute black, it didn't matter. He felt around with his hands out in front of him, judging the size of the opening, determined to stop before the tunnel got so narrow he couldn't retreat. After a while, he knew he'd come too far to go back. If he couldn't find a way out ahead, he would die here encased in a rock grave and nobody would ever know what had happened to him.

The fresh air was his only hope. There *was* fresh air ahead of him, there was no doubt about that now. The tunnel got more narrow. He had to suck in his belly to squeeze through. Hope was draining out of him and a black void of despair filled—

The tunnel ahead was bigger. He scooted forward with

his toes and when his elbows cleared he could feel the extra space. He dragged his body forward with his arms …

And his upper body tumbled out into a cavern.

He lay there for a moment, gasping big lungfuls of air, rejoicing in the space around him, and the wind …

He turned in the direction he felt it coming from.

And there was a glow. A pinprick of light. He crawled toward it. Though he was sure the cavern was tall enough to stand, he wasn't sure his knees would hold him up. The light grew until he could make out images around him. He had crawled along the trail for thirty or forty feet before he realized that's what it was. An old trail his grandfather'd made when he first opened …

It was light now, real light. He stood and could see walls and a floor and a ceiling. There was enough light to walk — *to run!* — and he did. The light grew. He turned a corner in the passageway and could see a fully lighted open space ahead. It wasn't an entrance. Bright sunshine streamed into the cavern through the roof—

Double Cellars Sinkhole! A gigantic dent in the ground where the cave roof had collapsed hundreds of years ago. How could he possibly have gotten here? He didn't even know there were passages that connected Broadway to this one. Relief flooded through him that felt like warm molasses.

Down the cavern beyond the sinkhole a hundred yards or so was the Historic Entrance. But Noah didn't go down the cavern beyond. For the first time in his life, Noah wanted out of the cave *now*! He hurried across the cavern and climbed up the rock pile that the collapse had dumped in the cavern and up into the light above. There was a metal barrier at the top of the sinkhole to prevent people from climbing down into the caves through it. But he was able to squeeze between the sets of bars on the barricade and out into the open field beyond it. He just stood there for a moment taking it all in, the sunlight and the trees, the breeze lifting his sweaty hair off his brow — and the pall of black smoke rising into the air from below. There was nothing down below the Natural Entrance except a winding road that ended in the Cricket Bottom Entrance two hundred feet above the river and the visitor's center there. Was the visitor's center *on fire*? Is that what happened to the lights?

Noah didn't know and right now he didn't care. He had made it out!

How?

No time to consider that now. He needed to hurry. The Double Cellars Sinkhole was probably half a mile down a hiking trail from the Historic Entrance, which was where the academy group would be exiting. The academy bus would be parked at the edge of the parking lot. The upper lot was bigger, so tour buses disgorged their passengers at the Cricket Bottom Visitor's Center, parked above, and returned to pick their groups up at a specified time. Maybe the bus was still parked up here. Maybe because of the fire below, they'd kept the buses here.

Noah had no idea what time it was, how long he'd been lost, and no way to judge whether his group had made it back to the entrance before he had. If they were already out of the cave, then they had noticed his absence and had sent out guides to look for him and he didn't want that.

He ran down the trail, passed a few hikers, but they weren't walking. They were standing on the trail, looking at their phones. He suspected if he'd stopped, he'd have seen they were glued to the Astral app.

The trail opened up onto the back side of the parking lot and he ran across it, looking to see if the academy bus was still here, but couldn't spot it among the others. There was a stitch in his side from the exertion when he finally made it to the Historic Entrance and stood panting at the top of the concrete steps — there were 314 of them — that his family had installed where people had gone in and out of the cave for more than a thousand years.

Tourists streamed out, most of them older people, a couple in wheelchairs. They had been on one of the short tours that stayed in the large chambers that were handicapped-accessible. The people hurried past him, not acknowledging his presence, intent on their own hushed conversations centered around the phones most of them had out and in their hands. Once they were past, no one else came out. He sat down on a rock to catch his breath — and remembered his stuck zipper. Out in the daylight, it wasn't hard to work the fabric from his underwear free. He realized he'd gone running past that group of hikers with his pants unzipped and they hadn't even noticed when he saw another group of people coming out of the cave. At the head of them was Ranger Thomas and Dr. Weiss, looking like moles emerging from a hole into the daylight.

Noah was so relieved to see them that he leapt down the steps to greet them and threw himself into Dr. Weiss's surprised arms. The old man peeled him off and signed rapidly.

"How did you get here?"

Noah signed back that he'd gotten separated from the group, so he'd taken a different route through the tunnels that led him here. He knew he must look a sight. Hot, sweaty, dirty, with the knees torn out of his uniform pants, scratched up and bunged up.

"There is no route that connects where we were to this entrance except the one we were on," said the guide.

Noah just shrugged and signed, "I found one."

He would certainly have been the subject of much more scrutiny under other circumstances. Right now, Dr. Weiss was more interested in getting the children to the bus and away from the cavern and the ugly black column of smoke bruising the blue sky.

Dr. Weiss motioned for the children to follow him up the final steps, and once outside the cavern their hearing aids worked and they could hear his instructions. Noah, of course, was still wrapped in profound silence. Several children, including Astrid, were signing questions at him — asking how he'd gotten separated when they were all holding hands. And how he had managed to find his way in the dark cave to this entrance. He had signed back that this was, after all, *Matheson* Caverns. He'd gotten a little lost, and had had to crawl through some passageways to find his way out, but it was no big deal.

Not until they were seated in the bus, with Dr. Weiss standing in the front counting heads, did Noah really relax. And he was soon forgotten. There were much more exciting things for the children to talk about.

Aliens.

Chapter Twelve

THE SUN HAD ALREADY DROPPED behind Tucker Mountain when Sheriff Sawyer Matheson pulled his cruiser up under the portico of the administration building at Zion Academy. He killed the engine, but didn't get out at once, just sat massaging his temples. It had been a … bad day at the office. He suspected you'd be hard pressed to find anybody on the planet who'd had a good day today.

He'd cherished the hope that his first altercation of the day, his run-in with Monty Phillips, the owner/manager of Phillips Foodtown, wouldn't be indicative of the mood of the townspeople and that other store owners would be more reasonable.

Wrong.

"What do you mean closing my doors!"

Monty came at Sawyer like a hornet that'd been shaken up in a Mason jar.

"This is my grocery store, private property. You have no legal right to send that lummox deputy of yours" — he was talking about Roger Hawkins and Sawyer had to admit the man was lacking in certain social graces — "to march in here like the Gestapo and tell me I gotta lock up and not sell nothing to nobody."

"You're right, Monty. A sheriff does not have that kind authority."

That stopped him, or at least slowed him down.

"Then you better call off your—"

"But I have declared martial law in McClintock County," Sawyer continued, "and that *does* give me the authority to close you down."

Monty was shocked into momentary silence. A small, squat man, Monty Phillips was roughly the size and shape of a mailbox, with a round, bald head that sat directly on his shoulders.

"You can't declare martial law."

"Well, I did. And maybe the town council will rescind that declaration at the emergency meeting tonight, but between now and then I am in charge and your doors will stay locked."

"But why—?"

"Are you kidding?"

Sawyer gestured toward the crowd of angry shoppers who'd gathered in the store's parking lot.

"You think those people came here for a gallon of milk and a loaf of bread? They'll clean you out. Every one of them intends to buy everything they can carry. And they're the first wave, the ones who plan to *buy* what they take. The looters won't be packing Mastercards."

"Looters? Here, in Jessup?"

"I guarantee you there are folks out there gearing up to find, pillage and hoard whatever supplies they can lay their hands on. If it makes you feel better, pretend I'm protecting you from a rabble of strangers."

The other three supermarket owners were no easier to convince or mollify. Howard Hansford, who ran the local

Buy Low, threatened to sue Sawyer, then seemed to realize how much weight a threat like that carried now.

Sawyer continued to rub his temples, trying to relieve the tension of the day's contentious encounters, each kicking a bruise that got more and more sore as the hours wore on, and night was coming. Darkness had a way of heightening fears, pulling knots of tension tighter, and emboldening those with dark intent.

He'd come out here to Zion Academy to talk to Dr. Weiss about security measures. Today, people were scared and scattered. Tomorrow, they'd be more scared and less scattered and it wouldn't be long before it occurred to somebody that there was a place in McClintock County with supplies to rival anything available in the Foodtown on Main Street. Warehouses full of farm produce, a dairy, cattle, sheep, chickens and a spring with pure water. Why, there was enough provision at Zion Academy to see 120 students, a teaching and admin staff of twenty-one, and four couples who served as full-time houseparents through a nuclear holocaust — or so the townspeople would speculate.

And it was unguarded.

The academy wasn't particularly popular with local residents, partly because the man running it was clearly from "Away From Here," that hell-hole somewhere out in the wide world where folks lived who didn't grow up in McClintock County. And the children who attended the academy weren't garden-variety youngsters. They were the offspring of the rich and powerful, used to luxury the citizens of McClintock County couldn't even conceive, arriving in black town cars, helicopters or stretch limos with tinted windows. Everything about them shouted "upper crust" in a town mostly devoid of class structure.

The real bone of contention was how the students

behaved when they came into town, which was blessedly seldom. The locals didn't have any use for arrogance, for children who clearly had not been properly disciplined to respect their elders. The only saving grace, and a source of smug satisfaction for the town, was the fact that the children had to work at Zion, probably for the first time in their pampered lives.

The academy had partnered with Gethsemane Monastery, whose monks ran a gigantic farming operation, raised crops, tended animals, made beer and wine — bad wine, as the growing season here wasn't long enough to produce flavorful grapes. The monks provided the land, equipment and expertise, and the academy's students provided the farm labor. If the students' rich parents didn't like that, they could find somewhere else to place their pampered pooches, which, of course, they wouldn't, because just about any sacrifice was worth a hearing aid that made it possible for totally deaf children to hear normally.

The lone exception was Sawyer's son, Noah. The Weiss implant did not work for Noah.

An ache of sorrow welled up in Sawyer's chest at the mere thought of the boy. Thin, pale, a shadow of the boy he'd been before his mother and sister had been killed in the fire that had very nearly killed him, too. When the boy had finally awakened from the coma where he'd languished for more than a week after the fire, Sawyer had been standing by the window on the other side of the room. He saw the boy's eyes open and cried out, "Noah!" But the boy hadn't turned to look at him. Because he hadn't heard.

Though the doctors couldn't find a specific injury, it was clear the blow to the head that put the boy in a coma had robbed him of his hearing. Dr. Weiss had graciously offered to take the boy as a scholarship student at the academy, but after four years there, the miracle hearing device still left Noah in silence.

Sawyer got out of his cruiser, walked up the steps to the administration building and into the office of the academy secretary.

Lucy Pruitt's demeanor always reminded Sawyer of Tweety Bird's grandmother, though she didn't have enough hair for a proper bun. That was, in fact, the first thing you noticed about Lucy. Her gray hair was so thin her pink scalp showed through like a bad paint job.

She looked up from her desk and saw him, pulled the telephone headset off her head and tossed it on her desk, then put her head in her hands and began to cry.

He crossed the room in two long strides, sat down on the edge of the desk and put his hand on her shoulder. He realized he could no longer employ the balm of platitudes that even if they hadn't always been true when he said them they had at least given him something to say.

It's going to be fine.

Everything will work out.

You'll get through this.

So he said nothing, just let her cry.

She finally lifted her head, took off her granny glasses and wiped them with the tail of her sweater.

"I have been on the phone every second since … since …"

"I know."

"Parents — scared, demanding, *angry*. Like all this is *my* fault. They want me to pack up their precious child and put him/her on the first plane to … wherever. Like we could do that with all 120 students at once. Some said they were sending cars or planes to pick the children up, that I should personally see to it that they were packed and ready to go."

"I'd be scared, too, if Noah were a thousand miles away and I couldn't get to him."

"Oh, I know that. I get it. I'm just venting. They're even more freaked out that they can't reach their children on their cell phones."

"Phone service has been blinking on and off like a Joe's Beer Joint sign since nine this morning."

"I tried to explain to them that some of the children had gone on a field trip today to Matheson Caverns and the phones—"

Sawyer had forgotten that Noah's class had been in the cave today, had walled off all thoughts about the fire that had apparently destroyed the Cricket Bottom Visitor's Center.

"They're not back yet?"

"No. And they're hours late. I've tried calling Dr. Weiss."

Then Lucy's face broke into a smile and he followed her gaze, watching the Zion Academy bus pull into the driveway and head toward the portico.

Sawyer walked out past the line of children rushing into the building and stood at the bus door looking for Noah. He was the last kid off the bus. And he looked like he hadn't ridden in the bus but had been dragged along behind it.

"Noah, what—?"

The boy spotted him then and launched himself at his father, grabbing him around the waist in a death grip. Sawyer looked helplessly at Dr. Weiss, who had gotten off behind Noah, looking distracted and disheveled, his normally immaculate suit with dirt on the knees and down the front of his coat.

"The electricity to the cave went off and the lights went out," Dr. Weiss said. "There was some kind of explosion at the visitor's center, something about a tour bus. I don't know the details, but I think it was totally destroyed. So sorry. Terrible. Terrible thing."

The old man stood shaking his head, looking … befuddled.

"What happened to Noah?"

"Ah yes, Noah. Well, he got separated from the group—"

"Separated?"

"I don't know how. I have asked him but he's just … vague."

"If he got separated, how did he—?"

"I don't know that either. He got out before we did. He was waiting for us outside, and as you can see, he had obviously been crawling around on the ground. I know the boy practically grew up in the cave, but how could he possibly have found his way *in the dark*?"

Noah continued to cling to his father, wouldn't let go. Sawyer patted him reassuringly, didn't know what else to do.

The old man took a deep breath and let it out in a long sigh, looking up at the darkening sky as he did. Though it wasn't yet sundown, the mountain was to the west and the sun had passed down behind it, granting the valley a shadow twilight until real nightfall spread black into the gray light, filling in the spaces with darkness.

"And so, we are like Masada," Dr. Weiss said.

"Masada …?" Sawyer scrambled to recall what the word meant.

"Like the Jews watching the Romans build the ramp up to the fortress. The world watches and waits for the ships to arrive … and destroy us."

Now, Sawyer remembered. Masada was where Jewish resistance fighters held out against the Romans. He also remembered how the story ended. The night before the Romans breached the wall, the Jews committed mass suicide — something like two hundred of them.

"You believe the destruction part?"

"And you don't?"

"It ain't over till the fat lady sings."

The old man looked at him sadly and shook his head.

There was a sudden noise in the sky, the sound of a swarm of bees.

"Ahh, someone has come for their child," Dr. Weiss said. "With what is to come, the children would be better off staying here."

A helicopter suddenly appeared, flying low over the trees. A helipad had been built behind the school, but the pilot of this chopper chose instead to set the machine down on the vast front lawn. It had barely settled to the earth when the back door flew open and a woman leapt out. She was dressed in designer jeans and a red blouse made of some clingy fabric. She ran, bent over beneath the chopper blades, crossed the lawn and up the service road to where the sheriff and Dr. Weiss stood outside the bus.

"I've come for Gretchen Hampton. Where is she?" she demanded without preamble, pushing her tousled hair back out of her face. "I have called and called but there's no answer — the phone rings but—"

"Many of the children lost their cell phones today," Dr. Weiss said. "I'm sure all their parents are frantic. They put their backpacks in lockers at the visitor's center at Matheson Caverns and there was an explosion—"

"But Gretchen's alright? She wasn't hurt, was she?"

This woman was teetering on the edge of panic and the ground was crumbling out from under her.

"She's fine. She just went inside. If you—"

The woman turned and raced up the stairs and disappeared into the building.

Noah was still clinging to his father, but no longer in a death grip. Sawyer peeled him gently away and knelt on one knee in front of him. The boy was a wreck, his arms were scratched and dirty, his pants torn at the knee. There was dirt in his hair.

"Noah, how did you get lost?" Sawyer signed. He wasn't as clumsy as he'd been when he first started learning sign language four years ago, but he was still totally incapable of communicating on the kind of deep level he wanted to with his son, communication the boy desperately needed.

Noah just shrugged and shook his head.

The chopper pilot left the engine idling, got out and walked across the grass and up the road toward them. Sawyer got to his feet.

"Uh ... you do know that the Federal Aviation Authority grounded all aircraft, don't you?" Sawyer said.

"Yeah, but ... there's the law, and then there's Elliott Thurgood Hampton."

He gestured with his chin toward the building where the woman had disappeared.

"I can't let you take off," Sawyer said. "I'm sorry."

The pilot was a little surprised, but took it well.

"Fine by me," he said. "I'd rather be here than Chicago anyway." He turned toward the chopper. "I'll go shut her down."

The pilot headed back out across the field and Sawyer got back down on his knee in front of Noah. This time he spoke as well as signed, slowly, pronouncing every word carefully.

"Tell me what happened to you. I want to know."

"I got lost," Noah signed back.

"How?"

"I don't know."

Dr. Weiss touched Noah's shoulder and the boy turned to him. "I told you to hold hands. You were between Derek and Kareem. Did you let go?"

Just then, they heard the engine of the helicopter fire up. The sheriff stood in surprise, but there was nothing he could do. The pilot lifted the machine off the ground in seconds, turned in place and headed back out across the trees.

"What ... where's he going?"

The cry came from the woman who now stood on the front steps, holding the hand of a little girl about Noah's age.

"I told him the chopper was grounded, but I guess he decided to make a run for it. Hope some fighter jet doesn't shoot him down."

The woman hurried down the steps.

"Get him back here," she demanded, watching the spot where the chopper had just disappeared over the trees. "Call him or radio him or whatever — just get him back here. He can't leave us."

Sawyer sighed.

"Ma'am," he said as kindly as he could muster, and he was scraping at the dregs of his store of kindness, "I have no way to communicate with that pilot. And even if I did, and I somehow convinced him to come back — which I couldn't — it wouldn't matter. I wouldn't let you leave, either. All air traffic is grounded. Period."

"But ... but I'm ... That means we're stuck here."

"There are a whole lot worse places to be right now than in the mountains of Kentucky," Sawyer said. "It's safer here than it'd be in — where'd you come from?"

"Chicago."

"I imagine most of the residents of that fair city would gladly exchange places with you right now. The news says the outbound roads from every major city in the country are parking lots, jammed with people fleeing the cities."

"But we have to go—" She stopped, as if she hadn't really planned out where she intended to go from here.

"Welcome to Zion Academy," Dr. Weiss said expansively. "Come with me and we'll find you a room."

He turned and started to walk her up the steps.

"I need to talk to you about security, Dr. Weiss," Sawyer said.

"Tomorrow," he said without looking back. "There'll be plenty of time to talk about that tomorrow."

Sawyer knelt back down in front of Noah.

"You need to stay here," he signed.

"No, I want to go home with you!"

"Mrs. Bailey and her husband went … somewhere. They left town today." Mrs. Bailey was the housekeeper who looked after Noah when Sawyer was at work. A lot of people had left town today. He suspected most of them would be sorry they'd left, and some of them would try to get back. But going from Point A to Point B in America was likely to become exceedingly difficult in the coming days.

"Will you be alright here?"

Noah nodded solemnly, then turned his back on Sawyer and walked up the steps.

Sawyer watched him go. It was hard now even to remember the cheerful, bubbly, full-of-mischief little boy who'd crawled with him through hundreds of miles of unexplored caves. That boy had died with his mother and sister.

The radio in his cruiser crackled.

"Unit One, 911 dispatch reports a ten forty-seven on Miller Pike." A ten forty-seven was an injury accident.

The sheriff jumped behind the wheel, turned on his lights and siren and sped down the road away from Zion Academy.

Day Two

Chapter Thirteen

"SHHHH, IT'S OKAY, KIDDO," Uncle Clyde said, smoothing Star's hair and rocking her gently back and forth. "I won't let the Boogie Man get you. I'll punch him in the gizzard."

Uncle Clyde had been telling her that since she'd awakened in the grip of a paralyzing nightmare her first night in the chaotic Baker family's seventy-foot-long trailer in Sunny Vale Mobile Home Park. But even then she had known there were no real Boogie Men in the world, and probably no gizzards, either. It was a part of the human body Star had never had been able to locate.

Now, there might really be Boogie Men in the world. Not now, but soon. In five days. And she thought she might know what they looked like.

"Their teeth are like needles," she said, as Pumpkin snuggled closer to her in the bed and laid his head in her lap, whining, sensing as only he could her upset mood and need for comfort ... and hoping she'd rub in that special spot behind his ears.

"The Boogie Men in your nightmare got needle teeth?"

Uncle Clyde was a big man and she could imagine him perched on the edge of her single bed in the small bedroom at the far end of the trailer. Though Star had never "seen" him, she knew his face as well as her own. She had run her fingers over it a thousand times. Bushy eyebrows that almost met at the top of his nose. His broken nose. It had a lump on it and below the lump it bent slightly to the left. When she'd asked him how he broke it, he'd just told her, "You shoulda seen the other guy."

His broad face had little holes in it, on his cheeks, where he'd had chicken pox as a child and he had a turkey-neck flap of skin that dangled down from his chin. His shoulders were thick, muscular, and the belly that protruded out over his belt buckle was so big she couldn't get her arms all the way around him when she hugged him. He was probably not very tall because her face was on his chest under his chin when he hugged her and she wasn't very tall. He always wore cowboy boots, genuine Tony Lama boots and she had polished them for him so many times she knew every scratch and mark on them.

"I don't think it's just the Boogie Man from a nightmare," Star said, trying to get her breathing under control. She had awakened shrieking, with her sheets in a sweat-drenched tangle and her heart was still pounding, her breathing coming in short sips of air. "I think … I maybe it's — you know, *them*." She gestured toward the ceiling. "I think they're the Boogie Men."

Uncle Clyde didn't say anything for a moment so she pushed ahead.

"I've been having this dream for a month. Every night the same one. Not the same dream, just the same things in the dream. There are silver balls that just hang in the sky like they're weightless, only they're huge, big as the mountain almost. And smaller little balls whiz around them. I heard the newscaster last night say they think those space-ships, the ones that are coming, they think they're round."

"So you think you been seeing 'em … the aliens?" She could tell it was a struggle for him to get the word out.

"Uh huh."

She should have told him sooner, but she didn't want to burden the man who always seemed to be scrambling with foster children flowing into his life and back out again like surf on a beach. And Aunt Mary Ellen … them not getting along. Her whining and complaining and Uncle Clyde always trying to make it right but nothing ever suited her for long.

"But this time it wasn't just … in all the dreams, the monsters are there." She shuddered. "Some of them are giants, white, with no hair and it looks like their eyes are just black but they're not. They're blue." She took another breath. "But it's the other ones, the ones that look like … giant bugs. Or lizards with too many legs." She shuddered again and Uncle Clyde pulled her tighter to him.

"You don't have to talk about it if—"

"It doesn't matter whether I want to talk about it or not, everybody's going to be talking about it pretty soon. That's what's in those silver balls — white giants and insects with teeth like needles. They glow blue, the insects and the blue eyes of the giants glow, too, sometimes. And the insects make this sound, this horrible sound, a sucking sound."

She literally lost her breath at the memory of it and couldn't continue.

"Is there anything else in the dream?"

"No, just the boy."

Uncle Clyde knew about the boy. Star had told him

about the boy many times, how he just stood in her dreams in the background mostly, never said anything. Just looked at her. But she liked having him there, liked it when she saw him in a dream. He always made her smile. And when she saw him, she felt safe, comforted in a way she couldn't have begun to explain.

But there *had* been one other thing in the dream.

"There's a skull. A spider, a big one, like a tarantula, is crawling out of the right eye socket and a snake is slithering through the left."

"You been having this dream for a month, you say? You never cried out before."

"It was different this time. The monsters weren't just there in the dream. Just scary to look at. This time the bug one was chasing me, and he moved so fast, I couldn't get away, then he grabbed me and opened his mouth and it was like he was purring. And his teeth …"

She had no air to continue. She shook her head from side to side as if to fling the image out her ears. Then she buried her face in Uncle Clyde's chest and cried.

Finally, the crying passed and she pulled back out of his arms.

"What time is it? I didn't mean to wake you."

She hated it that she had awakened him in the middle of the night when he had to go to work in the morning. Or did he? Was there going to *be* work in the morning?

"Aw, it's almost time to get up anyway. You wash your face and get dressed and I'll open up a Breakfast Magic." Breakfast Magic came in a box. You pulled back the flap of the box to activate the heat, waited ten seconds and then pulled out a hot breakfast of eggs and toast and bacon or pancakes.

"You want pancakes or—"

Uncle Clyde's cell phone rang in the family room where he had left it on the charger.

"Who'd be calling before the sun's even up?" he said and got up off the bed and went to answer the phone.

She could hear his voice getting louder and louder as she washed her face and when she turned the water off she could hear what he was saying. She froze, listening.

"Everything? The freezer, did they break into that, too?"

He waited, listened.

"Can you fix the lock?" A pause. "Then nail it shut!"

"What happened, Clyde?" Aunt Mary Ellen had gotten up and gone into the living room. His voice had risen as he spoke, probably woke the whole house up. He ignored her question.

"You get my shotgun — it's locked in the storage room." Every night before he closed the store, he took all the weapons and locked them away. It didn't sound like last night's thieves had gotten into those. "Get it and go out to the gate and stand there with it." A pause. "I don't care if you feel foolish. Do it. Folks'll just drive on by if they see the gun. At least, until I can think of something better to do."

Uncle Clyde seldom cursed, but he let out a string of rank profanity as he stormed down the hall toward the bedroom, apparently to get dressed.

"Uncle Clyde said a bad word," said Liza. Or maybe it was Laura. The voices of the five-year-old twins were so similar that even though they'd been at the Bakers' since right after Christmas, Star had trouble telling them apart.

She went out into the hallway that ran the length of the trailer and told the girls to go into the kitchen.

"Keenan picked some fresh grananas last night," she said. Keenan was a nine-year-old boy who'd only arrived

— in the middle of the night — a month ago. Then she went down the hall and stood outside Uncle Clyde and Aunt Mary Ellen's bedroom door. It was open. She wasn't snooping. Uncle Clyde would want her to know what was going on.

"Al saw 'em," Uncle Clyde said. "Said they was four of them in a camper with Michigan plates, just pulled off the highway and parked right in front of the store. Didn't even try to hide. Broke the door window out, reached through and opened it and hauled all kinda stuff out."

"What was Al doing out there in the middle of the night?" Al was the man who operated the machinery in the Retro Amusement Park. Uncle Clyde had called him "a Slinky" once and when Star asked what that meant, he'd said, "you know, a Slinky — not really good for much, but amusing to watch when it tumbles down the stairs."

"He didn't say." Uncle Clyde paused. "Shoot, might be he went out there last night to break into the place his own self and they beat him to it."

"Al wouldn't do a thing like that."

"Who knows what anybody'll do anymore."

"What are *you* going to do?"

This time she sounded genuinely alarmed, not just her normal whiny.

There was a long pause, then Uncle Clyde sighed.

"Ain't but one thing we can do — we're moving."

"Moving?"

"This here's a *mobile* home, ain't it? Got wheels under it, ain't it? We got to get out there to the world so we can look after things around the clock. So we can make sure don't nobody else come along and steal our supplies. I should have thought about this sooner. The food, water and stuff that's out there. We need it for ourselves."

"But … but," Aunt Mary Ellen was stuttering in surprise, "… the porch … the back deck …"

"Be glad it ain't a double-wide."

"… the flowers and fence." Her horror quickly morphed into anger. "You can't *move* this house."

"Watch me."

Chapter Fourteen

PACO AWOKE to the smell of bleach, shit, piss and vomit. He didn't know where he was until he lifted his head off the pile of towels he'd used as a pillow and reality slammed down around him with the clang the prison doors made when they banged shut.

He sat up, remembered that the others had forced him to sleep on the side of the room where Tiburón had had diarrhea, the spot they'd turned into a latrine because there wasn't a bathroom in the laundry where they'd spent the night.

The door to the room that the guard had locked behind him last night suddenly flew open and an inmate came in pushing a cart with a tray on it. It was the guy missing a thumb who had reached through the bars and grabbed Paco's nuts the day before, squeezed so hard they ached still and he stifled a groan of misery at his bruised testicles.

"This place stinks!" the inmate said. "What'd you do, spend the night shitting in here?"

He indicated the cart with trays.

"This here's breakfast and it's all you gonna get so you better eat it. Only reason you get room service is the mess hall's closed on lockdown. And the only reason I'm the one bringing it to you is half the guards didn't show up this morning and the cons got to pick up the slack."

He stepped back, indicating the trays.

"Go on, eat, I ain't got all day. I got other places I gotta take food."

Paco started toward the cart and the big con moved to block his path.

"Not you, piss ant." He pointed to the filthy floor on the other side of the room. "You gonna clean that up 'fore you eat." He called to the con who was standing outside the door with another cart that was obviously bound for a cell block to feed cons who wouldn't be going to the mess hall.

"Go get him a mop and a bucket."

The other boys grabbed food and sat down on the other side of the room with the trays on the floor in front of them. Paco could see toast, maybe eggs or maybe oatmeal, some glob of something. Cartons of juice sat on each tray. None of them had a word of complaint about the food, though. A night on the floor in the shit-smelling room had tamed even the most belligerent of them. Tiburón sat off to the side, though, at least with a show of independence to indicate he was the meanest dog in the junkyard.

The other inmate returned with the mop and bucket and the thumb-less dude shoved it at Paco.

"Get to work."

Paco took the bucket on wheels that had a mop, with rollers in the middle of it to squeeze the water out.

"You know what's good for you, you'll have that mess

cleaned up 'fore I get back." Then he went out, closed and locked the door.

Paco had no idea where to start. There was pee all over the floor and clumps of feces. The pile of diarrhea was dried, near the back. Then he looked at the piles of linens, and went for it. Grabbing armfuls of towels, he threw them down on the mess, soaking it up. Then he scooted the whole mass of them off to the side while he used the mop and bucket to clean up the floor.

The other boys jeered at him as he worked. Paco on one side and everybody else on the other — that was nothing new. He'd just finished the job when the laundry room door burst open again and the big con from the first day — the one the others called Spade, stepped inside and gestured for the boys to follow him.

"Come on."

"We getting out of here?"

"Where you taking us?"

"We ain't supposed to stay locked up here. We got rights," said the black kid with the huge 'fro and it was the wrong thing to say. Spade turned on him, jacked him up against the wall and snarled into his face.

"You ain't got no rights of any kind. You got that, kid? None."

Then he threw the boy back into the line and marched along at the end, right behind Paco.

The no-thumb inmate led them through a maze of hallways and locked doors, with the guards in plexiglass-enclosed stations all along the route to open doors by tapping icons on their control console, then closed the doors behind them.

They finally entered a large room with a partition down the center made of some kind of see-through glass. It was divided into cubicles, with chairs in each and an ancient handset telephone receiver. It was where visitors came to visit inmates, who could only see them through the glass and talk to them through the phone.

The room was empty.

"You're staying in here 'til they send a van for you," Spade told them.

"What about them spaceships?" asked Jamal, the smallest of the three black kids.

"Yeah, the ones they seen on that app," said the fat, pimple-faced white kid. "That was all a joke, right?

"It wasn't no joke, punk. Why you think I'm dragging your sorry asses around instead of the guards doing it? 'Cause there ain't no guards to do it. Half of 'em didn't show up this morning 'cause they musta decided their jobs didn't matter anymore, not with the world about to end."

"Them aliens ain't gonna blow us up or something, are they?" the scrawny Hispanic boy called Hector wanted to know.

"How the hell do I know. They gonna do whatever the fuck they decide to do! That ain't your problem. And you ain't gonna be my problem much longer."

He turned toward the door but purposefully walked close to Paco as he left the room. He put his hand on Paco's shoulder and leaned close.

"You mine, sweet meat. All mine. I'm gonna get the pick of the litter and that's you. You gonna service me twelve ways to Sunday."

His touch revealed to Paco that the big con was terrified of snakes. And that he had a thing for boys, was pretending to be a good guy, but was filled with murderous intent. He was a dangerous man, maybe the most dangerous of them all.

Spade laughed, then walked out of the room and slammed the door.

Chapter Fifteen

THE PRE-DAWN LIGHT filtered through the lacy curtains on the window, warming dark corners and ascribing color and form to shadowed objects that were merely indistinct lumps in the unfamiliar room.

Ellie watched the room slowly fill with light, lying on her back in the bed that wasn't hers in a room she'd never seen before last night, in a world that in six days — no, five days — would be swarming with monsters from another galaxy.

It would be funny if it weren't real. And the thought of those aliens should have filled her, as she was sure it did everyone else, with a horrible foreboding and growing terror.

It didn't. Well, it did, but that fear was so overshadowed by the greater fear of what she would feel when she could gather the courage to touch her left breast that it seemed fairly insignificant by comparison. Which was silly. It was nothing, really. A node, whatever a node was. A swollen gland. Weren't there glands in the breast? A cyst. Or ... okay, a tumor, but benign. There was no reason to leap to the conclusion that it was cancer. That she had breast cancer on the eve of the end of the world.

She willed her hand to move under the covers to the left corner of her breast where she could swear she could feel it from the inside now, which was crazy because you couldn't feel anything inside your breast. But she could swear she could …

It wasn't there! Gone! Oh holy Jesus, Joseph and Mary it wasn't—

No, there it was. She had to feel around to find it, but the bigger-than-a-pea, smaller-than-a-marble-sized whatever was still there. Solid. Was it bigger than it'd been yesterday? It couldn't be, that was her terror talking.

And she would remain terrified until she did something about it. She *had* to see a doctor. There was treatment for breast cancer. It wasn't a death sentence anymore, not with the super chemotherapy drugs that—

Was there chemotherapy now? Was there anything like that now?

She sucked in a breath as the realizations washed over her. Would hospitals operate when the aliens came? Would there be medicine, which had to be manufactured somewhere and shipped to somewhere else, all of which required people doing their jobs. Just one break in the chain … a truck driver or a lab tech or … no electricity because the guys running the power plant—

Stop it!

Maybe people were still hanging in there doing their jobs or maybe everything in the country had already fallen apart. She didn't know. But she did know that it would get worse the closer it came to the aliens' arrival. She needed to act fast, find a doctor *now*. Where, in this little Kentucky mountain valley?

Well, if there was one, she'd find him.

She saw Dr. Weiss in the hallway of the administration building before she got to his office.

"Dr. Weiss, I need to talk to you."

The old man didn't look good. Like he hadn't slept last night. But who had? He looked at her, well, pointed his eyes at her, but she never felt like he actually saw her.

"Oh, I would love to stand and chat, young lady, but I have to—"

"I need a doctor." That stopped him in his tracks.

"Are you sick?"

"No, I mean yes." She said nothing. What was the point in hiding it? She blew through her reluctance and embarrassment.

"I found a lump … in my breast yesterday. I have to see someone right away."

The face under his mop of unruly white hair flushed scarlet. Clearly, he wasn't accustomed to that level of frankness.

"I'm afraid we only have one doctor in Jessup," he said. "Oh, and we have a chiropractor, wonderful man who … but I don't suppose a chiropractor would do you any—"

"Jessup. That's the nearest town?"

"Yes, you could drive another thirty-five miles to Bardstown, it's bigger."

"But Jessup is closer."

"Oh, my yes, right down the road."

"Will you please give me the doctor's name and telephone number?"

Dr. Weiss pulled his phone from his pocket, then paused.

"Trying to call … the service isn't very good now, not since …" He let the end of the sentence dangle.

"Since the world found out we're about to be invaded?"

"Well, yes." He looked around. "I am trying to shield the children from as much of the news as I can," he said softly. "Poor Lucy. She's my administrator and her phone has being ringing off the hook, calls from frightened parents. They want to come and get their children, but how — from New York or Miami or London? No planes in the air and the roads turned into parking lots?"

"I guess I'm fortunate I came when I did. The name and number, please. And … the number of a taxi service."

"Oh, McClintock County is not nearly populated nor advanced enough to warrant a taxi. You are welcome to borrow my car. It's parked out front. Here are the keys."

He patted his front pants pockets, his back pants pockets.

"Here somewhere …"

He finally pulled a bit of copper wire and a large bolt from his suit coat pocket.

"These are — oh, never mind." He found the keys underneath, dangling from a keyring with a Star of David pendant. "It's …" He got a funny little smile on his face. "My car, it's a humdinger."

She had no idea what he might mean by that. Then he gave her the doctor's phone number and hurried away down the hall. She punched the number into her phone.

All circuits are all busy now. Please try your call again later.

Well, she'd just have to go to the doctor without an appointment, sit and wait. He shouldn't be hard to find if he was the only doctor in a town too small for a taxi.

When she stepped out into the parking lot and saw Dr. Weiss's car, she understood what he'd meant by humdinger. The man must have quite a car fetish because the vehicle was a huge Hummer 5. She climbed inside and looked around. The vehicle had every conceivable bell and whistle, including a Mobil Eats in-dash printer that would provide her snacks, if she so desired, as she drove along.

The automatic driver's voice was British. When she told the machine the destination was Jessup, she was informed, "Oh, that won't take very long a'tall."

She looked out the windows at the view and discovered what hadn't been apparent from the helicopter. The place was as picturesque as a postcard. Towering hardwood trees, flowering pink-and-white dogwoods in the forests and wildflowers along a road as winding as a tangled string — all shadowed by the mountains beyond. Azalea bushes in full bloom, growing wild.

It was a beautiful setting.

A pretty place to die.

She slapped the thought out of her mind. She wasn't going to die here. In fact, as soon as she could get her ducks in a row, she was leaving, going … yeah, where? Back to Chicago? A city would be the worst place in the world to be at a time like this.

Right now, that really wasn't her primary concern. She reached up and felt through her blouse and bra, hoping irrationally that she really had been mistaken.

The lump was there. Bigger. She could swear it was bigger now.

The town of Jessup looked like the set for the old, old juke show her father watched, *The Randy Griffith Show*, or something like that. The town there was called Mayberry.

The folks on the street were few and she suspected that was unusual for a place like this. Many stores were not open. She passed a grocery store and saw an armed deputy standing out front and the parking lot empty.

She stopped at an intersection, rolled down her window and asked a woman where she could find Dr.

Stanhope. The woman pointed back up the street to a white house that had been converted into office space.

She pulled into the parking area beside the building and found only two cars parked there. Ellie's stomach jerked into a knot. She'd expected to find a crowd — only one doctor. There should be people standing out on the porch. Like at a restaurant that had just been selected the Dine-Out Solo of the week by the Chicago Dispatch.

A little bell jingled merrily when she opened the door. No one sat behind the counter enclosed in glass and no one sat in any of the chairs in the small waiting room. She went to the counter, tapped on the glass, then called out as politely as she could.

"Is there anybody here?"

A woman appeared from a door in the back of the reception area. She was a big woman — resembled a snowman with pudgy face, round cheeks, and a large upper body with pendulous breasts that rode atop hips that could have carried a float in the Macy's Thanksgiving Day parade.

"We're closed," she said as she approached, not even waiting for Ellie to speak. "The doctor isn't in today."

As she said the words, a man who was clearly the doctor strode down the hallway behind her. He was short, portly and had the most ridiculous goatee Ellie'd ever seen. Like maybe three chin hairs. He was carrying a cardboard box and he stopped at a cabinet and began shoving drug containers out of it into the box.

"Dr. Stanhope?" Ellie asked.

"I'm not seeing patients today," he snapped and kept working.

"Please, I ... found a lump in my breast. Can you just take a look—?"

"Ma'am, I don't have time to examine you and even if

121

I did, it wouldn't do any good. I have no lab where I can send a tissue sample."

"But … what am I supposed to do?"

"My best medical advice is … find a surgeon and get a mastectomy. That's your only safe option."

He shoved the last bottle into his bag and walked out of the room.

Ellie stood rooted to the spot in shock. The receptionist's face looked sympathetic.

"Our tissue samples always go to a lab in Louisville. Maybe you could just … you know, go directly there."

"Where?"

"I can give you the name of the oncology practice where we refer patients. You can call them. Tell them you're Charlotte at Dr. Stanhope's office, don't say you're a patient, tell them you want to schedule an appointment with Dr. Cheatham or Dr. Wong or Dr. Gillespie and you will be needing a biopsy."

Then the woman stopped her spiel and just looked at Ellie.

"But maybe they won't be there. Lots people aren't even going in to work. I mean, why bother when …?"

"You came in."

"I didn't have anywhere else to go."

She looked out past Ellie at the windows that faced the town.

"Folks are leaving, but I don't know where they're going. Dr. Stanhope's going to the Smokies."

"The smokies?"

"You know, the Smoky Mountains in Tennessee, said he had a cabin there. But I don't have no mountain cabin. Do you think they, the aliens … what do you think they want?"

Ellie had tried not to think about that. One horror at a time. But an answer burped out.

"Nothing good. It seems to me that if you're coming in peace, one spaceship will get the job done. What do you need a fleet of them for unless ... I don't imagine they've just come by to drop off a Welcome to the Universe basket."

"Will they ... you know ... kill us?"

"I don't know." Ellie said, thanked the woman and then walked out into the bright sunshine. Kentucky in the spring, a Chamber of Commerce day. She didn't get into Dr. Weiss's "humdinger." Just stood there staring up at the sky.

Another car pulled into the lot. It was the sheriff who had grounded her helicopter last night. If he'd let her fly away, she'd be ... yeah, where would she be? Her family owned houses in Palm Springs, Tahoe, San Francisco ... eight or nine different homes. She could have gone to any one of them. Which would have been better than here, her own place, her hired help ... if they came in to work.

Now, she was stuck here.

The sheriff rolled down his window.

"If you need a doctor, he's not—" That's as far as she let him get.

"What I needed you took away from me last night. If you had let me fly, I'd be—"

"Dead right now. The president pulled commercial and private planes, but not military. Fighter jets see somebody flying around up there after the grounding ... they might've blown you out of the sky."

"Shoot a civilian helicopter out of the sky? I'd gladly have taken my chances, but thanks to you, I didn't get any."

"I'm sorry about that. Look, you're new here. If I can help you …?"

He extended to her a card that read McClintock County Sheriff Sawyer Matheson, and three different phone numbers. She almost crossed her arms and refused to take it, but not only was that childish, it was stupid. He was parked crossways, blocking her path.

She snatched the card out of his hand without another word, stuck it in the case that held her phone, got into Dr. Weiss's H5, and took over the steering wheel. Using manual drive, she pulled out of the parking lot and sped away.

Chapter Sixteen

SUNNY VALE MOBILE HOME VILLAGE was the oldest of Roswell's three mobile home parks, with flowering shrubs and trees mature enough to offer shade on sweltering summer evenings when the smell of grilled hot dogs kissed the night breeze off the prairie and the symphony of crickets under the porch mingled with nearby laughter to fall on your ears soft as confetti.

Aunt Mary Ellen loved flowers, planted some everywhere she could find three grains of spare dirt. A profusion of gladiolas, cannas and iris outlined the railing of the broad deck Uncle Clyde had built onto the back of their trailer, and blood-red roses circled the sturdy wood porch out front. A serpentine road called Vale Drive wound around through the mobile home park, with driveways off it to each trailer. The bushes along Vale Drive had been planted by the builder and were now so big and thick they served as a privacy fence maintained by a lawn service that came every so often to trim the sides and lop off the top at a uniform eight feet. The lawn service mowed the lawn in the "common areas," pruned the gardens and maintained the playground, which was at the back of the park and held the traditional hard plastic tubes and mazes for children to crawl through and climb on top of a rubberized mat.

When Star stepped out onto the front porch she could see the fuzzy white blob that was the trailer next door, the green one that was the top of the tree, knew how many steps it was from the front door to the picket fence. The blobs formed remembered images crisp as a photograph in her mind. She couldn't imagine how Uncle Clyde intended to move it.

But he was intent on doing just that. She and the other children were confined in the far corner of the front yard while Aunt Mary Ellen was inside taking pictures off walls, setting breakables on the floor, tying cabinet doors shut and doing anything else she could think of to keep the whole place from being destroyed.

Uncle Clyde pulled his big double-cab diesel pickup truck up to the front of the trailer, where the frame that fit on the ball of his trailer hitch had been secluded from view for twenty years by white aluminum siding. When he started tearing away the siding, the neighbors began to suspect what he had in mind.

"You ain't thinking of trying to move that thing out of there?" asked Ralph Davies, whose family lived across the street.

"Yep," Uncle Clyde told him, and Star could hear the squalling, wrenching sound of him ripping away the aluminum siding.

"You can't do that," said Millie Cox, who had come out of her house next door and held a crying baby on her hip. "You'll tear up everything — the bushes and—" She called back into her house, "Mike, come out here. Tell Clyde he can't move his trailer."

"Of course he can't move it," Mike called from inside. Then he came out on the porch.

"Clyde, whadda you think you're doing? You can't just drag that thing out of here."

Uncle Clyde's voice was muffled, coming from under the trailer where he must have crawled to unhook the electric, water and sewer lines.

"Oh, yes, I can!" he called out.

Star could sense that a crowd was gathering, could hear the grumbling and mumbling that seemed to be turning nastier by the minute. It took Uncle Clyde a long time to get everything unhooked beneath the trailer, remove the chocks and concrete blocks from around the wheels. By the time he emerged to hook the truck to the trailer, an angry crowd of neighbors had gathered demanding that he stop before he tore out shrubs and fences and porches and God knew what all the way to the front gate.

Uncle Clyde was yelling at Tyler Wilson as the crowd shouted support for Tyler when it suddenly got deadly quiet.

"So ..." said Uncle Clyde. "You gonna shoot me if I don't stop? Is that what you're saying, John?"

John Mitchell was their next-door neighbor on the other side. The stillness was broken by the sound of him racking a shell into the chamber. Probably a 30.06, a deer rifle.

"I'm saying I'm not gonna let you vandalize this whole side of the park. You signed the park constitution, same as the rest of us. You ain't got no right to—"

"Then you're gonna have to shoot me," Uncle Clyde said.

Uncle Clyde must have gone on about what he was doing because John said, "Clyde, I'm warning you. You stop—"

"Dammit John, don't you get it." Uncle Clyde had finally lost it. "You think this time next week you're gonna care about this bush and that fence? Aliens will be here in five days! *Aliens.* For all we know there ain't gonna be a next week! It's all over — the way it was, living here, worrying about the roof leaking or your tax refund. It's done. The world ain't never gonna be like that again."

The crowd was silent. Uncle Clyde stopped yelling. His voice sounded tired and sad.

"I got to move out to Alien World so I can watch over it. Some guys from Michigan done broke into the store, stole half the canned goods, and I can't protect it from here. I got to look after me and mine … just like you got to look after yours. The best you can. As long as you can. That's what life is now. You can stick your head in the sand and pretend it ain't happenin', but that's reality. You got to change, do whatever you gotta do." Then Uncle Clyde spoke softly, some might have missed it, but Star heard. "You don't, John, and you and your family ain't gonna survive."

There was no other sound after that except the noise Uncle Clyde made banging on metal, and maneuvering his truck to put the ball of the trailer hitch beneath the catch. She could hear him grunting from the effort. Then heard him say, "Thanks, Mike."

Maybe others helped him, too. Star didn't know. But she could tell that the crowd had remained, silently watching, until he called out to her and the other kids to "get in the truck." Laura led Star by the hand toward the gray blob of truck. Pumpkin hopped inside into the back seat with the other children. Uncle Clyde went to the house to get Aunt Mary Ellen and when she was in the front seat beside him, he put the truck in gear and they began to move slowly. Star could feel the vehicle straining, heard the engine roaring.

There was a great grating, scraping sound as the trailer began to pull free of the deck on the back of the house. Uprooting and bulldozing the garden. Aunt Mary Ellen began to cry softly over the deaths of her cannas and irises. The truck must have been pointed at the hedge, to get the right angle to pull the trailer, and Star heard the cry of broken limbs scraping past the window as he ran through it.

Apparently, the front porch refused to let go of the house. The truck must have uprooted the posts but the porch itself remained attached because Liza cried, "The porch is tangled up in the fence," and she could hear the scraping sounds as the porch drawing alongside the trailer began uprooting all the fences on that side of Vale Road.

The left side of the truck bumped into something hard and scraped along the side of it. Mr. Brown's storage building, probably. She heard the mirror on that side of the truck snap off.

And as a background to the scraping, screeching, grating sounds was the sound of Aunt Mary Ellen, sitting in the front seat, crying.

The tangle of trailer house and whatever else was still attached to it, dragging along beside stopped before it went out onto the road. Star heard no traffic, not a single passing car, and couldn't imagine why the road would be empty at this time of day. Uncle Clyde got out and she could hear him hammering and banging and the sound of splintering wood and bending metal. It took almost half an hour for him to wrench all the collected debris free of the trailer. When he got back into the cab, he was panting.

"You see that smoke," he said to Aunt Mary Ellen, who was still sniffling softly.

"Wow," said Liza.

"What is it?" asked Star.

"It's a black cloud of smoke," he said. "Something big's on fire in town. Big enough to stop traffic so there ain't no cars coming out this way."

"But there aren't any sirens," Star said. "I didn't hear any trucks."

"Ambulance service never answered when I called 911 yesterday either. I guess there ain't no fire department anymore."

That chilled Star to the bone.

Then Uncle Clyde turned his big truck and pulled the trailer house out onto the road for the trip to Alien World. There were no cars behind them. And few coming toward them must have moved off to the side of the road to let them pass. When they got to Alien World, the railings and the first two steps of the front porch were still attached to the trailer.

Chapter Seventeen

Opportunity had come knocking. Yessiree it sure had for a fact and when opportunity knocks on yo door, you're a one-eyed wing nut if you don't break both your legs getting to the door to throw it *wide* open.

You don't answer it fast enough, opportunity gonna go next door and see do them folks welcome it.

And you got to invite opportunity in when you see it standing out there on your porch. You got to drop whatever else it was you'd got planned, no matter how important it might have sounded before you heard that knock, because you got to give your *undivided* attention to what's standing hot and stinking on yo front porch.

Cornelius Tyrone Jackson hadn't got to where he was today by turning a deaf ear to the knock of opportunity. No, sir! The man who had decided about age seven that his name was Spade, and then beat the shit out of every kid in the neighborhood who dared to call him anything else, had spent his life doing his dead-level best to squeeze every drop of juice out of whatever fruit of good fortune life handed him.

Though there had been some inconvenient bumps in the road of his life — like partnering up with the trigger-happy ass-wipe who'd shot that security guard — Spade had managed to come out on top in most of the circumstances he found himself in his whole thirty-five years on Earth.

On top here at RC, Radcliffe Correctional Facility, had required sucking up to every guard, social worker, special programs director, or anybody else with a badge or a gun who had crossed his path in the past nine years. He'd figured out early on that if you was a big man, you'd better convince the world you was a "gentle giant" or you'd be in a shitstorm noon to midnight, so he hadn't so much as raised his voice here. Well, except yelling at them Scared Straight kids and it was his job to yell at them.

It'd been his "unassuming" manner that'd earned him the privilege of yelling at those snot-nosed little punks. And that had made it possible for him to work his way out of security Level A, through Level B in the cell blocks and all the way out to Cell Block C, the barracks unit, where the inmates weren't locked behind bars but lived like soldiers — or Boy Scouts — with nothing but their own self-discipline and good judgement to keep them from killing each other. That part wasn't near as hard as keeping his hands off the necks of the stupid guards who acted like your "friend," hung out and talked baseball with you like the two of you was just sitting on stools side by side in a bar, having a beer with the boys before you went home to the wife and kids. Of course, the guards *did* go home to a wife and kids while you lay in your bunk in a room full of men just *thinking* about it.

Spade was the most trusted of all the trustees in the prison — which earned him privileges his fellows locked up by themselves twenty-three hours of every day, let out for

precisely sixty minutes in a concrete block exercise yard —
would have given both nuts for.

He worked in the laundry — was the inmate supervisor
of the whole inmate crew who washed the prisoners'
uniforms, sheets, pillow cases, towels, underwear and jock
straps — and served as the receiving dock for smuggled
drugs, cigarettes and booze and every other sort of contraband some con might be willing to pay for. He'd spent
several years as the head man in the small factory that
made license plates, along with all manner of weapons,
from shivs thin as an ice pick to that machete Carlos
Castillo had stashed behind a wall tile under the latrine in
the exercise yard crapper.

He also headed up the crew of other tough-looking
inmates tasked with scaring the shit out of the teenagers
the bleeding hearts had sent to RC to see first-hand the
consequences of making bad decisions. Spade had to exercise his well-muscled self-discipline as well as his biceps and
triceps to keep from rolling his eyes or busting out laughing
at the do-gooders' stupidity. Shit, you didn't get locked up
in a place like Radcliffe for making bad decisions. You got
locked up because you got caught!

But that wasn't what they wanted the boys to hear,
wasn't on the script, and Spade played the part they'd
assigned him. In the beginning, he was the meanest-
looking and sounding of the inmates allowed into the big
holding cell across the hall from the laundry room, where
they could yell at the boys and grope whichever ones got
thrown up against the bars of their cell. Tell 'em what
you'd like to do to them, which wasn't a part of no script
'cause it wasn't hard to remember. The fresh meat aroused
all the cons and without the guards to protect them the
cons would have fallen on those boys like attacking lions,
fighting for their own sweet piece of ass, nice even if you

hadn't been locked away from women during the best years of your life.

And Spade could swing either way. Boys, little girls, women. He'd hump anything with a pulse, got his rocks off with them all. In actual point of fact, though, he thought boys was the juiciest of them all.

After a while, he'd worked his way out of the holding cell and into the elite squad of badasses actually allowed to touch the boys, get up in their faces, grab a handful of sweet meat — oh, just to scare 'em, that's all. Just playin' the part he was assigned. He was a man who knew how to play whatever part was needed to get what he wanted, had his future *outside* all mapped out — the men he intended to take out for one good reason or another, the step-by-step approach to moving in on some dealer's territory and making it his own. With five years knocked off his sentence for all his good behavior, he was looking at being released before he had to pass another change of seasons locked up in RC.

Until yesterday, that is.

Everything had changed yesterday morning when them spots showed up out there in space and the telescope on the far side of the moon beamed pictures of them down into every cell phone on the planet.

Wasn't nothing in life ever gonna be the same again. Nothing.

And if you was real quiet — and Spade knew how to be so quiet he could sneak dawn past a rooster — you could hear the knock, knock, knock of opportunity on your door.

Spade didn't give a gallon of rhino piss what the little green men out there did when they got here. They'd blow the world to hell and back or they wouldn't and either way Spade didn't have no say over it. What he did have say over was his response to how the world was at this very moment shitting its pants about it.

That was the opportunity that had come knocking at his door, offering all manner of possibilities to a man willing to take action and move fast. Ole Spade had greeted that sucker on his porch with open arms and a can of beer.

That's why he was standing outside in the receiving area, waiting for the van from the California Department of Corrections to arrive to collect the Scared Straight boys. Ordinarily, they wouldn't have let nobody but a guard out into the receiving area, but seeing as how more'n half the guard staff didn't show up to work this morning, they was severely shorthanded, and in times like those, they looked to their most trusted trustee for assistance.

They knew Spade Jackson wouldn't let 'em down.

Just then, the big gate at the end of the driveway leading to the receiving area began to slide back. When it was open, the gray DOC van pulled through it and drove up to the spot where Spade was waiting for it. He'd been waiting, as a matter of fact, for more than two hours.

"Don't give me no shit about being late," the driver said as the van rolled to a stop. "You better be damn glad I made it at all. You seen the traffic out there? Everybody's on their way to somewhere and that somewhere is out of the city. I would be, too, if I had anywhere to go."

"Hate it that you went to all this trouble for nothing."

The man had been opening the van door but stopped and stared at Spade.

"What are you talking about?"

"Them kids is already gone," Spade said. "When you didn't show up on time, the warden got his panties all in a wad, didn't want to be responsible if something happened to them. So he sent 'em off about an hour ago in one of the prison paddy wagons."

"Are you shitting me!" Then he let out a string of obscenities as he slammed the door shut hard enough to shatter the window.

Spade just shrugged.

"You'll have to take that up with the warden," he said, but the man wasn't listening. He had already shoved the van into reverse and pulled violently backward out of the receiving area drive, then swung the vehicle around and shot out gravel behind the tires as he peeled back down the access road.

Spade smiled, but didn't go back into the building right away. He'd wait another hour at least — the whole prison was going to shit and nobody would notice or care that he hadn't returned. Then he could just say he'd waited three whole hours and that damn DOC van never showed.

Chapter Eighteen

NOAH's first thought when he opened his eyes was that he'd had a horrible nightmare about aliens and being in the dark in the caverns and—

Then Noah came full awake and knew he hadn't been dreaming.

Aliens. *Aliens?*

That was something that happened to people in sci-fi movies like the vintage ones his father had shown him from his collection of old movies and shows on his juke. *Invasion of the Body Snatchers. War of the Worlds. Independence Day. Star Wars. Signs* had been his favorite.

This couldn't be *real*.

People died in those movies. Monster aliens attacked and covered the world in human blood, or showed up quietly and grew a pod beside your bed that became you.

That didn't happen in real life.

It couldn't.

Noah wanted to cry. He wanted his father, wanted to run into his arms and then maybe sit in his lap like a little kid. He wanted to tell him about the nightmares, the silver marbles hanging in the sky and the monsters, and to ask him if … was it possible he'd been dreaming about aliens? Was that what the white spots were — the silver marbles in his dreams? And the monsters … were they …?

But Dad was in town, trying to be a sheriff in a world about to be invaded. Noah needed somebody …

Brother Sebastian. Yes! He was the monk most proficient at ASL so he could understand Noah and communicate with him. But even if he hadn't been able to sign a single word, Noah would have just hung out with him in silence.

He seemed to be about as wide as he was tall. In his brown robe he looked like a milk chocolate fire hydrant, bald except for a soap ring of brown around the bottom. It took him a while to find Brother Sebastian. The Gethsemane order of monks had several hundred, he didn't know exactly how many, and ran a fully functioning farm. Even with the children used as what some of the kids called "slave labor" there were still gardens to till, cattle to milk, chickens to feed … no end to the number of chores — and the monks swapped out jobs.

Finally, Brother Luke said Brother Sebastian was working in the mill. The mill was one of the original buildings on the monastery property, hundreds of years old. A modern, high-tech hydroponics building had been squeezed in between the mill and the barn with a hole knocked in the old mill wall to make a doorway into it. But Noah went around to the front of the building and pulled open the heavy wooden door. When Noah closed the door behind him, he felt pressure in his ears.

Brother Sebastian saw him grimace and signed to him.

"The old brothers knew how to build," he said, gesturing around the cavernous room with a low ceiling. "They cut these rocks by hand and then fit them together so snug this room is just about airtight. I suppose it needs to be, wouldn't do to have wind blowing through a window" — he nodded toward the lone small window on the wall, the kind that didn't open — "into a room full of flour."

He made a sweeping motion with his hand in front of his nose.

"Sneeze hazard."

Noah smiled.

"Want to see how it works?"

Noah nodded.

The monk pointed up.

"The grain is in a big hopper above the ceiling. It runs down that chute there" — he indicated the thing that looked like a pipe without a top where grain slid slowly down — "into this small hopper." He pointed to a cone-shaped metal bowl resting atop a great round stab of rock incased in a round wooden frame.

"That's the grindstone," he said. "There are two of them, but you can only see the top one, the one that moves. There is one just like it below that stays still."

Brother Sebastian spoke as well as signed, so the combination of reading his lips and his signs made him easy to understand.

"So the grain runs down between the stones, and the movement of the grindstone pulverizes the grain into flour, which comes out here." He pointed to a long flat open-toed wooden box with a metal box inside.

"What makes the grindstone move?"

"That rod," he said, pointing to a slowly turning rod that went down into the stone.

"What makes the rod move?"

"Gears," the old monk said, as if they were a wondrous thing indeed. "Want to see?"

Noah nodded and the monk took him to a ladder that went up the side of a big metal box at the back of the room.

"Climb up and look down into the box. Don't go all the way to the top and out on the catwalk. That's too dangerous. If you fell off, those gears would grind you up like hamburger."

Noah climbed high enough to look over the edge and saw a tangled maze of metal gears in graduated sizes with the biggest being six feet across. He looked back but didn't sign because he had to hold onto the ladder with one hand.

"And you want to know what makes the gears move?" the monk signed. Noah nodded.

The old monk smiled. "Historically, it would have been water, like from a stream, moving a paddle — you've seen pictures of those."

Noah nodded.

"But old dogs can be taught new tricks. There are solar panels on the roof that keep it moving non-stop all day, even with no grain to grind if I forget to turn it off when I leave." He gestured toward a switch on the far wall.

Noah felt a vibration in the metal of the gear box, like maybe some kind of buzzer had gone off. The metal rod stopped turning and the door into the hydroponics lab slid instantly open.

"Come on back down," Brother Sebastian said. "Something's got stuck in the gear box. Whatever it is, it's bigger than a rat to trip the alarm. You could have spread the last rat that got caught in there on toast — not that you'd want to." Brother Sebastian wrinkled his nose.

When Noah got to the bottom of the ladder, the monk was gathering up his robes to climb up it.

"Let's have a look." he said.

He went slowly up the ladder and climbed out onto the

catwalk that ran across the top of the gear box. It was probably three feet wide but there was no railing and the old man wasn't terribly steady on his feet. Even if the gears weren't turning to grind him into hamburger, a fall down into them would surely be fatal.

After getting down on his hands and knees and peering off the edge of the catwalk, the monk climbed back down the ladder.

"I can't tell what's jammed," he said. "Would you mind going over to the kitchen and asking Brother Thaddeus to come have a look while I bag up the last of this flour?"

Noah liked Brother Thaddeus, too. All the kids did. He was almost like a cartoon character, never quite seemed to know where he was, but was a mechanical genius, could fix anything, had once broken his nose running into a wall when he tried to demonstrate a bat's sonar. And he was so kindhearted he'd devised a painless way to kill the spring lambs by putting them to sleep so they wouldn't cry out.

Brother Sebastian suddenly turned toward the big wooden door Noah had come in, then visibly relaxed.

"Glad I didn't lock it," he said. "If I had, Brother Thaddeus would have been replacing a broken lock as well as fixing whatever's gummed up the works in there."

He could see Noah wasn't getting it.

"Whenever something goes wrong mechanically, something stuck in the gears or the hopper comes loose, this awful buzzer goes off and the door into hydro zips open all on its own."

He held up his hand to forestall Noah's question, though he hadn't been about to ask one.

"I have no idea why."

Clearly Brother Sebastian was not a fan of new technology. Most of the monks weren't. Noah didn't think any of them even had cell phones. "Things opening and closing automatically — tearing the locks right off the doors. I'm afraid to scratch my nose around here for fear my underwear will *automatically* fall off."

Noah smiled broadly.

"That smile looks good on you, son."

Noah felt the smile drain away. He hadn't noticed that the knot in his belly that made it hard for him to eat or sleep had untied while he was talking to Brother Sebastian. It was a physical pain when it suddenly yanked back tight.

Brother Sebastian laid his arm around Noah's shoulder. When he did, the monk's calm and peace spread out through Noah's whole body as warm and comforting as hot chocolate on a cold morning. That was one of the things Noah liked most about the monks, particularly Brother Sebastian. They were serene, and when he touched them, their emotional well-being flowed over him like a wave climbing the shore.

The wave always receded, though. When Noah felt the emotions of others, they always struck him hard and then receded, which was a good thing when he happened upon someone who was sad or angry. But he wished he could hold onto the feelings he could sense from the monks.

"I get it. Aliens. That's scary stuff, isn't it?"

Noah nodded, wanted to ask about the dreams, but didn't know where to start.

"Everybody on the entire planet Earth was surprised when those ships suddenly showed up on the telescopes … but you know who *wasn't* surprised."

Noah shook his head.

"God. He separated the light from the darkness, created the heavens and the earth. Nothing … *nothing* happens that he didn't either cause or allow. There's no need to be afraid."

But Noah was afraid. Terrified.

The monk gently patted Noah's shoulder.

"He's got this, son." The monk's tender smile spread out into wrinkles all over his face like cracks spreading out from a broken windshield. "Off you go now. Brother Thaddeus will be glad to see you. He much prefers to tinker with machinery than to hang laundry on the line."

Noah remembered Father Sebastian thumbing his nose at the dryer the housekeepers used in the dorms.

"That's why God created the sun," he'd said. "I have it on the highest authority that solar panels are a personal affront to His dignity."

Chapter Nineteen

HANKY'S TAVERN WAS QUIET, everybody speaking in subdued voices, soft, like they was in church. Like maybe they thought the aliens on them ships out there in the sky could hear 'em if they spoke up any louder.

Ancil Wickliffe lifted his beer and took a big swallow, looking up at the juke screen that'd been put above the bar so Charlie Daniels could call the place a sports bar, so the guys could come in here and watch the game, the Cowboys and the Steelers, or the local ENMU — Eastern New Mexico University — against Baylor, drink their beer and let their wives stay home as true football widows.

Wives.

Edith.

Ancil's throat tightened. He had got where he couldn't even picture her face. Couldn't call it up in front of him. Kelly Ann and Stephanie, too. He had to struggle to remember what they looked like and it'd just been two years. Now, when they stepped onto centerstage in his mind — the three of them were always waiting in the wings, only a thought away — what he saw were the faces in pictures. He'd stared at the pictures of them for so long he'd about looked the images right off 'em. But now that's what he saw, not how Stephie looked when she giggled, or Kelly Ann when she was little and got the hiccups and every time she'd hick her whole little body would shake like she was having a seizure.

Or how Edie looked, staring up at him, her eyes wide open when he made love to her. Men said their wives closed their eyes during sex but Edith always kept hers open. Said she wanted to see his face, watch it register the pleasure she was giving him.

They were gone now. Not just the three people he cared most about in the whole world, but even their images were gone. Blown away by the wind.

At just that moment, a gust of prairie wind banged the sign out front, set it to squeaking where the S hooks affixed it to the screws in the porch ceiling.

He hadn't felt the wind that day. He'd been safe in Roswell. Had not even been concerned when he saw the sky darken. Who worried about storms anymore? The SWSS would give plenty of warning if there was going to be trouble and the Meteorological Management Center made sure there wouldn't be trouble. Controlled the whatever it was in the atmosphere so them big thunderheads that spawned tornadoes couldn't even form.

But one had formed that day. Easter Sunday. He and Edie and the girls had gone to church, then he'd dropped his "three favorite ladies" off at home while he went to work in the car lot in Roswell. Even Easter Sunday was a busy day; folks had time on their hands to browse and you had to get them on the lot to get their names on the dotted line.

He had been closing a deal, in fact, when the sheriff came to tell him. The twister, the one that little Indian squaw had told Edie would strike, had done just that, exactly like she'd said it would. It had wiped Slidell, New Mexico off the map and taken from Ancil his whole world.

He hadn't listened to Star Yellowhorse's "prediction." Why would he? Why would anybody? She was nothing but a fake fortune teller in that circus Clyde Baker ran out on Route 28. Alien World. Claimed she could see the future in them alien rocks from out in the desert where that ship had landed.

Alien rocks.

It was a joke.

When Edie'd said she and her girlfriends had their fortunes told and the squaw said she seen a tornado blowing Edie away, he had laughed right out loud. Edie hadn't seen as much humor in it as he did. It had made her uneasy. That was one reason he'd dropped the girls off and went on in to work that day. He was showing them he knew everything was gonna be fine and they didn't need to worry about no stupid predictions.

Except, of course, it hadn't been fine.

He lifted his eyes to the screen above the bar. The sound had been turned down. Nobody wanted to hear what the newscasters were saying. The pictures told the story sure enough. There really were aliens. They were coming, little white specks on the Astral app, everybody could see them, flying in some kind of formation. They were just specks, of course, but they could tell they were flying in formation. Meteors didn't line up in neat rows.

It was aliens.

Not a joke.

Shoot, the other aliens probably weren't a joke either. They'd probably been real, but the government hauled them off to Area 51 and put out that it was a hoax and everybody believed what the government said.

But them aliens had been real, too.

He took another swig of his beer, set it down and looked at the screen. There was nothing there but spots, but he stared at them same as everybody else.

When he picked the beer back up and put the glass to his lips, he couldn't swallow. He couldn't even breathe. It was like he'd been struck by lightning. It came to him, all at once. Poof! Like he'd been in a dark cave somewhere and then somebody'd lit a lantern. Dark, then light. Can't see, then everything's clear.

Them other aliens, the ones back in the 50s, they'd been real. *And them alien rocks, they was real, too.*

And *that* explained everything.

He turned to Billy Rodriguez, sitting one stool away to the right, sipping something clear in a shot glass — vodka or tequila. It was tequila.

"You know where they're going, doncha," Ancil said.

"Yeah. Earth. That's what the news said."

"I don't mean that. *Where* on Earth?"

"How would I know where—?"

The bell on the door rang and Ray Phillips came in, strode to the bar and sat down on the stool between Ancil and Billy. He crooked his finger for Charlie — Charlie Daniels — the bartender's name wasn't even Charles, but he'd glommed onto the "Charlie Daniels" name because of some famous country western singer a long time ago. The young men these days, they weren't impressed because they'd never heard of him.

"Gimme a Forrester," he said.

"Light?"

"Full octane. What's the point in watching your waistline when the world's gonna end altogether in six days?"

"Five," Ancil said, and looked around Ray to continue his conversation with Billy.

"You may not know where they're coming, but I do. They're coming *here*, right here to Roswell, New Mexico."

"Who's coming here?" Ray asked.

Ancil ignored him.

"Why do you think they—?"

"Because they've been *summoned*, that's why."

"You mean 'cause that spaceship crashed out in the desert back in—"

"I mean because somebody's *calling* 'em. Bringing 'em here. Somebody who's been talking to 'em all along except didn't nobody believe it was real."

"You talking about Star Yellowhorse?" Ray asked. Just the way he said her name made it clear he didn't have no use for her, neither.

"What makes you think she's—?"

"Don't you get it?" Ancil said. His raised voice turned heads in the too-quiet bar but he didn't care. "Don't you understand that it was always real, just so preposterous we all thought it was fake. Star has been in communication with the aliens for years. Through them rocks."

Owen Alexander got up from the nearby table where he'd been sitting, listening to the conversation as his wide eyes remained fixed in wonder and horror on the juke screen. He walked to the bar and sat on the stool on the other side of Ancil.

"You really b'lieve that?" Owen asked. "You think she's been talkin' to them aliens?"

"You tell me," Ancil said. "You tell me how else she could do the things she done, know the things she knew."

He took a swig of beer.

"How else did she know about that twister?" Nobody had to ask what twister he was talking about. He'd bragged to his buddies here that he wasn't gonna take his family and crawl into some hidey-hole just 'cause that little squaw said he ought to. So he never brought it up at the bar. But he did tonight.

"The only possible way a twister could have slipped past the SWSS, the only way a storm could have formed in the first place was if Star got her alien friends to jam the satellite feed or tinker with the meteorological management stations that regulated the weather."

He realized that the murmur of conversations in the bar had quieted. Everybody was listening to him.

"That little Indian squaw knew there'd be a twister Easter Sunday because she *orchestrated it* through her alien buddies."

Nobody said anything then. Probably because nobody wanted to argue with Ancil, seeing as how he had lost his wife and two daughters in the twister.

"You don't believe me?" he said, suddenly belligerent, directing the comment at nobody in particular. "Well, you're gonna believe me in five days when them alien spaceships start dropping out of the sky and landing on Main Street."

"Why would they come here?" somebody asked. He couldn't tell who.

"Why do you think? Them aliens is here for payback. One of their own crashed out there in the desert and the government hauled them away and cut 'em up like they was cleaning fish. You don't think they're pissed about that?"

There was an uneasy murmur of assent. Nobody liked the thought of that scenario, but they couldn't argue the logic of it.

"Star Yellowhorse has been chatting away with them little green boogers for years and the first thing they're gonna do when they get here is even the score. Hone in on Star to lead them to—"

He stopped in mid-sentence, mid-thought.

Yep, Star would lead them alien spaceships right here to Roswell, New Mexico unless … unless Star wasn't around to do the leading.

"Them aliens is gonna use Star as a beacon," he said, "like them fellas with the flashlights in both hands directing airplanes into the gates."

"You don't think they could find Roswell without some flashing light guiding them?" That was Roger Willingham, sitting at the far end of the bar.

"Duh," said Owen Alexander, "they found it once before, didn't they?"

Ancil stopped talking then. Turned around on his stool to face the bar and looked down into the dregs of his beer in the glass, his mind churning.

Owen got up and went back to his table, but Billy Rodriguez leaned over Ray, his voice quiet.

"Are you thinking what I'm thinking?" he asked

Ray Phillips, sitting between them, couldn't miss what they said. And he was of the same mind.

"Maybe they didn't need Star to guide 'em," he said, "but you're right about one thing: they're gonna come here. And they're gonna be *pissed*."

Day Three

Chapter Twenty

ELLIE SAT on the side of Gretchen's bed, holding her as she cried.

"I can't hear, Mommy," the little girl wailed.

"Not at all?"

"Sometimes I can. But it blinks on and off. Before ... *I could hear.* I wasn't deaf anymore, and now—"

The communications network that made Dr. Weiss's famous hearing system work had become totally unreliable.

Things all over the planet were rapidly going to hell in a handbasket.

Las Vegas had burned. *Burned!* The whole city, up in flames. There was news footage of food riots in Omaha. *Omaha, for crying out loud.* Who riots in Omaha?

Ellie had had no real hope that anything would get better, unless ...

Unless the aliens just flew by, waved and went on their merry way.

Or they came offering peace, putting daisies in the gun barrels all over the world that would be trained on them.

Or...

Who knew?

An hour later, with Gretchen calmed, Ellie got ready to go to Louisville.

She had spent some time in Jessup yesterday, buying the bare essentials, since she had literally arrived in Kentucky with nothing but the clothes on her back. She needed everything. She tried several of the dress shops along Main Street that appeared to be upscale establishments, as upscale as anything got in Jessup, Kentucky. But all of them were closed.

And that's how she ended up ... at *Walmart*. Elliot Thurgood Hampton at Walmart! The place was jammed. The hardware department was chaotic. Everybody wanted a generator, and there were no generators to be had.

This Walmart only had a few rows of essential food items and Ellie noticed when she walked in the door that those shelves were completely bare. No, not bare, there was a single box of Frosted Asteroids cereal. Appropriate. As she looked at it, a woman snatched it up and completed the sweep.

Ellie wasn't shopping for groceries or generators. She left with three huge bags — clothes, toiletries, socks, underwear, several kinds of shoes, which, though they were certainly not brands she'd ever heard of, looked like they'd hold up under some rugged wear. She bought pajamas, shampoo, toothpaste and dental floss — everything.

After that, she went to the lone car dealership in town and bought a car. There was only one salesperson and maybe a couple of people working in the back. The garage portion of the building was closed. She'd walked briskly past the new cars, picked one out and handed the salesman her credit card. He had been a bit flustered. Apparently, the good people of Jessup, Kentucky, didn't customarily purchase vehicles with credit cards, but he ran it and it went through.

How long would *that* last?

She had wanted to get a few thousand in cash out of the bank, but it was closed. The ATM still functioned, but it had a thousand-dollar limit so she withdrew that much and figured she'd go by on her way out of town and withdraw more. Maybe there'd be banks open in Louisville.

Her car had been delivered to the academy early this morning, fully gassed up. She had signed the car dealership's paperwork, but the manager had told her he wouldn't be able to go to the courthouse to transfer the title until ... well, until the courthouse opened back up.

So technically, the car didn't even belong to her. Like that mattered.

Ellie left Zion right after lunch, let the car drive itself, watched the scenery out the window and allowed her mind to wander just a little bit. She kept a tight rein on her emotions, had to for Gretchen, and that required she not think about ... certain things. She turned on the radio but the news was too depressing. Riots. Fires. And the alien vessels ... they were still coming. She turned it back off and tried to consider what the future might look like.

Not the future medically. She had those thoughts in straitjackets, locked away in stone dungeons deep in the guts off her mind. Just ... the future. She was a billionaire stuck in a little town ... like most people jamming freeways out of the cities were trying to escape *to*.

Getting back to her world was important, of course, but she had to focus on what mattered most right now. There would be time for other things later. Now, she had two priorities: Gretchen and getting medical attention. Everything else in her life was below that on her to-do list.

She had heard such scary things about the roads that

she was apprehensive about going to Louisville today, but she didn't have any choice about that. She had spent the whole of yesterday afternoon wrangling an appointment with Dr. Wang or Wong or some other Asian name. She'd written it down. The woman she finally got to talk to in his office said the doctor was expected to be in, seeing patients. But there was no guarantee that the support services he typically used would be available. All the laboratories in the University of Louisville Medical Center, where biopsies were typically performed, had been closed yesterday with no guarantee they'd be open by today.

Ellie had no choice but to drive to Louisville, park her butt in the doctor's waiting room until … Dammit, she had a lump in her breast.

She'd made herself a promise that she wouldn't keep touching it. She was making it sore just from fingering it. And if she did that she wouldn't know if it really began to hurt from some other more sinister reason. But she couldn't help herself, and even as she thought about her promise, she was touching it, feeling the lump that she could swear was bigger.

It couldn't be.

It *was*.

She encountered very little traffic as she passed through stereotypical "rural America." The three convenience stores with gasoline pumps had lines of cars waiting to fill up. Gratefully, she had enough gas to get to Louisville and back to Jessup without having to stop.

As she neared the ramp onto Interstate 65 north toward Louisville, traffic began to back up. She edged onto the interstate, drove perhaps half a mile and then traffic stopped altogether. She waited. Ten minutes. Twenty. Was there a wreck up ahead, something barring the road? There was no way to tell and she was boxed in, a guard rail on the right and cars in front, behind and on the other side. Cars in the southbound lane were stopped, too. In one of those cars filled with people abandoning the city, was there a lab tech from the University of Louisville Medical Center who wouldn't be at work today?

She sat without moving for three hours. Then, traffic began to inch forward, agonizingly slowly. It was late afternoon before she even reached the city limits of Louisville, almost evening before she came upon the cluster of hospitals on the east side of the interstate right before the bridges that crossed the Ohio River into Indiana. Jewish Hospital, Kosher Children's Hospital, the University of Louisville Medical Center were all within sight of each other, separated by buildings that must house medical offices, rehab facilities — and, please God — tissue labs.

The rising hope that surged in her breast ebbed as she exited the interstate and vanished altogether before she'd driven two blocks. The streets were full of people, most of them ragged, dirty and unkempt. Communities of homeless people apparently lived under the Interstate 65 overpasses, which looked like garbage trucks had stopped there to dump their day's pickups. Trash was everywhere, not just in the gutters, but strewn out across the street so she had to drive through it. And there was furniture, appliances, "all the comforts of home" shoved up high in the dark recessed beneath the freeway.

She didn't like the way the people on the street looked at her as she drove past. There was a desperation in their eyes that chilled her to the bone. Fear grabbed her belly and squeezed. She got off the street as quickly as possible, drove into a parking garage with no attendant manning the little box office and parked on the side facing the building with U of L Medical Center emblazoned on the side in red letters.

When she walked purposefully through the milling throngs, even her Walmart clothing, new and clean, set her apart. She realized as soon as she entered the building that everything was all wrong. No receptionist at the information desk. People who clearly had no business being here wandering in and out of rooms marked "staff only." Stubborn resolve and her own desperation carried her. Dr. Wang's office was on the fourth floor. She eschewed the elevator for the stairs — she didn't want to be sealed in a small box with any of these people — and wound her way up.

As she climbed the steps, she steeled herself. Okay, she was hours late for her appointment, but that was *not* her fault. They'd just have to understand. She refused even to countenance the idea that the doctor might already have left for the day. There were so many people … he'd be too busy to leave. She would march into his office and *demand* to see him. She would refuse to be silenced until—

When she stepped out into the fourth-floor hallway, she realized she'd made a mistake. Perhaps only the elevators went to the floors with medical offices because clearly she was on the fourth floor in a hospital. And it was chaos.

The people in the hallway were the street people she'd seen — and worse. A woman cried out from the hospital room on the right, begging for help, but Ellie saw no nursing staff in sight and there was a brawl going on at the nurse's station down the hall — two big men clutched armloads of boxes while a third held off a crowd of half a dozen other people, hammering at them with a fire extinguisher. A man with wild eyes peeking through a mass of hair and beard burst out of a room between her and the nurse's station and raced toward her. He held several IV bags with tubing attached, dangling behind him as he ran. She stepped out of his way or he'd have knocked her down, and he hit the stairs door at a dead run. When the door closed behind him, it caught one of the tubes and Ellie could see a needle on the end of it. Had the man stolen bags attached to patients …?

She turned and ran, too.

The crowd in the hospital lobby had doubled in just the few minutes she'd been gone and she had to shove her way through it to the doors. The crowd outside in the growing dark was even bigger and as she stepped out into it … something snapped. Some spark ignited the fuel of desperation, the fumes of nothing-left-to-lose and between one heartbeat and the next, the whole world exploded in a riot.

Ellie bolted in full-out panic. A man grabbed her, groped her, but she jerked away, spun around and faced another man with a knife. A bloody knife. As she stood frozen, he stabbed the man who'd grabbed her, plunged the knife into his belly without provocation. An angry rumble of voices — screams, shouted obscenities — ate up the world around her and she pinballed off people, staggering, almost tripped over the body of a woman lying on the sidewalk with blood spreading out around her. Smoke. Someone had set a car on fire. More than one.

And so she ran. People grabbed at her. A man caught her shirt and shoved her against a wall and she bit him and he let go. She kept running. Away, only away. But the riot had spread out like burning gasoline into the people wandering the streets, and she couldn't seem to get out ahead of it. She heard gunshots in the distance, and then nearby. Everywhere she looked people were fighting, women were screaming. Teenagers were throwing Molotov cocktails at houses, buildings, cars, setting the streets ablaze, sending sparks spiraling up into the night sky.

The gang of teenage boys spotted her when she staggered to a stop beneath a street light at an intersection and put her hands on her knees, gasping for breath. She saw a big black kid elbow an even bigger white kid and point to her, then both of them — along with two or three others — crossed the street toward her. She turned and ran down the sidewalk beside a restaurant, turned into the dark alley behind it and was halfway down it before she saw the chain-link fence topped with razor wire blocking the end.

Trapped! She looked around, frantic, panic gripping her chest so tight she could barely breathe.

A dumpster stood behind the restaurant. She ran to it, lifted the black lid, clambered up over the side and dived into it, letting the lid fall shut above her. The stench was unimaginable, triggering a gag reflex Ellie had to grit her teeth to resist. Putrid food, rotting there in the heat of the sunbaked dumpster.

"… she go, man?"

"Could be anywhere, it's too dark to—"

"Fuck it, there's other hoes around."

"I want that one, classy white bitch, rip her clothes off and fuck her blind. Hurt her, too. Hurt her bad."

"Bitch's gone, let's go—"

"She hidin' in the shadows. She'll come out."

"You gonna sit here and wait—?"

"Gimme some of that weed!"

The boys were at the head of the alley, not twenty feet away! They must have lit joints because they stayed where they were talking and laughing.

They were making so much noise, in fact, that Ellie barely heard the squeak of the first rat.

Chapter Twenty-One

At least the visitation room had a bathroom. The boys didn't have to make a latrine in a corner somewhere. Paco waited his turn to use the facilities. He was last, shoved around by the other, bigger boys, but eventually they'd all taken care of business and he had a chance to do something about the stench of feces and urine that still clung to him from cleaning up the mess Tiburón and the others had made in the corner.

He stood in front of the sink and looked into what passed for a mirror in a prison, a piece of polished metal that gave you a general idea of what you looked like. Now, in here by himself, he allowed himself to feel some of the emotions he'd been stuffing since he passed through the doors of this hellhole two days ago.

He looked at his face and practiced making it totally impassive, showing no emotion at all, then relaxed and watched his own fear appear in the haunted look in his eyes. Paco'd never been afraid like this. He'd glided through life and situations, manipulating other people, knowing shit he couldn't know, making his own way. He could have done that here, should have done it or something like it, but he'd been too rattled and frightened to concentrate. The world had shifted under his feet and he wasn't sure of anything anymore. There had been rules, people in charge, the comfort of knowing that the rules limited the behavior of the inmates toward the boys. The guards would step in if something got out of hand. The guarantee on the bottom of the form Grandma Rosa had signed said the boys would not be physically harmed.

All bets were off now.

Half the guards had failed to show up for work yesterday and even fewer showed up today. They weren't here to enforce whatever rules had been in place when the boys arrived. It was all breaking down and Paco had no illusions about who was likely to be at the bottom of the pile if things went south. He'd come here at the mercy of the guards and the inmates. Now, he was at the mercy of the other boys, too. They didn't know he'd saved their asses by confessing to something he didn't do. Instead of respecting him for having the balls to fess up, they ostracized him for creating the mess in the first place and made him the outsider. They would turn on him without the slightest provocation and there would be no guards to step in and intervene until the bus returned and took them back

…

Yeah, back to what?

That was the other thing he was afraid of.

Aliens.

It was crazy, absurd, the kind of shit people made up in bad movies. There couldn't really be aliens on their way to Earth. That couldn't be. Could. Not. Be.

But apparently it was.

Aliens … like the monsters in his nightmares.

He didn't want to make the connection, but there it

was. He'd spent every night for a month "seeing" monsters, white ones and bug-like ones. Over and over. Then, suddenly, there are "aliens" about to invade Earth.

How was it possible the dreams and the aliens were related?

How was it possible they weren't?

There was a juke mounted on the wall — out of reach, of course — in this visitors' room but the off-on switch was locked up somewhere outside because there was no way to turn it on. If he could see the news, find out what those ships looked like now that they were bigger than white dots. Find out if they were silver balls.

Maybe it was a good thing he couldn't find out. Reality was scarier than it had ever been in his life, and …

And what!

So it was hard. Well, suck it up, buttercup. Life had always been hard. Always would be hard. So he was scared — well, he would just have to live with that fear and manage not to show any sign of weakness to the other boys. He had to get his mojo back, drill in on the other boys. Just happening upon random images wasn't enough. He had to find their weaknesses and exploit them. Do some "pushing" of his own, inside their heads where nobody could see. The other boys were likely to be even more dangerous than the prison inmates because he was locked in here with them, and the inmates, at least for the time being, were locked on the other side.

"Hey, motherfucker. You in there jacking off or something? I got to shit. You don't open the door, I'm gonna shit on the floor and make you clean it up."

Paco opened the door to find Jamal, a black kid who wasn't a whole lot bigger than Paco. Though Paco was small, he was wiry and fast and he could probably take Jamal if he had to. And he might just have to.

The boy purposely shoved his shoulder into Paco as he walked past him into the bathroom. In that brief encounter, Paco saw the image of a pretty Asian girl with a rose tattoo on her neck.

The other boys were sitting around … doing nothing. There was nothing to do. The room had no windows, a juke that didn't work, chairs and booths with phones and nobody on the other side to talk in them.

Paco spotted a chair on the far end, a short distance away from three boys in a heated discussion about the alien invasion.

Tiburon was also seated by himself, had dragged a chair over into a corner and tipped it back on two legs so he was leaning back, reclining, just watching. He brushed off any attempts by anybody to talk to him.

The biggest and meanest, and the smallest and … well, meanest, too, but nobody knew it, had pulled themselves out of the tribe and isolated. Paco knew why he had stayed off by himself but he couldn't imagine why Tiburón had. He had seemed to thrive on strutting his stuff, doing his tough-guy routine, intimidating the others, making sure it was completely without doubt who around here crowed and who laid eggs. But he had been silent and standoffish ever since he had shit the floor instead of his pants the day they arrived. Paco couldn't figure why that was.

"I figure they come here to take our resources," said Randal, the black kid with the big hair. "You know, like in that movie where they're on a planet that died and so they have to find another planet—"

"Bullshit," said Hector, the scrawny Hispanic kid who'd been standing beside Paco in line in the laundry the first day.

"They come here to kill us, that's what I think," said the pimply-faced white kid whose name was either Rob or

Bob. "They ain't gonna let us live 'cause they know we'd fight back if—"

"Reckon we're gonna fight back?" Hector asked, "gonna launch missiles and shit?"

"We could knock those motherfuckers out of the sky, just zap the bastards with a cruise missile," Randal said. "Ain't nothing can stand up under a nuclear warhead."

"Yeah, we could shoot them out of the skies and when they crashed, we could take over their ships and have all their technology," Rob or Bob said.

"You know how to fly a spaceship, do you?" Jamal wanted to know.

"We could figure it out," Hector said. "There are pilots that could figure that shit out."

"I don't think they're gonna land at all," said Jamal. "I think they're just gonna stay out there in space, maybe surround the planet and launch death rays down on us until there's nobody left and then they can come in and take whatever—"

The door that lead into the hallway of the prison opened and the big black trustee con, Spade, stepped inside.

"The van ain't coming today," he said.

That was dripping a drop of water into hot grease and the room exploded. The boys, stormed over to the door yelling and cursing, demanding to know what the fuck was going on.

"We got rights," somebody said, who apparently had forgotten what saying that had gotten Hector yesterday.

"Why ain't they coming?" Jamal demanded.

"They got to come get us," Randal said.

"Can't they just let us go?" Rob/Bob asked. "We could find a ride into town, take a bus or something."

'We didn't do nothing, didn't commit no crimes," Hector said. "They can't keep us locked up in here."

"Shut the fuck up, all of you!" the con roared and there was instant silence. "There ain't nobody to take you anywhere and there's a whole lot more important things going on here than you. Whole bunch of guards didn't show this morning and we ain't even got to second shift yet. It's going to get interesting." He paused. "And you boys are gonna be right in the middle of how interesting it gets, whether you like it or not."

Then he stepped back out of the door and slammed it.

The room was a riot of anger and fear, boys hollering about—

And then the juke set came on. Maybe the big con had decided they'd be easier to handle if he gave them something to watch. The distraction did calm things down, but there was nothing to watch, just a series of talking heads, describing the invading fleet of ships and what it all meant.

There was speculation by some scientist or other who talked about where the aliens had come from, how they had bent time and flew through wormholes or some shit like that.

Another scientist said that technically the armada wasn't aimed at Earth, which caused a brief burst of hope that was quickly quelled by his explanation.

"From that distance, if they were on a course to Earth, they would get here and we would be gone. Earth isn't just hanging motionless in the sky. We're moving. They know that, of course. They didn't make it all the way across the universe without figuring out they would have to aim not for where Earth is but where it will be in four days when they get here."

Four days.

Shit.

Paco curled up beside the chair in the corner and tried to nap. He was tired, had not gotten a lot of sleep last night, as none of them had. But as the day wore on, their anger and frustration with being kept against their will began to be replaced by a more basic instinct. They were hungry. Particularly Paco. The rest had at least had the nasty gloppy breakfast the trustees had served early this morning. He hadn't had a bite of anything.

It grew later. There was a big clock on the wall, apparently to make it clear just how much time visitors had, and as it neared evening, some of the bolder boys pounded on the door, demanding to be let out or at least to be fed. There was water in the fountain, but unless they were interested in trying to consume the plastic chairs, nothing to eat in the room.

Shortly after six o'clock, the door opened again. It was a different trustee this time. He had a garbage bag and he just threw it on the floor in the middle of the room.

"Hope you wasn't counting on three hots and a cot like in jail," he said. "There's bread in there, a couple jars of peanut butter and some jelly. That's what you get and be grateful Spade thought to have you fed at all."

Then he left and the boys descended on the green plastic bag, grabbing out loaves of bread and jars of peanut butter.

"There ain't no knife to spread it with," Hector wailed. "How the fuck are we supposed to eat peanut butter if we can't get it out of the jar?"

Paco stayed back, on the outside of the pack, let the other boys grapple for theirs before he went for something himself. When they all were eating something, he went to the sack and found only leftover pieces of bread that had fallen out of loaves in the boys' scramble to get at them.

No peanut butter. No jelly. The other boys had control of those and Paco had to pick his battle.

He picked the scrawny Hispanic kid, Hector, who was leaned against the wall by the door digging peanut butter out of a jar with his finger.

"Gimme some of that," Paco said.

Hector looked up.

"Fuck you."

Even skinny as he was, Hector was bigger than Paco. But Paco "pushed." As Hector bent at the waist to get another piece of bread out of the loaf at his feet, Paco "bumped into his mind" with his own, stole his equilibrium and made him dizzy, so he was unable to respond when Paco landed an upper cut square under Hector's chin that had every ounce of strength he possessed.

The blow slammed Hector against the wall, his legs went boneless and he collapsed. Blood poured out of his mouth. He must have bitten his tongue. All conversation in the room turned off like a water faucet. Paco hadn't seen that Hector was particularly chummy with any of the other boys, but there was always the chance that one of them would be pissed by what he'd done and he did not want to have to "mind fuck" and fight any of the others.

Into the silence came the sound of clapping. Exaggeratedly slow clapping. If applause could be sarcastic, this was.

Clap.

Clap.

Clap.

Everyone turned toward the source — Tiburón. His face was totally expressionless.

Paco leaned over and picked up the half-full jar of peanut butter that had fallen to the floor when he hit Hector. Casually, not letting on that his hand hurt like he'd busted every bone in it, he took it and the bread and walked to an empty visitation booth, put them on the counter, sat down in the chair and busied himself making a sandwich, using his finger to spread the glop on the pieces of bread.

"I'll get you, motherfucker," Hector said, trying to talk around his bitten tongue. There was no force to the words, though. He sounded confused and kept shaking his head, still dizzy from the psychic blow that had preceded the physical one. "You better watch your back."

Chapter Twenty-Two

STAR WAS FEEDING the animals in the petting zoo. It was one of her favorite tasks because the lambs always nuzzled up close to her to get at the rubber nipple on the bottle Aunt Mary Ellen had made for them.

She was tossing feed to the chickens, which technically weren't a part of the petting zoo. No little kid wanted to pet a chicken. And the rooster was mean, took after Uncle Clyde once.

"Whoever it was decided *chicken* meant coward never made the acquaintance of that rooster!" he'd said.

"Here, chick, chick," she said, tossing out a handful of grain, imagining as she did so their little beady eyes, and their heads moving forward in an odd rhythm with their feet, a herky-jerky dance as they peered at you with first one eye and then the other. Uncle Clyde didn't like chickens even before his run-in with the rooster, or any other bird for that matter. He said he couldn't trust any creature that only looked at you with one eye at a time.

She reached into the small metal bucket and took out another handful, but she didn't toss it. She just stood there.

Pumpkin was beside her, as always, as much a part of her as her own arm and she had felt the dog tense. Then he let out a low whine and she knew at once who had come.

"Papa Eagle Feather!" she cried.

"You make an old man feel bad," he said from behind her and she turned to face him, resisting an urge to throw herself into his arms. Papa Eagle Feather wasn't a hugging kind of grandfather, but just his presence was enough to make her feel better. "It is impossible to sneak up on you."

He always tried, though. Had explained to her about the Indian tradition of counting coup on their enemies. Of touching them without harming them. She didn't know if that was an Apache tradition or if all tribes did that. Or it was even possible that Papa Eagle Feather had simply made it up. Uncle Clyde said Papa Eagle Feather was "not the most reliable source of information out there."

"Where have you been?" she asked.

It was a stupid question. Papa Eagle Feather was like the wind. He blew in and blew back out and she had no idea where he was in between visits or what he did while he was away. She had gone to his hut on the Mescalero reservation only one time and it was hard to imagine he actually lived in it full-time, with its dirt floor and potbellied stove for heat. What he did for a living, she had no idea.

He smelled like worn leather and horses and she heard a rattle when he moved, unless he was trying to be quiet and she heard nothing at all. The rattle came from the beaded necklace he wore around his neck.

"Away," was his response to her question. It was always his response when she asked where he'd been. She could feel Pumpkin's tail swishing frantically against her leg and knew her grandfather had leaned over and was scratching him behind his ears.

As she conjured the old man's face in her mind she remembered the first time she realized his face was like the buffalo nickel in Uncle Clyde's coin collection. The image of the buffalo on one side had been worn almost flat and it was hard to feel the outline and make out the shape. But the head of the Indian on the other side had been clear and distinct and the face her grandfather had allowed her to trace with her fingers when she was younger had the same wide forehead, the strong nose, flat lips and a clear, prominent jaw. He wore his hair in braids, too, with feathers in it, and most Indian men didn't do that anymore. And the skin on his face was weathered with deep grooves around his mouth and nose, and two dents on either side of his nose in front of his eyebrows that she knew had to have formed by a scowl, which she assumed was probably always on his face.

She threw out the last of the chicken feed in a clump, knowing as she did so that Aunt Mary Ellen would not approve. The feed was to be dispersed randomly throughout the yard. If you dumped it all in one spot, the chickens pecked each other to get at it, fought for the feed. But Star didn't care. She reached out her hand and her grandfather took both her hands in his, as close as you were likely to get to a hug from the old man.

"You heard?" she said. "About the … you know—"

For some reason she had an aversion to saying "aliens." Maybe because saying it made it real or maybe because she still hadn't quite made the mental leap from years of pretending to connect to the aliens to the reality that they were out there in the sky, steaming toward them, full steam ahead. People had started calling them "Astrals" and that rolled more easily off her tongue. "The Astrals."

"I heard," he said, and she felt foolish for asking such a question. Of course he'd heard. Was there anyone on the planet who hadn't heard? But her grandfather lived far outside "the loop" of the modern world — didn't even own a truck that drove itself, had no phone, no electricity.

Though he never said it in so many words, it was clear that her grandfather revered the old ways and lived as much of his life as he could in the manner of his ancestors. As far as she could determine, he lived off the land, hunted mule deer, elk and antelope for food and traded their tanned hides for whatever else he needed.

According to Uncle Clyde, he was always one step ahead of the game wardens because he thumbed his nose at "seasons" and hunting restrictions and "deer tags." But even her uncle granted that there was no better shot with a rifle — and even a bow and arrow — than her grandfather, said he'd once seen the old man throw a bowie knife fifty feet through the center of a knothole on a fence.

But Papa Eagle Feather probably hadn't watched more than ten minutes of juke in all his seventy-one years and it was actually conceivable, in her mind at least, that he hadn't heard about the invading armada.

"They've come back," he said.

"Back?"

"I have seen them coming in my dreams for a long, long time."

So had Star! Well, for a month anyway. She was certain now that her dreams of silver marbles, white giants and monster insects had been about the aliens.

"But you said 'back.' When they were here before, the spaceship that crashed in the desert, did you know they were here then?"

"I'm not talking about then. They came long, long ago when the world was young. Our ancestors speak of white giants from the skies who came and destroyed the world."

"Destroyed the——?"

173

"Just legends. Stories. Indian fairy tales."

She had heard Uncle Clyde coming. His footsteps were unique, big boots on gravel, a purposeful step, almost like he was marching.

"And hello to you, too, Clyde," said Papa Eagle Feather. "Yes, I'm fine, thank you. And you?"

You'd have to be a special kind of blind not to see that here were two men who did not like each other.

"I figured it wouldn't be long before you showed up."

"You think they haven't come before?"

"I think you don't need to be scaring Star, filling her head full of—"

"She is Apache. The white gods from the sky came to her people—"

Uncle Clyde made a sound in his throat, a grunt of contempt. "You come waltzing in here doing your shaman gig, plant all kind of nonsense in her head, then you waltz back out, leaving her with a million questions and you don't show up again until—"

"There are cave drawings in Sedona where white giants—"

"We don't know if these Astrals are—"

"*Astrals.*" Papa Eagle Feather spit the word out like it tasted bad.

"—are white giants, little green men or big balls of see-through ectoplasm. So how about you don't lay claim to being their second cousins, twice removed, until—"

"They were the ancestors of all mankind, Clyde. Surely even you are willing to admit that now."

"The only thing I'll admit is that they're up there in the sky right now. Beyond that — all bets are off."

Star knew full well her Uncle Clyde believed the aliens had been to Earth before. The two of them had talked about it. But if Grandpa Eagle Feather had said water was wet, Uncle Clyde would have spent his dying breath arguing it was dry.

"Stonehenge. Easter Island. Machu Picchu. Ringing any bells yet, Clyde?"

Star didn't normally get between the two stubborn bulls, but she wanted to know, had to know what Papa Eagle Feather was talking about.

"What did you mean, 'before'?" she asked while Uncle Clyde was sputtering to come up with a zinger. "About them destroying Earth?" She couldn't keep a tremble out of her voice. "Is that what you think they're going to do?"

"See, I told you you were scaring—"

"They come to Earth. They look at the works of man, the race they placed here. They see the evil. They wipe us out."

"Wash, rinse and repeat, right? The end-of-the-world chorus, second verse."

"Not second ... verse. The cycle has repeated itself for—"

"How do they know we've been evil? Have they been watching? Left something like a nanny-cam behind, did they?"

"They have eyes to see—"

Star couldn't stand it anymore.

"Are we all going to die?" she cried. "They're going to blow us up or do what that man on TV said, ram into Earth and knock it out of orbit so we'll all freeze to death or burn up or—"

"Happy now, Eagle Feather?"

Papa Eagle Feather had probably said more than he intended to say. That didn't mean it wasn't true, it just meant he hadn't likely planned to drop the whole load on her at one time.

"I am saying they hold our destiny now as before. I didn't mean they would destroy us *now*."

"Then when?" It came out in a tear-clotted cry of fear.

"I don't know—"

"Eagle Feather, I think it's time for you to climb back into that rat trap of a pickup truck and haul out of here." There was genuine menace in Uncle Clyde's voice.

There was a beat of silence. Two. Star could imagine the two of them standing there, chests out, glaring at each other.

"I'm sorry, Star," Papa Eagle Feather said. That was a conversation stopper. The old man had never, in her presence, admitted he was wrong about anything or had done or said anything that didn't need doing or saying. It did momentarily shut Uncle Clyde up. "I didn't mean to frighten you. There is much we don't know about what happened in the past. We can read the cave paintings and see the result … but when? Who can say. A hundred years from now? A thousand? Time is not to them what it is to us."

"So basically, they're gonna blow us out of the sky, but they might wait a week, ten days maybe, to do it — that about cover it?" Uncle Clyde growled.

"I will not lie," the old man said, his voice as hard and cold as a hammer left out in the snow. "They are many, but they think as one. One being, a single purpose — to judge our civilization. What do you think, Clyde? You think we'll pass muster?"

"What I think," his words were slow and measured, ground out between clenched teeth, "is that you're going to be in a world of hurt, old man, if you don't shut up *right now*!"

Star couldn't help a little squeak of dismay and Uncle Clyde took a deep, shaky breath. "How about we all do the sensible thing and wait to see what they have in mind when they get here."

"Yes," Papa Eagle Feather said with his typical lack of emotion. "And when they do, Falling Star Yellowhorse will have a special part to play in what happens then."

"What will I have to do with the—?"

"It was foretold by your ancestors. That is why you were named *Falling Star*."

"Did those ancestors also foretell that Eagle Feather Yellowhorse was going to meet an untimely death, because that's for sure gonna happen if you don't—"

"You will see, what our forefathers saw in their visions will be clear ... *in three days*."

Chapter Twenty-Three

IT WAS INSIDE-A-LUMP-OF-COAL dark but for a thin slice of light that came through the opening where the hinges held the lid on the dumpster. Ellie could see nothing, but she could hear the squeaking, hear the rustling as the rodents picked through the garbage around her.

The boys at the head of the alley had been joined by other people but all their voices wouldn't mask the sound if Ellie lost her grip on one of the black, hairy-legged screams crowded in the back of her throat, clawing and scratching to be released into the world.

A rat brushed by her leg, *touched* her, and she reflexively jumped, lurching away and thumped into the side of the dumpster. She froze and held her breath, but apparently no one heard. There were more squeaks now, more sounds of movement.

This dumpster's full of rotted food!

The realization froze her breath. Of course it'd be full of rats, too.

A sudden burst of squeaking and rustling sounds on the other side of the dumpster could only be rats fighting each other, and something seemed to be … she slapped at a rat *climbing up her pants leg*, knocked it away.

Out. She had to get out of here. She didn't care what the boys did to her, she couldn't stay … As she reached with her right hand to shove the lid up, her left hand felt something leaned against the wall behind her. A rod. A pipe! Her fingers closed around it and in one motion she swung it at the rustling garbage beside her foot where the rat she'd knocked off her leg had landed. She felt it connect, heard a squeal.

With her back against the side of the dumpster, she used the pipe to shove away the garbage from around her feet until she was standing in a small clear space. When she heard a squeak near her foot, she brought the pipe down as hard as she could, must have hit the rat a glancing blow because it scurried noisily into the mounds of trash.

She was panting. Sweat rolled down her forehead into her eyes. She held her weapon now in both hands. Time telescoped. Life became a string of single seconds, connected like paper dolls, each separate and distinct, each identical, full of nauseating stench and terror and … *Rage.*

"Come on," she whispered. "Want your heads smashed? Come and get it!"

She might have been in the dumpster for an hour or for ten. She killed one of the little fuckers! Felt the pipe smash into its skull! Knocked the others away. Defended her little slice of dumpster turf.

The silence outside the dumpster seemed sudden and she wondered how long the people had been gone before she noticed. She lifted the lid an inch and peered out. The alley was empty. She grabbed hold of the panicked need to throw the lid back and leap out of hell. Instead, she raised it slowly, watched with every ounce of concentration. Her eyes were so adapted to darkness she would have seen anything that moved out there. Nothing did.

She let go and threw the lid back then, jumped up onto the side of the dumpster and down to the ground and had made it maybe three steps when she heard voices. She still had the pipe in her hand, and she would use it to fight whoever was coming. She would *not* climb back into the dumpster. She would rather die.

Then she spotted the silver trash can sitting next to it with the lid propped against the side.

WHEN SHERIFF MATHESON's phone vibrated in his pocket it was the first time it had rung in hours. He was certain it was not because he wasn't getting any calls but because the calls weren't making it through. He wondered how long it would be before there was no cell service at all. There were landlines, of course. Some. And it wasn't like Ma Bell had come into town and taken down all the lines strung from one pole to another and dug up the buried ones. It would take some doing, but there were ways to forge new communication out of the old.

He didn't recognize the number.

"Sheriff Matheson," he said, and heard a garbled sound on the other end.

"Oh thank God, I've been trying and trying, called 911 but there's no answer."

"Who is this?"

"Ellie. Ellie Hampton."

It was a moment before he placed her.

Then she gushed out words in a torrent, so fast he had trouble following her.

"You have to help me. Please, help me. It was horrible.

Everybody was fighting and a man shoved me up against a wall, but I bit him. I actually bit somebody and then I was running and running."

"Where are you?"

"In a trash can."

"What?"

"I'm hiding in a trash can. I've been here for hours. Before that I was in a dumpster but there were rats ... *rats!* I used a pipe to fight them off. I heard gunfire. And ... a man grabbed me and another man ... he just *stabbed him.* There was blood everywhere. And I think a man in the hospital was stealing IV bags, yanking the needles out of patients' arms. Everyone was screaming and—"

"Ellie."

"I didn't know what to do."

"Ellie."

"I had to get away."

"Ellie. Where are you?"

"I don't know. I ran down streets — just *away.*"

"What streets? Where?"

"In Louisville."

"You're in Louisville? What for?"

"Because I had to see a doctor." She barked out a little laugh. "Except I didn't see a doctor. I didn't see anybody. Came all this way and there was nobody."

"So you went to Louisville. How?"

"I drove. What difference does it make how I got here? I don't even know where the car is. I parked it in a lot, but I couldn't find it now. I don't know where I am."

"So you're safe now?"

"Right this minute, yes. But I can hear them. There are gangs, just walking the streets, hitting people and taking whatever—"

"I thought you said you were hidden."

"I am. I scrunched down in a trash can and then put the lid on. It's in a dark alley. Why would you go down a dead-end alley and take the lid off a trash can?"

"I want you to stay right where you are. I will come and get you."

"Oh, thank God!"

She started to cry.

"You have to tell me how to find you."

"I told you, I don't know where I am."

She was teetering on the brink of total hysteria.

"Tell me where you were going."

"The University of Louisville Medical Center. The nurse in the doctor's office in Jessup said that's where they refer all their cancer patients, where they get biopsies."

Cancer. No wonder she'd been so desperate to see a doctor in Jessup.

"She gave me names and I called and got an appointment so I bought a car and drove here."

She bought a car. Just like that. Of course, she had come here in a chartered helicopter, and all the kids in Noah's school were rich. Except Noah.

He looked over at his son, who had nodded off leaning against the door.

Sawyer had gone out to the academy and picked him up. There had been a lull, just a little one and he knew the boy was scared, so he'd taken him to the house and made him a sandwich. He drove around town after they ate, checking on his deputies, and Noah fell asleep. He probably hadn't gotten a good night's sleep since Astral Day. That's what they were calling it now. Astral Day.

Sawyer was scared and he'd admit that to anybody who asked, but how much scarier must it be to be a little kid, not knowing what was going to happen, the people you counted on in life to protect you, seeing that they didn't have any more say than you did over what happened.

Ellie was talking and he focused back on what she was saying.

"... sat in traffic for hours. Not moving at all, stopped. Missed my appointment. But I had to see the doctor. I *had* to."

She paused for just a moment.

"There's a lump in my breast. I found it two days ago, the day I came to pick up Gretchen." She burped out another half sob. "I was trying to get an appointment with my gynecologist, and I turned on the juke to find out what was wrong with the phone. And there were pictures of the little white dots, every channel, little white dots."

"Focus, Ellie. So you went to Louisville ..."

"The streets were full of ragged people, looked homeless. And I couldn't find the doctor's office, wound up in the hospital instead. That's where it started. The riot started right outside the hospital."

She did sob then, cried for a few moments.

"Ellie, walk me through what you did next, where you went."

She sniffed, took a breath. "I was in a daze, walked out the door of the hospital and the crowd went off like a bomb."

That was not good. The University of Louisville Medical Center was located snug up against Phoenix Hill, second only to Southland Park as the worst neighborhood in Louisville.

"People were screaming ... I heard gunshots ... men tried to grab me ... so I ran until I couldn't run anymore. And then I stopped. There were some teenagers across the street, boys. They started toward me."

"What could you see? What buildings?"

"In the distance there was a building shaped kind of like a giant cash register."

"Yeah, Commerce Bank, on the river."

"The boys were crossing the street, so I turned and ran down it to the alley and—"

She stopped abruptly and for a moment he thought the connection was broken.

"Ellie… Ellie, are you there?"

"Somebody's in the alley," she whispered. "I hear them, voices."

"Tell me what you saw, the last things you saw before you hid. Anything at all."

"A tattoo place. There was a dragon on the sign, and a pawn shop."

"Jiffy Pawn?"

"Maybe. I don't remember. Most of the street signs were missing, poles but no signs. The last one I saw said Blackwood Street."

"Were you on Blackwood?"

"No, I was on another street that crossed Blackwood."

"What was the name of that street?"

"I didn't see a sign. I was running and—"

"Then what?"

She didn't answer.

"Ellie."

"I can't talk." He could barely hear her. "They're close."

He couldn't ask her anything else, but he pulled a U turn in the middle of Parker Street, flipped on his lights and siren and headed out of town on Bardstown Road. He wouldn't even try the interstate. He knew all the back roads. He'd go in through Bardstown, turn toward Mount Washington and go into Louisville up US 31E. And then …

Well, he'd have to see what conditions were like when he got there. He would probably have to wind his way downtown taking side streets if the expressways were clogged.

"Ellie, don't answer me. Just blow on the phone if you're still connected. I can hear that."

He heard the sound of her breath. But he could also hear voices. Angry voices that were getting louder.

He absolutely did not want to take Noah with him to Louisville. The city could be dangerous. But the academy was in the opposite direction from Louisville. The boy had awakened when he whipped the U-turn and was looking at his father questioningly. That was the problem with signing. It took two hands and was really hard to do while you were driving.

He keyed his radio.

"I'll be 10-28 for a while." A 10-28 meant unit out of service.

"Yes, sir, 10-28."

There was still a dispatch. Betty Hawthorne had come to work. In fact, all but two of his deputies were on duty just like he was. The initial shock had sent people all over the place. It was like the whole town leapt on their horses and rode madly off in all directions. But it had settled a little since. Not equilibrium. There was no possibility for that until … well, until the world found out what the aliens wanted. But there was a tight lid screwed on most people's panic right now.

It appeared that the populace of Louisville had figured out, as had the people in every major city in America, that they'd be better off somewhere else, just about anywhere else, than in a city where supplies of everything would run out. There were reports of riots in New York City the first night, and half the power grid there had failed. There was electricity in Jessup. And running water, at least for the time being. They'd go down. He didn't doubt that. Eventually, most everything would go down.

Then he heard a crashing sound from the phone. After that, silence. The connection was broken.

Chapter Twenty-Four

SHE'D HEARD the sound of them coming as she whispered frantically into the cell phone.

"... just bust out the glass. Who's gonna know or care?"

"What for?"

"Diamonds, man, you know how much—"

"Don't nobody need diamonds now, moron."

"I ain't seen Spuds. How he even gonna score? He gets it from somewhere and that somewhere—"

"We gotta find somebody, man. I'm starting to itch."

"What about the CVS Pharmacy on Third Street?"

"Ain't nothing in that place anymore but aspirin."

"One of the hospitals, then. Kosair. Ain't nothing but little kids in Kosair and we got guns!"

"We gotta get water and food, too. The Aldi on—"

"Ain't nothing in that place. Shelves is bare. I told you we come too late. We shoulda made our move that first day."

The voices were angry and scared, sounded like teenagers maybe, coming down the alley on the other side of the street toward her. Surely, they'd turn off. This alley was a dead end. But they didn't. She heard bangs and crashes, like maybe they were knocking over things, kicking trash cans as they passed by them.

Oh, please, no ...

Suddenly, there was a thump on the side of the can, knocking it over on its side. She barely kept herself from screaming. The lid flew off and clattered on the asphalt and the can rolled over twice before it came to rest against a brick wall. The voices were no longer approaching, they'd passed and were moving on.

"There was some'm in that can. It was heavy."

She heard footsteps approaching.

"You wanna go digging around in trash cans or get some smack?"

"Imagine how much smack there must be in a hospital."

The approaching footsteps stopped.

"Maybe hasn't nobody thought about that yet."

The footsteps headed off in the direction of the others down the alley. There must have been a way through the fence she hadn't seen.

"Ain't nothing but fat old security guards guarding the place. I went to see my cousin and there ain't even a metal detector. We can go in with guns blazing, mow 'em down."

The voices got farther and farther away.

If they had stopped, looked into the can ...

The lid was gone now, but she was still jammed down into the can lying on its side. The can was more disgusting than the dumpster had been, the inside slathered with unspeakably filthy goo and she was crouching on top of a small amount of mashed garbage, which stank like meat gone bad. It was gooey, squashing up between the toes on her right foot. She had lost her shoe ... somewhere.

But she didn't move. Heard the voices receding, but didn't make any effort to get out of the can, didn't even peek up over the edge.

She heard a sound — a squeak — and when she looked out the top of the can the pile of garbage beside the wall moved.

Rats!

Let 'em come! She still had her pipe.

SAWYER MATHESON DROVE like a madman down country roads, past deserted houses, some with front doors standing ajar. Most were silent and dark. It wasn't that late. On any normal night he'd pass houses with the porch light on, maybe somebody sitting out in a rocker, or in the swing, and in the distance little patches of light in far-off houses. The countryside was as black as the inside of Matheson Caverns.

Maybe the electricity was off, but Sawyer thought it just as likely that the people had fled. Going somewhere, anywhere gave the illusion of control, gave you a sense of purpose when all purpose had drained out of the world as soon as little white specs were spotted out by Jupiter.

From the outskirts of Louisville, he saw the fire in the distance and as soon as he crested a rise, two things were clear. One, this fire had been deliberately set, even though it was staged to look like an accident, like a tractor trailer had lost control and jackknifed. And two, if he stopped to offer assistance when nobody else had, no fire trucks, no police officers, no other stopped vehicles, he would become a statistic, though he doubted anybody was keeping track anymore of the number of violent crimes. Sawyer turned off onto a side street a quarter mile from the burning wreck and made his way downtown by way of Brecken-ridge Lane to Taylorsville to Bardstown Road to Broadway.

He turned toward the University of Louisville Medical Center, hoping to retrace Ellie's steps. She'd said she had gone there for an appointment. Doctors' offices were in the annex building and she'd gone to the hospital instead. When she left, she'd run into a riot and he could see evidence of it — the still-smoldering husks of burned auto-mobiles and furniture that'd been dragged into the street and set ablaze.

The lights in all the hospitals — Jewish, Kosair, U of L Med Center — were on. They must be using auxiliary generators because nothing else near them, no street lights or signs, were lit up. There were no ambulances parked at the emergency entrances and the front lobbies had been looted and vandalized.

He began to cruise the streets adjacent to the tall silver medical center building, made a mental grid and went slowly along it, using the search light on the top of his car to peer down dark alleys near the hospital, though Ellie had made it clear she had run a long way from it. When he was about three blocks out from the hospital, he began cruising up and down every alley he could negotiate, but evidence of rioting was everywhere. Not a single unbroken window in sight.

He saw a glow a couple of blocks up. A car there was still burning but nobody was around. He passed several small grocery and convenience stores, moving slowly down the deserted streets. They all had doors ajar and broken windows. He was sure there was nothing left on the shelves.

He saw few people, certainly not the rioting mobs Ellie had seen. There should have been streetlights, passing cars, but there was only darkness, figures flitting away whenever his car lights or search light touched them, like ghosts, evil spirits of the night, all of them guilty of some horrible crime or skulking around on their way to commit one, creatures of the night, running into dark holes.

When he was about five blocks out from the hospital, he began to use the megaphone on the top of his cruiser calling out, "Ellie, where are you?"

He turned a corner and saw approaching headlights. He had his own red-and-blue light bar flashing but the metro police car that approached did not. He pulled up and stopped beside it and the two rolled down their windows.

"What's a county sheriff doing in my fair city?" the officer asked.

"Looking for someone. She came to Louisville to see a doctor and called me, said there was a riot."

"Yeah, there was a riot. We couldn't do a thing about it, had to let it burn itself out."

"What are you—?"

"I just came from Kosair Hospital. A bunch of teenagers went roaring into the lobby shooting people, after drugs likely. Security guards dropped three of them and the others ran off. Seven people dead altogether."

"And you're here now because …?"

"Because at least the presence of a police car might help calm the fears of the poor people who are stuck in those apartments, the ones who aren't out looking for drugs, the ones just hunkered down, scared. Waiting."

Sawyer drove on, calling out, up and down streets and alleys, getting farther and farther away from the hospital. Maybe he'd missed her. Or maybe … She had heard someone coming, something crashed. He hadn't let himself think about that on the drive to Louisville, but it was front and center of his mind now. She might not be hiding anymore. Maybe she'd been found, dragged out off and …

He called her name over and over again. Nothing. Half an hour passed. He caught sight of a few people scurrying furtively down the darkened streets, but no sign of Ellie.

He stopped in front of the opening of an alley behind Giuseppe's Little Italy, shone his light down it and could see a dumpster and trash cans. "Ellie. El—"

"Here!" a voice cried. "Here!"

He threw the car into park and turned to Noah, who had been riding along beside him in silence, the terrible silence of the deaf that had settled over the boy like a cloud — a silence in his own head and all around because there was no reason to talk to him when he couldn't hear.

"Noah. I'm going to leave you here for a few minutes." The boy looked instantly alarmed. "I'm leaving the light bar on and the doors locked. I'm only going over there." He pointed down the alley. "Won't be more than fifty yards from the car. You'll be fine."

The boy nodded. He was frightened, but not clingy. Noah had never been clingy.

He instinctively pulled the boy into a hug, let him go and kissed his forehead tenderly. Then, with both hands free, he signed, "I love you."

Noah signed, "I love you, too."

Then he got out of the car, closed the door, drew his service revolver and started down the alley.

Chapter Twenty-Five

SAWYER LET HER CRY.

She was semi-hysterical when he'd dragged her out of the trash can, clinging to him, crying "Rats!" He could see them scurrying around the trash in the alley. "There were rats in the dumpster, but I got 'em." He'd had to pry a bloody pipe out of her fingers.

At first he thought she was bleeding, that there was blood smeared on her face and in her hair. Then he realized it wasn't blood. It was … either catsup or … no, it was pizza sauce. And that chunk of something in her hair was a piece of pepperoni.

She said other things, too, as he half-walked, half-carried her back to the car and deposited her in the front seat. Then he got in on the driver's side and waited, signing to Noah, who'd climbed into the backseat, that she was upset and needed to cry it out.

He didn't start the engine until the sobs were no longer wracking her body in great heaving gulps, then he asked her softly, "Is there anything I can get you?"

She lifted her head immediately and her eyes were blazing. "A car wash."

"What?"

"You have to take me to a car wash. I have to get this" — she made a gesture of revulsion that swept her whole body — "off. *I can't stand it.*"

"But you don't have anything else to—"

"Please. *Please!*"

She was on the razor edge of hysteria and he couldn't say he blamed her. He'd have to find one of the older car washes, the ones that still had slots where you inserted change to make the water turn on. The fully-automated ones certainly wouldn't do, even if they'd been working, which with no electricity he was sure they weren't, and she couldn't very well walk through a series of the spinning pieces of — what were those things made of that they guaranteed they would not scratch your car? — on rods that moved up and down and all around the vehicle.

He drove out of the city down the route he'd driven in, quickly leaving downtown behind. It was a warm evening for May, but even so, once Ellie's clothing was soaked she'd get cold quick. He thought he remembered where — there it was, set back from the street next to a Home Depot, across vast parking lots from a row of street-side restaurants — Joe Bob's Steak House, the Laughing Dolphin and Rafferty's, that had once been a good restaurant before the neighborhood declined and it was turned into a second-rate bar. It was doing a land-office business tonight. The fish food and steak houses were dark and empty, but the parking lot was full of cars in front of Rafferty's and loud, old-time country music was wailing from inside.

"… fine time to leave me, Lucille. Four hungry children and a crop in the field …"

Men stood outside the front doors or leaned up against

their cars, openly drinking in defiance of the city's ordinance that forbade it. They watched his cruiser pull into the street leading to the stores beyond and not a one made any effort to hide his bottle.

"There's no car wash here," Ellie said. "Why——?"

He gestured with his chin toward the Bed Bath & Beyond.

"You're going to need a towel."

All the plate glass windows in the front of the Bed Bath & Beyond were shattered, the interior dark. But there were several cars parked in the lot in front of the building — still between the lines, leaving the handicapped spaces open — and he could see light sabers of flashlight beams in the building.

"Who loots a Bed Bath & Beyond?" Ellie asked.

"Must have figured they needed to get the house spiffy for the arrival of guests from the other side of the galaxy so they took a baseball bat to the windows of their neighborhood BB&B and made off with new curtains and a shower caddy."

A ghost of a smile crossed Ellie's face, aborted before it was born.

The Home Depot next door was dark as well, but the front glass was broken and people could be seen pushing carts full of tools, batteries, lanterns, flashlights and other kinds of emergency supplies out to their cars. Sawyer watched them for a moment. Normal people. Not a mob — you'd need another couple dozen people for that. Then you could add water and stir — some guy grabs the pair of pliers some other guy saw first — and you've got yourselves a riot.

Other cars were pulling into the parking lot, had maybe been driving by and realized they'd better get their hands on what they needed "now while supplies last." Or they'd merely waited to "do their shopping" now, under cover of darkness, when no sin seemed nearly as heinous and morning light was a long way off.

"You guys wait here," he both said and signed and saw apprehension on Ellie's face and an instant look of something like panic cross Noah's. Before either had a chance to protest, he pushed a button and an ear-splitting *whoop, whoop* sound shattered the darkness.

Everyone jumped. the people pushing carts raced with them across the parking lot and several people came barreling out of Bed Bath & Beyond, their arms full of who knew what, and raced away, like roaches when you turned on the kitchen light.

"I'll lock the car and if you see anybody, anything out of the ordinary — anything at all — push the button. That's probably all you'll need to scare the salt off their crackers, but I'll come running. Will you be alright?"

"Sure." Ellie's voice was still cry-shaky.

Noah merely nodded, his eyes open wide, so like a baby rabbit Sawyer longed to take him in his arms again.

He needed to get this done fast. Louisville was getting less safe by the minute, and though they'd left the real low-rent district behind they were still in a less-than-prosperous neighborhood.

He drew his weapon. He certainly had no intention of shooting looters. But there was fear in the air, danger on the night air, and a sense crawled slowly up his spine that anything — literally *anything* — was possible.

Once inside the building, Sawyer realized there were more people in the store than he'd first thought. Flashlight beams shone out down aisles and from behind shelves. The store looked like there'd already been a riot. Merchandise was everywhere, neat rows of linens now piled in the floor, a whole row of women's makeup mirrors, methodically smashed — what's up with that? — and the shelves containing cookware mostly bare.

In the twin beams of his cruiser's headlights shining in the front door, he discovered little he could use. He was not in the market for fine crystal, drapes and shades or kitchen appliances, though that seemed to be a popular spot where half a dozen flashlights dueled in the darkness.

A woman came out from behind a tall shelf unit into the glow of his flashlight, caught enough of a glimpse of him to see the uniform, cried out and dropped the toaster oven she was carrying. What use was a toaster oven without electricity?

"Officer, I … you can't arrest me … everybody else—"

"I'm not here to arrest anybody." Then he added, "Not my jurisdiction. I'm a county sheriff."

He said that because he couldn't bring himself to say out loud that he wasn't going to arrest anybody because the days of enforcing looting laws were so far back in the rearview mirror it was hard to see them clearly anymore — though the world-shattering/changing event that had put them there had only happened three days ago. And the worst was yet to come.

The woman hurriedly picked up what she'd dropped and vanished into the darkness.

In the dark hole of the opposite corner of the store, he found the linens. Moving so his back was against a wall, he holstered his weapon, opened a king-size pillow case and stuffed into it what he needed. Then he threw the bag over his shoulder like a Santa's pack, picked up his flashlight and began to make his way back across the expanse of darkness to the twin headlight beams slicing through the front door.

He didn't see it coming in time.

Out of the corner of his eye, he saw movement,

dropped the sack and moved his flashlight in that direction as his other hand went for his weapon. But the dark form launched itself at him out of the darkness above him to the right, like someone had been crouching on top of a shelf, waiting. For what? What did he have that—?

He had a gun. Ammunition. Another weapon and more ammunition in the car. A police cruiser.

Then the full weight of someone enormous slammed into him and knocked him off his feet, flattened him, knocking his flashlight out of his hands and it hit the floor and spun, creating a freak show of dark and light shadow figures, dancing jerky-jerky like people in a convenience store surveillance video.

He struggled to reach for his gun, but he was pinned down by the form on top of him. The best he could do was jam his elbow between the gun and his body, making it impossible for anybody to release the catch and pull the weapon from the holster.

In the darkness, he couldn't see the fist coming at his face until it connected a glancing blow on his jaw that knocked his head to the left and pulled at the drawstrings of darkness, closing it all around him. As the world faded, he heard the *whoop, whoop, whoop* of the siren on his cruiser. Then it was as dark behind his eyelids as it was in front of them.

Chapter Twenty-Six

Paco had been expecting it for so long it was almost a relief when the attack came. He had noticed the boy named Enrique staring at him on the first day. He was white, would have been handsome but his features were too pronounced, big eyes, a large nose and pouty lips. Clearly, the dude was gay, which nobody cared about. But it was equally clear the guy had a thing for Paco, and they were *locked in* here together.

Paco didn't just see it, he felt it, felt Enrique watching him when he wasn't looking, felt the hungriness when their eyes happened to catch and lock. Paco had done his dead level best, every possible thing he knew to do to send the message to Enrique that those were not his inclinations and he would not welcome sexual advances.

But you could send out all the messages you wanted — you only got say over the messages you sent, not what the other dude received, and Paco could feel the tension building. He knew the guy was going to make his move soon, so he wasn't surprised when he felt a hand on his shoulder as he sat in one of the chairs with his head leaned up against the partition faking a nap.

"Hey, sweet thing," Enrique purred close to his ear.

Paco saw images, a collage of lurid sexual encounters, and a striking Hispanic man named Manuel who resembled Paco.

Paco leapt to his feet. "Maybe I look like your whore, Manuel, but I'm not."

Enrique looked like Paco'd slapped him.

"Manuel's out there fucking" — another face, a white boy with red hair — "that red-headed slut while you're locked up in here, but don't expect me to take his place. I'm not interested."

Enrique's face went as white as a gym sock and Paco knew instantly he'd screwed the pooch. His jab about Manuel hadn't staggered Enrique, distracted him, knocked him off center as Paco'd planned. Instead, Enrique responded like he'd slammed his thumb in a car door. He literally roared, "Now!" And before Paco had time to push for an advantage, shove his way into Enrique's mind, before he could leap on Enrique, or retreat and defend some piece of turf, before anything, he felt strong arms grabbing his. Hector was on his left, Jamal on the right.

"Hey, what the fuck—? You guys queer, too?"

They weren't, they were straight, but Enrique had elicited their support and Hector probably hadn't required a whole lot of convincing.

That part was bound to happen, too. Allegiances formed. Fact of life. People gravitated to other people. It was hard to navigate life solo. Paco's cold eyes put people off, and nobody ever warmed up to him, which was how he'd always wanted it, but it was a definite disadvantage here.

Paco lurched backward forcefully, trying to shake

Jamal's hold on his right arm. The hold held firm. Hector had been joined on the left arm by the fat white kid with pimples, Rob/Bob, and though he wasn't strong, he was leveraging the one thing he did have going for him. Size. Girth. Weight.

"How you know about my Manuel, huh?" Enrique asked. "You gonna wish you was Manuel. I treat him nice and gentle. You — I'm gonna get me a piece of you."

"I ain't no ass-fucker. Let me go!"

"Oh, that means you're a virgin! Excellent. You are about to lose your cherry, oh yes you are. And I get to do the picking."

It was clear quickly that the rest of the boys in the room wanted no part in the conflict. If three guys wanted to fuck Paco over, that was fine with them so long as they could stay out of it and not get hurt.

"You such an ugly motherfucker you can't get a piece of ass unless you force it, that the way it is, Enrique?" Paco snarled, his thoughts too scrambled to focus on seeking an advantage, looking for a place to "push."

Enrique doubled up his fist and landed a blow in Paco's belly that knocked all the air out of him. As he bent double from the blow, Enrique took an upper cut with his left fist that caught Paco square in the mouth — just like he'd hit Hector, but Paco didn't bite his tongue. It knocked him backward, though. The two boys holding his arms let go and he fell on his back and slid a few feet toward the wall.

Enrique took two steps, leaned over him, grabbed his crotch and squeezed hard and the agony that shot up into his belly and down his thighs made breathing impossible even if his diaphragm had been willing to cooperate.

"Get him up," Enrique said. Jamal took his right arm and Hector his left and dragged him upright. He could not stand on his own, could not breathe, felt blood pouring down his face and dripping off his chin but could do nothing to stem the tide.

"You about to get yours, sweetie pie," Enrique said. "Lean him over."

The boys holding his arms shoved him forward, draped his body over the back of a chair and slammed his face down on the desk. He felt fingers fumbling at his waist for the tie on his pants, tried to struggle and could do nothing as his pants fell around his ankles. He still had not drawn in the breath that had been knocked out of him, still couldn't breathe for the agony in his balls.

He knew what was about to happen was going to hurt, too, but it wasn't the pain he feared. It was the degradation, the humiliation. He struggled to focus his mind, to exert some control somewhere, shove someone hard. But the pain and — admit it, the *fear* — so distracted him that his mental strength failed him for the first time in his life. Whatever was going to happen was going to happen. He sure wasn't going to stop it.

He could hear the other boys now. They'd been silently watching. Now, they began to join in. They laughed, called him names.

"Got an ass like a little girl, punk."

"You such a coward you shit your pants just being here."

"I want me some of that little-girl ass, too!"

If the others got aroused, and that seemed to be exactly what was happening, this nightmare would get uglier quick.

He could feel Enrique behind him, snuggling up close, gritted his teeth, wanted to cry, "No!" but had no breath.

"I got him thirds," someone called from behind Enrique. He could see movement around him and realized that other boys were moving to get in line. He wasn't about to be raped; he was about to be gang-raped.

Four, five, maybe—

Suddenly, Enrique wasn't standing behind him anymore and the grip of the boys holding his arms loosened. Before they even had a chance to let go completely, he saw massive hands, beefy hands, Tiburón's hands grab Jamal by the back of the shirt, rip him away and throw him across the room. Hector let go of Paco's arm and tried to run. He didn't make it far, but Paco couldn't see what happened to him because as soon as they were no longer pinning him in place, Paco collapsed off the side of the chair and slid down onto the floor, struggling as he did to reach down and pull up his pants.

With his cheek on the floor, he watched Tiburón go after Enrique. He grabbed him by the front of the shirt, jammed him up against the wall, and slammed a fist the size of a toaster into his face. Enrique went immediately limp, but Tiburón held him there, hitting him again and again. When he finally did let go, Enrique collapsed on the floor. Tiburón turned, daring anybody else to approach.

"You want some of that," he indicated Paco with his chin, and shook his fist, "you get some of *this*. Anybody? Whatsa matter — ain't got no guts now, afraid to fight unless it's two or three against one?"

He took two steps and lifted Jamal off the floor where he lay on his back, where Tiburón had thrown him. Without even lifting him all the way up, Tiburón hit him in the face, then let him drop.

Hector literally collapsed to his knees in front of Tiburon.

"I'm … please … I didn't … I didn't know he was yours."

That was absolutely the single worst thing he could

have said. Tiburòn launched himself at Hector, who was struggling to his feet to run. He grabbed his shirt and began to punch him mercilessly in the belly, again and again. He was doubled over when Tiburón came up with his knee into his face and Paco could hear the sound of his teeth breaking.

Then it was quiet. He had managed to pull his pants back up to his waist, but his balls and belly were still in so much pain he couldn't get up. Tiburón approached him, grabbed him roughly by the upper arm and dragged him to his feet. He had to remain standing. He understood that he absolutely *could not collapse now.* In some strange way, he thought it would disappoint Tiburón if he did.

He wobbled, but remained upright.

Tiburón shoved him toward a chair. "Sit down." And Paco gratefully collapsed. Then Tiburón pulled up a chair beside him, leaned it back against the wall and sat, his hands between his knees, not talking.

The other boys who had been frozen in place by the fight began to thaw out. Somebody went to Enrique. It seemed clear even from this distance that Tiburón had hurt him bad, real bad. On the other side of the room, Hector was on his hands and knees, blood pouring out his ruined mouth to the floor.

Minutes passed. Jamal and Hector found some supporters who helped them into the bathroom to clean up. But Enrique lay unconscious and nobody would get anywhere near him. Half an hour passed. The tension in the room abated. They gave in again to the merciless assault on their senses of the juke set that showed every conceivable angle of the approaching silver spots, and hauled out one expert after another to explain what the spots were and to contradict the previous speaker's interpretation of their intentions.

"What'd you do it for?" Tiburón asked.

"Do what?"

"Why'd you say you done it? I'd ate some bad shit and wasn't no stopping it."

Paco thought of various answers but decided to go with simple truth.

"They was gonna blame me anyway, and if I didn't fess up, all the others here would have been pissed at me." He looked into Tiburón's face. "And I was so popular with the other guys I really hated to give that up."

"They ain't gonna bother you no more," Tiburón said, gesturing with his chin toward the other boys. "You ain't got nothing to worry about from them."

"Yeah," Paco said. "Just from the convicts."

"And the guards."

"And the aliens."

Tiburón smiled a little. "No problemo."

"Piece of cake."

Paco reached up to finger the two teeth Enrique had loosened. Enrique remained unconscious on the floor.

Chapter Twenty-Seven

THE BRIGHT LIGHT that suddenly shined on his face pulled Sawyer back out of the darkness he had fallen into, but he didn't open his eyes, just squinted up through a forest of eyelashes to see a flashlight aimed at him ... not at his face, his chest. A figure was standing above him with one foot on each side of his waist.

"Got me one," the man was calling out. "Some county mounty—"

A *whoop, whoop, whoop* bellowed into the cavernous building and echoed off the walls. Sawyer had to get to the car, and to do that, he had to take out an enemy in the light-and-shadow ballet dancing around him while darkness blanketed the rest of the world thick as a shroud.

Nobody rises to the occasion. Everybody defaults to the level of their training.

Drill instructor at boot camp at Camp Lejeune, first week of Marine training. No, training instructor Faversham his first day at the state police academy. One or the other. Both had trained him to do what he did next, reflexively. He didn't have to think or plan, it just happened.

He curled his left hand into a fist and drove a round-house punch with all his strength into the femoral nerve in the inner thigh of the dark figure's right leg, and the man's knee collapsed out from under him like a tent when you yank out the center pole. The other knee responded in a sympathetic reflex and in seconds the man who'd been towering above Sawyer was now on his knees straddling his waist.

Off balance, and with the flashlight in his right hand, the man had caught his fall with his left hand. Sawyer knocked that out from under him with a blow to the inside of his elbow. As it collapsed, Sawyer lifted his left leg and the man tumbled over onto his side and Sawyer rolled over on top of him. His flashlight flew out of his hand and rolled away lighting up piles of sheets, towels and bedspreads.

Sawyer instantly got to his knees astraddle the man and landed two punishing blows to his chest, using his right elbow, a harder, sharper weapon than a fist. He actually heard ribs snap and the man shrieked in agony. He slammed his elbow down again, hoping to jab the broken rib bones into his lungs. He hammered another elbow shot into the man's sternum and a fist into the front of his neck, hoping to fracture his trachea.

His movements had been so lightning fast the other man, a fat man who must have weighed three hundred pounds, had yet to land a defensive blow. Sawyer rolled off him, grabbed one of the flashlights with his left hand and continued the roll, freeing his gun hand to draw his weapon so he ended up on his belly, weapon drawn a flashlight beam sweeping the area around him 360 degrees. A figure not fifteen feet away was sprinting toward him, holding something aloft to hit him with, like a fire place poker. He shot the man in the chest and he folded up and fell to the floor. Then Sawyer leapt to his feet, training his gun on the fat man lying on his back, groaning in agony, blood bubbling out with every breath.

Sawyer swept the flashlight in an arc again and it lit other people, several of whom had flashlights of their own. None of them looked menacing.

"You move and I will mow your asses down, you hear me," he yelled at them as he took off running, leaping over aisles clogged with small appliances, broken pictures, storage boxes, and shattered glassware.

When he raced outside, there was no one anywhere near the cruiser. He leapt into the front seat behind the wheel and Ellie babbled, "—three of them and one of them had a tire iron and when I hit the button and the siren went off they jumped back, but then they were coming again until the gunshot. Was that you? Did you shoot somebody? It scared them off."

"Stay put," he said, he reached up, grabbed his service rifle off the rack, then leapt back out of the car and slammed the door. This time when he entered the building, he went in like a tank, his rifle to his shoulder and the flashlight in the left hand holding the barrel, pointing wherever he pointed the gun.

"This is the police. Do you hear me, *the police.* You are looting. That's a Class D felony punishable by up to five years in prison and a ten-thousand-dollar fine. Come near me and I will drop you on the spot. No questions asked." Then he fired the rifle at the ceiling, the sound not as loud as he'd hoped it'd be, muffled by the fabric all around.

That gunshot was totally off the reservation. You never, *never* discharged a weapon without a target in mind. Every bullet goes somewhere, Faversham had said a thousand times, and you are responsible for where every bullet lands. Hopefully that one would fall back to earth harmlessly, drop onto the roof of the building. He couldn't let that be his problem right now.

"Get to the back of the store. All of you. NOW!"

He watched flashlight beams all turn and point away from the store front, lights bobbing as people ran to do his bidding.

His head on a swivel, moving low and fast, shining his flashlight beam all around, he made his way back to where he'd been attacked.

He found the fat man where he'd left him, wheezing and groaning. Punctured lungs. He would die without immediate medical attention, was drowning in his own blood. Sawyer looked around, trying to figure how he might be able to ... But the man was huge. There was no possible way for Sawyer to get him out of the building, couldn't even drag him, the aisles were clogged. And in the time the useless effort took him ...

You couldn't save every puppy in the pound. And even if you could, you didn't start with the one that bit you.

He couldn't let this guy's fate be his problem. The man had chosen his road and paid the price for his decision. Sawyer would dial 911 when he left the building, but he knew there'd be nobody on the other end to respond.

He made another sweep with his flashlight, then set his flashlight on a pile of towels pointed toward the door and slung the rifle over his shoulder by the strap. He stepped over the man he'd shot, didn't look at his face, didn't want to know what he looked like, didn't want to wake up with that face staring at him wall-eyed out of the darkness. He merely reached down and placed two fingers on the man's neck. No pulse, not that he'd expected to find one.

Grabbing the Santa bag, he looped it over his arm, picked up the flashlight, and without a backward glance made his way to the front of the store where twin beams of light shone through the broken windows. He stopped at the front counter. The electronic cash register lay on the floor beside it, ripped out of place. He felt in his pocket, drew out his wallet and extracted the last bill he had, the only bill in it. A fifty. He placed it on the counter.

It felt necessary to him to do that, important to adhere to the last trappings of civilization and the rule of law and he didn't question it. He had just killed a man, no, two — as a law enforcement officer, acting in self-defense. He was not a looter.

Outside, he opened the back door of the cruiser and tossed in the bag, got behind the wheel, put the vehicle in reverse and squalled backward. He hit 911 speed dial as he shifted into drive, and a not-voice informed him — big surprise — that all circuits were busy and he needed to hang up and try his call again later. Laying rubber, the cruiser raced across the parking lot toward the street, passing the revelers at Rafferty's, having a beer together to toast the end of the world.

The strains of a song drifted out of the bar into the night.

"I live back in the woods, you see. My woman and the kids and the dogs and me. I've got a shotgun, a rifle and a four-wheel drive. And a country boy can survive."

The wind blew the last words away in rags, "Country folks can survive."

Chapter Twenty-Eight

ELLIE SAID nothing as they sped away from Bed Bath & Beyond, still so shell-shocked she couldn't form a coherent thought. In the silence, she tried to get a grip on herself, sort out the jumble of images, stop shaking so hard. It would help if she could get control of her breathing that was hitching in and out of her chest like a little kid after a crying jag. They wound their way out of town on back streets through residential neighborhoods for what seemed like an eternity before getting on a main artery. She read a sign. Bardstown Road. Hadn't she come through the town of Bardstown earlier today?

Today.

It couldn't have just been a day. She had lived a lifetime since she ... two lifetimes. She hardly recognized the person who had climbed into a brand new Chevrolet that she had charged on her no-limit American Express Gold Card, and headed out in blind determination. Why hadn't it registered with her that there was probably a reason all those cars were *leaving* the city — that maybe those people had a reason to leave, were perhaps fleeing something. But she had been so single-mindedly focused on finding a doctor.

A doctor.

Because she had a lump in her breast.

She couldn't stop her hand. Unbidden, she lifted it to her breast and felt around in the lower left corner.

It was there. Hard. Bigger.

Oh, *no, no, no* — she couldn't go there right now. If she did—

That's when she spotted the car wash. It was what they'd been looking for, the old kind where you dropped coins into a slot and—

"I don't have any money."

"Look in there, I think there's enough."

The sheriff indicated the little drawer on the dashboard of his cruiser. She opened it to find sunglasses, salt and pepper packets from Bob's Burger Barn and on the bottom, a pile of coins. She grabbed a handful and began picking out the quarters while he pulled the cruiser up to the first stall and parked outside it, the headlights lighting it.

She practically leapt out of the front seat, so desperate to get the goo off, *get the damned goo off!*

The sheriff opened the back door and pulled out the sack he'd brought out of Bed Bath and Beyond, and it occurred to her, with her mind so muddied it had taken a while to get around to this point, that the sheriff might actually have shot somebody — she'd heard a gunshot — might even have killed somebody to procure for her what was in that bag.

He was already putting coins down into the slots. The water turned on, a hard spray of it coming out the end of a three-foot-long wand. She hurried into the open enclosure.

"Spray me off. Please hurry, spray me off."

He did. Standing about ten feet away, the sheriff used the wand of water, starting at her head and moving slowly down her body as she turned so he could get both sides. The force of the spray knocked her off balance at first, but she braced herself while he made two full circuits up and down her body.

"I've got shampoo and soap," he said, and unbelievably, he reached into the pillowcase where he'd stuffed his purchases from Bed Bath and Beyond. And they were *purchases*. She'd seen him clearly in the spill of the headlights. Watched him take out his wallet and put a bill on the counter.

He set the wand on the ground and went to the sack, taking out two bottles and handed them to her.

She poured rich, sweet-smelling shampoo into her palm and lathered her hair until there was so much foam it was running down into her face thick as whipped topping. Then she slathered her clothes with the body wash that smelled like mangos. She made a lather on her body, clothes and all, until she must have looked like a piece of cotton candy. Then she stood as he washed up and down her body again until the soap was gone.

The force of the tiny bbs of water stung, but she didn't care. It felt good. She covered her face with her hands and asked him to make one more full circuit up and down her body.

He put the still-spewing wand down on the ground again and pointed to the bag.

"There are towels in there and also a terrycloth robe — might not be your size, it was the only one there — and some terrycloth slippers. I'll move the car to block the entrance while you get dried off." He reached into the sack and withdrew a wash cloth. "And I'll clean off the seat."

He started to turn, then remembered.

"There's a hairbrush in there, too, if it didn't fall out."

Then the water turned off automatically, the money had run out, but she was clean.

He got back into the car and moved it crossways across the opening to the bay of the car wash, then turned on his flashing lights. She stepped gingerly out onto the gravelly concrete and picked up the bag, then stood just inside the opening of the bay and peeled off her clothes.

In the throes of some unidentifiable emotion, she wadded up her shirt and threw it as hard as she could toward the back of the bay where she heard it hit the concrete wall. She did the same with the other garments, so glad to be rid of them she shivered in loathing as she heard the splatting sound of her jeans.

She used the pile of towels to dry herself and combed through her hair, savagely yanking out knots she imagined were pieces of unmentionable nastiness even though she was sure the stinging water had removed all the foulness from her body. Then she pulled the terrycloth robe around her, secured it with the belt and hugged herself, aware for the first time that she was chilled. No, cold wasn't why she was shaking. The trembling had made her think she was cold, in the same way she always thought of something sad when she was cutting up onions, making the tears real. Why waste a good cry?

A good cry.

Would there ever again, from this day forward into whatever future lay out there for all mankind, be any circumstance simple enough to be assuaged by a good cry? She doubted it.

Her hand reached up without her bidding and felt the lump in her breast. It was bigger. It really was. No, it was her imagination. No, it genuinely was bigger.

She almost screamed "stop it" out loud. She could not think about all that now. She could feel how tentative was her hold on … what? Her emotions? No, more than that. Her hold on herself as a human being. How did she even know who she was anymore? She was Elliot Thurgood Hampton, the woman whose father had given her a thirty-foot yacht for her twenty-first birthday and threw a dinner party for more than a hundred friends and family. That had been before little specks of light had suddenly appeared next door to Jupiter. She had only just met the new Elliot Thurgood Hampton, the woman who had defended her dumpster turf against rats with a bloody pipe and then spent three hours cowering in the filthy muck of a trash can.

She hardly knew that person at all.

She shuddered so violently she almost lost her balance. She had to sit down. Now, before she fell down, and she hurried in slippered feet across the parking lot to the cruiser, clutching an armload of wet towels.

"Where are your clothes? You didn't wash them off?"

Loathing colored her words. "I bought those clothes in *Walmart*" — which would once have been all the explanation anybody needed. Anybody in her world, at least. But she could tell the uniformed man before her wasn't making the same connections she was, not looking at anything from the same point of view. A chilling awareness came to her then, not for the first time: her world didn't exist anymore. No telling how long it would take, or what the world would have to go through, before it did exist again. If it ever did. And the voice of realism whispered in her ear that it never would.

"I couldn't get all the … I couldn't get them clean, so I just left them. I can get more … you know, at Walmart."

She was suddenly struck dumb by a horrifying realization. It knocked the breath out of her because it made a statement about the essential core human being who was Elliot Hampton that she didn't want to hear right now. She'd been beat up enough for one day. But it was what it was.

She had spent less than five minutes of her life with this man before she'd pulled her cell phone case out of her pocket with trembling hands and the card he'd given her fell out when she opened it. She'd dialed the number in the dark, had demanded that he drop whatever he was doing, drive for an hour and a half over God only knew what kind of roads, perhaps into the meat-grinder of a full-bore riot. *Demanded*, not asked.

If he hadn't come, if she'd had to stay the night in the trash can, battling the rats and whatever the world of daylight might bring …

Sheriff Sawyer Matheson had saved her life.

And she'd never even thanked him for doing it.

Chapter Twenty-Nine

Spade Jackson lay in his bunk in Number Two Barracks, watching the shadows the revolving light on the guard tower made as it passed over the window next to his bunk. It looked like somebody was walking, the lines moving in unison across his bed, down onto the floor and up the wall.

He was smiling. Shit, he didn't think he'd stopped smiling since that guard burst into the laundry room three days ago and said there was an invading armada of spaceships headed toward Earth. He suspected he was in the minority in his feelings about the aliens ... what was it they were calling them, the *Astrals*. The whole world was shitting itself over the armada, everybody else saw it as a bad thing. But how you seen stuff was all about the angle you was looking from. If you's on top, and you seen them ships coming to take away all the shit you worked or lied or stole or whatever you had to do to accumulate your whole life, then yeah, you'd be shitting your britches to think them little green, big-eyed dudes was gonna take it all away. But if you's looking from the bottom up, as Spade was, you'd see them little buggers as locusts, maybe, that come along and stripped the leaves off everything so's you could go in and pick the fruit.

Them green motherfuckers was gonna give Spade the chance to come out on the top of things and wasn't nothing he liked more'n coming out on top.

He groaned a little. Thinking about being on top had made him think about that Hispanic kid, Paco, with them big brown eyes and long eyelashes. Shit fire and toast a marshmallow in it but he wanted to fuck that kid's ass. And he would. He would.

He'd get that boy as the cherry on the top of the banana split when he took over Radcliffe Correctional, when he made this hellhole his own private country and him the king, then yeah, he'd get whatever he wanted whenever he wanted it.

No, he wasn't gonna go out into the wide world in a couple of months as he had been prepared to do, with a hundred dollars in his pocket, a new set of clothes, a parole officer to suck up to and some dumb-fuck job to do.

Nope. Thanks to the little dudes in the sky, Spade Jackson would go out into the wide world with a gang … no, with an army. He would have a thousand troops ready to do his bidding *if he was the one let them out their cages.*

And he would be that man.

He had a plan to make it all happen.

The prison was always understaffed, never had enough guards to do all a guard was supposed to do. That's how he'd got to where he was today, because he stepped in and yes-sir'd and no-sir'd and please-and-thank-you'd his way into being the con the guards could trust to do … not just trustee things, but the little grunt jobs the guards didn't want to do.

This morning, the warden — if he had even showed up and Spade doubted it — was running the show with thirty percent of the personnel he needed. Guards didn't show up. Kitchen crew didn't show up. Admin staff didn't show up. Hell, the world was about to end. Wasn't nobody willing to pretend anymore to "do the best they could." Now, life was about getting whatever you could as fast as you could however you could and fuck that job as a garbage man.

Now, he and his band of trusties had been charged with all kind of duties they'd never been allowed to do before. It was them fed the prisoners, wasn't for them all them cons woulda starved.

Radcliffe was no different from any other prison, though from what Spade could gather, whoever designed it was more "safety conscious" than most. Basically, the whole place was a cage inside a cage inside a cage inside a cage. Doors on every hallway and leading into every room. All of them locked, of course, and an elaborate system for opening them. Some had keys. Some could only be opened electronically by guards in a control center — always on the locked side of the door. Those control centers could open and close individual doors or a bank of doors at will. But there were even failsafes on that system. In the event of an emergency, any guard could push a button and isolate any portion of the prison — and an "alarm close" required keys to open those doors, keys kept outside the cell block entirely, locked away in the administration building. That way, cons couldn't grab a few guards and force them to open up everything. Limited access, limited liability.

There were five cell blocks, an administration building, a cafeteria, a building that housed the laundry, the license plate factory and the three dormitory buildings where the trusties lived.

Most important of all to Spade's future, to the future

of all of them, was the Department of Corrections distribution warehouse building on the back side of the prison yard. RC was centrally located among the state-run prisons, group homes, juvenile facilities and halfway houses, and it was the only one with a railroad siding. So they'd made it the distribution point for the supplies for all of them. Kinda like an Amazon distribution center. Bulk loads of supplies showed up on train cars and trustee inmates unloaded the cars and sorted out the supplies so weekly trucks could load up and transport them to the other prison locations.

It was a high-priority job to work in the warehouse because the warehouse was the central distribution point for the drug trade to all the prisons in this part of the state and for every imaginable sort of contraband a con wanted and could afford the money, cigarettes or hooch to pay for, from fancy jukes to extra cigarettes, to MagnaPOWER bars, advertised as "a full day's food supply in a bar" — you name it. It really was like an Amazon distribution center.

The gangs strictly controlled the drug and black-market items, amid constant hostility and violence. But it was Spade who controlled the trustees who unloaded the shit, and push come to shove, he was really the man in charge. He'd stayed out of all kind of prison politics, of course, because his position as the highest-ranking trustee afforded him perks that mattered a whole lot more and wouldn't earn him a shiv in the back or a month in solitary if he got caught.

Now, that distribution warehouse had taken on a whole new significance, oh yes, it surely had. In the world that was evolving since Astral Day, it had become more valuable than any gold mine. Jammed full of enough supplies to meet the needs of a small inmate population like this one for … shit, *months*. Which would make Spade Jackson the richest, most powerful man for five hundred miles in every direction. Supplies to feed his army, if he could amass one, and an army to guard the resource.

Of the three cell blocks, two were maximum security. These where the cells where the badasses were kept, but Spade knew they was way more than badasses. They was *stupid* asses, didn't have sense enough to behave themselves and wound up in nine-by-twelve-foot cells and allowed out one hour a day into a courtyard that had concrete walls so you couldn't even see another human being.

That's where you ended up when you were a nothing-to-lose, life-without-parole dumbshit too stupid to see that it might be a plan to make your life behind bars as good as you could make it under the circumstances. Do as he had done and work your way into a tolerable existence.

But those dumb fucks didn't have sense enough to control their emotions. They bit the guards, threw shit at the guards. When the guards went into those cell blocks, they had to wear that protective clothing like you used when you was training an attack dog.

What they got for their ferocity was living out their miserable lives in concrete boxes.

The other three cell blocks were designated for inmates who had a few more social skills, ones who could play well with others — most of the time. Those three cell blocks were all alike, with four tiers of cells built in a U around a common area where there were tables and benches. Prisoners were free to wander around their tier of thirty cells which should have held thirty men, but now held forty, sometimes up to fifty. But there were locked doors on both ends of the U.

There were ten cells in each of the three sides of the U, designed to be one-inmate cells, so each tier should have held thirty inmates. Four tiers of thirty inmates made the capacity of each cell block 120 inmates. But the state had jammed 160 to 170 inmates into the blocks, one-man cells forced to accommodate two inmates, 'cept there wasn't no extra room for the extra body. Jammed in like that, men's fuses got short quick. Violence was a constant. One con beating the shit out of his roommate because the roomie snored, or a bigger con riding his little roomie too hard at night when the guards pretended not to hear the screaming. The competition for a cell all to yourself was stiff.

Though the inmates on the four tiers couldn't socialize with the other tiers, under normal circumstances the doors to the cells were left open and the inmates were free to roam around, hang out with a buddy or watch a juke in the cell of somebody lucky enough to have one, and use the common area on a rotating basis.

Each of the tiers had two guards walking the open hallway in front of the cells. They didn't have guns, of course, duh. That would have got them shot in about six seconds. The whole cell block was controlled in a booth that sat on the ground floor. With the open U-shaped design, the guards in the booth, behind unbreakable glass, could see up through the grate floors into the catwalks around all the upper cells, could watch what was going on in the common area on the ground floor in front of them and had CVT cameras to cover any area out of line of sight. The only access to that booth was from a door in the back of it, which only led to a hallway with locked doors on both ends. A cage inside a cage. There was also a door from the control room into the common area, which could not be opened unless all the cells on the ground floor were locked.

The three guards in the control center had control over all the cells. With the push of a button, they could seal off a whole tier of cells, close all the cell doors on a particular tier, or open them all, or lock certain cells and not others. They operated everything from monitors that enabled them to see who was where doing what at every second of every day. You wanted to jack off, get used to an audience.

And so, of course, the first shot fired in Spade's revolution would have to be one that got him inside that control center.

He smiled broadly. Yeah, he already had a plan for how he was going to do that, even though it'd be difficult with the whole place on lockdown. But the lockdown was slowly providing the motivation he needed to get control of the masses of inmates.

Lockdown created a logistical/manpower nightmare for the guards even with all hands on deck. How did you feed a thousand men when they couldn't file by cell block in an orderly fashion into the cafeteria to eat their meals?

The last meal the cons in cellblocks had had was breakfast on Astral Day. Even under normal circumstances, there weren't enough guards to take prisoners individual meals on trays and with fewer guards showing up every day, the difficulty became an impossibility.

And the cons knew it. The Astral armada had sentenced every inmate within the walls to death — slow death by starvation. Unless Spade swooped in and saved them.

The inmates who hadn't eaten in going on three days were going to be fed tomorrow *because he and his trustees would take them food.* And he would make damn sure every mother's child of them knew and understood what side their bread was buttered on.

But still ... even though he could position himself as the savior of the whole inmate population, that wouldn't guarantee their loyalty to him a week from now. His takeover plan needed to be preceded by — how should he put it? — some ethnic cleansing. Spade had made his decision years ago to be a trustee, which in essence made him one of the guards. You was either one of the guards or one of the inmates. You couldn't be both. As chief of trustees, he couldn't be the leader of any of the groups and gangs in the regular prison population.

Every street gang in Los Angeles had a representation in Radcliffe. The Bloods, the Crips, El Cajones, Aryan Nation, Westside Locos, White Fence, Armenian Power, Mexican Mafia and Asian Boyz. Their leaders ruled supreme over their little tribes. Just because Spade took over the prison, didn't make him the leader of all the groups within it. Unless he got the second part of his plan right, he'd just be the guy who brought them sandwiches and eventually unlocked the doors, thank you very much, next.

To rule supreme, he had to rule all the smaller groups. Which meant he had some "team-building exercises" to conduct to develop the loyalties he'd need so that when everybody could bolt out the door and go wherever the fuck they wanted, he'd have an army who'd decide they'd be better off where they were … with thirty-five hundred people, the whole population of the town of Clarksburg, as their servants.

He'd have a good time in that little town. But Spade wouldn't have to wait until then to take his pick of the litter. The little Hispanic kid Paco was *his*!

Day Four

Chapter Thirty

NOAH MATHESON WAS SIGNING SO FRANTICALLY Dr. Weiss was having trouble following his "words."

The old man shook his head to clear it, couldn't remember the last time he'd slept more than an hour or two — sometime before Astral Day —. and it was becoming increasingly hard to focus, to concentrate. During the day, he had the academy to run, a school full of 120 children who were suffering varying degrees of panic, with parents who would have moved heaven and earth to get to them, but found neither movable. Thank God for the monks. Literally. They had stepped in, serene and competent, and took over cooking meals when the cafeteria ladies stopped showing up. They were the only reason Zion Academy was still functioning.

Dr. Weiss fell into bed every night exhausted, but instead of shutting off in desperately needed sleep, his mind went to work on a monumental mechanical conundrum, a project he'd been working on for almost twenty years. He was certain that *someday* he would find a way to miniaturize the patented Weiss Implant hearing device that had enabled thousands of people to hear. But as soon as the little white dots were spotted out by Jupiter, "someday" was no longer soon enough. It had to be *now*. The current implants were hooked via communications satellites to a device that he'd named "Dumbo," for a cartoon elephant from his childhood. The device flawlessly converted sound to brain waves for thousands of people worldwide as long as there were functioning communications satellites. Now that the satellites were no longer reliable, the hearing of thousands was blinking on and off like a digital clock left unplugged, and he was sickeningly sure the implants would stop functioning altogether soon.

And so his mind churned, night after night.

It broke the old man's heart to watch children who'd laughed, talked and played like normal-hearing children slowly descend into silence again. No, it more than broke his heart. It broke something deeper than his heart. It broke his soul.

Of course, the little blond boy signing in front of him had never left the silence. Noah Matheson was the only person on whom Dr. Weiss's hearing device did not work, and he was slowly coming around to the belief that something more than a physical injury had made the boy deaf. But he had no time to ponder that mystery now. In fact, he had no time for Noah at all right now, but he had stopped the boy to talk to him because he was so anxious to hear what on earth had happened to Ellie Hampton. She had left the school yesterday afternoon driving her own brand new car, and was returned by Sheriff Matheson and Noah in the dead of night last night, barefoot, wearing only a robe. Where had her clothes gone?

The boy's hands flew through the air and Dr. Weiss gleaned out the words from the motions.

"People fighting ... riot ... chased Mrs. Hampton ...

hid in a trash can. Dad said that … *it* … was falling apart."
The boy didn't know how to sign "civilization," or how to
spell it, but Dr. Weiss knew what the sheriff meant. The
boy paused, then attempted to quote exactly what his
father had said: "The thin blue line between society and
chaos won't hold much longer."

The boy paused again, then signed, "Dad said everybody has to get ready to fight now."

The doctor walked slowly back to his office after his
talk with Noah, his heart heavy — through hallways that
were silent. At this moment, the doctor's hearing device
wasn't connecting to the children's hearing aids. They all
were deaf.

Everybody has to get ready to fight.

Was it true? Had it come to that? Apparently it had.

And he thought about his aunt.

David's father, Jakob Weiss, had been smuggled out of
Warsaw after both Jakob's parents, Moses and Sarah Weiss,
died heroically fighting the Germans there. The day Nazi
tanks finally rolled into the Jewish ghetto, Jakob's father
blew up three of them, jumped on top and dropped
Molotov cocktails down into the turrets before he was
gunned down. His mother, Sarah, was an elementary
school principal and before the Nazi soldiers could storm
her school, she poisoned herself, her own older children
and all of her students so they couldn't be captured and
taken to the concentration camps and gas chambers.

But David's older sister, Maya, only pretended to drink
the poison. There were not enough doses to go around and
she gave hers to another child. Maya was marched with the
other captives out of the city to train cars to haul them off
to Treblinka. One of the soldiers took a liking to the beautiful ten-year-old, separated Maya from the others and
dragged her into the woods to rape her. They found his

body later, his throat slashed with his own knife, Maya gone. She survived the war living in a Polish farmer's chicken house and was reunited with her little brother Jakob years later in Israel.

Jakob's only child, David, grew up in Israel listening to his great aunt Maya's stories about the heroism of her parents.

Everybody has to get ready to fight.

Dr. Weiss squared his shoulders and strode purposefully into his office. He would be prepared to fight as his ancestors had fought. He sat down at his desk, pulled out a detailed topographical map of the school grounds and set to work.

Chapter Thirty-One

ONLY ONE GUARD in the kitchen.

Just one.

The detail of four during mealtimes and two the rest of time had dwindled to one guard. Like one guard could do jack shit.

He was supposed to patrol the rows of cutting boards, check to see that all the knives were still safely chained to the walls as they ought to be. And if they weren't? If he found one missing, or two. Or ten? What could he do about it?

Spade shook his head and smiled.

Why did they keep up the charade?

There would be aliens in spaceships landing on the planet in two days — shit, you could practically see the ships with a pair of binoculars — and still a handful of diehards showed up at work to keep men in cages like it mattered, like keeping these men out of civilized society made any difference at all since in another week there would be no civilized society to protect. Give it another week and you wouldn't be able to tell the criminals from the citizens … well, except the citizens would be clumsy and inept at taking care of business and the cons would kill anybody who got in their way.

But Spade had to admit that the slow death of the prison was making it possible for him to take it over in a — how should he put it? — *bloodless transfer of power.* Well, not bloodless. Just less blood than there'd be in a riot with every man for himself and every gang fighting every other gang.

As far as Spade could determine, the prison was now operating on a staff of less than twenty-five percent of its employees. And every shift, guards were supposed to relieve the guards who had done their eight hours … only they never showed. Some of the guards just stayed on, which meant there were a handful of them who had worked thirty-six hours straight. And for what?

Again Spade shook his head.

Frank Gillespie, the lone guard in the kitchen, approached him. He looked like he hadn't slept in days and maybe he hadn't. But the stress of living with Armageddon five … then four … then three days away would make anybody look like they hadn't slept in days.

"The delivery trucks that were supposed to be here last night never came," Gillespie said. He looked around help-lessly. "We have enough supplies here to last a few days, then we're going to have to start hauling stuff over here from the warehouse."

He stopped, like he expected Spade to say somethings comforting like, *oh, everything will be fine in a day or two*, or *the world is going to right itself by Friday morning at the latest.*

"We got this, boss," was what Spade did say. "Me and the boys. We can keep everybody from starving. Ain't gonna say it'll be three meals a day like it should be, but we'll see they got food."

"You're a good man, Spade," Gillespie said, relief coloring his voice.

You just about to find out how good, when I'm running things. Spade planned to let him live. He was one of the good ones. Shit, there weren't any good guards, but he was better than most. He'd be one of the few who'd still be breathing by the time the little greenies showed up in two days.

Gillespie was covering the kitchen and the infirmary, which was to say, he was making sure the infirmary stayed locked. The guards had had the good judgement in the first twenty-four hours to take every conceivable drug that could be abused out of the prison. But there were stashes the guards didn't know about, of course.

When Gillespie left the kitchen, Spade motioned for Sandman and Bobby. They'd already talked it out. The heads of the Bloods, the Crips, El Cajones, Aryan Nation, Westside Locos, White Fence, Armenian Power, Mexican Mafia and Asian Boyz, plus first lieutenants in Bloods, and the top three in Mexican Mafia — they'd kill them all.

And special doses for another ten inmates who for one reason or another the world would just be a better place without. Four of them weren't human in any way that mattered anymore. No way was he going to let *them* out. They'd kill somebody inside five minutes after their release just for grins. And another handful — personal grudges of Spade's. And then another two dozen randoms. Spade couldn't take out only the gang leaders — there had to be enough other deaths to disguise the purpose. Convince the cons that the guards intended to kill all of them, and they were lucky to have survived.

"You got the sauce?"

Bobby pulled from his pocket a small bottle of white powder. Rat Poison. It was kept with the cleaning supplies, just labeled Rat Poison, not in the original containers so there wasn't any way to know exactly what specific poisons were in it. Maybe arsenic, maybe cyanide or strychnine. Maybe some combination of all three. The shit was deadly, that's all that mattered, but Spade wasn't no chemist. He didn't know how much it would take of the poison to kill a man, whether or not he'd die right away or linger, and what the dying would be like.

The cons would only get one meal today, sandwiches and chili. And it would be the hottest chili this particular kitchen had ever made, two or three times the normal amount of chili sauce and jalapeños. Surely to God, you couldn't taste poison if your mouth was on fire from chili sauce. Locked up and only gonna get one meal today, and no guarantee when the next meal would be — they'd eat whatever was put in front of them even if it tasted a little wonky.

"Once we doctor this shit up, don't get any of it on your hands," he said. "For all I know, you can absorb the poison through your skin."

They all nodded gravely.

Only the three of them were in on the takeover plan. The other men on the crews working with them would quickly fall in line, though. They'd worked with Spade long enough to know that he was smarter and more clever than any of the idiot guards he cow-towed to. The trustees would follow Spade down the barrel of a howitzer.

"And make sure you tell all your people to make a big deal about it to the cons, that *the guards were all over us* while we were fixing the food, fooling with it themselves. Can't blame it on them unless everybody already knows they was the ones made the food."

"We good," Sandman said and grinned. He had a wide space between his two front teeth that made his grin either particularly endearing or sinister, depending on how you looked at it. Bobby was the skittish one. Spade put his arm around the little white man's shoulders. "You sure you good?" Bobby nodded again, but couldn't manage a grin.

"Then let's *do* this."

Chapter Thirty-Two

STAR WAS SITTING at the kitchen table in the trailer folding towels when she heard the first car pull up out front of the closed gate of Alien World, but she didn't hear a car door open. Couldn't they tell the place was closed? Who wanted to play miniature golf or ride the merry-go-round now? Even Star wasn't interested. She'd taught Pumpkin how to turn on two of the rides so she could ride in them when the park was closed and Uncle Clyde was working in the store or the restaurant. On the Tilt-A-Whirl and the Ferris wheel, she'd lift the metal covers off the switches, get in the car, then tell Pumpkin "On!" and he'd stand on his hind legs and push the button. When she'd had her fill, she'd call out "On!" again and he'd punch the button and turn the ride off. The merry-go-round turned on by pushing a lever down, and she could have taught him that, but he probably couldn't have pushed it back up. With the trailer here at Alien World and the three other kids always around, she couldn't have gotten away with it now, but it didn't matter. Sneaking a ride on the Tilt-A-Whirl didn't hold much appeal when the world all around her seemed to be coming to an end.

After Uncle Clyde dragged the trailer through the gate yesterday, he closed the swinging bar to traffic, and padlocked it to the pole on the other side of the entrance. He'd even set out orange traffic cones in front of it. Surely, whoever was parked out front could figure out that meant they weren't open for business.

Star felt around in the gigantic mound of clean linens — not the end of them by any means, Aunt Mary Ellen was still running loads through the ultraCLEAN machine that washed and dried clothes in less than five minutes.

She'd had to wash every linen they had, towels, washcloths, bedspreads, sheets, you name it. Everything that had been jammed in the linen closet beside the back door when the wheels on the trailer had slipped off the asphalt about two miles from Roswell and the back door had flown open. The jolt had opened the linen closet door a few feet away, too. They had deposited towels and sheets along half a mile of NM Route 84 before Aunt Mary Ellen spotted a sheet flying out the door and told Uncle Clyde to stop. Then she went running down the roadside, trying to collect them, darting out between cars, with Uncle Clyde standing beside the door of the truck, cursing.

"She's gonna get run — *watch out, didn't you see* — leave the towels!"

Gratefully, the cars weren't going very fast because they'd had to slow down behind the parked trailer house, which took up the whole right side of the road and half the oncoming lane. Uncle Clyde said it should have required all kind of permits to move that thing down a state highway, an over-wide load sign on the back of the trailer in letters at least twelve inches tall, and cars with signs and lights and red flags driving in front of it and behind it.

There wasn't a lot of traffic going out of town, but it backed up quickly and every car that passed them laid on the horn. Where were the people going that they thought would be safer than Roswell? How could anywhere be safe now? They were all in a hurry once they got around the trailer; dashing off to what was probably no safer than where they'd come from.

Once they finally made it to Alien World the night before, Uncle Clyde had simply parked the trailer inside the gate, then this morning he'd moved the little trailer Welcome Center that sat right by the gate out of the way and used its hookups to fit onto the mobile home. So there the "house" sat, just inside the gate.

When he had finally gotten the trailer situated, and the water hooked up, Aunt Mary Ellen had started doing laundry and had pretty much done it non-stop. It was Star's job to fold and the little kids took what she'd folded and deposited it back in the closet where it belonged.

Star tried to picture in her mind what the new and definitely unimproved Alien World must look like. The gigantic Alien World sign unlit. Just inside the gate, a banged-up trailer house sitting at an odd angle because the hookups weren't exactly in the right places for it.

There was barely enough room for a vehicle to drive between the end of the trailer house through the open gate, which Uncle Clyde said was the good news because nobody needed to be driving in there anyway.

Then she heard another car pull up. She didn't hear anybody get out of that vehicle, either. How odd.

A little tickle of ridiculous fear fluttered in her stomach. And she thought of the dream she had last night of the boy crouched in the darkness, looking out a window into darkness. Was the image from the past or the future? Or a fantasy that meant nothing at all? She couldn't have explained what was so sinister about the image, but it terrified her. No, as she thought about it, she realized that she was frightened because the boy had been so scared. He knew what was going on and knew there was something terrifying out there in the darkness.

But it was broad daylight now. What was scary about——?

Well, everything, as a matter of fact. The spaceships that were at that moment streaking across the sky toward Earth might be coming to destroy the world.

A third car pulled to a stop in front of the closed gate and then Star heard the doors on all the cars open and several people get out. Women. They must have been waiting for each other. She could hear their voices greeting each other.

Then she heard Uncle Clyde, too.

"What can I do for your ladies? As you can see, we're closed."

"We didn't come out here to ride the merry-go-round, Clyde," said a voice that was familiar. That was Susan Lester, one of the tellers at New Mexico Federal Bank.

"What *did* you come out here for?"

"Clyde … we didn't come here to see you," said another voice that also sounded familiar but Star couldn't dig the woman's identity out of her mind. She was very, very good at telling who people were by their voices, but not so much when they were out of context. Recognizing the dentist's receptionist at church, for example — back when they used to go to church.

"We come to … see Star."

"What on earth for?"

"We want her to … tell us what's gonna happen."

"You what?"

"A couple of years ago, I got her to read my fortune

with them alien rocks. She told me I was gonna have a baby, a little girl with red hair," Susan said. "And she was right. She got it just right and there wasn't no way she could have known a thing like that. I wasn't even pregnant yet."

"She told me about Joe's leg," said Darlene Littlewood. She was easy. Her voice was annoyingly high and squeaky, like talking to someone who'd just breathed helium. Her husband was in an oil field accident about six months ago and his leg was crushed so badly the doctors had to amputate. "I didn't believe her. Nobody did. But …"

"And you know why I believe her," said the third woman and then Star did recognize her. It was Rose Harrington. "Star knew." Rose was one of the survivors of the tornado that had wiped out Slidell Easter Sunday two years ago.

"So let me get this straight. You come all the way out here because—"

"She knows," blurted Rose, who seemed close to tears. "You know she does. She can tell us—"

"Don't you think if she could tell where them alien ships was gonna land and what was gonna happen the government would have swooped in here and scooped her up and hauled her off to Area 51?"

"I ain't wanting to ask her about what the aliens is gonna do to the world. I want to ask her what's gonna happen to me and mine," Darlene said.

"And me," Rose chimed in.

"And me," said Susan.

"Please, Clyde," Darlene begged.

The sound was so pleading, so full of fear and sorrow it broke Star's heart. Apparently, it had the same effect on Uncle Clyde because she could hear him coming back to the trailer house. He'd had to stack concrete blocks in front of the door of the trailer because it stood four feet off the ground and only the top step and part of the railing had stubbornly hung on during the move. He stepped into the living room that opened onto the kitchen.

Before he said a word, Star said, "They want me to tell their fortunes."

"Yeah."

She wouldn't be able to do for them what they wanted. It wasn't like registering a dollar credit and touching the screen and out of the bottom of the machine dropped UltraFizz Cola. She saw whatever she saw. Random images. She couldn't answer questions like "will we this or that?" because she had no control over what she saw, and lots of times didn't even know what the images meant, if they were of the past or what hadn't happened yet.

"I told them before that I couldn't—"

"They know that, but they don't care. Knowing what's gonna happen, even some small inconsequential fact — I think it gives them back a little control and right now the whole world is spinning out of control."

"Okay," Star said.

Uncle Clyde didn't bother to take them and Star to the astral reading room that was located beyond the Alien Museum. He just brought them into the trailer one at a time, had to help them up the makeshift concrete block steps, and set them in the living room.

And Star took each of their hands in turn — they all were cold and clammy — smelled their fear, and tried to see into their lives. What she saw sickened her, jabbed a cold dagger of terror into her belly so deep she couldn't get her breath from the pain of it. Was this what was …?

She couldn't speak, couldn't tell them …

So she swallowed hard and started making stuff up.

She told Susan that she saw her sitting down to a big

dinner with her family, Christmas or Thanksgiving maybe, and everybody was laughing. What she really saw was Susan in some kind of mob scene, fighting with two other women to hold onto a loaf of bread she was crushing to her chest. One of the other women hit her in the face with something, a piece of the metal rack off the shelf unit, slicing twin gashes across her forehead and cheek, and she staggered. The woman snatched the bread out of her hands and instantly had to fight for it with another woman as determined to have it as she had been. Susan staggered back against a wall, then sank slowly to the floor, where the fighting women knocked her over onto her side and stepped on her as they battled it out.

She told Darlene that she saw her sitting serenely on the porch in a mountain cabin watching a sunset, and Darlene had squealed, "We have a cabin near Vail, Colorado and we're packing right now to go there. See, she *can* see what's coming."

And Star *had* seen Darlene in the mountains, but not sitting serenely on a porch. She saw her turning from an ice-encrusted stream carrying buckets of water in each hand. She stopped, looked at her footprints in the snow leading back up the hill, registered the red blotches where she'd stepped. Then she looked down and her feet were wrapped in rags, not shoes. Pink rags.

She scrambled for something to say to Rose, then finally spit out that she was riding down the street in Roswell, in the back seat of a car on auto-drive, and she was painting her fingernails, her phone was on speaker and she was chatting happily with Stella, her little red-haired girl.

Rose had been in a car when Star saw her, alright. Or in some kind of vehicle. But it wasn't moving, on auto-drive or any other way. Rose was in the back seat, but not

painting her fingernails. The seat was piled high with —
blankets, clothing, a water bottle — she'd been living there,
in the car, in the back seat. And she wasn't talking to Stella.
She held Stella in her arms, rocking back and forth, twin
tracks of tears cleaning the filth off her bony face. The
little girl lay motionless as Rose cried. There was noise
outside, but Rose paid it no mind, just kept rocking the lifeless child back and forth, as explosions boomed out beyond
the windows, something ripping apart. Maybe the end of
the world.

The three women gushed their gratitude and Uncle
Clyde refused to take their money — what for? What good
was it anymore?

As soon as she heard the last car pull away from the
gate, Star burst into tears.

"I lied," she wailed, as Uncle Clyde stood beside her
chair, pulled her to him, her face against his rotund belly.

"I know you did, sugar."

"What I saw, they … they …"

"Hush now, you don't have to do that anymore. You
ain't never gonna have to do that ever again. I promise."

So she clung to him and cried, determined not to
concentrate on "seeing" him as she touched him. It was a
skill she had perfected as soon as she was old enough to
grasp that looking into the future of those you loved might
sound like a good idea but it backfired, every time. It set
you apart, made you different in a way that was as indefin-
able as it was real. People — even people you loved, started
being careful about coming near you. Nobody wanted
somebody else looking inside their head, seeing stuff that
hadn't happened yet. It wasn't at all hard *not* to see. In fact,
it had taken her years to learn how to do it in the first
place. At first, she just caught fleeting glimpses, a blur of
images that went by too fast and were too indistinct to

make out. She had to teach herself how to concentrate, how to blank out her own mind to see into the mind of someone else. When she'd tried to explain it to Uncle Clyde, he'd said it sounded like those pictures within a picture, images you could only see by un-focusing your eyes and trying to look through them. She couldn't imagine what something like that could possibly look like, but it seemed to make perfect sense to him.

Visions, though. Uncle Clyde had told her about people, psychics like she was, who saw huge, detailed visions of some catastrophic event in the future. She was always afraid that would happen to her one day, too, that she would have a full-blown vision. As she sobbed, she willed herself not to have a vision now. Star absolutely did *not* want to see what their future held.

Chapter Thirty-Three

ELLIE'S FATHER loved cars and had a collection of antique vehicles, some of them even older than the vintage Mustang. On Sunday afternoons when she was a little girl, he would take her out onto the grounds of the estate and let her drive. She had to sit on a pillow in the 1939 Buick, and even then the seat was so low she had to look through the steering wheel rather than over it.

These were not, of course, auto-cars. There was no one to guide the vehicle except the person behind the wheel. And there was more to do than just guide it. You had to push on the pedals on the floor to make it go faster or slower. And in some of them, there was even this extra pedal, and you had to push it in to change gears.

That had been the hardest part of all of it. It had taken forever to learn how to do it. She remembered how she'd start the car, push in that little pedal, it had a name — the *clutch*. Her father would tell her to "ease off" on the pedal, not to let it pop up. But she couldn't seem to get that part right. She'd let the clutch pop up, the car would lurch forward and the engine would die.

Seemed like it took her years to master that skill … easing off the clutch, easing on the accelerator. But once she did, she was able to drive even the oldest cars, changing gears as she drove. There were still issues, though, more things to know. You had to know how to shift gears, but you also had to know *when* to do it.

There was rumbling power in first gear. The engine would roar louder and louder, straining as the car climbed the estate's hills. As it did, her father would shout, "Shift, shift! You're going to blow the engine!" The louder the engine roared, the slower the car went. It would go slower and slower until it finally couldn't move upward at all.

Ellie thought about those cars, the clutch and the gears as she lay in bed while dawn painted the Kentucky sky pink and yellow. She had done that last night. She had shifted gears. Not smoothly. She had lurched forward, hopped and jerked and jumped, painfully jerky-jerky. But the car hadn't died. It had come close, but it hadn't died and the gear had shifted.

The horror of last night, the riot, the trash can, the rats, had changed the essential Ellie, put her in a different place than she had been before, going forward in a different gear. She no longer felt the rumbling power of her own engine, her wealth and prestige and status in the upper crust of American society. To move forward on the road she now traveled, she would have to leave that behind. She flat out could not go where she had to go without leaving that gear, letting go, moving on.

Ellie would either do that, shift, change, abandon the old self, or she would roar until her engine blew, or merely roll to a stop, unable to make it up the hill.

She looked down at the sleeping child beside her, dawn light granting her skin a pink glow, her dark lashes spread out like fans on her cheeks, her eyebrows feathered above them. She was a beautiful child, didn't so much favor Ellie as she did her grandfather. Gretchen was the image of Ellie's father, and Ellie felt a love so pure and powerful for the little girl it gripped her heart in a painful vice.

Somehow, she had to survive to take care of Gretchen in this new world order. But what if she was sick? What if it was …

Her hand went to the lump; she rolled it beneath her fingers and a strangled sob escaped her lips. The little girl stirred, then went back to sleep. Ellie got carefully out of bed, pulled open the drawer of the dresser, an antique, beautiful mahogany. All the furniture here was the best money would buy. She took from the drawer a pair of Walmart jeans and a tee shirt and quietly got dressed. Then she slipped into the hallway, went down it, her bare feet ruffling the soft pile of the carpet. Beyond the dormitory wing were the classrooms, and she went up the stairs to them, all of them still and empty.

It was near the end on the left, she thought, but when she opened the door there, she didn't need the light to see it was a chemistry lab. She tried the next door down and found what she was looking for. The art room.

The walls were decorated with student-produced art. From little-kid stick-figure families done by the second and third-graders, to moderately skilled skylines and portraits by the high school students. She had left Gretchen here with the kindly art teacher yesterday when she left for Louisville. And she knew where to find what she was looking for.

There were several lumps of sculpture clay in the drawer beneath a row of half-completed statues, some identifiable — an elephant, shoe — most not. She cut off a piece about the size of a piece of fudge, had to cut it because the clay was cold and hard. She put the piece of clay in the pocket of her Walmart jeans and was back in Gretchen's room before the child woke up.

She waited most of the morning, until Gretchen was playing with her friends. Then she came back to her dorm room, closed the door behind her and took the piece of clay out of her pocket. It was not as hard as it had been, warmed by the heat of her body while it was in her pocket. Still, it took several minutes of just working it in her hands to make it really malleable. Then she pinched off a small portion of the clay — it was blue, baby-boy blue — and rolled it around on the palm of her hand until it was round. She sat down on the edge of the bed, reached under her shirt with her right hand and felt the lump in her breast. She held the ball of clay in her left hand. The ball of clay was much, much bigger. So she pinched off a piece of it and rolled the remainder back into a ball again. It took half an hour before she was satisfied that she had made the ball of clay the same size and shape as the lump in her breast.

She would get a box for it, to keep the ball of clay in. A ring box maybe. And she could take it out of the box and check it anytime she wanted.

No more guessing. She could use the blue ball of clay as a measurement. No more needless terror, certain that overnight the lump had doubled in size. If the lump in her breast grew ... now she would *know*.

Chapter Thirty-Four

THE LONE MEAL of the day didn't make it to the rank-and-file prisoners until almost two o'clock in the afternoon, and by that time the natives were way more than restless. No telling how many men had been injured or killed in the violence. Spade was in charge of the A team, Bobby the B and Sandman the team in Cellblock C.

Sandman had wanted to know why Spade didn't just poison the guards, too.

"'Cause we poison them, they seize up and die in the guard control suite, how we gonna get inside? They got to let us in. And they got to be alive and well to do that. And we can't blame them for poisoning the food if they eat it and die, too."

Spade's plan required that the guards sealed in the control center unlock the doors at the ends of each tier so Spade and his crew could pass down the aisle in front of the cells handing out sandwiches.

"We made enough so you can each have four," he said, knowing as he said it that the men would eat only two and use the others as currency later. He started, of course, with

249

the gang leaders on that tier. Their "rank" afforded them special privileges — a little like being the first to board the airplane if you had enough frequent-flyer miles. It was a little thing, but even something like being served first mattered in here.

Starting on the first tier, Spade jibed as best he could with men who weren't in the best possible moods.

Soon as he walked in, they wanted to know what was going on in the outside world and outside in the rest of the prison. Those with jukes in their cells were no more informed than anybody else. The administration had cut the satellite feed to the sets before nightfall on Astral Day. No need to upset the inmates with bad news they didn't need to hear.

"Them aliens landed yet?"

"What they look like, anybody seen?"

"We still got government? We gonna blow 'em out of the sky?"

"Ain't no guards, why won't they just let us out? They gonna just walk off and leave us here to die?"

Spade responded to that, kept his voice low so only the cons could hear him.

"You ain't gonna be left here to die. Ain't none of you gonna be left in cages to starve. You got my word on that. Ain't gonna happen. I will *personally* see to it that it don't."

Carlos Hernández, leader of the Mexican Mafia who had a private cell in the middle of the row facing the guard console, grabbed Spade's wrist when he handed the sandwiches through the bars, and pulled him close.

"You get us out of here. You find a way. You hear me? Gotta be a way without no guards. You do that, and you gonna be my right-hand man. You understand what I'm saying to you?"

"I hear you. I'm already on it."

"You my man!" Carlos said, talking with his mouth full as he devoured the sandwiches.

Spade also made a big deal out of the fact that the guards were so antsy they had put extra guards in the kitchen. Trustee crews normally prepared the food, but every time they turned around they was tripping over a guard. Only a third of the guards had even shown up this morning and he didn't have no idea why they had put so much heat in that one place, for the life of him he couldn't figure it out.

Spade's crews brought the food up in the elevators and coordinated their efforts, so every tier got served at once. After they'd distributed sandwiches, they rolled in the carts with the vat of poisoned chili and bowls.

"Gillespie made gallons of this shit. I ain't tasted it yet so I can't guarantee it don't taste like cow piss. But you can have as many bowls as you want, long as it lasts."

Bobby rolled the cart down the aisle so he could serve the first bowl, of course, to Carlos Hernandez.

While he was handing out chili, Spade held up a paper sack to show the guards in the control room.

"These got double meat and double cheese," he said. "Gillespie said he thought you like provolone so he put that on one."

Frank Herndon nodded, punched the button that opened the door from the common area into the control room, and Spade walked right in.

He could see that Bobby was trying to take his time handing out bowls, so he wouldn't kill half the men in the cell block, but the con two cells down yelled at him, banging his cup on the bars, demanding that he hurry up.

So he obliged him. Ladled out a big bowl and handed it to him. The two men in the cells he'd skipped began to complain. So … hey, you want chili, I got chili.

As soon as Spade entered the room, his back to the cellblock, the smile dropped off his face.

"You seen the pictures, the ones from the Hubble Telescope? Them motherfuckers is ... you seen 'em?"

Herndon said he'd seen it before he left for work that morning. Charlie Rogers had not.

"What they look like?"

Herndon described them, while Spade glanced casually over his shoulder, watching the chili distribution.

"I ask you something?"

"What?"

"What the fuck are you doing here?"

"Ain't got nowhere else to go," Herndon said. "I got home Astral Day, Martha Jean was gone, took the kids to her sister's in Portland. Well, she was going that way. I don't know if she made it. I talked to her once from the road and the traffic was stalled dead on the freeway. After that, I couldn't get another call through."

"Truth?" Rogers asked.

Spade nodded.

"I came in today because ... I'm gonna give it another day, one more day, but if we don't get more guards showing for work tomorrow — and I don't think that's gonna happen — I'm ... we're gonna open the place up and let you guys out."

Spade was genuinely surprised.

"We talked about it, Harold Adams, Randy Barker, Stanley Johnkowski and me. It's not right, you guys locked up in here, no way to keep feeding you."

"Let *most of you* out. Not everybody, not the wack jobs."

"Shit, the world may be about to end. You guys got a right to—"

Then Carlos Hernández started to scream.

Spade could see Carlos on the floor of his cell, clawing

at his throat. The guard on that tier — there were supposed to be three but he was the only one who'd shown up — raced to his cell and motioned for the guards sealed in the console room to open Hernandez's cell door.

The guard knelt on the floor beside the writhing man but had no idea how to help him. He spoke into the microphone on his shoulder, seeking guidance from the senior guards. But before any guidance could be forthcoming, before anything could be done, in fact, a con two cells away began to cry out, doubled over in pain. His cellmate yelled.

"He's puking blood! Damn … there's blood coming out his eyes! Somebody do something."

Another con dropped on the tier above and two more on the third tier and another on the fourth.

As soon as Herndon and Rogers were both distracted, Spade leapt into action. He hammered a fist the size of a canned ham into the side of Herndon's face, grabbed Rogers's hair and slammed his head into the console. They were both incapacitated in seconds. The original plan had been to dump them into the common area. But Spade changed the original plan. He punched the button that opened the door out into the hallway and shoved the men out, then closed it.

They'd planned to be decent to the cons. That had earned them their lives. He told an only half-conscious Herndon he had exactly one minute to get out of the unit before he locked it down.

"Drag him out of here or you're both dead," he snarled. He didn't have to say it twice.

Then he hit the emergency red button that locked down all the end doors on every tier of cells in the whole block. A blaring alarm sounded, with alternate red and white lights flashing. Now, it would require a key from the administration building to open every locked door in the cell block.

Then Spade rushed out to the center of the common area and climbed up on a table.

"No more chili," he yelled to the three men on his crew who had been ladling it out. "Stop, now! Something's wrong with—"

He stopped in mid-sentence and did a pretty good imitation of shock and recognition.

Looking at the guards patrolling the four tiers, he screamed.

"You motherfuckers! You poisoned the chili. The guards are trying to kill us all."

A match on gasoline, the whole cell block went up in a full-bore riot. The cons were yelling and cursing, throwing things out of their cells at the guards, a roar of anger and fear that Spade could imagine was being replicated in Cell Blocks B and C if Bobby and Sandman had managed to get control of the guard consoles. That was the iffy part. But they were good men.

Then Spade fell on the lone guard walking the open area in front of the bottom row cells and beat him to death with his bare hands — a performance played out before a standing-room audience of caged inmates in the tiers above. The cellblocks were an unrestrained riot for hours, as those who'd consumed the poisoned chili got sick, convulsed, puked and shit blood, bled out their noses, eyes and ears and then died.

When Spade thought it was time for him to start exerting authority, he walked out into the center of the common area and climbed up on a table and yelled for attention.

Took a while for the men to quiet enough to listen.

"You got the control booth, why the fuck don't you

open the cells," a guy on the third tier called out.

"He can't, moron, didn't you hear the alarm?" another con called back.

Gratefully, as soon as men started getting sick wasn't nobody watching what was going on in the guard console, didn't see that it was Spade and not the guards who had hit the red button. The cons knew that as soon as the emergency system was engaged, the automatic controls shut down and the doors between different portions of the prison would only open with keys.

"I jammed the A Block entry door with my shoe," he said, lifting his socked foot for demonstration, "so I'd have both hands free to carry the food trays. Good thing I did, 'cause I got a way out, but the rest of you is stuck in here 'til I can get the keys. And I am gonna get the keys. In the meantime, I'll see to it you get fed."

"Just get our asses out of here!"

"Count on it."

Fifty-one convicts had died, some instantly, some after a couple of hours, all of them painful, ghastly deaths. Half a dozen convicts were still sick and wouldn't likely make it through the night. The other cons had remained locked in their cells, unable to do anything but watch the men die. The doors at the end of each cell unit had locked down tight, sealing the guards in on the catwalk in front of the cells.

They wasn't likely to spend a particularly comfortable night, given that the cons thought they'd tried to poison them and they had watched Spade beat O'Hara to death. As soon as those cell doors opened … whenever that was, the guards would be at the mercy of whatever cons had survived the poisoning. It wouldn't be pretty.

So far, so good. The first part of Spade's plan had gone off without a hitch.

Chapter Thirty-Five

SAWYER HAD HELD it together right well, had deposited a totally spent Ellie Hampton at Zion Academy, amid a torrent of praise and pledges of eternal gratitude. He'd talked her off a ledge on the way back to McClintock County, driving down winding roads through empty countryside, the twin swords of headlights slashing through the black silk of the darkness. It looked like the world had been abandoned by everybody but the three people in that cruiser.

He'd listened to her story. It wasn't rational, was totally garbled with the time sequences all messed up. She couldn't have gotten where she was when he found her if she'd only walked ten minutes. She had walked at least half an hour, probably a lot longer than that. But she'd squashed that time into a little space, had likely been a zombie, just wandering, so she'd contracted that period of time to fit neatly into her understanding of what had happened to her. And she had elongated the time she spent in the dumpster and then the trash can. In her mind forever after, she would believe she had spent almost the whole night, seven or eight hours there, a lifetime, where every moment was the longest moment of her life until the next, which was the longest then.

In her worldview forever after, she would believe that she had battled dozens of rats, fending them off, smashing and killing them with a pipe, defending her life against an attacking army. And there had been rats alright, he'd seen several as big as cats. But she had called him at nine o'clock and he'd found her before midnight. That was a horrifyingly long time to spend in a dumpster and a garbage can, hiding from murderous rioters. But it hadn't been all night.

She'd finally asked him what he thought would happen when the aliens landed.

"I don't think any farther ahead than the next crisis and there will be plenty more of them before the guano finally connects with the air conditioning."

"The world's going to fall apart, isn't it? Society, I mean. Civilization. It can't stand up under something like this."

"I suspect so. Most of it, maybe. In places. But there will be islands of sanity, too. I intend to keep my little corner of the world safe as long as I can."

"The cities are burning. People in the crowd were saying that Paris was in flames and that in London there had been explosions everywhere, gasoline tankers or something."

"Well, you know how it is, you can't believe everything somebody tells you in a riot."

That'd gotten a small smile.

"I suppose, all things considered, that Gretchen and I are better off here than where we'd have gone if a certain butt-in-ski sheriff hadn't chased off my helicopter. Everybody's leaving the cities, looking for somewhere they can feel safe."

He had deposited her at the academy and left a reluctant Noah with her. The boy wanted to come with him and he couldn't blame him for wanting to be with his father. But he really did believe the boy was better off there than anywhere else he could think of.

"I'll keep an eye on him," Ellie promised, "spend time with him so he won't feel … abandoned."

Sawyer appreciated that maybe as much as she appreciated him plucking her out of a garbage can.

He had dropped the two of them off, pulled out of the long drive and made it all the way off the property before he had to pull over and throw up. He heaved and heaved until he was panting, his eyes watering, his head on his hands on the steering wheel.

He had killed two men.

Killed them. No, they weren't the first men he'd ever killed. He'd been a Marine in Afghanistan. And though Ellie and the boy didn't know it, his knees had been so weak when he came out of the Bed Bath & Beyond, he might very well have folded up on the sidewalk.

He had *shot* a man. Watched the blood spurt out and never even saw his face. And he had beaten another man to death. No, worse, he had beaten him and then left him there to die.

That thought made his stomach heave again and he quickly closed the car door to keep the smell of his own vomit from filling the car, which still smelled more than a little rank from where Ellie had sat when she was slathered in trash-can goo.

He had killed two men!

Yup. He had. And it wouldn't likely be the last ones he'd have to kill before … well, before the world righted itself. And he had no faith at all that it ever would.

Chapter Thirty-Six

PACO HAD FINALLY MANAGED to drift off to sleep, curled up next to the wall in the visitor's cubicle on the end. There wasn't enough space for him to stretch out, had to remain curled in something like a fetal position, but he liked the walls on three sides of him. There was some small degree of comfort in that.

He'd staked out that piece of turf for himself earlier in the day after the cons who came with food noticed Enrique dead on the floor. They'd dragged his body away without comment, didn't ask what'd happened to him.

The juke controls were not in the room and whoever had turned it on had left it on. As the alien reports played and replayed and replayed, the boys had been beaten down by the sheer enormity of it. Knowing an invading army of aliens would be here in four days to kick ass and take names, was humbling, made even the toughest of them — even Tiburón, Paco suspected — feel small, helpless and insignificant. The room had gradually quieted, each boy retreating into himself, to wherever he went when he was forced to face harsh reality, without benefit of support, bravado or drugs. It was an uncomfortable place for most of them, a spot they had managed to avoid most of their lives. But there was no avoiding it here, now, and the solemn looks on their faces as the hours of news presentations began to sink in slowly morphed into dread that quickly dissolved into naked fear.

Then they'd sought their own spaces, their own corners, to deal with their fear or to keep the others from seeing it. Paco was self-aware and astute enough to figure out that the other boys were no less terrified of their situation than he was, they were just managing to hide it. He was hiding his, too, and he thought he was probably doing a lot better job of it than some of the others. He'd had lots of practice.

He was lying on his side, his head resting on his arm bent at the elbow, when Jamal suddenly let out a whoop.

"Holy fuck!"

The wall clock said it was 3:30 a.m. The announcer on the juke screen was standing outside in the daylight so it must be a broadcast from some other country. He was reporting that Earth's bigger telescopes could now make out details of the approaching armada.

Then the image through the Hubble Telescope was shown on the screen and Paco couldn't breathe. The shot was of a perfectly round craft, no flying *saucer*, a row of them, identical. They were the silver marbles from Paco's dreams.

Ever since Astral Day, he had resolutely refused to make a connection between his dreams and the alien invasion, but there was no denying it now. He'd been dreaming for a month about silver marbles, *these silver marbles.*

And about monsters.

He scrambled desperately, struggling not to make the mental leap, but there was no leap. Just the next logical step. If the silver marbles in his dreams were the alien spacecrafts, *then the monsters in his dreams were what was inside them.*

Those silver marbles were filled with white giants with glowing blue eyes. And bug-like horrors with mouths full of razor teeth.

The psychic blow knocked the breath out of him as surely as Enrique's fist to his belly. Never in all his not-quite-sixteen years had Paco been so stunned. And confused. What did it *mean*? Why had he been dreaming about the invasion, and the invaders, before they arrived? How could that be?

The juke showed the front row of ships, but the rows behind were blocked from view by the front row. What had looked smooth and featureless from a distance was revealed to be anything but smooth. Grooves and indentions, holes of different shapes, like seeing a pretty girl from a distance and close up she had bad acne. The image was mesmerizing and terrifying. The boys gawked at it, unable to look away.

"The guy said them marbles, they're like the size of a small town," Rob/Bob said. "And he said the fleet might have lots of other kinds of ships, different shapes and sizes. These might not be the biggest of them. They might even be the smallest."

Randal suddenly leapt to his feet and raced for the bathroom and the other boys could hear him in there vomiting noisily. Paco turned to go back to his sleeping quarters and saw Tiburón. Their eyes locked. Fear as real as a gust of wind passed between them. There was some small comfort in knowing somebody else felt the same way you did. That's what friends did, and he'd only ever had one friend, Vincent Singleton. Singleton and Sálazar. S & S. The spider and the snake.

They'd spent a single, glorious summer together in the mountains of West Virginia. Then they'd gotten drunk one night, Vincent had wanted to ride around and around in a laundromat dryer ... and the awful thing happened.

At eight o'clock on the night after Halloween four years ago, Paco had *rescued* his friend. And Vincent had given him a parting gift.

He pulled the baggy orange uniform shirt away from his body and looked down at his chest, at the tattoo of a skull with a spider crawling out one eye socket and a snake out the other. A tattoo that was merely connecting-lines, fill-in color. The picture was formed by scars.

Somebody had turned out the overheads so the only light in the room was the dancing light of the juke screen reflected off the boys' faces and the shiny tile floor. The faces the light revealed were not doing a good job at all of hiding their fear.

Paco sat back down on the floor on his piece of turf. Curling into something like a fetal position, he scooted back against the wall in the booth and tried not to hear the announcer's voice describing the alien armada — silver marbles filled with monsters — that would reach Earth in just three days.

Chapter Thirty-Seven

ANCIL WICKLIFFE HADN'T BEEN sober in three days. No, two days. No, it was three. He'd gotten drunk the night they spotted them white spots in the sky and hadn't been completely sober since. Oh, he'd shown up at work the next morning after, his eyes bloodshot and probably the smell of booze on his breath. But the boss didn't say nothing, didn't notice, spent most of the day in his office trying to make calls, then he took the keys to all the new vehicles with him, picked every one of them up off the board one at a time, a whole handful home with him. Guess he figured somebody'd break in and steal them, seeing's how most of the sheriff's department and half the cops on the city police force hadn't shown up for work.

Actually, come to think of it, he had gone into work the day after that. Staggered in to work. The boss wasn't even there but the assistant manager gave him the boot, the seeya-wouldn't-wanna-beya, and he had staggered back out the door he'd come in.

It was a good thing old Ancil lived close to Hanky's

Tavern. If he hadn't, he'd surely have hit something on his way there.

The usual crowd was mostly there. Mostly.

Owen Alexander had taken his family and fled north. Nobody knew where.

Billy Rodriguez had left for a day and then came back, said he'd gone into Mexico to get his mama and brothers and sisters. Said the border patrol wasn't even manning the crossing.

Ancil stepped unsteadily up to the bar and ordered a beer.

The bartender-owner didn't look so good himself. Charlie Daniels certainly didn't look like a famous country western singer now.

"It's warm," he said. "Best I can do. Sorry."

Ancil didn't know what it was that would have made the beer warm. The electricity was still on because there was lights on. But he didn't ask. He didn't care. He'd been drinking warm beer for three days.

"You look like death on a cracker, Charlie," he said, tipping the top of his bottle in salute and downing most of it in one swallow.

"Been here, had to be. Stealing liquor. Everybody wants liquor, thinking how maybe it's gonna be in short supply pretty soon."

That was the first time it had occurred to Ancil that maybe he wouldn't be able to get drunk and stay drunk as he had been. Certainly couldn't if there wasn't no beer to drink. He'd have to go to the store to load up on a couple of cases. But some part of his mind registered that when he'd passed the grocery store yesterday or the day before, it'd looked like there'd been a war in the parking lot. Maybe there wasn't no beer left.

"You wanna see 'em?" Charlie suddenly asked.

"See what?" Ancil replied.

"Them spaceships. You wanna see what they look like?"

"I got a Astral app same's everybody else. I done seen everything I need to see."

"I ain't talking about seeing them little fly specks on your phone. I'm talking about seeing them, really seeing them through a telescope."

"You can't see them through a telescope."

"Oh, yes you can! I done been up on the roof once tonight, soon's it got dark. You can see 'em alright."

"You got a telescope on the roof?"

"It belongs to my boy." His face clouded. His boy was going to college somewhere up east, Boston maybe, no, somewhere in Connecticut. Charlie'd talked to him on Astral Day — it still rankled, made him slightly nauseous to say the word, the pet name the media'd given the day the whole world and everything in it fell apart. The boy said he had to get out, wanted to come home. But it was a long way from Boston to New Mexico. Then Charlie'd tried to get in touch with him, musta called a thousand times, but he hadn't got no answer. He put a good face on it, though, would tell anybody who'd ask — and nobody would because they already knew the answer — that his boy was "on the way home." Would be here any day now. Would surely make it before the aliens did.

Ancil wondered if Charlie really believed that or was just saying it to convince himself. Them cities up east, the news showed them with riots and burning. They wasn't no place to be, but them jammed highways made it clear if you's there, you's gonna stay there.

"Your boy had a telescope?"

"Yeah, got it for him when he was in high school. He liked to go up on the roof and look at the stars, said it was clear here and when he'd tried at Columbia" — that's right, that's where he was — "the air was so polluted, or there was too much light, I forget, but anyway he couldn't see hardly nothing at all."

"You saying you seen 'em with your own eyes."

"Come on up and I'll show you."

He turned to Pete Harrington, the other bartender, who looked like he'd slept just fine thank you very much, but then the booze and the bar weren't his to take care of. And he didn't look fine, actually. He looked like he was high as a weather balloon on something and it wasn't booze.

"We're going up to have a look-see. Watch the bar for me."

The juiced-up kid nodded his head, up and down, more times than he needed to. Yeah, he was high on something.

When Charlie headed through the back of the bar, past the bathrooms to the stairs that led up onto the roof, he was leading a parade of people. Ancil, Billy Rodriguez, Hank Abercrombie and a couple of fellas Ancil didn't know.

The night was clear and too damned warm for May. Charlie went to the telescope that was set up on top of the metal air conditioning unit, so it could be angled up and you didn't have to lean over to put your eye on the eye piece. He looked through it, adjusted something with a nob and then stepped back.

"You try it, Ancil."

Ancil went to the telescope and put his eye to the eye piece. He saw nothing. He might be too drunk to be doing this, he allowed that he might be, but he squinted, tried to focus, settle his eyes.

There they were.

They wasn't little fly specks on a juke screen here. They were … they were …

Perfectly round, looked like silver marbles. Flying in neat rows, formations. Hard to tell how many.

As if he'd read Ancil's mind, Billy said, "Somebody at one of them big telescopes had got a clear enough image to count them. They's two hundred."

The thought hit home, landed like a dead weight in the pit of Ancil's stomach.

"Two hundred?"

"Yeah, two hundred."

"You say it like that's good."

"It is good. They could have been two thousand of them or ten thousand. Just two hundred. If you's the captain of one of them ships and there was only 199 others, wouldn't you put them over major cities? New York. Hong Kong. London and the like. I wouldn't think you could spare one of them for a little hole in the world like Roswell. All of us in fly-over country, we're better off here than them people in the cities."

Then he thought about what he was saying, with Charlie's boy being in the city and all, and he coughed and shut his mouth.

Ancil couldn't take his eyes off the little silver marbles. They were real — *real*. It was happening. Not that he or anybody else had ever doubted it was true. But seeing really was believing and he was a believer now.

But he didn't agree with Billy. He knew for lead pipe certain there'd be one of those ships had their name on it. "Roswell or Bust" painted on the side of the little ball. One of them ships was coming here, drawn here by that little Indian squaw.

"She's bringing 'em here," he said under his breath, still staring at the balls in the sky.

"Come on, Ancil, let somebody else look," said Hank Abercrombie. But Ancil didn't move.

"One of them ships is gonna come right here, one of them balls is gonna be hanging right over Roswell. You'll see. The Indian squaw will bring them here and then we'll all be out of luck."

Ancil felt the growing hatred of the little girl multiply by ten as he saw what she'd summoned, the destruction she was bringing down around their heads.

"I need a drink," he said, and staggered back, bumped into Charlie, who cursed.

"You gonna fool around 'til you knock somebody off the roof."

Ancil pushed past him for the stairs. He'd started off in search of a beer. But the images the telescope had put in his head made him dizzy. Then sick. He barely made it to the bathroom inside. And as soon as he stopped heaving, he stood up unsteadily and started running. Stagger running, out the door and down the street. Not going anywhere but away. No destination. Not going *to* but going *from*. But there was nowhere to go, no place to hide.

Them little marbles was gonna be here in two days. And that little Indian slut whore was gonna park one on main street in downtown Roswell. Just see if she don't.

Day Five

Day Five

Chapter Thirty-Eight

Zion Academy had a security system second to none.

Dr. Weiss was out at first light, walking the perimeter of the property studying how it functioned.

Because the academy served the offspring of some of the richest, most powerful people in the world, no expense had been spared on keeping them safe, using state-of-the-art equipment made to look like the native flora of the Kentucky mountains. No one but a professional in the field could have spotted the locations of the hidden cameras and sensors.

There was, after all, no reason to turn this idyllic old monastery into a fortress. The parents had, after all, sent their children here to live in one of the most beautiful settings on the planet. And it was, after all, so secluded that its very obscurity would be its best defense. Reasonable assumptions during reasonable times. These were not reasonable times.

The security system was all about identifying a threat before it had a chance to become a threat. The first of the heat sensors and movement sensors in the woods surrounding the grounds and farmland were located more than half a mile out from the actual property line, connected to a huge security console that pinpointed the whereabouts and movements of anything larger than a raccoon 360 degrees around the facility. The Acme Securities Systems, Inc. technician who installed the system had bragged that you could spot an intruder in time to knit him a sweater before he got to the front door.

The security console was monitored twenty-four/seven by security guards — *not* the old-man-in-a-bank variety who couldn't have held off a knitting-needle attack by the Little Sisters of the Poor. These were trained professionals. Dr. Weiss sometimes wondered if they were side-jobbing as a Navy SEAL team.

There were four of them, none local. Two didn't show up for work the morning after Astral Day. One bailed the next day. The most reliable of the quartet had promised to hang in there, but Dr. Weiss hadn't seen him since he left after his shift night before last. He understood. Their first responsibilities were to protect their own families, get them to safety, wherever the illusive "safety" was.

A brilliant scientist, David Weiss was, by nature, a sequential thinker: Do this and that happens. Reliably reproduce "this" and you can reasonably expect to consistently deliver "that." Though he had never thought of himself as a strategist, strategy was at its core sequential thinking, the orderly assembly of cause-and-effect reactions.

As the warm morning sun kissed the dew off the grass in the meadows where the dairy and beef cattle grazed, Dr. Weiss was assembling in his mind a catalogue of the academy's resources so he could then figure out how to allocate them to his best advantage. What have you got and where should you use it?

Well, he had firearms. Lots of them. Something of an arsenal, in fact. Zion Academy was located in an environment where the average man on the street probably owned a couple of rifles and a handgun or two, and Dr. Weiss believed it was part of the well-rounded nature of the education he wanted to provide at the academy that the students adapt to their surroundings. He had hired a registered firearms instructor for the first two years he was headmaster and he went to every class, watched and listened, intent on teaching the class himself one day.

The weapons were stored in the armory, and back when life had been normal, you could hear the sound of gunfire resounding against the old walls of the monastery every day. The professor had been pleasantly surprised at what good shots some of the students had become. Though all were excellent marksmen, a couple might well have qualified as snipers … if what they were sniping at were squirrels and rabbits. Therein lay the crux of his defense issues. He had an arsenal, but he had only children to fire the weapons.

As Dr. Weiss walked back to the barn, he saw Brother Thaddeus approaching, the oddest of the odd ducks at Gethsemane Monastery. The monk looked much like the stereotypical mad scientist. His eyes were a bit bugged, granting him a perpetual wild, just a half-bubble-away-from-chaos look. His eyebrows were two wooly worms parked in the handicapped spaces above his eyes and his hair stuck out in a finger-in-a-light-socket fringe around his head.

He was carrying his gas mask so today must be a slaughter day.

"Good morning, Brother Thaddeus," Dr. Weiss said.

"Yes, just so. Good morning to you, too, Dr. Weiss. Beautiful morning, indeed, beautiful. Yes."

Dr. Weiss indicated the gas mask.

"And you're on your way to—"

"Deliver death, doom and destruction. Yes. Harm without pain. No crying for the little ones. Just sleep."

"Well, then, I won't keep you."

"Indeed. Yes. Good morning."

Then the monk stopped.

"Did you know there are aliens out there in the sky?" he said. "Really are, yes."

"I did know that."

"Hmmm," the monk said, "just so," and he continued on his way.

Dr. Weiss watched him as he hurried up the path, clearly preparing to kill lambs. Lambs were slaughtered every spring, culled out of the herd of sheep, taken to the slaughterhouse and butchered.

Dr. Weiss had not tried to protect the academy students from that harsh reality. They ate lamb. They couldn't reasonably be expected to believe it had grown on trees. But he had never allowed them anywhere near the slaughterhouse during that season because the poor little creatures made such pitiful noises as they died, cried out like babies.

At least they had until Brother Thaddeus announced his determination to find a "kinder, gentler way." A week later, the monk had produced huge canisters of Nitronox X gas, the non-pharmaceutical, industrial grade of Nitronox III and Nitronox IV, the two most common forms of human anesthesia. Dr. Weiss had never asked, certain he was better off *not* knowing how the monk had managed to get his hands on the deadly gas, which surely was a strictly regulated substance. A few whiffs would drop a grown man in his tracks. It didn't take much more than that to anesthetize a whole herd of lambs.

Now, the spring slaughter was accomplished in silence. Brother Thaddeus gathered the lambs into a stall in the barn, donned his bug-eyed gas mask, pulled out his big red canisters of Nitronox X and put the little creatures to sleep before he killed them. Given a larger dose of Nitronox X, the lambs would merely have stopped breathing, but the monk used as little as possible to prevent the possibility of chemical residue in the slaughtered meat.

After his tour of the facility, Dr. Weiss went back to his office and before breakfast, he had come up with a defense strategy.

It was simple.

As he saw it, the first part of a good defense was to contain the threat to a limited area. The property owned by Gethsemane Monastery was enormous and for the most part unfenced — a farm with barns, equipment buildings, sheds, a mill, a hydroponics plant and acres of crop fields, vineyards, orchards and pastureland. About a hundred Jesuit monks lived in the abbey, a cluster of ancient buildings nestled in the trees between the walled monastery and the Twin Forks River. An order committed to education, the Jesuits had ceded the old monastery buildings to Zion Academy almost twenty years ago, and Dr. Weiss had converted the facility into a world famous school for deaf students who'd been granted hearing by the Weiss implant.

The academy, which consisted of dormitories, the classroom/administration building, gymnasium, cafeteria, storage buildings and the armory, occupied the historic Gethsemane Monastery buildings within the old monastery walls, tall rock structures three feet thick and eight feet tall. So sturdy even after four hundred years, they could probably withstand a tank attack. Of course, it would be a simple thing to climb over them, even though the security specialists had taken great pains to remove all trees near the walls and certainly to cut back any branches that might stretch out over them. The encircling wall met beneath an entrance archway where two huge metal gates swung inward. The gates were works of art, more for decoration than security, and would probably rip off their hinges under a heavy vehicle assault, or intruders could merely break the latch that fastened them shut.

As it stood, neither the wall nor the gates were much of a deterrent to attack. He had to fix that.

After the children filed past his office on their way to breakfast, he placed a call to Brother Sebastian, the abbot. Though external communication was spotty, almost nonexistent most of the time, their internal communication system and all things electric remained functional, courtesy of solar-powered generators. When the sun stopped shining … well, then they'd have bigger fish to fry than no blow dryers in the girls' dorm.

Brother Sebastian listened to Dr. Weiss's plan, then dispatched several monks to help him implement it. One of them went into town to Timmons Hardware Store. Stubby Timmons had kept the place open, though he had long since sold out of anything anybody wanted these days. Not a generator remained. But he had not sold out of Gloppy, since nobody was much interested in re-grouting or re-tiling their bathrooms in the days counting down to an alien invasion of the planet. The monk brought back two big drums of the adhesive. More sticky than its predecessor Superglue, it would bond anything to anything. *Permanently.* Stick any two objects together with Gloppy and the only way to separate them was with an ax.

After breakfast, he took five high school boys out to the three-bay garage and placed a tarp on the concrete floor, while another crew of boys went to the kitchen to gather up glassware — bowls, plates, glasses, anything glass. He placed the glassware on the tarp, covered it with another tarp, outfitted the boys in rubber boots, gloves and goggles and then handed the mystified lads sledgehammers.

"Break the glass," he said. "Do be careful that none of the pieces fly out from under the tarp."

Before lunchtime, Dr. Weiss had an assembly line going, collecting baskets of glassware to bring to the garage where one group of students shattered it while another gathered the broken pieces in baskets. The monks were already up on ladders spaced at intervals along the rock wall spreading Gloppy along the top and arranging the pieces of broken glass the students carted out to them.

By noon, the perimeter fence was topped with razor-sharp broken glass all the way around. Anyone determined to break into the facility would have to cross it, or come in through the front gate. Dr. Weiss could successfully contain the threat to that limited area.

The entrance road under the Zion Academy archway through the front gates lead directly into the quad, where it became the original flagstone path, circling around the statue of Brother Malachi, the monastery founder, and a fountain in the middle.

The dormitories were on both sides of the U-shaped central building, boys on the left, girls on the right with a gymnasium beyond the girls' wing and the library on the end beyond the boys'. The middle of the U featured a portico that opened onto the administrative offices in the front of the first floor, the kitchen and cafeteria behind them, classrooms on the second and third floors with Dr. Weiss's lab and Dumbo occupying the whole top floor.

He'd place a bus crossways in front of the gate — no real deterrent, just for annoyance factor. Anybody with a crow bar and a hack saw would make short work of the lock securing the gate latch and once inside the fence at the front gate, it was a straight shot to the buildings and no way to deter an approach that he could figure. But if he could bottleneck an attack there, focus it on the front of the building, he had an arsenal of weapons to use on any invading intruder.

Right. An arsenal. And nobody to shoot them except children. Sure, they all were good marksmen, some were crack shots. But they were kids. He couldn't expect a ten-year-old to shoot somebody!

He was stuck on that point until after lunch. The only solution that came to mind was not born of scientific acumen but of David Weiss's childhood as a card shark. He often thought he'd been born in the wrong century, had missed his calling as a riverboat gambler. When he was a boy, he routinely cleaned out whole buses full of tourists lured into a simple card game with the cute little Jewish boy in a yarmulke. And like every good poker player, he had learned early and well the power of a well-conceived bluff.

Dr. Weiss spent the next couple of hours setting soft drink cans, small vases, pottery, crystal wine glasses, the pieces from the gigantic chess set, and balls of every size — footballs, tennis balls, soccer balls and golf balls all around the quadrangle, almost like he was hiding Easter eggs. Except he wasn't hiding them. He was putting them out in plain sight.

Chapter Thirty-Nine

SPADE HAD SLEPT the dreamless sleep of the just, or maybe just of the successful. He stopped to drop off food for his boys, his special prizes, before heading to the barracks, watched the news and saw the satellite and Hubble Telescope pictures of the armada scheduled to pull into Station Earth tomorrow.

And he really didn't give a fuck. Spade didn't think the world was going to end, but he would be content if that was the way it had to be. He wasn't a man to look backward with regret and he looked forward to a bright future when the little green dudes showed up and mostly left the stupid humans to take care of their own affairs.

That's how he thought it would go down.

Just after dawn, he met Joe Morrison to give him a key that didn't exist except on the keychains of the captains of the guard and the warden, the key to the warehouse full of supplies on the back of the property. Spade had long ago made copies of all the keys that mattered in the prison. He could let himself into and out of just about anywhere — except places automatically locked down by guards operating console units. It had taken him the better part of three years, sending molds of the original keys out with the various truckers who came to the warehouse to deliver supplies and paying dearly for the keys they brought back.

Morrison was his go-to guard, the only one who actually worked for Spade, not the other way around, the man Spade had made rich with the proceeds of contraband sales over the years. Morrison had been quicker on the uptake than some others and had figured out all his paper money wouldn't buy jack now, that what really mattered was sitting on shelves and pallets in that warehouse. He just needed the key to get to it, and Spade needed Morrison to set the auto-lock timers in the prison that he couldn't get to. And so they'd made a trade.

"You got a truck?" Spade asked as he handed over the key.

"Hell yeah. Me and the wife and kids got a cabin up in the Sierras and we're heading out with the U-Haul soon as we get it loaded tomorrow."

"You cutting it kinda close, ain't you?"

"Had to act like a good little soldier today. Only ten or eleven staff besides me even showed up for work. Hell, the warden hasn't been here since Astral Day. They say he has a boat, and he's sailed somewhere … who knows. The plan of the guards who are left, if they got a plan, is to lock the place down from the outside — put all those doors on automatic so you're gonna have to break them down."

"They just gonna walk off and leave a thousand men locked in cages to die."

"Yeah, that's about it."

"You set all them timers like I said?"

"You know damned good and well I did, Spade. You wouldn't be here if you didn't."

True. Spade could get into the console and knew that

at least the internal timers had been set. He'd needed Morrison to set the others.

"Everything is on twenty-four-hour release with the timers ticking. All the auto locks, at least inside the buildings, will unlock at the same time tomorrow morning. That'll get you out into the yard. The rest is up to you."

"We'll work it out."

"After you took over the cell blocks yesterday, that was all they needed to know to 'clear their consciences" about walking out and leaving you locked up. You proved you could figure out a way to escape, some of you anyway. Come tomorrow morning, won't be no guards standing in your way. Won't be a living soul on this property except you cons."

"That's how we like it — the place all to ourselves."

"Good luck to you," Morrison said, reached out and shook his hand, firm, genuine.

"Good luck to you, too, Joe."

When the man turned around, Spade buried a shiv up to the hilt in his back.

Wasn't that he couldn't spare a couple of truckloads of supplies out of that warehouse to pay Morrison for setting the timers. It was just that if Morrison started loading up stuff tomorrow, might be somebody'd see him, figure out they'd ought to get themselves a truck and do the same thing. Right now, folks wasn't thinking about that building sitting quiet at the back of the prison. Spade had to keep it that way until he had the manpower to protect it.

So it was done. All the prisoners would be freed within the prison walls tomorrow by automatic unlocks. Of course, Spade had the keys that he could have used to free everybody yesterday after he killed off the gang leaders. But the cons didn't know that. And he wanted to engage in some more … team-building experiences … with them before they were freed. Wanted them to go hungry another day and then get what little food they got ... eating out of his hand. By the time they were outside in the yard tomorrow, he'd be the undisputed leader of his little kingdom.

Particularly, after he showed them the prizes he'd saved for them, the boys he'd kept here all this time so he could hand them off here and there to do a little extra persuading. Shame about Enrique, the gay one. He was a good-looking boy and would have pleasured somebody right well if the big boy Tiburón hadn't killed him.

There was still Paco, of course. Just as good-looking. But he was Spade's private property.

ANCIL WICKLIFFE HAD AWAKENED from his drunken spree the night before he gradually, painfully, surfaced like a body drowned last summer that'd worked free of the debris on the bottom of the lake that snagged it, and made its slow, ghastly ascent into the sunshine. To float there. Stinking.

Ancil lay beside his bed. Not in it, beside it. Like either he had passed out before he got there, or ...

And then he smelled it. Yeah, he'd rolled off the bed because he'd puked on it and had had the drunken good judgement to roll off the mattress rather than roll in the filth.

It didn't matter. Nothing in life mattered anymore now that the little silver balls was bearing down on the planet carrying little green aliens just like the ones that come last time, only nobody believed they'd come. But there was those that seen alright, maybe even some who had themselves a sit-down-how-ya-doin' talk with the little greenies, and might be one of them was Clyde Baker's daddy.

Clyde told folks he got them "alien rocks," the ones his Indian whore used to tell fortunes, out in the desert, that his daddy had seen the ship's crash landing and after the Army scooped it up and hauled it away to Area 51, his daddy had gone out to where it'd crashed and found all the sand had been turned to glass by something so hot it melted everything around it.

Clyde had the rocks to prove it and though nobody had believed him then, Ancil believed him now. He was lead pipe certain old man Baker'd seen that ship crash. And he'd bet his left nut the old man did a sight more'n pick up the rocks after the ship left. He'd bet the old guy had made hisself some little green friends while he was at it, maybe told 'em to come on back and see him sometime and they'd took him up on his invitation.

Ancil had spent the better part of the day nursing the mother of all hangovers, easing shut the gigantic crack in his forehead with a slow ooze of booze, down easy, a little beer, and Maker's Mark and Coke, and by the middle of the afternoon he was feeling as good as he could rightly expect to feel. Better'n he had when he woke up but not near as good as he would right before he passed out tonight. The brain was a blackboard and booze was an eraser.

He sat now on the back porch of the nothing rental house on the outskirts of Roswell. It was getting worse every day he lived in it, drinking, breakin' things and crashing his fist through the walls when the hurtin' got so bad his vision went red and he had to release the fury or else it'd blow off the top of his head. Moving was pointless. You took yourself with you wherever you went. Any place was as good as any other.

He took another big swig of beer, looked up into the sky darkening toward night and felt a hatred pure and bright, focused as a laser beam from a sniper's rifle. For them ships, them silver marbles screaming across the universe, and for the slut whore who'd called them here.

And some part of him was deciding even then that he wasn't gonna let the sun set on another day with her breathing the same air in the world as him. That part of his mind required a certain level of alcohol saturation before it would start spewing out poison into his reason, blackening his sight to everything but a foul purpose. But he would reach that level of drunkenness, oh my yes, he surely would for a fact.

Tonight.

Tomorrow.

Soon. Before them ships came and wiped out the world. Before her green buddies had a chance to swoop down and spirit her off, Ancil Wickliffe was going to END Falling Star Yellowhorse.

He would strangle the life out of that squaw slow, squeeze her neck tighter and tighter until her whole face popped and brains spewed out like pus from a boil.

Chapter Forty

DR. WEISS WAS PACING. He didn't realize he was doing it until he banged his shin painfully on the sticking-out rocker bar on the rocking chair. When had he started pacing? He had no idea. He could have been doing it for the past ten minutes or for the past hour. Time was squirrelly when you didn't sleep. He hadn't slept since … the night before Astral Day, maybe. He didn't know, couldn't remember.

The better question was *why* was he pacing? And he knew the answer to that, oh my, yes, he knew. He was pacing because he couldn't sit still. Simple as that.

He actually hadn't spent that long looking through the telescope on the top of the boys' dormitory. He had looked, seen and then come back down into his office.

But he didn't sit down behind his desk. He seemed to remember that he meant to sit down behind his desk, intended to sit down behind his desk. But he had started walking instead. From the fireplace, past the window to the bookshelves. Turn. From the bookshelves past the window to the fireplace, turn.

Back and forth.

Back and forth.

In truth, he couldn't actually see where he was going. Not really. Because everything was behind the overlaid image he had seen through the telescope. The little silver balls.

Oh, dear Jehovah, Elohim, it was true. Seeing was believing after all and Dr. David Weiss had seen. He had gone down to the river and bathed in the Jordan and his eyes had been opened and he had seen. Hallelujah.

He barked out a laugh that sounded so much like hysteria he put his hand over his mouth to stifle any other such strange outburst.

And kept walking.

From the fireplace past the window to the bookshelf. Turn.

They really were out there. Of course, he had never doubted it. Never really believed it was some kind of hoax. Some monumental practical joke perpetrated on the whole planet by … well, by somebody. But he hadn't believed that. He had believed the scientists who said the little white dots on the Astral app were spaceships, not meteors. They're flying in formation, they said. Meteors didn't fly in formation. They're slowing down, they said. Meteors didn't slow down. They're on a landing pattern. Meteors didn't …

He'd believed.

But now. *Now.*

Oh, dear Elohay Kedem — God of the Beginning — they really were coming.

The little silver marbles streaking across the universe would be here *tomorrow.*

To do what?

What else? He didn't believe they had come all this way to pat the world on the back and tell them: "Well done on your civilization!" A civilization that produced Attila the Hun. Stalin. Hitler. Pol Pot.

And a civilization in which a little desert tribe …

How odd
for God
to choose
the Jews.

He burped out another little not-laugh.

But God had. And from the moment he had, all the rest of the world was trying to destroy them. The Hittites and the Amorites. The Babylonians and the Egyptians. All trying to wipe them out.

And the Romans. But the Jews had beaten them at Masada. They'd won at Masada.

They'd watched the Romans building that ramp.

Coming up the ramp.

Coming across the universe.

To kill, to ravage, to enslave. Just like the Romans.

Coming.

But the Jews had won! The Jews had saved their own, decided their own fate. They had died at their own hands rather than live enslaved by monsters.

He remembered reading once that when the Romans transported their slaves, they didn't put a rope around their necks to walk in single file. They put hooks through their cheeks. A hook through your cheek that tied you to the next guy in front of you. If he tripped and fell, well, you both lost your faces.

To enslave. To murder. To kill.

There was no other reason.

The aliens would come and they would treat the whole of humanity as humanity had been treating the Jews for thousands of years. They would enslave. They would be the masters and mankind would be the servants. For all eternity.

But the Jews had won. At Masada, they had won.

From the bookshelves past the window to the fireplace. Turn.

He pictured the mountain stronghold overlooking the Dead Sea. An engineering marvel, created by Herod the Great. It had its own water supply that came from up in the mountains, through ducts that could not be sealed or polluted. It had land enough to grow crops. It had roman baths.

Just like Earth. Everything in abundance. Trees and water and sunshine and flowers. Everything a civilization needed to grow and prosper.

To be happy. To raise their children.

Now the masters were coming to take it all away.

He suddenly thought of the forms of the monsters in the ships. He had inadvertently been thinking of them almost cartoonish, little green men with bald heads and cute eyes and hands with too many fingers.

Now he saw them for what they were. They were *Romans.* They were *Nazis.*

There was a knock at his door, but before he had chance to answer Lucy Pruitt burst in. She looked at him funny and he didn't know why.

Had he done something strange? Again. He looked down at himself, unable to see what—

He was wearing his coat wrong side out. Why on earth was he wearing his coat wrong side out? Did he turn it wrong side out to wear it that way? Or had he simply taken it off and it had come off wrong side out and then he didn't notice and put it back on that way?

Which had he done?

Why had he done either?

He grabbed hold of his mind that kept skittering away from him like a water spider. He tried to grab it, to pin it down, to make it obey, and it just skittered away.

He needed to think, but the thoughts wouldn't be still long enough.

He realized he had said nothing to Lucy. She had come into the room and been so stopped by his appearance that … It was his jacket, that was what she was staring at, wasn't it?

No, she wasn't looking at his jacket. No, his jacket was fine. She was looking at … his fly was unzipped. He looked down, horrified. It was unzipped. And the front of his pants were wet.

That wasn't his fault! He was an old man. Old men had prostate problems. It wasn't that they wet themselves. It was that when they urinated, they thought they were finished. Shook it off — three shakes, any more than that and you're playing with yourself, that's what the other boys in Hebrew school said. But when old men put their junk back in their pants, they weren't finished after all. This little squirt of pee was still in there waiting to leak out as soon as you put your business away.

But he'd been taking the medicine the doctor had prescribed and …

No, actually, he hadn't been taking the medicine. He'd run out, and the pharmacist had hit the road on Astral Day. He couldn't get more medicine, so he was destined to spend the rest of his life with the front of his pants wet and smelling like piss. He reached down hurriedly and zipped up his pants, then babbled something …

"Oh, I am sorry. Spilled … spilled my coffee in my lap, don't you see."

Lucy didn't believe that any more than he did. But it

did release her from her slack-jawed stare so that she recalled the reason she had burst into his office.

"Sir, the surveillance cameras. They picked up … There are little spots on them, on the heat sensors. People. There are people in the woods beyond the cornfield. They're coming this way."

Chapter Forty-One

Oscar Higgins was pissed!

The motherfuckers had put broken glass on the top of the wall. A wall around a *church*, for God's sake!

He had a nasty cut on his forearm and Harold Windom had sliced open the palm of his hand, couldn't even hold a gun. They'd had to stop and bandage both of them, tore pieces off a t-shirt and made pressure bandages to stop the bleeding. Oscar knew about pressure bandages, he was a volunteer EMT with the McClintock County Rescue squad and he'd had to take training.

He knew he was gonna have to get stitches in that arm and right now it hurt like a flaming whore.

He'd make them pay for that.

Oscar had not considered even the possibility that he or any of his men might be injured on this raid. How could they? There were going after a school full of deaf children, run by a doddering old Jew. This was way on the far side of dangerous.

But the broken glass!

He had intended to take the place by surprise, planned

to sneak through the woods under cover of dark, climb over the wall in the back and approach the building from the rear. He understood tactics. He'd been in ROTC in high school, didn't go into the military because of his sinuses. They were always stopped up, stayed so swollen they'd made twin lumps on his forehead. The lumps were noticeable on a face as thin and sharp as his, like a hatchet blade, with a rounded chin that looked like the knob on the end of a femur. His features were all the more severe because they were punctuated by a hawk nose and lips so thin they were only visible when his mouth was open. Or when he smiled. And Oscar Higgins never smiled.

He didn't know a whole lot about the layout of the building. He had never been in it personally, but his sister had worked in the cafeteria for a while and she said there was a service entrance in the back and a loading dock where they took food supplies off the big trucks that hauled them in. He didn't have a big truck waiting to haul them back out again, though, but he did have a dozen smaller ones, pickup trucks. This haul would set them up with supplies for months.

And the guns. One thing his sister remembered was the guns. She said them deaf dummies had target practice all the time, and there was a room, she called it an armory, where they kept the firearms. Once he laid hands on those, he would be set.

He'd be the chief. That wasn't a good word, but he hadn't yet come up with a better one. Maybe just boss. Whatever you called it, Oscar Higgins intended to set himself up as the king of the hill of McClintock County. He'd seen the opportunity on Day One.

Them green bug-eyes on their way here probably didn't know what they was getting theirselves into. The military'd likely blow them out of the sky with nukes or something. But he really suspected they might be here for a while, like maybe they'd brought an army and they'd land somewhere and spew them out and the army'd have to fight them off, hand to hand.

He could think of any number of ways it would go down, but all of them contained the element of societal breakdown. Yes sir, society was gonna fall apart while the army fought off little green men, and even if the army lost, and the little green men won and took over, they'd never be able to get him and his men out of these mountains! They could hold up here for *years*, fight off whatever the little bug-eyes threw at them. At least they could if they had sufficient supplies and firearms.

And Zion Academy was a great start, the first step in setting up his empire. He had other targets, too, of course. There was the Sisters of Ophelia Motherhouse in Ridgehurst. They would likely have stores of supplies. But the biggest target was one he couldn't go after until he got the firearms. Once he could arm a hundred men — shoot, maybe two hundred men — he planned to march on the distillery, take it over. There might be some resistance there, but he would come with enough firepower to knock out whatever they threw at him.

And once he controlled the liquor, well, he would control everything.

But first things first. Get the goods and the guns here and take the next steps when he was ready.

He remembered what Rommel had said, or Patton or Eisenhower, or somebody. *No plan survives the first contact with the enemy.* After that, you had to improvise. He was down with that. He'd just have to march right in the front gate. Wouldn't be no hard thing to break the lock on the thing, if it had a lock. Once they had it open, he'd radio Simpson and they'd show up with the trucks to haul the goods away.

The motherfuckers musta put glass on top of the wall because they was expecting trouble, figured to stop folks from breaking in. Well, it'd take a sight more than a cut on his arm to stop Oscar Higgins. He might just find that old Jew and smash his face in. Maybe cut him a little, let him see how it felt. He winced as his arm howled with pain as he and the others hurried around the perimeter of the rock fence to the front gate. Yep, it was locked. Big deal. They weren't idiots. They'd come prepared.

"Buster, cut that off."

Buster had brought bolt cutters, but it was Oscar who'd thought to do that. He was in charge and it was his job to figger things like that out.

"What we gonna do about the bus?" Harold asked.

There was a bus parked crossways in front of the gate to block the road.

"We'll move it. What do you think we'll do with it? Mike, break out the window of that thing and get inside."

It didn't take but a couple of minutes before Mike was inside, put the bus in neutral, and six of the other men rolled it out of the way. With the road clear, Oscar motioned for his men to follow him up the road to the front of the building.

It was dark, and that was odd. If it weren't for the faint glow of some exit signs he'd think the electricity had gone off. He hoped not. He'd had the foresight to bring flashlights, and his men turned them on now to light their way. But he didn't want to have to find and load up the supplies by the light from a flashlight.

He made a hand motion and half his men cut off at the circle, one group moving along the circle from the left, his group from the right. The statue of whoever it was was white stone and it shone a little in the moonlight. They were about even with the statue when suddenly the lights came on. Blinding lights.

"What the fuck!"

Their eyes had adjusted to the darkness and the lights were so bright they blinded them. He squinted up into the lights. They had *spotlights*.

"That's far enough, gentlemen. Turn around now and march right back out the way you came in."

He couldn't see who was talking, but he was sure it was the Jew bastard. He was somewhere inside.

"Fuck that!"

"Fire," cried the voice.

A lone gunshot rang out and a soft drink can three feet from Oscar's left boot clanged and danced away.

"Leave now," the voice commanded.

"Oscar …?" The voice sounded frightened. That was Buster, ready to put his tail between his legs and run. Well, Oscar wasn't going anywhere. First order of business was to take out whoever'd fired that shot. He lifted his rifle, aiming at the windows, growling at the Jew bastard he couldn't see.

"You son of a—"

"Fire!"

Suddenly, gunfire rang out everywhere and he could see rifles sticking out all the windows. Bullets were pinging all around him, but he remained unharmed.

What the fuck was going on?

Chapter Forty-Two

DR. WEISS LOOKED at the shapes on the screens on the security console and felt the same revulsion he had felt for the shapes he could see on the telescope on the roof an hour before. An hour. No, no, no, much longer than that. Hours and hours.

He glanced at the clock on the wall above the console. It had been about fifteen minutes.

Couldn't have been only fifteen minutes. He had spent hours pacing in his office, he knew he had.

From the fireplace past the window to the bookcase. Turn.

The clock was wrong, that's all.

He realized he was staring at the spots and thinking about pacing in his office. About peeing in his pants. About his coat. He looked down. His coat was on right side out now. Had he changed it? Or had it been on right side out all along, and what Lucy had noticed was—

"Dr. Weiss."

The words penetrated. Became one of the water spiders of his thoughts but he grabbed the little sucker, grabbed hold of it and held on and even though it was wiggling to get free … the *thought* … the thought wiggling. He forced his mind to hold it, to hold on. And the rest of his mind seemed to right itself then, the thoughts to freeze where they were, instead of skittering around. He had the sense that he could go to any one of them now, pick it up and he could think it. He could think any thought.

"Dr. Weiss …"

He was doing it again. Thinking but not thinking.

Get a grip.

"When did you … how long since you first saw these?" he asked Lucy and Jocelyn Conner, who'd been waiting for them in the security screening room. And he sounded rational enough. Sounding rational helped him feel rational.

"A few minutes, sir," Jocelyn said. Then the two women looked at each other and spoke at the same time. One said three minutes, one said five.

Not long, though.

He studied the spots. The console was an amazing thing. It could show views of every angle from every camera and heat sensor in the woods and on the grounds. More than a hundred of them, from every angle.

Because it was dark, the shapes appeared in different hues. On the heat sensors, they appeared as fuzzy red dots, kind of outlined in orange. Like they were on fire. On the motion sensors, they appeared as blinking pings on a radar screen. On the infra-red cameras, they were a shade of turquoise. But all the shapes were moving, as coordinated as a Russian dance group. The red ones and the blinking ones and the turquoise ones, doing a coordinated dance, coming through the woods. Coming for them.

Just like the Romans.

The Nazis.

His mind settled like a hovercraft settles after it has crossed the water riding on cushions of air. When the air blowers turn off, the craft settles gently into the water. His mind settled like that.

These were Nazis. They had come for them. And his grandfather had beat the motherfuckers.

Oh, my goodness! He *never* said words like that. But he hadn't said it. He had just thought it. Mustn't let a nasty thing like that slip out of his mind into the world.

His grandfather had been a freedom fighter. He had faced down the firepower of the Nazis, and told them, "Fuck you!"

Words like that were … exhilarating. Empowering.

His grandfather had attacked them with what he had, not as powerful as their weapons, but he and the others had a weapon the Germans didn't. They'd had *courage* and they drove the monsters back with the power of their courage.

Moses Weiss had done that. He was the grandson of Moses Weiss and he would be no less courageous.

"So what do you think?" he said. And now he not only sounded rational, he felt rational. Thoughts lined up as neat and orderly as little West Point cadets. "How long do we have?"

The women looked at each other again. Jocelyn had spent a good amount of time in the surveillance room; she had a crush one of the security guards and had come up with every possible excuse to be near him. A young woman who had been pretty seventy-five pounds ago, Jocelyn was testimony to the "disappearing features" phenomenon — added weight stole features, so over time an overweight person came to look like every other overweight person. So sad. So — his mind snapped back into place. The almost-a-Navy-SEAL security guard had been a showoff, had wanted to impress Jocelyn, was constantly waxing eloquent about the capabilities and the functioning of the surveillance systems. Jocelyn knew how they operated better than anybody still on the premises.

"I'd say twenty minutes. Maybe half an hour."

She even sounded like the not-a-Navy-SEAL. Or maybe that was his imagination. Yes, he was imagining that part.

"It depends on how they approach after they reach the potato field," Jocelyn said. "If they come straight in, they will make the back of the wall in twenty minutes. If they go around the field on the dirt road, it'll take them another ten minutes or so.

"And they won't be expecting the glass on the top of the wall," he said.

She brightened. "No, they won't. That will slow them down considerably if any of them tries to climb and—"

He cut her off. No time for this. "So at maximum, we have thirty minutes to get ready for them."

She looked confused. "The sheriff can certainly get here inside half an hour," she said.

"We don't need the sheriff. We can take care of our own."

Again, the look. If Jocelyn looked at Lucy like that again, he would smack her.

"Sound the fire alarm!" he said.

The fire alarm in a place filled with deaf children consisted of several different elements. Harsh strobe lights flashed in the hallways and inside the dorm rooms. There were small air jets, too, mounted above all the doors. When the alarm sounded, hot air issued through the jets with enough velocity to scatter papers on desks. The hot air smelled like ammonia. It was just an added scent, but was as noxious and eye-watering as the real thing. There was a piercing siren, too, at a decibel level that would cause vibration in even the profoundly deaf.

You had lots of fire drills when you were responsible for 120 children who couldn't hear. The kids had been well trained; they'd go immediately to the cafeteria. The cafeteria was right next to the armory.

Dr. Weiss found himself running, his tie flapping over his shoulder, down the hallway that was filling with confused frightened children ... and they were talking to each other. They could hear! Oh dear God, thank you, the internet was functioning right now and they could hear. Well, all of them but one. Noah Matheson couldn't hear. Dr. Weiss would sign what he had to say as well as speak it. For Noah.

Inside five minutes the whole school, every man, woman and child stood before him in the cafeteria.

"Our security system has indicated that there are armed men coming through the woods, headed our way."

The cry that went up from the frightened children had to be quelled quickly and harshly.

"Hush!" he said. "This is the world we live in now. Adjust and survive. Or perish!"

There was silence.

"They are coming to steal our supplies, our food and water stores. And they will ... they will do whatever they choose to all of us ... *unless we fight back.*"

He paused, then continued resolutely, "And we *will* fight back."

"I want all of you to file in an orderly fashion into the armory. Get a weapon and come right back out here. We don't have much time."

Shocked into silent obedience, the crowd was soon standing in front of him again.

"You all know how to shoot. You are excellent

marksmen some of you. Hank. Reginald. Paul and Benjamin and Daniel.

"Are you saying we're going to ... shoot somebody?" one of the children asked.

"Don't be ridiculous, I don't mean anything of the sort." The room relaxed a bit. "I would never ask you children to do a thing like that. You know that. I know that." He paused. "But the men coming through the woods ... they *don't* know that. We are going to *bluff*. I have it all set up."

The children and a sprinkling of adults just looked at him, stupefied.

"Go back to your rooms. If you're on the side of the building facing the woods, go across the hall into the room there. Open the windows, but don't put your guns out until my signal."

They stared at him.

"The quadrangle is dark. When I flip on the lights. I want you to lift your weapons and stick them out the windows. But don't show yourselves. Don't let the people below see you. Can you do that?"

A room full of heads bobbed as one.

Then he explained to them what to do when they got his signal, repeated himself until he was sure every child understood.

"Now go."

They went.

"Paul, Hank, Reggie, Benjamin, Daniel — come with me." Then he selected certain house parents, Lucy, Jocelyn, and, of course, Ellie Hampton. "I'll tell you my plan as we walk."

Chapter Forty-Three

WHEN THE BIG black guard named Spade brought two cronies to the waiting room where Paco and the other boys had lived for the past five days, there wasn't a one of them believed anything good was about to happen.

But shit, after five days, it felt good just to get out of that one room, where the juke droned on and on about the invasion and they'd been forced to watch and listen twenty-four/seven since the day after Astral Day.

"We going for a little stroll, boys," Spade said.

This time, nobody questioned him. They were sufficiently cowed, no showoffs among them anymore. The boys might still have hoped to be "rescued" by a van, come to take them back to the juvie jail, but that hope had died when they found out the administration and the guards were no longer running Radcliffe Correctional Facility. The cons were. And the cons answered to nobody.

The boys were guided again through a labyrinth of hallways and corridors, past guard posts now unmanned and empty guard consoles. Spade had keys he used and the doors closed and locked automatically behind him when he used the key on the next door.

When Spade used his shoulder to shove open a final door that had been prevented from opening by a shoe, the stench on the other side was overwhelming and the boys cried out in horror.

"Mother fuck!"

"Shit, what is *that*?"

It smelled like the room in front of them was filled with dead animals. Jamal started involuntarily gagging. Spade stood looking at them, a smile on his broad face.

"This ain't as bad as it gets, boys." His eyes were deep pools of foul water with the shiny fins of piranha at the bottom. "Your worst nightmare ain't even close."

Then he shoved the boys ahead of him through the open back door of a guard console and out the other side, through an open door into a common area with tables, chairs and benches. The stench was so thick and noxious the air looked green.

As soon as the cons saw Spade they began to holler at him, demanding to know when they'd be free, cursing him for not getting them out sooner, screaming obscenities and threats.

"You boys can have what's left of that," he told Paco and the others, indicating a garbage bag on one of the tables in the common area. When nobody approached it, he stepped to it, lifted it up and dumped out the contents. Half sandwiches, pieces of bread, meat, cheese, obviously the leftovers of what must have been what the cons had just been fed.

The boys had no stomach for food. Not with that smell. It was the stench of blood and shit, vomit and … something else more foul. Death and putrefaction.

On the floor in the cell across from the guard console,

the only cell that was open, was a bloated body lying in a puddle of nastiness. Obviously the man had shit his pants. Bloody diarrhea had stained his prison orange uniform and run out both pant legs onto his feet. There was blood and vomit on his chest, and his face was contorted, such a look of horror and pain Paco instantly looked away.

He glanced up into the four tiers of cells where he could see caged men at the bars of their cells, and there were other bodies lying there, men who obviously had met similar fates. What had all those men died of? And nobody had even moved the bodies, just left them lying there.

The body of a guard, his face caved in, lay on the side of the common area. Three other guards, one each on the second, third and fourth tiers were still alive. One was seated on the catwalk as far as it was possible to get from the cells. The second was leaned against the locked door at the end. The guard on the highest tier stood looking over the railing at them.

Paco shuddered. His grandmother and whoever it was who had designed the Scared Straight program had been horribly right. He and other boys had no idea the level of horror that resided behind prison bars. They'd glamorized it, told themselves they were tough, they could take it, they weren't scared. They weren't boys, they were *men*.

They were boys now, though, as scared as they had every right to be. Everything in the world had turned to shit and they were up to their necks in it and nowhere near shore. In here was blood, filth and death. And out there … well, out there, the aliens would land on Earth tomorrow.

"Listen up," Spade cried, and the cons slowly stopped their yelling and the cat calls they'd been making at the boys. "Progress report. You gonna be outta here first thing in the morning." The cheer was deafening, though there was muttering, too.

"What's taking so damned long?"

"You out walking around, doing as you please and we locked in here."

"All the timed auto locks will expire tomorrow morning," Spade explained. "And when they do, I can get out of here into the admin building. We'll fight our way to the guard captains' offices and get the keys to unlock these doors, one at a time."

"Shit, that'll take hours!"

Others yelled but Spade quieted them.

"Maybe not. It *might* be that once the auto locks expire, I can engage the controls in the console and unlock the whole cellblock. I don't think so, but maybe. Either way, keys or console, I'm getting all of you out tomorrow."

Another cheer arose, with a little less dissension than the first.

"Now remember, that just gets you out *into* the prison. Not out *of* the prison. They got it locked down outside twenty ways from Sunday and if these were normal circumstances they'd have state police and county mounties spaced three feet apart all the way around the outside walls."

He paused.

"But it ain't normal. You ask me, ain't gonna be a cop anywhere near here come tomorrow morning."

Then the cons wanted to know about the aliens and Spade spent half an hour answering their questions. Much of what he said was wrong. The ships were round, not flat and saucer-shaped like Spade said. Las Vegas had burned, much of New York was on fire, along with half a dozen other cities, but Spade told the cons every major city in the country was burning to the ground. Paco and the other boys were veritable experts on what was happening and what was about to happen. But none of them interrupted or corrected Spade.

"My guess is — since them alien motherfuckers is gonna land tomorrow, there ain't gonna be a mother's son in the admin building, manning the guard towers or anywhere else on the grounds. I'm betting they'll all be long gone. Their last shot was setting the maximum time on the lock timers. But them timers will expire tomorrow. In the morning, we'll be out into the yard — food in the kitchen — and we can figure out a way then to get the gates open."

There was a murmur of assent.

"So what's the fresh meat doing here?"

Spade smiled and gestured toward the boys.

"If I could get them cells open, I'd let you have at these pieces of ass, auction off the little fuckers."

Caucus laughter rumbled.

"But you can't get at them until tomorrow."

Spade grabbed his own crotch and squeezed, groaning. "Me and the other boys in the barracks'll break 'em in for you."

Laughter, applause and more catcalls.

"But I kept these boys here all week 'cause I knew how horny you'd be, in serious need of some entertainment when you finally get out of these cages."

He turned to Paco and the others.

"After I finish with 'em tonight, I'm going to turn 'em loose in the yard. They'll be out there all by their lone-somes when the auto locks go off tomorrow morning."

He smiled wickedly. "And you can do with them what-ever the fuck you want!"

Chapter Forty-Four

STAR JERKED AWAKE, sat bolt upright in the bed, so suddenly Pumpkin started and whimpered, almost got dumped onto the floor.

The Astrals.

She had not dreamed. She had not awakened from some horrible nightmare about white giants with the blue eyes, and the monsters with needle teeth. They weren't chasing her. They weren't there at all. She didn't see the skull with the spider crawling out one eye socket and the snake out the other. She saw none of it. She just saw the boy. The boy with hair so blond it was almost white. He was looking at her, concerned, talking to her but she couldn't hear what he was saying. She could hear his voice, but it seemed so very far away, she would know that voice anywhere, but she couldn't make out the words. It had been that way in her dreams for years. She would hear the boy, but like he was in another room with the door closed, she couldn't hear what he was saying.

She hadn't dreamed anything horrible.

So why was she so scared? And she was scared. More scared than she had ever been in her life. There was a sense of foreboding hanging over her like a cloud, a thick sickening blanket of terror, the certainty that something terrible was going to happen, something unthinkably terrible was about to happen. And she wouldn't be able to stop it.

She saw no vision. But she knew. She knew this was going to be the worst day of her life.

And maybe the last day.

"Star, sugar. You doing alright, hon?"

Aunt Mary Ellen had walked past in the hallway and seen her sitting up in bed, the covers clutched in her hands, balled into fists, pulled tight around her neck.

"Sure."

"No, you ain't, but none of the rest of us is, neither."

Aunt Mary Ellen had gotten quieter and quieter as the week wore on. The waiting, the wondering, she had not spoken about it, not once. She kept the juke off when it was working at all, which wasn't often. She didn't want the little ones to see what was happening. At least Star had assumed that was why. But it occurred to her now, hearing the fear in Aunt Mary Ellen's voice that maybe she had kept the juke turned off because she didn't want to frighten herself.

Star reached down and pulled Pumpkin up into her arms and he dutifully slathered her face with wet doggie kisses. Pumpkin didn't seem right either. He felt tense in her arms, apprehensive, and he kept sniffing the air, searching for …

Sometimes Pumpkin knew things before the people did. He sensed the bad coming.

Star heard the juke in the living room and after she

dressed she went in to sit down. Apparently, Aunt Mary Ellen had decided either it wouldn't do any good to protect the little ones from the news or she had finally decided to face it herself.

The ships were visible even with small, cheap telescopes, and every store everywhere in the country had sold out of telescopes. Images from the bigger telescopes now showed details of the armada that was "decelerating" for its Earth landing.

Different announcers, different places. The same story. Chaos.

Louisville, Kentucky was burning. Louisville!

In New Orleans, rioting gangs had looted the French Quarter, dragging shop owners out of their stores and beating them with their fists and clubs.

"Turn it off," Uncle Clyde said.

The sound went dead.

There was no sound in the living room either.

"Come on, Star," he said. "We got animals to feed."

Uncle Clyde never fed the animals. It was Star's and the littles', sometimes hired hands' and occasionally Aunt Mary Ellen's, but it had never been his job. He got up and went to the door anyway and she obediently got up and followed him. He had to help her down off the makeshift porch to the ground.

Aunt Mary Ellen followed them to the door but didn't come out onto the porch. She just announced from the doorway.

"I'm gonna go see Ruth."

Ruth was her sister. She lived on the other side of Roswell in a little house on a few acres, raised cattle and those black sheep. That's where they got the lambs for the petting zoo.

As far as Star knew, Aunt Mary Ellen hadn't even talked to Ruth in years. They'd had a falling out over, of all things, the recipe for bean dip, their mother's recipe. They had dug in their heels and refused to speak. Christmas came. Thanksgiving. Easter. The rest of the family thought that at one or another of the holidays one or the other of them would thaw out and make amends. They never did.

It took an alien invasion to get the sisters back together.

"She called this morning, said she and Harvey are going to that cabin they got in the mountains."

She paused for just a beat.

"And I'm going with 'em. I'm taking the littles with me."

She said nothing else, waiting, Star supposed for Uncle Clyde to say something. Finally, he did.

"Me and Star got work to do."

Then he turned and walked away and Star heard the announcers' voices again. Aunt Mary Ellen had turned the juke back on.

Star walked with Uncle Clyde back to the petting zoo. It was located between the miniature golf course and the amusement park.

"If Aunt Mary Ellen goes to the mountains ... how will you two ...? You can't call. How will you ... find each other again?"

"Likely won't. I think maybe that's why she's going."

He said nothing else, just kept walking with Star beside him.

"What did they look like?" Star asked. "The ships they could see with the big telescopes."

"Little silver marbles."

"Shiny."

"Yeah, kinda. But they wasn't smooth like they looked

when they was farther away. They had ridges and stuff, gouges."

"That's what I saw."

"In your dreams?"

"Uh huh."

They walked along in silence.

"So that means the rest of what I saw is real, too. It's accurate."

He didn't say anything for a moment.

"Yeah, I guess it probably does."

"White giants. Their eyes were bright blue. Not like that was the color of their eyes, but like a blue light, like it was shining out holes in their heads. They were not so much scary-looking. Just big and, you know, lumbered when they moved, kind of like an elephant."

She didn't say anything else. She suddenly felt a tightness in her chest. Uncle Clyde waited. He knew there was more. Finally, he asked, "And the others?"

"They were monsters. They looked like bugs."

"Bugs, like stink bugs?"

"No, longer, shaped like grasshoppers kind of. And their eyes were blue, too. And they made this sound, like … like a cat purring. And they had teeth, sharp teeth like needles and …"

She lost her breath and couldn't keep talking.

He didn't ask her to finish, just reached over and took her hand, the way he did when he led her somewhere when she didn't have Pumpkin to guide her. But the dog was right there on the end of his leash, the special halter. He wouldn't let Star run into anything.

Uncle Clyde's big hand felt warm and soft.

They got to the gate of the petting zoo and he opened it; when they went inside it seemed too quiet.

"I don't hear—"

"The sheep are gone."

"Gone?"

"Yeah, I turned them out last night."

"But why?"

"I don't know if we'll be able to get food for them. They're sheep. They'll be fine, wandering around. There's grass out there."

"And the others."

"The chickens stay. I want fried chicken, aliens or no aliens."

He led Star over to the bench and sat down with her.

"I'm scared." Her voice sounded very small.

"I'm scared, too."

"What's going to happen?"

"I don't got no idea."

"It's going to be bad, though. I know it."

"Because of what you seen when you was reading them palms, telling them ladies' fortunes?"

The image of Darlene Littlewood looking down at bloody rags on her feet in the snow blew through her mind.

"No, something else."

"What else?"

"I don't know. The boy, he came to warn me about something."

As soon as she said the words she realized that it was what he had come to do. He had come to warn her about something.

"What?"

"I don't know. I couldn't hear him. But there's something bad … out there."

He put his big beefy arm around her.

"I can't promise there ain't gonna be nothing bad happen. I ain't got no say about it. But we'll get through it together, you and me. I'll …" His voice got thick, sounded strangled and she realized that he was holding back a sob. "I'll protect you long as I can, sweetie pie."

Star had never loved anybody as much as she loved Uncle Clyde at that moment. She leaned into his hug and shivered.

Chapter Forty-Five

DR. WEISS WATCHED the intruders at the gate through night vision field glasses from the window of his fourth-floor office, saw them cut the lock and push the bus aside. Then he hurried downstairs and was waiting for them at the front door. Literally. He had opened it, then stepped back into the shadows where he couldn't be seen when the quad lights turned on.

The men approached down the main road, then split into two groups to approach the front door from both sides of the circle.

What for? It wasn't like they were hiding behind anything. They were carrying flashlights, for crying out loud, surely they didn't believe nobody'd notice a dozen men creeping up a darkened driveway carrying flashlights.

It was like they were playing GI Joe's Action Attack game.

It seemed to take a very long time for the men to walk from the gate to the circle of the quadrangle. Dr. Weiss didn't know if it really had taken a long time or if it had just seemed like a long time to him.

But his mind was stable, his thinking sharp. No thoughts flitting around, too wiggly to think. His mind was calm, his thinking ordered. His resolve firm.

He was the grandson of Moses Weiss. His back was straight. His shoulders squared. He would fight to the death to keep the children safe. If he had to, if the situation warranted it, he would gladly lay down his life to protect them.

And leave them alone, at the mercy of the monsters?

"Who said that?"

No one answered. The voice was not one he recognized.

You cannot let the monsters take them, the voice said and he looked around frantically, scanning the vestibule. But no one was there.

Fight bravely, David, the voice said, *but don't give your life needlessly. You are the only thing standing between the precious ones and slavery, murder and death. You can't let the monsters have them.*

Dr. Weiss' heart had begun to hammer in his chest as frantic as a caged bird. His temples pulsed, his vision blurred.

Who had spoken to him?

Then the two groups drew about even with the statue, and his mind focused there. Dr. Weiss gave the signal and the lights were suddenly shining so bright it looked like daylight in the quad. He took one step farther back into the shadow of the open front door, and called out in a firm voice — it didn't tremble or shake. His words rang out with righteous authority.

"That's far enough, gentlemen. Turn around now and march right back out the way you came in."

"Fuck that!" cried a man, tall and skinny, leading the group on the right.

"Fire!" Dr. Weiss cried.

A shot rang out and the soft drink Dr. Weiss had set carefully beside the statue exploded with a direct hit and spewed out foam as it skittered away to the left.

Reginald Hawthorne had done it, had hit the can dead center. It wouldn't have mattered if he'd missed, not really. The point was the gunfire, the show of force, but the can demonstrated it wasn't random. Reggie was the best shot of all the kids, sixteen years old, could hit a sparrow on a tree limb fifty yards away.

"Leave now," Dr. Weiss said.

The men stood rooted to the spot, had not even raised their own weapons, didn't dive for cover. Clearly, this was not a well-trained adversary.

"Oscar …?" one of them called out plaintively.

The skinny man lifted his rifle then, aiming it at the windows where the rifle shot had originated. But the lights were in his eyes, and Dr. Weiss had instructed the children, above all else, to stay out of sight.

"You son of a—"

"Fire!"

A deafening volley of shots rang out. Bullets hammered the quadrangle from more than a hundred guns, all firing at once. Cans, balloons, tennis balls, chess pieces, vases, and golf balls danced or exploded like fireworks in the glare of the bright security lights. The ceramic angel he had set on the statue, the coffee mugs he had laid in a line by the sidewalk. They all went flying, exploding in every direction.

He had told the children to take careful aim at one of the targets he'd left and to fire on his command, and he had carefully explained the firing squad rule.

"Only one of the rifles in a firing squad is actually loaded with a live round," he'd said. "The others are firing blanks, so no one ever knows for certain whose bullet has fired the fatal round."

He said that some of the rifles they would be firing had live rounds, some didn't. So if one of them missed their intended target and actually struck one of the men standing there ... well, no one would ever know whose bullet that was.

They were to fire only one shot, so the volley was loud, ferocious, but brief. It was followed by stunned silence.

"It ain't nothing but a bunch of kids," the skinny man yelled, but his voice sounded a bit tremulous. He turned toward the men behind him. "They are just a bunch of snot-nosed kids, shooting at cans. They ain't gonna hurt nobody."

"The children fired warning shots," Dr. Weiss told him, his voice calm and firm. "The adults will shoot you where you stand if you do not do as you were instructed. Leave. Now."

The man spit in the dirt.

"You want me to leave, Jewboy — make me."

He stood defiant. Dr. Weiss said nothing else. But time at that moment elongated, everything that happened after that stretched out like a rubber band. Longer and longer. Tighter and tighter.

The man took a step toward him, lifting the barrel of the weapon that had been pointed absently at the ground.

You have to shoot him, David, said the voice.

Dr. Weiss looked over and saw who had spoken this time. It was a man dressed in ragged clothes, his face dirty, holding a bottle in his hand with a rag sticking out the top of it.

Kill him.

The man whose name might have been Oscar took one more step forward and Dr. Weiss fired.

The expression on the man's face was quizzical. Surprised more than alarmed. He actually looked down, saw the red blossoming on the front of his white shirt. Then he collapsed in a heap in the dirt.

There was stunned silence. No one spoke. No one moved.

"We have more than two hundred weapons." A bluff. "Fifty of them in the hands of grownups." Another bluff. "Leave now, or as God is my witness we will mow every one of you down, riddle your bodies with a dozen bullets each."

That was all it took. The men turned and bolted back down the road toward the gate.

No one moved inside the building.

David Weiss's vision was throbbing in heartbeat bursts.

Some part of his mind, the analytical, the imminently sane and reasonable part of his mind knew immediately what was happening to him.

It was an adrenaline rush. When your body's fight-or-flight mechanism kicked in, your body was flooded with adrenaline. Your vision narrowed, your peripheral vision all but vanished, your hearing became more acute, your sight sharper. Your heart actually slowed, as he could feel his slowing now.

Scientific facts.

He found himself walking back into the spill of light in the front hallway. He had not willed his feet to carry him out the front door of the building and down the steps, but they did so without his bidding. He walked to the man who was lying in the dirt, the only one of the intruders still here. He had fallen on his back. The red splotch on his shirt was huge and there was a puddle of blood growing under him.

Dr. Weiss had been shooting an M4 assault rifle and he postulated that the bullet had been a through-and-through, that it had entered his body, probably right below the sternum — if the blood had not obscured the hole he could have seen that for certain — that it had passed through his lungs and heart, ripping the organs apart as it tore through them and then exited the middle of his back, probably between the third and fourth vertebrae.

Then the world, reality, reason, clanged down. He knelt on one knee, reached out his hand and touched the man — touched his chest, the red front of his shirt. He drew his hand back and looked at his fingers smeared with the man's blood.

He was aware of other people gathering around him, aware that a crowd had formed, but no one moved toward the body. No one.

Then Ellie Hampton stepped out of the crowd, knelt in the dirt beside the fallen man and put two fingers to his neck. She sat there. It was silent, no one spoke or moved.

Then she looked into Dr. Weiss's face.

"He's dead," she said.

The rest of the world began to spin, the faces blurred as if he were on a merry-go-round going faster and faster. Not all the faces were blurred, however. One was clear. The man who had stood beside him in the darkness out of the spill of light in the door. And the man was no longer alone. Standing next to him was a woman with a high, wide forehead and her hair pulled back into a bun at her neck. Their faces were clear, everything else spun around and around, but they remained still. They looked deep into Dr. Weiss's eyes, as if searching for something there.

They said nothing, just stared. The eyes of the man were so very old in one so young, lines of care and worry and fatigue slicing, gouging ravines down his face. The eyes were alive, though, clear and alert. They were an extraordinary color. Jade green. He recognized them instantly, of course. They were the same eyes that had been looking out the mirror at David Weiss for seventy-one years.

Chapter Forty-Six

ANCIL DIDN'T EVEN HAVE to plan it. Shoot, it wasn't even his idea.

He'd been sitting on his regular stool at Hanky's, not near as drunk as he wanted to be but getting there. The crowd was smaller now, much smaller than usual. Either the guys — and it was mostly guys — had stayed home or they'd left town, but less than a third of the regular crowd had showed up. They wasn't talking much, just watchin' the juke that hung over the bar.

They didn't have the sound turned up. Charlie said the TV was broke and the sound didn't work anymore, but it didn't matter. You didn't need to have some talking-head narrate it for you to see what was going on.

London burning. Flames licking at the bottom of gray clouds. He supposed it was already night there. He didn't know about those things, about what time it was in other places in the world, but it was good and dark there now and the fires were bright orange and yellow flames eating the city.

There were pictures of looting and rioters they said

was in Paris, or he thought the words at the bottom said Paris. But he didn't care what was going on on the other side of the world. Why didn't they show the United States?

And then they did show it and he was sick to his stomach.

The White House was on fire. The president's house was burning!

The scenes in New York didn't look like the crowds was as wild and panicked as the ones he'd seen in old film clips, running away on 9-11 when them towel-heads crashed planes into the World Trade Center. They was just running. Scared. Some fighting. He could see cars on fire back behind. And the news guy was just standing there, narrating the whole thing like it was some movie going on behind him.

And then some guy with a brick — *oh, holy crap* — some guy with a brick come up behind him, right there on camera. Only the camera was turning away, the guy holding it musta been yelling at the guy on the screen and he was turning.

But you could see it. You could see the guy smack the news guy in the head with a brick! You could see the blood.

"You see that?" cried Billy Rodriguez. "You see that guy!"

Then the bar got loud, everybody hollering at once. He wasn't even sure when somebody started talking about the Indian whore, or who it was who said it. But everybody acknowledged that she was gonna call them aliens here for a fact and that wasn't right. Then somebody, he wasn't sure who, was saying they'd ought to go out there to that Alien World and kick some ass.

And then everybody was running out to their cars and trucks. He got in the back of Billy Rodriquez's pickup truck. They all had guns in gun racks, but he didn't have his gun. It was in his truck and he'd walked to Hanky's.

Then they were roaring down the highway, three, no, four pickups, winding down the road, the drivers all drunk or seriously on their way there, whooping and hollering and laughing. But it was scared coming out as laughter. They was all scared, wanting to do something, anything to make the scared go away.

They wasn't no lights on in the buildings at Alien World, the big sign was dark, but the lead pickup, he thought it musta been Ray Phillips, went flying through that closed gate, hollering, and then he heard gunshots. Once the gate was down, they all drove through.

Old Clyde's truck was there, but his car was gone. They'd left. Maybe for good, but he doubted it. No, he was sure of it. They might not be here now, but they'd be back. Star wasn't going off somewhere. She was gonna stay right here so she could stand out in the desert to welcome her little friends when they come.

The truck careened past the arcade, then the museum, then that little building that said "astral readings." Though the buildings was dark, the lights on poles like street lamps was working, and he could see blinking lights, like strings of Christmas lights in the back. They made a roaring circuit around the thing in the middle Ancil thought was a puppet stage. Beyond that building was the amusement park with all them old rides so dangerous it was a wonder hadn't no kids got killed there yet. The petting zoo was in between the amusement park and the miniature golf course, then the store and the restaurant and the gate again.

The gunfire was deafening. Almost sounded like somebody had theirselves some kind of automatic weapons that just kept on shooting. They roared around again. Sam

Donavan was right next to Ancil, shooting from the back of the pickup and Ancil was afraid he was gonna turn and mow down everybody in the back with him, the way he wasn't aiming at nothing, just shooting and whooping and hollering.

The headlights just lit up dark buildings as they flew around and around the circle, the dust hanging in the air after the second or third time through was so thick you couldn't hardly see nothing. Ancil wanted to help, to shoot something but he was so drunk he could barely stand and would probably have shot himself or one of the others if anybody'd given him a gun, which they didn't.

Then the first truck, Ray Phillips's truck, stopped and all the other trucks stopped, too. The brakes on Billy's trucks squealed like he needed new brake pads. Everybody poured out of the vehicles though it wasn't clear what the plan was — if there was a plan.

Then Ray shouted, "Find the little whore!" And Ancil was down with that. He was totally down with that!

The men spread out, searching the place, but with all the buildings dark, he couldn't imagine how they was plannin' on finding anybody without flashlights.

"She's gotta be here somewhere," called Billy Rodriguez from the direction of the museum. "Where else would she be?"

Billy and some fella Ancil didn't know went running — best as they could run — toward the back of the place, the amusement park where the Christmas lights was strung. Ray Phillips and somebody else was searching the minia-ture golf course.

Ancil was winded from all the running and pulled up short under the Ferris wheel.

"I'm telling you, she ain't here," the man said. "We've searched the place. How does a blind girl hide?"

He wanted to reply that it wasn't hard *in the dark*, but he hadn't got his wind back enough to talk yet.

"Come on! I left my beer in the truck," the guy said, turned and headed back to the front of the place, with Ancil in tow.

When they got back to the trucks, Ancil realized there must have been some plan in mind after all because the men who'd stayed behind at the trucks had cans of gasoline and they were splashing it on the walls of the museum and that stupid little puppet theatre. Billy ran up on the porch of the restaurant and splashed gasoline around. Ray took a can to the store. Somebody was probably doing the same thing at all the buildings.

The arcade went up first. The old boards used to construct all the buildings were dried out like tinder and the fire caught with a pleasing, satisfying *whump* sound.

The museum caught, but not as well. A good part of it was built with concrete block, but the wooden parts caught. Wouldn't do no good to put gasoline on the astral readings building where the whore used the rocks to call her alien buddies. The whole building was made of concrete block.

The store caught and the restaurant. And before long everything was burning except the trailer. Everybody'd used up their gasoline by then so they consoled themselves by firing into it, emptying their weapons, riddling it with gunshots.

They stood still then, the glow of the fires lighting their faces, grinning goofy smiles as they watched the buildings burn. Then the smoke got to them. With fire on three sides, the smoke billowed out into the middle, choking, making it impossible to breathe. So they got back into their trucks and went roaring out the gate again, whooping and hollering. All of them felt better, stronger. They had done something. They'd fought back.

All the hilarity calmed down on the way back into town. They could see the huge ball of flames that was Alien World blazing out, lighting the night sky, sending little sparks up to join the stars.

But the chilly wind in the back of the truck sobered Ancil so that he knew it wasn't enough to burn the place down. It wouldn't be enough to keep her from calling the aliens, summoning her buddies.

No, it wouldn't be enough as long as the little whore lived.

Them aliens would be here *tomorrow*, might completely destroy the world. Oh, they might not destroy the whole world, but they'd destroy Roswell. They'd show up in the sky and shoot down some kind of ray gun and blow the place off the map.

Ancil was not going to sit around in Roswell waiting for that to happen. He might not be able to stop it from happening. But he could at least extinguish the beacon, put out the light that was calling the motherfuckers.

And he would.

He had a beer in his hand, but he threw it out of the truck half-drunk. He wouldn't be doing any more drinking tonight or tomorrow. He was going to be sober, cold sober when he went after the little whore and strangled the life out of her.

Chapter Forty-Seven

UNCLE CLYDE MADE A DISGUSTED GRUNT.

"What?"

"The electric's out again."

Uncle Clyde had told her once that one of the perks of being blind was you didn't know when the lights went out.

The two of them were sitting at the kitchen table finishing supper. Aunt Mary Ellen and the littles were gone and Star knew they wouldn't be coming back.

Uncle Clyde had heated up a couple of cans of soup and the two of them had that along with the last of the cold cornbread Aunt Mary Ellen had made last night. They could have nuked it — she liked it hot enough to melt butter — but Uncle Clyde liked his cornbread cold. He crumbled it up in the soup. And she didn't ask him to heat hers up because she wasn't hungry anyway. Her stomach was so tied in knots with foreboding that the smell of the soup almost made her nauseous.

Yesterday, Uncle Clyde had moved the trailer away from in front of the gate, snuggled it close enough to the restaurant so he could jerry-rig some electric lines to bring in electricity and hoses for water. They'd still be using the septic tank on the trailer. It wasn't full yet, and when it was, Uncle Clyde would have to detach it — it came with a dolly you could use to haul it off somewhere and empty it. She was sure he wasn't looking forward to the task.

"I ain't fixing it," he said. "Not tonight." There was emergency power stored in batteries connected to solar panels, but it only lit the big lights on poles around the property, and the string of colored lights that surrounded the carnival rides. "Hard enough to keep from electro-cuting myself working on them wires in the daylight." She heard a click. He must have switched on a flashlight or one of the electric lanterns they'd brought from the store to light the place before he'd got all the hookups working.

"Let's go sit … want to?"

He had gotten out two lawn chairs from the store, and set them off to the side in front of the trailer. They'd had chairs on the front porch when the trailer was still in the trailer park and he had liked to sit out in them in the cool evenings, no lights, just looking up at the stars.

They had no porch, just the staggered pile of concrete blocks leading up to the door. But the chairs were out there with a little table between them where he could set a beer.

He helped her down the steps to the chair and Pumpkin plopped down at her feet.

"Want a drink?"

"No, I'm good."

Even the thought of a soft drink made her sick. The knot in her stomach was winding tighter and tighter. Fear building. If this kept up, by the time the ships actually arrived, she'd be bent double with the pain in her belly.

He went back into the trailer for a beer, came back out and she heard him pop the top, and the protest of the wicker in the chair as he eased down into it.

"The stars tonight," he said. "You ought see 'em. They're big as," she thought he almost said marbles, but instead he said, "chunks of ice. I's in Dallas one night, went for a walk in the park, me and Mary Ellen, and when we looked up there wasn't hardly any stars to see. I guess it was the glow of the city lights, reflecting off—"

He stopped. But she'd already heard it. The sound of engines coming down the road. There had been almost no traffic on the highway all day and when it got dark the occasional car was all you'd see on a normal night.

The sound was loud, more than one vehicle. And it sounded menacing. Star couldn't have said why she thought so, but it sounded—

"Star, sugar, maybe you'd ought to go in the house."

Uncle Clyde had sensed it, too. He took her hand to lead her to the step.

But the engines were coming fast. Way too fast.

He stopped. Then saw something. She didn't know what it could have been, but whatever it was, it scared him.

"Not in the trailer," he said, and pulled her back off the bottom row of concrete blocks. "You need to—"

The engines were loud now and she could see a blob of light coming like a freight train down the road.

"You need to *hide*, sugar," he said, his voice tight and frightened. He shoved Pumpkin's leash into her hand.

"Run," he said. *"Now!"*

The sound was almost on them. Pumpkin pulled on the leash — he understood — and dragged her, and Star went running off into darkness.

The terror that gripped Star's heart was all out of proportion to the fear of running wildly through the dark. Her apprehension, her sense of foreboding, burst like a giant explosion, spewing out terror in every direction.

She was suddenly disoriented, had lost her sense of

direction. She was just running. Pumpkin wouldn't let her bang into anything, fall off a cliff or hit her head but she didn't know where she was going. She could hear the engine noise behind her louder, engines revving up, and knew she was running away from that sound but she hadn't counted steps. She knew where she was by counting how far one thing was from another. But she was just running.

Just running.

She heard a loud bang and stopped in her tracks, like she had been shot. It was a gunshot. Behind her. Someone was shooting.

She sucked in a breath, breathed out and couldn't make her diaphragm breathe back in.

Then the night exploded with gunshots. There was a rumble of gunfire, revving engines. She heard a whap sound and knew something, or somebody, had run through the gates, and now the engines were in the inner circle. It wasn't a road, just an open area in front of the various buildings. In the center was a concession stand and a puppet theatre. But someone, lots of someones, were *driving* in there. She could hear the engines getting closer.

Pumpkin slowed, blocked her path. Something was in front of her. She reached out and felt the cool of concrete blocks. She knew where she was then, behind the astral readings building.

Then gunshots began to ping off the museum, only a few feet away.

The whole world blurred into a nightmare of darkness and sound and terror. Gunshots, laughter, raucous laughter. She could smell dust, apparently cars were driving around and around in the circular area in front of the buildings so fast and furiously that they were stirring up a dust cloud.

Then the engines changed tune. The vehicles had

stopped. One of them had brakes that squealed, like the brakes on Papa Eagle Feather's did before he got them fixed.

Where was Uncle Clyde? Had they seen him? Had he been able to hide? Gunshots. Oh, dear holy God *had he been shot?*

She heard the voices of people, all men, loud, angry drunk men.

A voice cried out, "Find her. She's here somewhere. Find the little Indian whore."

They were looking for her. Why? Who on earth would be looking for—?

It didn't matter who. What mattered was that she had to do what Uncle Clyde said. She had to hide. Where? How could you hide when you couldn't tell what other people saw?

Then she thought of a place.

She leaned over and spoke softly to Pumpkin, and he led her to the back of the property where she could detect the faint glow of the string of colored lights. He stopped at the gate of the amusement park and she counted twenty-eight steps to the platform in front of the Ferris wheel.

Gunshots. Loud voices. Coming closer. Laughter, mean laughter.

"She's gotta be here somewhere. Where else would she be?" someone called, their voice coming from near the museum.

She quickly felt her way to the seat that had stopped on the platform, waiting for the next person to climb on the ride. She didn't get into the seat, but scrunched down on the floor in front of it and shoved the bar across the seat above her.

"Go!" she told Pumpkin.

A few seconds later she felt the machinery begin to

hum and the car where she knelt began to lift up into the air. She felt the car go up, higher and higher.

"Go!" she cried out again, and the car stopped moving just as it was about to descend on the other side.

"Pumpkin, kennel."

Star prayed he'd still respond to the command. He'd had a kennel when he was being house trained as a puppy. Uncle Clyde had bought one big enough for an adult dog. He'd been taught the command "kennel" in the service dog training he'd taken to be certified, would go there and remain there until he was released. But after he was house trained, Uncle Clyde had moved the kennel to the back of the petting zoo and sometimes kept baby lambs in it. Pumpkin hadn't used it in years. She waited, heard nothing. The kennel was behind the fence in the dark and nobody would see him if he went there. But if Pumpkin didn't follow the command, if he stayed beside the Ferris wheel, he'd protect her from anybody menacing who came near. And they'd shoot him! The men who'd come here to — what? Find *her?* Why? What did they want her for? — they'd *shoot Pumpkin!*

She squeaked out a little cry of terror at the thought, then clamped her hand over her mouth because she could hear men approaching.

"I'm tellin' you, she ain't here. We've searched the place. How does a blind girl hide?"

The men were standing directly below her. Clearly, Pumpkin was nowhere nearby.

"Come on! I left my beer in the truck!"

Several minutes later Star smelled smoke. She looked out over the top edge of the box seat and saw a blob of red and then another. It must be ... it was either the restaurant or the store. Burning.

The smoke carried up and up, but the wind was

blowing the other direction so the smoke was not overpowering. But she could smell it. She watched in horror at the red balls — there were more of them. The museum. The arcade. Maybe even the trailer. She couldn't tell anything about the blobs but their general direction.

Uncle Clyde.

Where was Uncle Clyde?

She was so frightened for him she was afraid she was going to be sick. She listened to the men, loud and laughing, the crackle of the fire as it devoured the world. Not Alien World, her world. Everything she knew about all the sights and smells of her childhood had been here. It was forty-one steps from the concession stand to the Moon Glow Restaurant. You followed Pumpkin to the sign, felt along the edge of it until your foot struck the raised wooden walkway, stepped up on it and followed the railing to the porch where there were rocking chairs for people to sit in while they waited for a table. From the restaurant porch, it was twenty-five steps to …

It was all gone now or would be soon, all going up in a ball of flames that surely must be visible for miles in every direction.

She heard the engines of the vehicles start again, heard them drive away. Heard the silence. Nothing but the rumble of the blaze eating up the world. The heat from it stung her face, sparks fell into her hair.

She waited. She didn't know how long, just sat huddled there smelling smoke that strung her eyes but wasn't the reason for her tears. Finally, the called out as loud as she could, "Pumpkin, come." He came and barked once. She told him, "Go," and the machinery clanked again until the seat was lowered to the platform where it had started.

She had to find Uncle Clyde, but it was crazy to go walking out there into fire you couldn't see. He would come looking for her, she was sure of it. Now that the men were gone, he'd come looking, calling her name. She made her way to the merry-go-round and climbed up on one of the horses. She sat there waiting for Uncle Clyde to call out to her. For him to come and find her and wrap his big arms around her and tell her everything was going to be fine.

She waited.

And waited.

It must have been hours, had to be. The fires burned ferociously. The buildings were constructed of old barn wood, because it would look rustic and before the place was Alien World it had been a trading post with Indian relics and teepees and barn wood buildings. The timber was dry and burned fast and hot. The fires eventually tamed, though. The light from them got dimmer and dimmer. But nobody came.

Uncle Clyde did not call her name.

No one else came either. The fire was bound to be the only bright light, visible for ten miles in every direction. Of course, the fire department didn't come, not this far out, where there was no water for their pumper trucks.

But the police didn't come, either. Neither did anybody else. If cars passed by on the road out there, they didn't stop. The usual gawkers and looky-loos just kept on driving.

It was probably close to dawn before the fires had settled into dull red blotches on the ground, and the smoke was no longer a gagging, choking wall of poisoned air.

When she finally decided it was safe to leave the merry-go-round and go ... looking for Uncle Clyde, she didn't want to do it. She was afraid, oh so horribly, terribly afraid of what she would ... her stomach was tied in such a knot that she could barely breathe.

He would have come for her, would have come looking for her after the men left unless …

She climbed carefully down from the merry-go-round horse and walked along the side of the ride, from there to the back fence, then she traced the fence around the outside edge of the compound. The circle of it went behind the rollercoaster, behind the astral reading room and the museum and the arcade — except none of those things was there anymore. It went all the way to the gate. The astral reading room would remain, she thought, because it was made of concrete block. The museum and the arcade were beds of glowing coals. The fence ended in a post. The gate should have been closed, but it wasn't. She held out her hands and walked forward and found it twisted on its hinges, as if it had been struck and knocked out of its socket.

Ahead of her, along the fence line, she could see the glowing remains of the restaurant and to its left, a pile of red ash that was once the store. But there was no glowing red …

She urged Pumpkin forward until her hands finally reached out to it. The trailer. *It hadn't been burned.* It was there, right there.

So where was Uncle Clyde?

Chapter Forty-Eight

"Uncle Clyde," she called out, so softly he'd have had to be three feet away to hear her. But she couldn't find enough air to speak louder. Her whole middle was so tied in a knot she couldn't seem to draw in enough air to call louder.

"Uncle Clyde, where are you?"

No answer.

"Uncle Clyde!" There was a sob on the end of her words and she bit her lip not to cry.

Then it hit her. She had been so upset, so scared and knocked sideways that it hadn't even occurred to her.

She leaned over and patted Pumpkin on the head. Their game, the one he'd played since he was a puppy, when Uncle Clyde would hide and she'd tell the dog: "Go see UC."

She leaned close to Pumpkin and spoke softly into his ear. She didn't know why she felt the need for quiet, but she did. She felt the presence of some big, ugly evil, like a black twister bearing down on her, and in the presence of a monster, you whispered.

"Go see UC," she said.

The dog obediently trotted along the side of the trailer house with Star in tow, around the makeshift porch on the front and stopped about halfway down the other side.

He barked once.

"Uncle Clyde?" Star called. "Where—?"

She heard a sound. A small sound, a groan, a moan, something like that. It was coming from nearby, but down lower and she dropped to her knees and began to crawl under the trailer house.

"Uncle Clyde? Uncle—"

She touched a shoe.

Uncle Clyde. She felt frantically up the leg from the shoe.

He was lying on his back. She felt up his legs and across his—

His chest was wet. His white shirt was soaked.

He must have spilled his beer, that's all. He spilled his beer on—

She felt up his chest. His hand was lying across it with his phone clutched tight in his fingers. She continued feeling up his neck to his face. She found his lips, held her fingers there. Breath. She felt a breath.

"Uncle Clyde, talk to me, I'm here."

"Star."

It was a whisper on a breath, so soft only someone with the acute hearing of a blind person could have heard it.

"I'm here. Yes, Uncle Clyde."

She leaned over and kissed his cheeks, his chin, his forehead.

"I'm here. I'm here, Uncle Clyde. Talk to me."

"Star."

Again a whisper on a breath. She put her ear down

near his lips, felt his breath, such a little thing, not even like the breath of a baby.

"I'm sorry. I ..."

But there was no more. Just a sigh.

And no more breath.

Uncle Clyde? Why had he ...?

"Uncle Clyde!"

Still no answer

No.

Oh dear holy God in heaven, no.

"No," she said the word out loud except she didn't. No sound came.

"Dad-eeeeee!' she screamed and threw herself on him, holding his big body, her arms around him, crying, sobbing.

"Please no. Oh, please no. Don't be ... Don't—"

But he made no more sounds. He didn't move.

Uncle Clyde was ...

Uncle Clyde was dead.

Star snuggled up beside his big body. She used to do that when she was younger — and he was thinner. She'd cuddle up next to him on the couch while he watched sports on the juke. He loved the Dallas Cowboys and he'd explain to her what was going on, but she never ... She put her head on his shoulder and her arm around his chest. Pumpkin curled up behind her. He knew. He always knew things before humans did, and he knew she needed him close, needed to feel his warmth. And he was warm, the feel of his regular breathing a comforting presence. Uncle Clyde was not warm, and as time passed, he felt colder and colder.

But still, Star stayed where she was, cuddled next to him. The smoke from the dying fires all around wafted under the trailer sometimes to sting her eyes and make them water.

It wasn't the smoke, of course. The tears that flowed down her cheeks weren't smoke tears.

Shock overtook her, all her breakers tripped and she was wrapped in the fuzzy cotton of unreality. Pumpkin lifted his head up and licked her face tenderly. He was trying to offer reassurance, and only knew to move close, to be there, to lick her face and let her smell the warmth of his doggie breath.

She didn't want comfort anyway. She had nowhere inside to put comfort. A howling wind was blowing through the hollow frame of her body and there was no solid substance there anywhere.

She tried to cry. She knew she should cry. She needed to cry, but she couldn't make it happen. When she tried, the vast hole in her belly gobbled up the emotion before she could engage the muscles of her diaphragm.

It was quiet here, under the trailer. No sound but the breathing of her dog and the quiet crackling of the still-burning fires. At one point, out of nowhere, there was a scream. It went on and on, a wail, an agony given voice, but in the silence under the trailer the scream shattered and pieces of it clattered into the dirt. The screaming went on and on but Star wasn't sure who was doing the screaming, until her throat was raw and her voice so hoarse she could only croak. and cry.

Finally, Star cried — great gulping, heaving sobs that wracked her body like seizures.

Day Six

Chapter Forty-Nine

STAR HEARD voices that roused her, then she came full awake with a start from a horrible nightmare. She had dreamed that—

But it hadn't been a nightmare. She was lying on the cold ground, beside Uncle Clyde and he was as cold as the ground she lay on.

The voices were coming from overhead and for a moment she couldn't get her bearings, didn't know where … who was talking.

It came back to her then, all of it, all the horror, and she realized that the muffled voices above her were coming from the trailer house. The juke. Aunt Mary Ellen must have left it on and apparently whatever had knocked out the electricity was functioning now. She sat up slowly, with Pumpkin right there beside her, overly close, leaning against her, not for his comfort but for hers.

She had to get up. She had to go to the bathroom and she was thirsty. Her throat was so raw and parched it hurt with every swallow. And she was sure Pumpkin needed water, too, and access to his food dish.

She was stiff, sore, crawling out around Uncle Clyde's feet, and out from under the trailer. She had to feel her way along the trailer and up the makeshift concrete block porch to the door. She let herself inside and now the voices were clear.

"… hanging over Houston. There are similar ships over Chicago, San Francisco …" A woman's voice.

"As far as we know, we have heard no reports of the ships doing anything. No reports of them landing. The smaller ships were released from the larger ones over Dallas and they seem to be flying in a formation." It was a man talking.

"Switching to the news anchor in Dallas," said the woman again. "Are you there, Stan?"

"Yes, Sarah. As you can see in the background, there are smaller ships cruising in the sky, like they are in formation. Almost … almost like they're walking guard duty. When the—"

He stopped in mid-sentence. There was a moment of silence, then static, then the voice of the first news anchor.

"We have lost the feed from Dallas. But we can show you pictures of Tel Aviv. And London. The ships in London are hanging over the Thames River above the Westminster Bridge with Parliament in the background where the House of Commons is right now in session. Prime Minister Hadley said they would be issuing a statement to the country later today, urging citizens to remain in their houses and remain calm."

"As you can see in the background, there's smoke. There had been rioting for the past three days and much of the west side of London is burning.

"In Paris—"

Star stepped forward and switched off the juke, went to

the sink, drew a glass of water and gulped it down. She could hear Pumpkin lapping up water out of his dish.

She found her way to the bathroom, and when she was done she ran warm water in the sink and splashed it in her face.

Now what?

She had no idea. She came out of the bathroom and Pumpkin was right there, determined not to get more than a couple of feet from her. Animals could sense pain, sense human moods. She had read about dogs that could sense when an epileptic was going to have a seizure, so they could warn their owner to get down on the ground so they wouldn't fall and injure themselves.

And of course their sense of smell was astounding.

After Uncle Clyde brought home the cuddly teddy-bear bundle of love Star named Pumpkin, she had listened to online audio books to learn everything she could about service dogs, and dogs in general and found out that her pitiful sense of smell paled in comparison to what an ordinary dog could tell about a person with a single sniff.

She'd read that a dog's sense of smell was like 100,000 more acute than a human's. A famous researcher at the Sensory Research Institute at Florida State University had tried to make that number understandable. "If you make the analogy to vision, what you and I can see at a third of a mile, a dog could see more than 3,000 miles away and still see as well. Make an analogy to taste, and a human can taste a teaspoon of sugar in a cup of coffee and a dog could do the same thing if the sugar were dissolved in two Olympic-sized swimming pools."

Meaning Pumpkin could smell enzymes and chemicals, a book full of information given off by any person's skin.

That was a whole lot more impressive than touching

somebody and picking up a random image from their mind.

Pumpkin knew she was hurting. He wanted to help. But there was no help.

Star didn't know what she should do now, only knew that she wanted to comfort Uncle Clyde. She went to her bedroom, pulled the bedspread off the bed, and dragged it behind her out the front door.

As she carefully eased herself down the steps, she discovered she was crying. Or was she? Was it crying if there were tears streaming down your cheeks but you weren't making any sound? Star didn't know.

She got down on her hands and knees and crawled back under the trailer and tenderly covered Uncle Clyde with the bedspread. She didn't want to touch him now. He didn't feel real, felt like a mannequin or a big cold doll.

Then she crawled back into the sunshine and made her way to the porch. She sat down, let the feel of the sun on her face warm her. It was probably nine or ten o'clock in the morning. She could tell by going into the house, where the clock beside her bed had no face. Uncle Clyde had removed it so she could feel where the hands were pointing.

Uncle Clyde, who was dead now.

What should she do?

She thought then about Earl, Earl the husband of Mildred who'd had a heart attack when she heard the aliens were coming and had died right there on the floor in the astral readings building where Star told fortunes. Earl had picked her up and taken her out to his car and driven away with her. To where? What did Earl do with his dead wife? Star couldn't imagine. What could she do with her … with Uncle Clyde? She couldn't … bury him, not by herself. What should she do?

She sat with the sun in her face, trying to think what she ought to do but her mind felt like it was packed in cotton and her eyes, they were still running, tears streaming down her face and dripping off her chin. The pain in her belly, the loss, the grief, hurt worse than any pain she had ever felt in her life, worse than that time she tripped over one of the littles' roller skates and fell and broke her arm.

It was pain and grief and sorrow all tangled up with fear.

They were here. The aliens were here now, their ships were up there in the sky, maybe up in the sky right above her and if she could see, she could look up and see it hanging there. But she imagined the ships were over big cities. Though there were those who claimed they had been to Roswell before and they would come back.

The aliens were here. Uncle Clyde couldn't protect her from them, from the bug monsters with needle teeth and bright blue eyes. The ones that purred.

Star was all alone.

Chapter Fifty

MAYBE IT HAD BEEN WORSE for the other boys last night after Spade handed them off to the barracks full of inmates who grabbed and clawed at them like wild animals as they carried them away.

But how could it have been worse?

Spade had raped Paco repeatedly all night long. He lost track of how many times. The sheets on the bunk where he lay when the sun came up, with Spade asleep on top of him, were stiff with his own dried blood.

As dawn lit the eastern horizon, the sun rising into a stormy sky as bruised as Paco's body, Spade yanked him upright and shoved him staggering in front of him, patting his butt and pinching him. Paco could barely stand. Walking was agony. Spade directed him through hallways to a door that lead out into the yard. It looked like every prison yard Paco had ever seen in some old movie. The east wall stood out against the sunrise, a massive stone edifice with guard towers every two hundred feet, and topped with coils of vicious razor wire with bright serrated edges that would have winked and twinkled if the storm light had not been so gray and dull. Huge spotlights were located in every guard tower and the beams from them could be directed into the yard or out over the wall to the outside perimeter, that Paco remembered was an empty area enclosed within another fence, electrified, with razor wire on top. He'd been told that guard dogs patrolled the open area between the fences, but he bet there were no dogs there now, just like there were no guards in the towers.

The building formed one side of the yard, with the wall enclosing the other three sides to make a square space bigger than two football fields that right now was completely empty. No one stirred.

The dark clouds boiled and bubbled and flashes of lightning strobed the dirty concrete.

Spade shoved him out the door and ahead of him alongside the building and then back in another door farther down. There were other cons there who made sick jokes with Spade about his bitch — jokes Spade found riotously funny.

"Soon's I get him broke in good, I'll let you have a ride," he told an ugly man with a twisted nose, bulbous eyes and ears with hair sprouting out of them. His body smelled worse than the dead men in the cellblock last night.

Spade shoved Paco into a chair and he bit the inside of his cheek to keep from moaning at the impact, then consulted with the other cons about … Paco didn't know what. Or care. He tried to order his thoughts, tried to think what might be happening next. Searched listlessly inside himself for the Paco who knew things about people, could "push" others, who was able to control situations and circumstances. That Paco was nowhere to be found.

Maybe Paco would die. A large part of him hoped so

because the larger part of him thought that he wouldn't die, that he would be prisoner here, a whore to all the nasty old men, raped and raped until … what? He died, maybe. Or killed somebody.

Killed. Somebody.

That thought brought such vitality to his body it felt like hot water had been flushed into his veins.

He would kill Spade!

He would. He would butcher that motherfucker, gouge his eyes out shove them down his throat. He *would* kill him. Somehow, someday. And he didn't give an ounce of rat piss if he got killed in the doing of it. He would willingly pay whatever the cost in the currency of self-sacrifice to watch that bastard choke on his own nuts.

When he thought of killing Spade, he began to feel alive again. He straightened in the chair. Though the pain in every part of his body from the waist down was excruciating, he sat erect. He could feel the color return to his face, sense the fire in his eyes. Felt his own personal power returning. The future was a black hole opening up in front of him lit only by the image of Spade's face twisted in death. He would live for that. He would die for that.

Then one of the cons turned on the juke mounted on the wall. The room fell instantly silent as the announcers narrated the scene. Not that any narration was necessary.

A gigantic silver ball hung over the Los Angeles skyline, hung suspended in the air, motionless. Of course, Paco had seen the image before. Announcers had described the ever-clearer views of the ships for every hour of every day since Astral Day. He'd seen the image before that, of course. Before the world stood gawking at their Astral apps at indistinguishable white spots out by Jupiter, he had seen the ships in his dreams. He and the two children, the blond boy and the dark-haired girl, had stared together at them hanging in the sky.

But he was surprised by the size. It had never occurred to him they would be so big, the size of a whole town.

"... shuttles that seem to be on patrol around the mothership," the announcer was saying as the camera swung to a closeup view of a smaller round cylinder — a row of them — flying in formation.

Paco looked away from the screen and saw the terror and confusion on the faces of the cons and he wanted to laugh out loud. Even Spade looked stupefied. Yeah, motherfuckers, take a look at what real scary is.

Want to piss your pants? Got shit running down your leg? So scared you want to puke? *Good.* These motherfuckers are gonna eat your guts out, if I don't do it before they get the chance.

Spade turned to Paco, his face somber, trying to hide his fear.

"Let's go get your friends," he said, and shoved Paco ahead of him down another hallway.

Randal, Rob/Bob, Hector and Jamal were huddled together on the floor of some kind of supply room. There was no sign of the others or Tiburón.

The boys looked like they had lived a thousand years since last he saw them. Their eyes were hollow, their faces wracked. It was clear that his own experience through his dark night had been replicated in theirs. They'd all been fucked. Royally.

"Out you go," said one of the other cons. He opened a door, grabbed Randal and shoved him forward. The other boys followed and they were back out in the open prison yard. Alone.

A blush of lightning lit the dark clouds, caissons of

thunder rumbled across the embattled sky and Paco could smell the scent of ozone.

"There'll be some friends coming along soon," one of cons said. Spade said nothing. Just winked at Paco, stepped back inside and closed the door behind him. The boys looked at each other, confused. That's when Paco saw Tiburón on the other side of the yard, in a bit of an alcove formed where the outside wall joined the wall of the building. He was leaned up against the wall smoking a cigarette.

Paco approached him. Somehow, *somehow* managed not to limp, not to show the agony each step caused.

Tiburón said nothing, just let his eyes slide over Paco and then away. He had a large scratch across one cheek and it looked like maybe one of his eyes had been blackened. But he said nothing and neither did Paco. What was there to say?

Paco stepped up to the wall beside him and leaned against it, grateful not to have to keep his body balanced on his wobbly legs.

"Today's the big day," Tiburón finally said. "Showtime."

He was talking about the Astrals, but Paco couldn't even make himself care. Let the bastards come, maybe they'd blow the prison off the map and kill everybody. That definitely sounded like a plan to Paco.

A buzzer sounded from deep in the guts of the building, followed by similar buzzers in different parts of the building adjacent to the yard and it echoed in other buildings farther away.

The other boys were still standing together in the middle of the yard, just standing there, when one of the doors leading into the building burst open and convicts came pouring out it like a flood after a dam had burst. A couple of them noticed the boys, but most didn't. They

were in some kind of riotous delirium that defied description. They were screaming, hollering, chanting, an angry,
rioting mob with nowhere to go and nobody to fight. It was
surprising how quickly the whole yard filled with something like a thousand hungry, tired, frightened, pissed-off
men. The tension in the air was palpable. It was a bomb,
ticking, and the whole thing would go off with the slightest
provocation or none at all.

The first fat drops of rain splatted down into the
crowd.

Then Spade appeared on top of the wall next to the
guard tower near them. He had a megaphone and he
addressed the cons.

"It's over. We free!" The crowd cheered, but not whole-
heartedly. There was angry muttering because it was plain
to see they were anything but free.

"We're working on the front gates now, should have
them open within the hour. My crews are cooking up piles
of eggs in the kitchen if you're hungry."

That elicited a genuine cheer.

"Spade! Spade!"

Someone started the chant and it spread like a wave
over the crowd.

Spade! Spade!

He was their hero, their savior. The ugly motherfucker
was revered. Well, he would die at Paco's hand, no matter
how long—

Then the chanting stopped as if someone had turned
off a faucet. There was an audible, communal gasp and
the crowd of cons fell back like wheat hit by a strong wind.

One of the round ships, the ones the announcers were
calling shuttles, had appeared in the sky above the prison.
It didn't "arrive" in the air above them; they didn't watch it
zip across the sky from somewhere else. It was just

suddenly there. Not there, then there. In an instant. Apparently traveling so fast it was impossible to track the movement.

The shuttle lowered slowly until it was dangling right above the yard, maybe three hundred feet off the ground. It did nothing, then began to rise and—

The *rat-tat-tat* sound of gunfire exploded in the stillness of the morning, an angry grating sound that bounced off the stone walls and carried up into the air.

Paco and the others looked around, trying to figure out—

There! In the guard tower, the one on the far end. One of the cons had climbed up into the tower, and — the exiting guard must have left the rifle, or maybe the con brought it with him. Didn't matter which, he definitely had a gun and he was firing it.

At the shuttle!

It took a second to grasp. The stupid bastard was *firing at the shuttle.*

Everyone could hear his laughter. Spewing obscenities and laughing hysterically, the con fired round after round at the craft overhead.

The shots didn't ping off it like metal. It was hard to tell what did happen to them. The bullets were just … gone. Vanished. They never made it to the surface of the craft. Maybe they had been intercepted in flight by … what? Maybe they'd been vaporized or repelled by a force field or … nobody could tell.

The only thing that was obvious was that the gunfire did absolutely no damage to the silver ball hanging above.

The man emptied his whole magazine. Not a shot landed. Not a mark appeared on the impervious, perfect surface of the ball.

When the man finally ran out of ammo and the firing

stopped, there was a beat of breathless silence. Thunder rumbled, closer now, and the few drops of water became a shower.

Then the silver ball began to descend slowly into the prison yard.

Chapter Fifty-One

DR. DAVID WEISS didn't sleep a wink that night. No, he didn't just "doze," or sleep fitfully. He had not closed his eyes, not one time. He hadn't even gotten ready for bed. After he shot the man—

Killed the man.

Yes, killed the man that Sheriff Matheson said was Oscar Higgins.

He had come into his lab and closed the door and sat alone in the darkness. He had done well when the sheriff came. He had held it together. Had let a little burst of inappropriate laughter burp out, but he'd covered it with a cough. The sheriff had tried to be comforting, telling him the story of the first time he ever killed someone. He had waited patiently through it, feigned interest, but in truth this wasn't the same thing at all. This was ... he had killed that man because ...

He lost it for a moment, couldn't get to the answer right away, then he found it again. He had killed the man to protect the innocents, as his father had done when he jumped on top of Nazi tanks with Molotov cocktails. He had been defending others, he had fought, he had stood up and said, no, *you won't come here and take what is ours. You won't harm my precious children.* He had stood up to the man called Higgins and all his buddies and he had …

Killed him. Shot him. Dead.

Dr. Weiss looked down at his hands and he was glad he had gotten the man's blood on his hands because that seemed to center him. To keep his mind from water-spidering away from him, his thoughts from slipping out of his grasp and dancing into the shadows. When they threatened to do that, when they tried, he looked at the blood on his fingers. Smelled it.

He killed the man because they had told him he must, they had come to him across space and time, not like aliens but like the ancestors of all humanity could do if the need arose. His grandparents had come to him, had held up his arm as Joshua had held the arm of Moses.

Moses had stood on the shore, holding his staff aloft, parting the Red Sea so his people could cross safely to the other side, escape the Nazis … no, not the Nazis, the Romans. No, it wasn't the Romans — the Egyptians.

But Moses's arm grew tired and whenever he weakened, when his arm began to sag, the waters threatened to return to the sea bed. So Joshua had come up beside him, a young man, strong, he had held Moses's arm aloft, helped him lift the staff high so his people would survive.

Just so. Dr. Weiss's grandfather was Moses, too. Moses Weiss. He and David's grandmother, Sarah had done that for him as he stood in the shadows while the armed men outside threatened … They had stood with him against those men, against the one he killed. Or the Romans. The Nazis. Or was it … was it the creatures from the big silver balls that were barreling at this moment across the sky, that had slowed down somewhere on the other side of the moon and now were, at this very moment, coming in for a landing on Earth?

Dr. Weiss suddenly noticed that everything seemed too bright. He turned off the light over his desk because it hurt his eyes. All the lights had shiny circles around them like headlights seen through a car windshield in the rain.

He wondered if his vision had become messed up somehow because he hadn't slept at all last night. He had not slept the night before either, come to that. Or … He hadn't really slept, fallen into a deep dreamless sleep the second his head hit the pillow since Astral Day.

That was, of course, why his thoughts were water spiders, skittering across the surface of his mind, going too fast, dodging away, not letting him think them. That was lack of sleep. But once he caught the thoughts, concentrated and grabbed one, the others stopped running, lay there on the shiny surface of the water waiting for him to pick them up one at a time and think them. Once he had done that. Well, then he knew.

He knew.

It hadn't been sudden. His awareness of their presence grew on him as the big clock ticked, ticked, ticked away the night hours, the last hours before the sun rose on the day the aliens landed.

He knew they were in the room with him even though he didn't see them. Not at first. He just felt their nearness. As he had felt their nearness when he had—

Killed a man, shot him dead, blood on his fingers.

And it was a while before he acknowledged the reality of it and turned to face them. The young man with his own eyes and the young woman with her hair in a bun, the image of his Aunt Maya. He remembered Maya. Remembered her telling the story of what had happened the day …

But he wanted to hear it from the source.

So he turned to the couple, standing there in tattered, dirty clothing, their faces worn with care, their eyes so very old for those so young. And he asked.

"How did you do it? How did you make yourself do it?"

And she had smiled. It was a little smile, not a rueful smile.

"By the time I was putting the poison in their juice, it was easier to do it than not. To have stopped, to have given in to … what, pity? Pity for children who would become slaves if I did not … it was harder then to stop than to continue."

"When it is right …" She looked deep into his eyes as she spoke. And he noticed that her eyes, too, were the same color as the eyes that looked at him from the mirror. How could it be that both his grandmother and his grandfather had the same eyes?

They did, though, and she looked at him with those eyes and they were on fire.

"You must come to the point where you understand the consequences of your cowardice. The consequences of being too timid to do the hard thing, of being too compassionate to be able to bestow real compassion, the consequences of inaction.

"Death. No, worse than death. Death is a gift to those who face slavery at the hands of monsters. The Nazis were monsters. I couldn't let them have the children."

She looked at him hard then, but he saw compassion in her eyes.

"You can't either, David. You know that, don't you. You can't let the monsters take your children."

"I know," he heard himself say. "I understand. I can't let the monsters take them alive."

As the sun was peeking over the mountaintop, he left his office and went to his apartment to dress. This was an important day and he must look the part of the courageous man he was determined to be.

Moses and Sarah went with him. Not walking along beside him, but there, standing on the edge of his vision, or behind his reflection when he passed a window, or in the water glass he used to take his medicine … He stopped. Why take his medicine? No need for such now.

As he dressed for work, his mind was finally as peaceful as a still pond, not a spider skittering across the surface but still and dark and deep as the pond itself, where you could see all the way to the bottom, watch the turtles swim with the minnows. His heart beat comfortably, slow and steady, pumping blood around and around his veins for the last few hours before it could rest. Before he could rest. Before they all could rest, could remain free, un-enslaved forever.

He looked at himself in the mirror and noticed that he still had blood on his hand. He had taken a shower, lathered his whole body. How had he managed to miss the blood on his fingers? But he couldn't go about the day with blood there. the blood of …

The man he killed, gunned down, shot and the bullet went all the way through and out the other side and then blood puddled under him.

When he was dressed, Dr. Weiss was neat and tidy, his tie on straight, his … well everything. Nothing as ridiculous as his coat on wrong side out as it had been yesterday. That was from the day when his mind was in turmoil and it wasn't today. It was peaceful. Not just peaceful, it was clean and eerily crisp, sharp, supremely aware. His sense of his surroundings was in such a heightened state he could see the individual cracks the blood had painted on the skin of his fingers. Hear an individual drop of from the faucet go splat in the sink. The glorious aroma of his last pot of coffee was so intense it took his breath away.

It was only his vision that was screwy. Circles around lights and everything so bright he felt like he needed sunglasses. He ached for the velvet darkness of Matheson Caverns, the absolute blackness, total silence, too, except for the echo of his own heartbeat. And even that was peaceful.

He squirted soap from the canister on the sink into his hands and lathered, then rinsed them in hot water to get the blood off.

He dried his hands on the white hand towel hanging by the sink. And there was blood on the towel. So much blood. Had he cut himself — how? He hadn't shaved, hadn't even trimmed his beard. It was the blood from his hand, where he had touched …

The man he killed, shot, blew his lungs and heart out through a hole in his back.

But his hands were clean. Or he thought they were until he reached out his hand to turn the knob on the doorway of his bedroom. When he did, he smeared blood on it. Looked at his hand, looked at the blood.

He stared at it for what seemed a very long time, wiggling his fingers. Then he felt the two of them come up beside him. Moses on his left side, Sarah on his right. Moses put his hand on his shoulder.

"It doesn't matter," Moses said. "The blood is a mark of your courage to stand and fight for those you love. When you look at it, see it as a badge of honor. Let it bolster the resolve you will need to do the hard thing, the thing you must do to save them all."

The Romans coming up the ramp. Camped outside the gate of the city, waiting for dawn to come inside.

The Nazis storming the school, ready to drag out the children.

All dead. All escaped.

You can't let the monsters take them alive.

"I won't," he whispered. "I swear it. I won't."

Chapter Fifty-Two

PACO COULDN'T BREATHE. He couldn't think. He couldn't engage his senses to feel or see or touch. He was so stunned by what was happening in front of him that he almost forgot to be afraid.

This was the silver ball that had decorated the dreamscape of his mind night after night. It was here. Now. Right in front of him.

He was seized with an incredible curiosity, like a sudden itch in the place between your shoulders where you can't reach it and he wanted so much to know about this thing, this silver thing that had obviously traveled a gazillion miles to show up right here, not twenty feet away.

There was a hush. A pause. Like everybody in the prison yard had been playing the childhood game of sling the statue and they were frozen in the forms where they'd landed. Nothing happened, nobody moved.

One heartbeat. Then two.

Paco felt an uncontrollable urge to walk toward the silver ball, to touch the side of it. Was it metal? Of course, it had to be metal, but what kind? In the glow of dawn light, it was almost pinkish and it could have been silk. Silk stretched tight. Was it warm to the touch, carrying with it all the fury and fire of the thousands of suns it had passed on its journey? Or cool? Maybe even cold. Maybe so cold, that if he touched it, his fingers would stick to it, like putting your tongue on a frozen flagpole.

He forgot about his injuries, forgot his pain, forgot his anger, his humiliation, his indignation, his pure hatred and the living fire of revenge in his guts. He forgot about everything in his overwhelming curiosity about this—

He felt a hand on his arm, turned to see that Tiburón had reached out and grabbed him because he had taken two steps *toward the silver sphere* without even realizing it.

Tiburón said nothing, just held on with his strong fingers and shook his head slowly from side to side.

Paco was released from the force that had snatched his soul and hung on, trying to drag it out of his chest. Whatever it was had reached out to him with such power he had been unable to withstand it. It was calling to him, this silver ball. Had been silently calling to him night after night after night. Drawing him forward. But as soon as Tiburón touched him, as soon as another human being laid his hand on this arm, the pull and attraction froze, fractured like fine china and clattered into the dirty concrete of the prison yard. It was such a visceral image that Paco was surprised when he didn't hear the sound of the glass hitting the concrete.

He stepped back against the wall.

As he did, the ship opened. It wasn't like there was a door that opened, either in or out. And he didn't actually see some kind of panel withdraw into the sides of the wall of the sphere, like a pocket door. An opening just … appeared, almost like the wall melted. A portion of the wall dissolved and beaded into the edges like liquid racing from the center. The side of the ship had been flawless and cylindrical and the next instant there was an opening.

Then something appeared in the opening.

Some *thing*.

It was so foreign that it made Paco's skin crawl. Somehow it seemed more horrible than if some tentacled sea monster had emerged from the ship. That would have been totally *other* and it would have been easier to accept *totally other* than this thing, this gigantic white thing that was somehow humanoid.

The giant from his dream.

It must have been ten feet tall, built like a sumo wrestler. It was more than merely pale. It was as white as a tissue paper. No hair, totally bald, and huge eyes, a startling bright blue. It had arms and legs, and ears like a human's, was similar in a hauntingly, horrible way. But this ... this *thing* he was seeing before him was an alien.

An Astral.

A single shot rang out.

The sound was so raw and grating it tore a hole in the air, seemed to rupture his eardrums, ripped open the silence. Not holy silence. There was nothing holy about this thing. Paco had gone to Catholic school. He knew what was holy and this absolutely was not it. But there was such a silence, the creature and the sphere and the whole event had been wrapped in such a blanket of silence that the razor edge of blasting metal was an affront, ugly and not pure. Like finding a cigarette butt in the offering basket at church.

The creature recoiled and blood squirted out of its massive upper arm, as big as a ham or a small pig. The blood was red, like human blood, and the sight of it sent a strange quivering sensation up Paco's spine. The blood was red, *red*. Somehow, this being was like ... us. Somehow. It bled. It bled red blood and it recoiled in pain. It was injured. The creatures he had seen in his dreams had none of these characteristics. They were perfect. They would have been impervious to injury, unable to feel pain. Any being that could cross the galaxies must be so much more advanced than mankind that it would be impossible to harm it.

But this creature had been shot. The bullet had entered its body. It had jumped back in pain. And it had bled. That reality spoke two completely opposite truths into Paco's soul.

There is hope for us, for mankind. We can prevail.

There is no hope for us, for mankind. They have evolved beyond our ability to prevail.

Then the creature was gone from the doorway and another creature took its place.

Paco knew this creature, too, had awakened in sweat-drenched sheets, a scream on his lips from encounters with it. This was what humanity had been expecting, totally *other*, foreign and horrifying. He found he was screaming now, but he couldn't hear his own screams, drowned out as they were by the screams of the other thousand men in the courtyard.

The storm struck then, and black rain, as if from a dissolving sky, poured down.

Chapter Fifty-Three

HE WAS out before first light, gathering up what he would need. It was not much, took almost no time at all to set it up. No one saw him. If they had, he had a plausible explanation ready for why he needed … but nobody stopped him.

He dispatched Lucy to gather up the staff and the houseparents in the wine cellar. She had looked at him funny, not as if what he was saying was odd but because … he didn't know why.

"Dr. Weiss, you look … well, you look good today, sir. Rested."

"Yes, rested. Slept well last night."

"You are probably the only person on the planet who did, then," she said, and burped out a little nervous laugh. "Today is the day."

"Indeed, today is the day. I need you to gather all the adults, everyone, in the wine cellar and all the children in the cafeteria. Can you do that?"

"Yes, sir … but may I ask—?"

"No, you may not ask. But you may know that I want

us all to gather as a group and acknowledge that today is the most special day in all our lives. We must plan what the future will hold, not what will happen to us but what will happen within us."

She was impressed. It was the old Dr. Weiss, the scientist who had devised the most spectacular invention of its kind in all history, a device that converted sound to brain waves. Until it didn't. But the children could hear today, or so it seemed. That was good. It didn't matter one way or the other, but he was glad they would be able to hear him, hear his voice.

He went from his office to the armory. It was particularly warm for a morning in May and he'd worn his suit jacket. It would surely be genuinely hot before nightfall. But by then, a too-warm coat would no longer be a concern and he needed the jacket because of its huge pockets, so he could carry loaded pistols, one in each.

He passed Jocelyn in the hallway, leading a line of obedient students to the cafeteria. They seemed so timid, so frightened. He smiled at them, called out encouragement.

"Stella, it will be fine, dear, I promise."

"Everything's going to be so much better soon, Harry. Trust me."

"Today is not going to be the terrifying day you have been expecting, Miguel. It will be not frightening at all and after today, nothing will ever scare you again."

Jocelyn looked at him quizzically when he said that. He merely smiled serenely.

"Get them seated and put the hall proctors in charge and meet me in the wine cellar. I promise what I have to say won't take long."

When he got to the wine cellar, he was surprised at how few people were there. Once, there had been thirty-one people on the staff and though there had been considerable attrition since Astral Day — God, how he *hated* that word! Astral Day. Nazi Day. Death Day!

"Where are the Hendersons?" he asked when he stepped into the room. "And Margaret ... I don't see—"

"We're it," Lucy Pruitt said. "The whole staff of Zion Academy — you're looking at it."

Perhaps a dozen people. That's all. How were that many people supposed to look after the physical and emotional needs of 120 children during the most trying times of their entire lives? His decision had not come a moment too soon.

He saw Ellie Hampton sitting away from the others, lost in thought. She had something in her hand. From here, it looked like a small blue ball.

"What is it you need us for?" Lucy asked.

"And why here?" asked Jocelyn. "It's a strange place to have a staff meeting."

"Oh, it's not odd at all," he said. "It's the perfect place. Absolutely perfect."

Then he thought of something.

"Oh, no. I forgot ... just wait here, I'll be right back."

He walked out the door, turned and closed it behind him, and twisted the deadbolt. It made a loud clunking sound.

"What are you doing?" Lucy asked. "Why'd you lock the door? We're the ones who stayed, remember, you don't have to lock us in."

"Actually, I do have to lock you in. So very sorry, but it is the only way. You will understand it all, soon."

"Dr. Weiss ... what are you—?"

Someone banged on the door.

"Let us out of here, Dr. Weiss."

"I can say what I have to say from here and the only

way you can hear it is from there. I want to thank all of you for your years of service to these incredible children and your loyalty to them even in the worst of times."

"Dr. Weiss …?" That was Clive Phillips, who'd taught history and coached the girls' tennis and softball teams. He rapped his knuckles on the door.

Bang. Bang, Bang.

"Open up, Dr. Weiss," he demanded.

"Afraid I can't do that, Clive. I am dreadfully sorry to have tricked you, but it was the only way to ensure that none of you tried to interfere."

"Interfere with what?"

"Masada."

For a moment, he felt something akin to vertigo and the thoughts in his mind spilled out, like marbles on a hardwood floor, rolling off in every direction. He stared, unable to think anything. Unable …

Sarah took his hand.

"You will be alright, David. It is a hard thing, but you can do it. We did. You are of our blood."

He looked at them both and wanted to cry. For loss. For time. That he never had the opportunity to get to know them. That their lives were taken from them so young, when he had been granted a good long life. He'd had no children of his own, had always believed that was because he had been too busy, had dedicated himself to all children everywhere. But he recognized the truth now for what it was. He'd not had children because he had understood in his soul that he had nothing to give them, no legacy of courage to hand down to them as courage had been handed down to him. At least, that's what he'd thought. Seemed he was wrong. Now, he ached for the loss of the children he should have had, little ones he was now strong and brave enough to save.

His thinking cleared. He almost giggled because he had the sense of a film shown in reverse, like watching the puffy dandelion fronds carried away by the wind move backward and reattach to the head of the flower. His thoughts did that now. The marbles rolled backwards, gathered in a bunch and his mind was neat and orderly again.

But Sarah and Moses were gone.

Oh how he hoped they would come back, that they would be with him at the end.

"Dr. Weiss, what's going on?"

"What are you doing? For God's sake, man, let us out of—"

"I do hope you won't have to stay in there long, but I have no way of knowing how long it will be before somebody comes looking and finds ... what I have done. It won't be so long that you will starve or die of thirst. It's a good thing to be locked in a wine cellar for all that."

"What are you saying?" That was Ellie Hampton. "You're talking crazy."

"No!" He shouted too loud but he couldn't help it. "I am not crazy. I am infinitely sane. I am sane enough to recognize the right, the moral thing to do. Until last night, I couldn't have ... But I have known all along this is how it must be. The lesson of Masada. Of Warsaw."

"Oh, dear God. Dr. Weiss, you're not thinking of ..." Lucy Pruitt's voice gave out and Jocelyn had to finish for her. "You couldn't be planning ... Let us out of here!"

"I have loved knowing all of you. I wish you godspeed in the months ahead as you fight for survival, struggle for the dignity of humanity amid subjugation and slavery. You are the brave ones, for choosing to go on. I ... don't have that particular kind of courage. Goodbye."

He turned and walked briskly away, aware that he had a lump in his throat and his eyes had filled with tears.

There was shouting and banging behind him, people screaming his name. He paid them no mind. Just walked with purpose to the cafeteria to meet the children.

And he felt them with him. Just a couple of steps behind. Moses and Sarah were with him.

Chapter Fifty-Four

When Paco'd dreamed about the monstrosity that now appeared in the doorway of the shuttle, it was just there. It didn't do anything, didn't move. And even then, even as still as a statue, it had so horrified him, he'd dream-screamed in terror. That's what always woke him up, the silent shriek.

His screaming wasn't silent now. And the creature wasn't a frozen horror. It stepped — no, not stepped. Not even leapt. It was so fast, so quick and agile that its movements couldn't seem to be characterized by the normal interpretations of leaping or running or diving. It *moved* out of the ship, splashed into the sea of screaming, sending sound cascading out from it in a symphony of horror.

There was nothing evenly remotely human about the creature. It was as big as a bull, but had too many legs, like an insect. It moved like an insect, shuttled across the ground like a cockroach across a kitchen floor. Its black skin wasn't skin but scales that grated like plates against each other when it moved.

It was black and its head was the definition of every

horror, every boogie man, the monster you dreamed about that was so absurdly horrifying that the very fact of its awfulness was overkill, like that somehow excluded it from possibility because it was too over-the-edge, a bridge too far. Its eyes … it had eyes that were changing color from yellow to bright blue, and its mouth was nothing but teeth that could slice into whatever its claws grasped.

And it did.

The first con the creature came to it ripped to shreds before the man could leap away. His blood squirting in every direction like you'd stomped a balloon filled with colored water. There was nothing left of him but gory chunks of flesh, guts and bones.

Pieces of his body were still falling when the creature had taken another man into its horrible maw.

That's when Paco heard the sound, a strange sucking sound coming from the bowels of the monster, like it was drinking … eating.

Paco and Tiburón were behind and to the left of the opening in the craft. Before Paco had time to think, to blink, there were two … three … five … half a dozen of the monsters — the smallest was the size of a Great Dane, the largest as big as a moose. They devoured the men around them, clawing, biting, rending bodies in a gory bloodbath that slathered the stone walls of the prison with disemboweled hunks of man meat, so thick even the pouring rain couldn't wash away the gore.

Shrieking filled Paco's head, a sound like bedsheets tearing, ripping his frayed soul into tattered rags.

A man's arm came flying at him and splatted against the wall, so close the blood splattered on Paco's face. He didn't move. Couldn't. If it had smacked him in the face, he would have remained transfixed, both feet bolted to the concrete. He had no control over his extremities, couldn't turn and look at Tiburón, though he could feel the other boy beside him, the horror pulsing off him in heartbeat waves.

None of the creatures had chanced to look their way. They all were weighing into the crowd, devouring bodies, a woodchipper grinding through a pile of humanity, throwing out bloody, dripping pieces.

But some functioning part of Paco's brain registered the understanding that when their killing spree was over, when they had sated whatever bloodlust the injury of the other creature had sparked, they would return to the silver ball. And when the monstrous insects turned around, they would be looking right at the spot where Paco and Tiburón huddled against the wall.

Tiburón must have come to the same conclusion because he pulled at Paco's arm, and Paco realized that Tiburón had never let go of it. The larger boy had grabbed him to keep him from stepping forward and touching the ship when it landed and he had held on. Through Grigsby shooting the white, hairless giant, through the buzz saw of dismemberment that followed, he had held on.

"Go!" Tiburón yelled and almost yanked him off his feet, shoved him toward — a doorway!

About thirty feet away was a closed door that led into the building, but it wasn't the one they'd come out. Paco stumbled over his own feet, slipped on the concrete wet with rain and blood, felt the agony of his injuries from last night in the distracted way you might feel a mosquito bite while you were battling a grizzly bear. He staggered, shoved forward by the force of Tiburón's terror. Then his own panic fueled his steps and he leapt ahead, his athletic agility on hyperdrive.

He gained a step on Tiburón, then two, then three. He

reached the door, grabbed for the knob, looked over his shoulder.

One of the creatures was scuttling behind them, closing fast, slathered in wet gore, its black scales glistening with blood too thick for the rain to wash away.

The world cranked down into slow motion. Every movement took a hundred years.

Lifting his hand to the knob. Brown stains on his fingers. Dried blood. His own from last night.

Closing his fingers around the knob.

The door was locked.

"No!"

He didn't recognize the high-pitched voice that shrieked the word. But the timing was off. His *no* echoed after the knob had already begun to turn and the door started moving inward.

He stumbled through the doorway, watched the dirty tile floor float up to meet him, felt its cold kiss on his cheek as his face smacked into it.

Rolling even as he hit the floor, he turned over on his back and slid into the room.

Tiburón was several steps away. The creature was seconds behind him.

Time stops, then. Doesn't slow, stops altogether, comes unhooked from the universe and leaves him, a boy lying on a filthy floor on his back, still bleeding from the repeated rapes that had torn much more than his flesh, that had ripped the whole fabric of his soul and being.

The boy lifts his eyes, sees the terror on Tiburón's face as he strains forward. And he slowly processes rational thoughts that can't have lasted even a millisecond in his mind.

If Tiburón is fast enough, he'll cross the threshold in front of the creature and Paco can use his foot to slam the door in front of the monster.

If the creature lunges before Tiburón makes the door, it will knock Tiburón through it and they both will land on top of Paco.

The world is still. Silent.

His heart stops beating. All life draws in a gasp and holds it, frozen in the horrified scream on Tiburón's lips and the agony of abject terror in his eyes as he lurches forward.

Paco lifts his foot and slams the door shut in Tiburón's face. Then he lies on the filthy tile floor and listens to the creature rip apart his friend.

Chapter Fifty-Five

"Why the mill?" asked Sarah Epstein.

Dr. Weiss wasn't surprised it was Sarah who questioned. It would be either her or Benjamin. They were always the ones who questioned authority. Born of privilege, taught since diapers that they were of a special breed, a cut above all the rest of humanity, many of these children displayed the traits of elitism that had so damaged all mankind's endeavors since time immemorial.

Noah never questioned.

He looked at the boy now, downcast, his blond hair in his eyes. He had a very special place in his heart for Noah Matheson. His only failure. The only child on whom the implant had no effect. He was deaf when he got here and he was just as deaf now, four years later, after countless different variations of equipment had been tried on him.

Noah had a humble spirit, a total lack of arrogance and as far as Dr. Weiss could determine, a totally other-centered worldview, where his own needs were not considered and the rest of the world mattered more than he. He was ... well, if Dr. Weiss had been a Christian instead of a

Jew, he would have seen many Christlike characteristics in the boy. It was a shame that he would not grow to manhood. With his incredible intellect and his gentle spirit, there was no telling what great thing he might have done.

But the monsters had come. And all such gallant innocents would be gobbled up in the terrible maw of their hunger for dominance. It was best it end here, now. The Noah Mathesons of humanity were totally unequipped to live in a world ruled by monsters.

"Why the mill?" Dr. Weiss echoed the question as he walked at the head of the line of students leaving the back door of the cafeteria and crossing the baseball and soccer fields on their way to the old stone building that would have been a water mill but what was actually powered by the sun.

"Because I say so," he said amicably. "And last time I checked I'm in charge and you're not. Is that the way the rest of you remember it?" he said to the others and a couple laughed.

"Aw, come on, Dr. Weiss. Why do we have to traipse all the way over to the mill? Whatever it is you want us to do, can't we do it—"

"If we could do it somewhere else, Benjamin, don't you think I would be taking you somewhere else? And since I am not, it would be the wise and astute student to deduct that the mill is the best place to do what I have in mind."

"You're talking in circles," said Elizabeth Jacobs. Her mother was a Supreme Court justice, and a more sour and unpleasant child he had yet to encounter.

"Circles are better than squares, my dear," he said. "Or triangles or parallelograms."

The banter went on, annoying but gentle. No one actually challenged his authority, just pushed at the edges of it, as was their birthright as teenagers. As it was his duty to push back, make sure they stayed secure within the boundaries.

That would make them into good, decent, caring human beings.

Which they would never have a chance to be.

He couldn't let himself think about that, though. If he did …

The monsters won't let them grow into good, decent, caring human beings. He didn't turn to see who had whispered in his ear. He knew. *The monsters will turn them into monsters, too. Better gone now, as innocents. That is an act of pure love.*

And so it was.

He didn't lead the children through the hydroponics lab and into the mill. Instead, he took them around to the side and they went in through the old wooden door fashioned by monks centuries ago. He went first, securely locking the door into the lab on the other side of the room.

"How long is this going to take?"

"I need to go to the bathroom."

"Michael shoved me."

"Children, children," he said. "Not now. Just keep it together for a few more minutes and I promise you will never have to … come here again. Ever."

"Our whole life? Not even when it's our turn to help Brother Sebastian with the flour?"

"Not even then, Shamus. I promise. Now, sit down."

"On the floor?"

"It's dirty."

"Sit down!" He hadn't meant for it to come out harsh, but his emotions were so heightened, it was hard to keep the calm, still water on the surface.

The small outburst surprised the students and he felt an unease spread through them. But they sat down as he had indicated.

"It's just so the little ones can see me," he said apologetically. He was signing as well as speaking, though he knew that right this minute at least, the hearing aids were working. But not all the children had been here long enough to master the use of the hearing aids. And then there was always Noah Matheson. He looked for him, spotted him seated by himself in the back. Such a sweet, sad boy.

He stepped up onto the stone base of the mill so he was a little taller.

"This is a very special day in your lives, in the lives of every man, woman and child on the planet. On this day, we will make ... contact ... with life from another galaxy."

"Are they going to kill us?" Cindy Roberts asked plaintively, and Dr. Weiss smiled his most kind, fatherly smile. "No, Cindy, they are not going to kill you. I promise you that. You will not die at the hands of these ... aliens."

"Astrals," Sarah corrected.

"*Aliens!* They are *aliens!*"

There was a pause, then he went on with his speech.

"I've brought you here because we're going to have a service to commemorate your acts of valor fighting our enemies last night and to encourage even greater courage in the battle against a more formidable foe in the days to come."

A sudden fierce chill gripped his whole body, as if someone had poured ice water on his head. No, *into* his head, so the cold sunk down into his bones.

How had it come to this? To planning something so monstrous?

How ...?

Before he could consider further, a door banged shut in his soul, as a man might slam a door in the face of an intruder on his porch, some bald, stinking terror come to murder his family in their sleep.

Only it was wrong-side-out. The intruder was inside the house. It was reason that stood outside knocking. But it was too late now, the terror was already poised. It drooled as it awaited the kill. There was no way to put the Boogie Man back in the closet. He was in charge now. Dr. David Jakob Weiss was just along for the ride.

"Now children" — even as he said the word he felt the teenagers in the group cringe — "I want all of you to face forward and close your eyes. We're going to say the Twenty-third Psalm together."

He'd had his way with that as he had with so many things over the years when the parents of some rich child objected to him requiring the children to work on the farm alongside the monks, to say grace before meals and to memorize Scripture. He'd said it nicely, he had a very kind, dignified rap down after all these years, but in essence, he told them, "If you don't like it, find someone else who can make your child hear." My way or the highway, said with a self-deprecating smile.

"The Lord is my Shepherd," he signed and spoke at the same time. "I shall not want …"

As he continued the Scripture, he moved from the front of the room to the back, patting Noah Matheson as he passed.

He stopped at the red canister and reached for the nozzle that would release the gas into the room. He glanced around and saw Noah Matheson watching him.

Chapter Fifty-Six

NOAH WAS THINKING about pregnant women, wondering about them. Mrs. Bland was pregnant. Mrs. Miller had said she was "ready to pop anytime now," and he'd been curious about that. Not the ready-to-pop part. He knew she wasn't literally going to pop and the baby burst out of her like the cork on a wine bottle. He had worked in the shed with the sheep, helped with the birthing of the spring lambs. He knew how the baby would get out.

It was gross.

What he was curious about wasn't about the baby being born but about what it was like to have a baby inside you. He knew women weren't hollow, didn't have a hole waiting for a baby to fill it up. So what happened to all the other stuff they had inside, livers and intestines and stomach, things like that? Where did they go when the baby kept getting bigger and bigger?

He'd asked and Mrs. Miller had told him that the baby gradually took up more and more room and essentially squeezed everything else in there aside. Squashed it, mashed it out of the way so in the end there was only room for the baby.

He was wondering about that because that's how he felt. Not pregnant, but something like that. His mother and sister, what had happened to them, what *he had done to them*, it was inside him all the time. And it seemed to be getting bigger and bigger and bigger, pushing aside all the rest of him, all the rest of Noah, the part that liked to play baseball, and liked to explore dark caves with his father and uncle, the part that enjoyed chocolate ice cream and hated beets and looked forward to Christmas because he'd been a good boy all year long. He supposed that stuff was still there inside him, but it was so squashed up, so shoved over to the side by the huge and always-getting-bigger thing that had happened the day after Halloween that he couldn't find any of it anymore. He couldn't find a desire to do anything, play baseball or scrabble or eat ice cream or crack open a ripe watermelon out in the field and dig the warm, red meat out of it with his hands.

He stepped into the building behind Astrid, and as soon as he did, he could feel the big machine running, the machine with intermeshing gears that moved the stones on the other side of the room to grind the wheat into flour. He could feel the hum through the stones, through the soles of his shoes. Powered by the sun, not by water, grinding away twenty-four seven. He moved to the right to allow others in through the small door after him and that's when he saw the two red canisters leaned up against the wall. He knew what they were for. They were to put the slaughtered animals to sleep before the monks killed them. But what were they doing in here? Was Brother Sebastian storing them in the mill for some reason? That didn't make any sense.

He stood near the back and watched Dr. Weiss sign

from the front of the room. He was pretty sure everybody's hearing aids were working because he could see the other children talking to each other, but Dr. Weiss always signed when he talked. Always. It was one of the things Noah liked best about the man.

"The aliens that have come to Earth."

The aliens were here. Today. Right now. Somewhere on the earth, human beings were looking at them, seeing them not through a telescope but with their own eyes. He had looked up at the skies as the group walked from the cafeteria to the mill, not really expecting to see a spaceship, but thinking maybe … He had no desire to see the aliens, didn't even want to see news footage of them, because he knew it would confirm what he had long been suspecting. The aliens were the monsters that had invaded his dreams before they invaded Earth — white giants with blue eyes and the bug things that had teeth like needles.

Nothing with teeth like needles had come all the way to Earth to be peaceful. If you had teeth like that, they were to eat things with and the thought of those needle teeth made him shudder.

And his gaze went back to the red canisters.

After Dr. Weiss said the part about closing your eyes and saying the words together, Noah didn't close his eyes, of course. There wasn't any way for him to keep his signing in sync with other people's if he didn't watch their hands and his.

"The Lord is my Shepherd," he signed. "I shall not want …"

The others spoke and he signed in unison with Dr. Weiss.

"He taketh me …"

Dr. Weiss moved from the front of the room toward the back and Noah's eyes followed him. When he passed by

Noah, he kept speaking but stopped signing long enough to put a hand briefly on Noah's shoulder.

Noah felt such a powerful jolt of emotion from the touch that it almost knocked him off his feet. Pain and fear and sadness and loss — all tangled up with a fierce joy and exhilaration. Noah had never felt an emotion like it from anyone he'd ever touched in his whole life.

Dr. Weiss stopped on the far side of the back wall and stood beside the red canister. Then he leaned over and put his hand on the nozzle. If he opened it, the gas in the canister would fill the room, couldn't leak out because Brother Sebastian said the walls here "were almost airtight." The gas would put everybody in the room to sleep. Why would Dr. Weiss want them to sleep?

His confusion must have shown on his face because when Dr. Weiss glanced his way their eyes connected and locked.

Why?

Noah hadn't realized he'd mouthed the word until Dr. Weiss signed the response.

"Masada."

That fortress place in the mountains in Israel where the Romans were coming and before they broke down the gate all the Jews inside killed themselves.

"Warsaw."

Where his aunt or grandmother or somebody had killed her students before the German tanks rolled into the city.

The old man's face displayed none of the emotion Noah had felt boiling inside him. It was just … blank.

A frozen dagger of terror ripped open Noah's belly. Dr. Weiss didn't intend to put them to sleep. *He was going to kill them.* Because the aliens were coming, Dr. Weiss had decided they all had to die. That was crazy. And as he looked into Dr. Weiss's eyes, as cold and lifeless as jade green marbles, he realized Dr. Weiss was insane. Dad had talked about that, how some people were losing it, doing crazy things. How the fear and waiting and not knowing ... it drove some people mad. Dr. Weiss was one of them.

"No!"

Noah spoke the word, screamed it out into the world. The first word he had said aloud since ...

He didn't hear the word but everybody else did. Dr. Weiss was stunned and the other kids turned to look at Noah.

He continued to talk out loud, using words. He didn't know if he was whispering or shouting, he had no way to judge the volume or even if he was saying the words right. But they came out his mouth, not his fingers.

"Don't do it, Dr. Weiss. Don't ... please. Don't kill us."

The other children reacted to that. He could feel the explosion his words caused in the crowd. The children leaped to their feet and he could sense what must be a mighty commotion of sound all around him. If any of the children happened to notice the red canister, they all knew what it was used for. And even if they didn't know, as Noah did, that the mill was airtight, they understood the threat.

Then Dr. Weiss took something out of his pocket. It was a pistol.

"Stay where you are," he said. He didn't sign, but Noah could read his lips. He looked at Noah, his face full of sorrow.

"Why did you have to spoil it?"

He shook his head sadly, then anger replaced every other emotion.

"Sit back down. Every one of you. Now."

Slowly, the children all around Noah sat back down on the floor. Some of them were crying, the girls. And some of the boys. But Benjamin didn't sit down. He turned and bolted for the door leading outside, tried to open it, threw his shoulder against it.

"The door is locked," Dr. Weiss said. "Both the doors are locked and I have the only keys. *There is no way to unlock them.*"

But that wasn't true. There was another way to open them.

Noah turned and looked at the ladder that lead to the catwalk above the gear box. If he could climb up there and drop something into the machinery, something big, bigger than a rat, the alarm would sound and the door to the hydroponics lab would open. Brother Sebastian had said it would open even if the door was locked.

"Don't want to shoot ..." Dr. Weiss was saying as Noah's gaze washed over him as he scoured the room for something ... anything to drop. "... not want blood and violence ..."

His mind was racing. Shoes were too small. A stick, a rod, a broom handle maybe, but that might not be big and strong enough. The gears had chewed up the body of the rat, so it would take something pretty good-sized—

Noah stopped breathing. Stopped thinking. Stopped being. Nothing moved within him — no heartbeat, no blood flow. Nothing moved outside him in the room. Every person was frozen as a statue. Astrid with her mouth open, crying. Hank with his face so distorted by fear he was hardly recognizable. Dr. Weiss, his face serene, holding a pistol in each hand — when had he gotten another pistol? — and pointing them at the children.

He did have something he could use to drop into the gear box and stop the machine.

He was not conscious of considering the decision, of deciding if it was what he should do, or even if it was something he could do. There didn't seem to be any thought involved at all, just intent and urgency.

He leapt to his feet and dashed across the room to the ladder leading up the wall to the catwalk that spread out over the gear box of the press. He wondered if Dr. Weiss would shoot him. He'd said he would shoot anyone who moved. But he didn't think Dr. Weiss would go through with it. Or at least that he would hesitate to do it long enough for Noah to get to the top. He just needed those few seconds to get to the top.

But time turned strange. It slowed down. He watched his right hand let go of the rung of ladder and reach upward for the next rung. His hand slid through the air as slowly as a goose sliding forward as it lands on the water. It took an eternity for his hand to reach the rung, for his fingers to spread out and clasp it, then for his other hand to let go and go through the same gradual, unhurried movement upward to grasp the next rung.

Then elongated time snapped back to reality and he was at the top of the ladder, had no memory of climbing more than the first rung and reaching for the second. But he had done it and now he was at the top, stepping carefully out onto the narrow catwalk leading across the open top of the machine. He turned around slowly and looked at Dr. Weiss and they signed a conversation. Most of it. Noah spoke aloud once, one more time before the end.

Chapter Fifty-Seven

PACO COULD HEAR the carnage outside the closed door, the heavy wooden door that stood between him and death.

Tiburón was on the other side of that door. The creature was butchering him, ripping him apart. Eating him. It took only seconds. Tiburón didn't make a sound.

There was a hard *thump* and the door trembled on its hinges. Then scratching, a claw raking the wood. Could the monster *open* ...?

The scraping stopped; the screaming and screeching continued. Farther from the door, though, not close to it.

He lay where he was, unable to move. Unable to breathe. Then he saw the peephole in the door, the slat that moved to the side so someone inside could check to make sure they wanted to open the door to whoever was standing on the other side.

He did not command his legs to move, didn't will himself to get to his knees, then stagger to his feet. He purposed nothing, just found himself pulling back the slat a quarter of an inch. He peeked through the tiny opening, saw that the fray was not directly in front of the door and slowly inched the slat all the way across, producing a hole about the size of a quarter though which Paco could see the eviscerating slaughter of hundreds of men.

He watched, mesmerized, couldn't feel his own body. His whole being was concentrated on that quarter-sized hole through which he witnessed and recorded images that surely would one day drive him mad.

Then the creatures stopped … hunting, stopped chasing the panicked men clawing their way through a huge tangle of writhing humanity jammed against the far wall of the yard, clawing each other, climbing over live and dead bodies to escape the carnage.

As if on command — like they'd heard a silent dog whistle — the creatures turned and scuttled back to the shuttle, scrambling over the slimy gore of mutilated dead bodies, through puddles dark with blood.

Would they get blood on that shiny ship?

Would the white giants be mad at them for not wiping their feet, making a mess on their clean floor?

Paco didn't see them enter the ship. And the next thing his mind recorded was the shuttle beginning to move upward. It floated, like a balloon. It made no sound, no roar of takeoff, no whump-whump of blades. It just moved upward. When it was about three hundred feet above the prison yard, it halted, hung there and the bottom began to glow red. Paco felt/heard a humming sound that grew louder and louder. A sudden bright light flashed down from the bottom of the ship. It was like lightening, so intense the images after it were burned away and Paco couldn't see what the bright light had done.

And then there was silence and the ship was gone. Vanished, as if it had never been there at all.

He moved his head and looked back through the slot in the door with his other eye, the one that hadn't been blinded by the light. He couldn't countenance what he saw. A huge chunk of the wall on the other side of the yard was gone. Just not there. Like a missing tooth on a first-grader, there was a gap fifty feet across, an opening. No pile of rubble, broken stones, smoking pieces of a shattered structure. There was just nothing. The earth was black and he could see blackened lumps of charred humanity, or pieces of humanity, all around it.

The Astrals had obliterated the guard tower on the far wall where the con had been firing, the tower and the wall around it.

It always seemed to him later that he didn't make the decisions that took him away from that place. He had no memory of the decision to open the door.

Don't look down, don't see what's lying on the ground outside.

He leapt over ... something. *Don't look down.* And then he was running.

He didn't decide to race across the bloody battlefield to the break in the wall, had no memory of willing his feet to fly like the wind. He saw nothing, heard nobody, felt nothing.

The next thing he remembered was leaning against the side of a building, heaving, the stitch in his side from sprinting nonstop for — how far? — so intense he couldn't make it another step. Rain pouring on him in a chilling waterfall. He turned then, still leaning against the building, and looked back the way he had come.

In the storm-shrouded distance, above the rooftops, he could see a wall topped with razor wire and guard towers. With an empty spot where the light from the shuttle had struck the tower.

Then he turned and splashed on through the storm.

Sawyer Matheson was standing on the porch of the municipal building in "downtown" Jessup, looking into the sky. Waiting. He could see people up and down the street doing the same thing. It was today. The aliens would arrive today and it was almost impossible not to stand staring, waiting for them to actually show up in the sky above.

He'd seen the newscasts, of course, the big ship hanging over Westminster Bridge in London, the one near the Eiffel Tower in Paris. Huge marbles, not smooth but with indentions and grooves that he was sure were necessary, performed some function his mind probably couldn't have fathomed if it'd been explained.

No place had broadcast any pictures of actual aliens. Not yet, anyway. As the sun crossed the Atlantic and made it today in America, the ships could be seen hanging over New York, Atlanta, Boston and, of course, Washington, DC. He wondered where the president was, because he sure as Jackson wasn't anywhere near the White House. It had burned to the ground yesterday, if rumors were to be believed. He understood there were bunkers in the Blue Ridge Mountains of North Carolina, where the seat of government was moved … in times like these. No, not like these. Not for an invading armada of aliens.

Still couldn't believe it. He shook his head and forced himself to stop watching the skies. Clearly, the ships had come to hang over big population centers and it would take some time, if they gave the planet any time, for them to spread out into the hinterlands to a place like Jessup, Kentucky.

If the aliens allowed the humans to continue to exist on their own planet, of course, and that was by no means a given. All bets were off. Literally *anything* could happen today. Or tomorrow or all the tomorrows stretching out there in front of humanity. The aliens would very likely be calling the shots from now on and it was exhausting to stand around wondering … what they looked like … what they'd say … what they wanted. He wished the creatures would beam down out of one of the marbles and answer some damned questions.

But, so far, all they did was hang there motionless in the sky.

He rubbed his eyes. They felt like he had poured a bucket of sand into them and he knew he shouldn't rub them, knew they must be red and angry-looking, but he rubbed them anyway, remembering back in the day when red eyes gave you away, let your parents know you'd been smoking dope.

Sawyer had not gotten his current state of red-eye in any activity as pleasant as kicking back with a joint. He had gotten it the same way the rest of his officers had gotten theirs. A week of no sleep. Not entirely accurate. He had slept some since Astral Day but he couldn't remember anymore which nights. Time had smeared together. From the moment the first newscaster broke the story …

He'd been making a cup of coffee, he remembered, even remembered how it had smelled. When Hardesty had burst into the room with his phone out, Astral app on the screen, telling the officers they had to see this. He remembered that he had spilled coffee grounds and he noticed just yesterday that the grounds had never been swept up. Footsteps had tracked them everywhere.

Then he had gone into his office, closed the door, and told his deputies not to interrupt him.

It was that way with all life-changing events. You remembered where you were when …

The first man walked on the moon.

The Challenger space shuttle blew up. Did the aliens have accidents like that, setbacks, before they were so advanced they didn't hop a rocket to their own moon but traveled unthinkable distances? He hoped they did, but wondered if the setbacks mattered to them. He hoped they did. It would mean they were capable of feelings and if you were about to be overrun by a race of technologically advanced aliens, it'd probably be best if they were aliens with feelings.

Feelings were a good thing, a normal human thing. That's what had been so strange about last night — the lack of feeling. Dr. Weiss had shot and killed Oscar Higgins. Sawyer knew the man slightly, knew he had people back up in Ferguson Hollow. It would likely take him all day today to find them.

More important than telling a maybe-family that they'd lost a second cousin was going back out to the academy today to check on Dr. Weiss. He was seventy-one years old and had shot and killed a man in cold blood, which should have been a devastating experience. It hadn't been. And that was wrong, all wrong.

As far as Sawyer could see, the old man didn't seem the slightest bit upset about it. Which meant, of course, that he was holding his feelings inside and it had been Sawyer's experience that a man who tried to quash emotions that powerful usually got totally bowled over when the emotions surfaced. And they *would* surface.

The old man hadn't looked good the last couple of times Sawyer saw him, but had looked better last night. On Astral Day, when he'd gone out to Zion to talk about security, the old man seemed befuddled, sort of a Mr. Magoo, only he could see. Of course, everyone was rattled, but it seemed to Sawyer that Dr. Weiss's foundations had taken a bigger hit than most.

He had only seen him one other time since, the night he went to Louisville after Ellie. He had barely recognized the man. He'd been an impeccably dressed man, always polite, almost courtly and just a little too uptight and stuffy. That day, he had greeted Sawyer with his tie askew and his wrinkled shirt tail untucked, dangling out beneath his suit coat. His eyes never actually landed on Sawyer. It wasn't just that he didn't make eye contact. He never really looked where Sawyer was standing, just spoke, launched words, conversational words out into the air. He knew the old man had been devastated when the wonder hearing aid that he'd developed no longer functioned reliably, and Sawyer didn't think—

His cellphone buzzed in his pocket. That was always an interesting experience. His phone had rung non-stop before Astral Day, but after, it only popped out a call every now and then, when the stars were in the correct align-ment to put a call through.

The caller ID identified Ellie Hampton. That was ironic — a woman he barely knew had been able to reach him not once, but twice now when his officers and the rest of the world at large had tried dozens of times and failed.

"Hello, Ellie. What can I do—?"

"Oh, thank God I reached you. I've been trying and trying — all of us have but there's been no service."

"All of who has been trying to reach me?"

"All of us here at Zion. You have to come. Now! Oh dear Jesus, he's going to kill them!"

"Who's going to kill whom?"

"Dr. Weiss. He's going to kill the students."

A boot of fear drew back and slammed itself into Sawyer's belly.

"What makes you think—"

"Just come, run! *Now!* Get in your car and come. I'll tell you what happened as you drive."

Sawyer was already running. His cruiser was parked a

little way down the street and he was sliding behind the wheel and slamming the door as she told him about the ruse of getting all the adults to the wine cellar and then locking them in.

"He keeps talking about Masada." She was sobbing now. "The whole settlement committed mass suicide. Then about his grandmother when the Nazis marched into the Warsaw ghetto — Sawyer, he plans to kill the children!"

Dr. Weiss had mentioned Masada last night and it had seemed so out of context. His calm when he should have been upset. The coldness in his eyes.

"He said he wouldn't let the monsters take them alive!"

Her words stabbed a dagger of terror into his chest. Noah was there, all Sawyer had left in the world. The loss of Noah's mother and sister had driven Sawyer to his knees, had almost punched his lights out. He had held onto the world, held onto life itself for Noah. Every time it seemed too much, that the pain of their loss would overwhelm him, he would consider the little blond boy who never smiled anymore, and he knew he had to make it through another day.

Noah was there. A hundred-twenty other children were, too.

He should have seen it coming.

I won't let the monsters take them alive.

Dear holy God.

Sawyer flew down the road, lights flashing, siren wailing, pushing the car way up past the speed he could reasonably expect to keep it on the road.

Noah!

Chapter Fifty-Eight

NOAH INCHED backward on the catwalk until he was standing over the middle of the grinding machine below him. Right over where the big gear mated with the smaller red one that connected to the even smaller blue one.

"Get off there," Dr Weiss signed. "What are you doing? Come down from there."

Noah said nothing, just shook his head slowly back and forth.

"It won't matter. Climbing up there won't matter. This room is air tight. The gas will reach you even if—"

"No, it won't."

That stopped Dr. Weiss. He was confused.

"I'm going to stop the machine." And Noah realized that he was crying. He hadn't intended to cry, hadn't even been aware that he was doing it but apparently he'd been crying the whole time he climbed up the ladder because his cheeks were wet with tears and his nose was running down his upper lip.

He reached up and wiped his nose with the back of his hand.

"You can't stop the machine. Why would you want to—?"

"Brother Sebastian told me. He said if something gets stuck in the gears," he pointed down to the moving pieces of precise metal below him, grinding slowly along, "the alarm will sound and the door into the hydroponics lab will open."

Dr. Weiss's eyes shot open wide at that.

"No, Noah, you're mistaken. I have the keys to the doors."

"Brother Sebastian said the door would open automatically even if it was locked."

He thought of what else the old monk had said and he smiled. Sobbing, he smiled. "He said his underwear would drop off automatically, too."

"Noah, you aren't making any sense. Come down off there. You have nothing to drop into the gears to jam—"

"Yes I do. I have me."

It took Dr. Weiss a moment to grasp what he was saying and when he did, the horror that registered on the old man's face made Noah feel terribly sorry for him.

He was sorry for his father, too. It was a terrible thing to take away the last of his family, but it was right. It fit. As soon as the idea had formed in Noah's mind, it felt like a piece of a puzzle, the lone missing piece, the one with strange edges and corners, the one that left a hole no other piece could possibly fill. The puzzle was the picture of his family that his father kept on his desk at the sheriff's office. Mom, Rosileigh, in that cute little yellow dress that made her look like a munchkin. They were all looking out at the camera, smiling. The puzzle of that family had shattered the day he had killed his mother and baby sister, had broken into a million pieces so sharp they would slice you open if you dared to touch one, dared to try to pick them up and reassemble them into family again.

But he had tried to put it back together again, or it seemed like he tried. All his effort had done nothing but cut his hands until they were bleeding, dripping blood into the rest of his life. But now he saw the picture was assembled, with some smudged blood on some of the pieces but back together. It lacked only the one final piece. This.

Noah would give his life as a payment for theirs. He had taken lives, now he was giving lives back. It was unarguably right. Justice. His life for theirs. A more than even trade.

He looked down into the grinding gears and considered what it would feel like to be crushed to death by them, ground up into hamburger like Brother Sebastian had said had happened to the rat. And he was so afraid he began to shake all over.

He'd been shaking that day, too. His hands had been trembling, but not from fear. From cold. It was so cold he couldn't work. That's why he'd done it, because it was so cold. That's why he'd started the fire. All the memories flowed over him in a series of images that ripped open his soul. His mother's screams, his baby sister's ... He couldn't stand the sounds of their screams, their shrieking. He had dropped to his knees on the porch and put his hands over his ears, shaking his head back and forth, blotting out the sound of their screams and his own.

Memory stopped there.

The next memory was not knit to the others. It had been a clean break. That had happened and then he had opened his eyes and he wasn't on his knees on the porch anymore. He was lying on his back on a white pillow in a hospital bed where the sheets smelled like bleach.

His father was there, sitting in a chair beside the bed.

His head in his hands, looking haggard and devastated, his whole face a mirror of the pain in his soul.

Only one thing had remained the same in the two scenes. He had stopped up his ears so he couldn't hear the screaming, and his ears had remained stopped up. His father called his name, threw his arms around him, the nurses came in talking to Dad and to each other.

But he didn't hear them.

His world was silent, no screaming — packed in cotton. Totally deaf.

"Noah, no!" He saw Dr. Weiss's mouth form the "o," and watched him raise the pistol and point it at Noah. Not really aiming, like he really intended to shoot him. Just reflexively, a demand that he stop what he was doing immediately.

Noah gasped and spoke out loud again, he didn't know how loud.

"Yes, please. *Shoot me.*"

It would be so much easier if Dr. Weiss would shoot him. That would probably hurt. Probably a lot. But it couldn't possibly hurt as much as being mashed by a machine, the gears grinding your skin and bones and guts. If Dr. Weiss would just shoot him, he wouldn't have to feel the pain of the grinding teeth. Just the gunshot. Then he would die standing there, his body would topple off the catwalk into the gears, the alarm would sound and the doors would fly open.

Dr. Weiss could shoot the children, he supposed, some of them. He had two pistols but he couldn't possibly shoot them all. And Noah didn't think he would shoot them. He believed the old man was capable of turning a valve and making them all go to sleep — forever — but he couldn't shoot them, rip their bodies apart with bullets.

No, if he would just shoot Noah, all the others could go free.

"Noah," the doctor cried, gesturing with the pistol like he'd totally forgotten what it was, like it was a pointer in his hand and he was showing them how to work a complicated math problem on the blackboard. "Come down off of there, my boy. Come down here and go to sleep with us. You will feel nothing. Just sleep and the darkness of death."

"Shoot me!" Noah cried, pleading. Begging. "Please." He was speaking aloud, as he hadn't done in four years. He was sobbing, too, crying so hard it was hard to talk. "I'm scared of how bad it's going to hurt when it grinds me up. Shoot!"

Dr. Weiss started forward and Noah knew he was about to climb up the ladder, somehow wrestle Noah off the catwalk before he could do what he had to do.

"Stop," he said, and the old man stopped, the gun still pointed at Noah.

Noah lifted his foot to step off into death, whispering now, he thought. Or maybe talking out loud, but softly. He couldn't tell.

"Please. Just shoot me."

The sound of a gunshot shattered the silence.

SAWYER RAN some cars off the road. He didn't know how many. Lots of oncoming cars swerved to miss him because he had made a corner too fast and leaked into the lane of oncoming traffic. He willed his cruiser to go faster, willed the other cars to pull off onto the shoulder of the road or, by God, he would run them into the ditch.

The road stretched and elongated in front of him like those shadowy nightmare hallways where you're trying to get to the end but no matter how many doors you pass or how fast you run, the door final door always stays just out there ahead of you.

He didn't wait until the cruiser had come to a complete stop in the academy parking lot. He unfastened his seatbelt as he rounded the corner and careened into the long drive approaching the school, and when he reached the sidewalk under the portico, threw the transmission into park with a bone-jarring yank, and leapt out.

He didn't know where Dr. Weiss had taken the children. Ellie hadn't known and when she finally surrendered the phone to Lucy Pruitt, she didn't know either.

Nobody knew what method he intended to use to … execute the children. Perhaps he planned to poison them. If so, he'd have taken them to the kitchen or maybe the cafeteria. But it didn't seem likely that was his plan. There weren't that many poisons readily available in the quantities sufficient to deliver lethal doses to more than a hundred people. He'd have had to plan that out way in advance and Sawyer didn't believe he'd done that. He didn't think the old man had had any intention of committing mass murder even yesterday. It was the aliens coming, coming, coming that had unhinged him and shooting that man dead last night had knocked the old man off plumb and he was unable to right himself.

Dr. Weiss had decided sometime *after* he shot Higgins last night that he would not "let the monsters take the children alive." So given that amount of prep time, how did he plan to do it and where?

Maybe he intended to gas the children, in which case he might have taken them to the slaughterhouse. Slaughterhouse sent chills climbing down Sawyer's spine one vertebra after another. But that barn was on the far side of the farm, a long way to march a group of 120 children.

And it wasn't the best place for such an endeavor. It was fine for putting lambs briefly to sleep, but the building had cracks between the wall slats and under the doors. If the wind were blowing, it would disperse the gas and make it a dodgy business.

But the gas was already on site, available. It required no preparation time and no expertise. Just find a place that was airtight ...

Then Sawyer knew.

He sprinted across the playing fields to the back side of the mill where the only window was sunk deep into the old stone of the building. He stopped running then, could see children inside, knew he wasn't too late. He approached the window slowly, gun drawn. Then what he saw turned his heart to stone.

Noah was on top of the catwalk across the bank of gears that moved the millstones. What was he doing up there? And Dr. Weiss was standing beneath him with a gun! The children were crouched against the walls surrounding Dr. Weiss and Noah. They were also more or less in the line of fire. If he had to fire ...

Then Dr. Weiss raised the pistol and pointed it at Noah, who was crying, sobbing. Noah started to move, like he was going to take a step. Sawyer aimed and ...

Let out his breath slowly.

Didn't pull the trigger, squeezed it. Gently.

NOAH HEARD the sound of the gunshot and tensed, waiting for the agony in his belly, his chest, somewhere, the agony of the bullet tearing into his flesh. It would hurt worse than that time he had slammed the car door on his thumb, worse than ...

But he felt nothing and he swayed, off balance, teetered on the catwalk as he looked up. He saw two things at one time. That wasn't possible but he did anyway. He saw Dr. Weiss's head … *explode.*

And he looked out beyond Dr. Weiss, followed the line of sight through the hole shattered in the window and saw his father in his police officer stance, legs spread wide, both hands gripping his pistol, his arms extended straight out in front of him.

Dr. Weiss hadn't shot Noah.

Daddy had shot Dr. Weiss.

Noah trembled, suddenly terrified he was going to lose his balance and fall.

He looked at his father in terror, teetering. And his father grabbed hold of his gaze, hooked him to the world so he couldn't lose his balance, couldn't teeter and fall. He didn't look away, didn't look down into the guts of the machine. If he had, he'd have fallen right into it. Instead, he kept his eyes on his father, whose gaze held him firm with the fierceness of his love.

Slowly, Noah crouched down until he was on his knees on the catwalk. Then he lay down flat on his belly. He scooted on his belly to the ladder, but lay there for a while getting his breath, taking it all in.

He wasn't dead. The other children weren't dead either.

And today … the aliens were coming today.

Chapter Fifty-Nine

STAR DIDN'T KNOW where the day had gone, had not been aware of the passage of time. She knew that it was evening only because the light that she could see as a bright blob in front of her faded. The sun was going down. The trailer faced due west where she had sat out in the chairs with Uncle Clyde and felt the warmth fade and saw the light fade. It would be dark soon.

And still she just sat. She no longer felt any need to do anything. What was there to do? She wondered, some part of her did, if this was shock. She had heard people on the juke talk about being in shock, and it sounded like people just sat and stared when they were in shock and if that was what it was, then, yes, she was in shock. She didn't know what happened to people like that … did they just sit and stare until they … until they died?

And Star didn't think like that sounded so bad, not bad at all, as a matter of fact. Just to die. Not get killed by townies with guns shooting drunk and crazy. Not killed by some monster with needle teeth, or by some white giant who maybe killed you with his big oversized hands. Not killed by anybody. Just dying. Wouldn't it be like going to sleep? Just closing your eyes and not opening them again? That wouldn't be bad at all. She didn't want to go on in the world without Uncle Clyde with her. She was terrified about the future, of monsters and … just not knowing. She was blind. Who would want her? Who would help her?

She could hear traffic on the road in front of the trailer and the gate to Alien World, trucks mostly, when she sat with Uncle Clyde outside on the porch of the Greater Crater General Store where they sold rocking chairs, not very many, and the Moon Glow Restaurant, where people liked to sit and rock as they were waiting for a table. From the restaurant you could hear the hum of traffic on the road, cars, the rumble of big rigs, the whine of motorcycles.

Now the road was quiet. She hadn't heard a car.

And then she did. A car was approaching, and she could tell that it was slowing down, she could hear the gravel crunch under its tires when it pulled into the drive in front of the gate.

And she heard the shriek of brakes.

Her heart froze in her throat.

The brakes of the car squeaked, just like the brakes of that car last night, one of them that had come shooting guns, one of the ones that had carried the drunk laughing men who had shot Uncle Clyde.

It was the same squeal. The same.

She was suddenly too scared to move even if moving would have done any good.

Pumpkin stiffened beside her and a low rumble of growl came out of his throat.

The car doors opened, all four of them. Four slams, the sound of feet on gravel, approaching the porch of the trailer. Pumpkin in full growl now. He was standing beside

409

her, the hair on the back of his neck standing up, his growl as low and angry as a wolf. She was sure his teeth were bared.

"Well, would you look here what we found," said the voice of one of the people approaching. "Never dreamed it'd be this easy."

"Like coming out and picking up a package old Santa left under the tree. All done up in pretty ribbon." That was somebody else.

The men approached and Pumpkin tensed to attack.

"That dog looks mean," said one of them.

"Shoot it," said another.

"No," she cried, her first words. "Please, don't hurt my dog."

"You ain't gonna shoot that dog," said another of the voices. A man's voice, with a Mexican accent. "You didn't say nothing about killing no dog. I ain't gonna do it, you hear me, I ain't—"

"Fine, fine, we won't shoot the dog. Happy?"

"But the thing's gonna attack if we come anywhere near the girl."

"So here you are, little miss Falling Star Yellowhorse. The fortune teller."

She didn't know these voices, had no idea who they were. But she was sure they were the same ones who had been here last night, the ones who had killed Uncle Clyde.

"So where's that no-good, conniving uncle of yours?"

She didn't answer.

"He around here somewhere?"

She still said nothing.

"Look, you—"

The growl in Pumpkin's throat deepened, so the man must have looked like he was going to touch her.

"You got to do something about that dog or it's gonna bite somebody."

"Tell you what, sweetheart," said the first voice, the one that sounded the meanest, the one that sounded angry, furious, but she couldn't imagine what it was he was mad about.

He was the only one of them who didn't sound like he'd been drinking. He sounded cold sober.

"Here's the way of it. Billy here don't want to shoot your dog. I would. I'd put a bullet in that skull and blow his brains all over the front of your shirt. But Billy here has a soft spot in his heart for dogs. So here's what we're gonna do. You're gonna take that leash and tie that dog to this post. Tie it real tight. Tie it so tight ain't no possible way the dog can get loose. 'Cause if he gets loose, if he comes after us, tries to bite us, I will put a bullet in his brain and that's a promise."

"What do you want?" she finally asked.

"Well, first off, I want to know where that no-good uncle of yours is."

She said nothing.

"Answer me," said the sober man, the one who said he'd shoot Pumpkin.

"He's … he's dead."

"What? Dead? When?"

"Last night. Somebody …" Then she felt her own anger boil up inside her. The rage struck her like a bolt of lightning. She had no idea such a feeling could well up and take over so quickly. "Last night you came here, drunk, shooting. You burned the place down. You did it. I know it was your car. I know. You shot Uncle Clyde. You killed him."

She was screaming now and she had stood, like she might leap at the man, rip his throat out, and if she could see, she would have. She would have torn his throat out, punched his eyes out.

"He's dead? Shot?"

"You're lying."

"No, she's not," said the other one. "Look at her shirt, what's all over the front of it. That's blood."

"Where's his body?"

Star refused to answer, could feel Pumpkin trembling beneath her hand. The slightest provocation and he would leap at these men. And they would kill him.

"You tell me where his body is or I'm gonna shoot the dog." She heard the sound of a rifle racking a shell into the chamber.

"No you ain't," said the Mexican man.

"Oh, yes I am, gonna shoot the no-good mutt—"

"There." She pointed. "Under the trailer."

She heard footsteps, grunting, then a voice.

"Yep, that's him alright. Dead as a doorknob."

One of them laughed.

"We shot him last night and didn't even know it."

"Good riddance."

"Now little missy, you're coming with us."

"Where?"

"Out to meet your little green friends. They're real anxious to take up their acquaintance with you and you're gonna be waiting for 'em soon's they land."

"Tie up the dog."

She knew Pumpkin was seconds from launching himself at the men, so she reached down and took his leash.

"Down, Pumpkin," she said and felt him drop to the ground beside her. "Stay." And Pumpkin would do just that. He would stay where she put him until she spoke the release word. It was the Apache word for go, ch'ilháh, that

Papa Eagle Feather had given her when he helped her train Pumpkin.

"I don't have to tie him. He'll stay until I tell him he can get up."

"Then he's gonna be here till hell freezes over."

"Now you, little missy, come over here. I'm not getting anywhere near that dog."

Star got down on one knee and put her arms around Pumpkin, buried her face in his soft fur. She knew she would never see him again. These men meant to kill her. She had no idea why, but they had come here for that express purpose.

And she really didn't care. She was just grateful Pumpkin would be alright.

She hugged him tight, tears welling in her eyes.

"Goodbye boy, good dog, sweet boy. I love you."

Then she stood and carefully set her foot, feeling around for it, on the next step of the makeshift porch. Pumpkin growled menacingly and barked. But he didn't move. When she got to the ground, strong hands grabbed her upper arm, and she smelled the stench of men who hadn't washed, dirty men who were afraid. Yes, she knew what fear sweat smelled like.

When the man grabbed her, Pumpkin went postal. Growling, snarling, barking and snapping. But he stayed where she'd put him. He didn't move.

What a good boy. Pumpkin was the best dog in the whole world. Someone would come by eventually. Someone would find him, feed him and take care of him. If he got hungry enough, someone could entice him with food. He was, after all, a dog, an animal. Uncle Clyde told her once, "ain't no animal in the world ever voluntarily starved itself to death." Pumpkin would be fine. She believed that. If she didn't, she would not be able to breathe, couldn't do what these men said and they'd shoot him.

"Where we gonna take her?"

"I been thinking about that. They's all sorts of stories about where it was exactly that ship crashed. So ain't no sense in trying to take her back there. But we don't need to. Them creatures is tuned in to her, homing in on her. They know she's here. We don't have to take her nowhere. Just haul her out back, over the hill there."

Then he leaned close to her and his breath smelled worse than his body. The stink of rotted teeth.

"And then we'll make you ready to greet your old friends."

He yanked her along beside him as the men made their way through the remains of Alien World toward the back. There was a hill out beyond the Ferris wheel, where she had hidden last night while these men were killing Uncle Clyde. And then beyond that, prairie.

She could hear Pumpkin, barking, growling and snarling. The sound growing fainter as they walked. She was glad she'd trained him well. It was a tiny light in the inky darkness of her life that her training had saved Pumpkin. She was glad her dog would live to see another day, even if she wouldn't.

Chapter Sixty

ANCIL YANKED Star along beside him, almost pulling her off her feet with every step. Now that he had his hands on her, was actually touching her, he was only barely able to control the need to throttle her.

He'd got up this morning believing that maybe today, the day the aliens showed up on Earth, maybe he would be able to see Edith, Kelly Ann and Stephanie again. Would be able to conjure up their faces in his mind.

He had lost that, had lost their images in a haze of booze and hatred, but now he would get them back, a little bit anyway. The little whore who had sent the storm to kill them would die at his hand and that would open up a window to those he loved. He believed that. He had to believe that.

When he decided last night not to take another drink, he'd thought at the time it would be hard to stop. That the pain and nausea of the hangover the night of drinking had earned for him would be so intense he would have to ease the pain with a drink.

He had awakened with a splitting head, nausea ... and

then he thought of what he would do this day, how he would finally wreak on the whore the vengeance he had held in check since the day he found Stephanie's body under a barn roof.

Hers had been the last body found. And for a gut-wrenching two days he had hoped that she was still alive. It happened, didn't it. People got blown away by tornadoes and still lived. He'd read that somewhere.

Oh, she would be injured, she'd be hurt bad if a twister had picked her up and dropped her, but she would live. He would care for her, he would devote his life to making her well.

And then they found her. She was wound up in chicken wire, couldn't even tell it was her except for the red hair, lying under the roof of the Henderson's barn, and they didn't find her until ... until the smell drew the dogs. It had been a hot spring.

And as he thought about that, about squeezing the life out of the murderer of his family, his headache had eased. Miraculously. It just went away. He wasn't nauseous. Wasn't anything. He felt fine. No, more than fine. Ancil Wickliffe felt fit as a fiddle, ready to do the job and laugh in the doing of it.

This might be the day the rest of the world had been dreading but it was the one he'd looked forward to for a good long time and he planned to enjoy it, yessiree bob, he planned to enjoy every minute of it.

Them little green men in them silver marbles was gonna show up to collect their little spy, their little buddy, and all they'd find was pieces of her. Little pieces.

As he yanked her along he felt at his side for his bowie knife. He'd spent the better part of the day sharpening it on the whetstone, smoothing the blade and smoothing it until it would cut a piece of paper. Shoot, he cut his finger just putting it in his scabbard.

He hadn't planned out the sequence of the deed, the killing. He wanted to strangle her, but she'd die easy that way. It would be better to cut her up into little pieces, a little at a time, let her suffer the way his little Kelly Ann and Stephie had suffered before they died, like he had suffered every minute of every hour of every day since the Easter Sunday morning when the sheriff come to the car lot and told him a twister had hit Slidell and he'd raced out there and … nothing. Nothing left.

He pulled up short about a quarter mile on the other side of the hill that stood at the back of the Alien World property. You could still see the huge sign from here. But it wasn't lighted, so it didn't light the evening sky.

But his eyes had grown accustomed to the darkness as he had turned away from the light and now the moon seemed almost over-bright, casting a silver sheen over the sand, the sage bushes and cactus.

Here would do fine. It was an area opened up wide, with no sage or yucca or cactus. A wide, flat spot.

He shoved her roughly to the ground.

"Put them lanterns all around so we can see what we're doing."

Though Ancil was sober, had been sober all day, Billy and Ray were not, but they'd been sobering up as they dragged the little girl out across the prairie and their bravado was oozing out of them as the booze leached out of their blood.

"Who you think it was killed Clyde Baker?" Billy asked. "It couldn't a been me. I was shooting a piddly little .22 and it'd take a couple or three shots to take a man down with a .22."

"I didn't have nothing against Clyde. He was a showoff,

a big mouth, but being a showoff ain't enough reason to kill a man."

"You sorry he's dead?" Ancil asked. "I ain't. If he wasn't dead, when we got here we'd a'had to kill him to get the girl anyway, so it just saved us the trouble."

"We wouldn't a'killed him. Just hit him over the head and tied him up or something. He ain't the one called them aliens."

They lit the lanterns, set them out in a circle so their light overlapped in the middle, providing a nice lit-up area for Ancil to work.

"What … what you planning to do, Ancil?"

"What do you think I'm planning to do? I'm planning to kill her."

He pulled the knife out of its scabbard and its blade sparkled in the lantern light.

"Then do it," said Ray. "Slit her throat and let's be done with it. I … I want a beer."

"I ain't gonna slit her throat. I'm gonna kill her slow."

He kicked Star where she lay on the ground, kicked her in the side and she groaned, doubled over.

"Hey …" said Billy. "You didn't say nothing about … that you gonna hurt her."

"She hurt me and mine. I'm gonna hurt her."

"I don't know about that. Look, just kill her and let's go," said Ray.

He turned on the two men, their eyes glowing in the lantern light.

"You signed on for this and we're going to go through with it just like we planned. You got that?"

The venom in his voice was as strong as a snake.

He turned around then. Got down on one knee beside the little girl lying in the dirt.

"Billy, you grab her arms, and Ray, you get her legs. She's gonna wiggle when I start to work on her."

Billy grunted, and dropped to his knees. But instead of grabbing her arms like Ancil'd said, he made a strange sound and toppled over on his face.

"What the fuck——?"

He turned full toward Billy then, saw the knife sticking out of his back.

Ray seen it, too, the whites of his eyes glowing in the lantern light. And then he fell backward, knocked over one of the lanterns and it rolled, casting an eerie light out around it, making shadows dance around the sage bush.

Ancil had time to think that, to realize he might have only seconds to do what he'd come here to do. He lifted the knife high above the little girl.

He felt a pressure on his back, that's all, like somebody'd hit him with something, but not hard. And just with a stick, not a bat or nothing like that. A stick, a pointed stick.

He felt his fingers open. He didn't open them, but they opened all the same and he let go of the knife and it dropped into the dirt beside the little girl. He couldn't hold onto it. His hand dropped down to his side. His head was suddenly heavy, his chin dropped forward, and he looked down, looked at the little girl curled in a ball, but it was getting dark. Hard to see.

That's when he noticed the thing on his chest. *In* his chest. Something pointed sticking out of his chest. An arrowhead.

Then the world went dark.

~

STAR SMELLED LEATHER AND HORSES.

But she heard nothing. No rattle. Papa Eagle Feather approached as quiet as a breeze.

Then Pumpkin was there, licking her face, doing the little whine he did when he was overjoyed to see her.

Pumpkin!

Strong, rough hands lifted her up to a sitting position.

Papa Eagle Feather.

"The men won't hurt you."

"Where are they?"

"Gone to the other side, the dark land where ghosts eat their rotten souls."

"Why … did you come? How did you know I—?"

"Your Uncle Clyde called and left a message."

"Called when?" She knew when. When he was hiding under the trailer, shot, bleeding, dying. She'd assumed he pulled out his phone to call the police, 911 or an ambulance. He'd called Papa Eagle Feather.

"What was the message?"

"Star needs you."

"That's all?"

"Just that. Star needs you. Half Moon said the line went dead after he said that. I came as fast as I could. Where is your uncle?"

A sob burst from her throat, exploded out of her body.

"He's dead. He's under the trailer, dead. They … they killed him."

And then she was sobbing again, crying like she didn't believe she could anymore. Like she never thought she could cry again. She thought she was cried out, that as she lay beside Uncle Clyde in the dirt she had sobbed until she had shed every tear she had in her body. But she was wrong.

Papa Eagle Feather sat on the ground beside her, drew her into his arms and held her as she cried. She smelled the leather and cigarette smoke. He rocked back and forth with her as he sat there, humming some nameless tune, or some kind of chant, she couldn't tell.

When she had cried herself out, he said, "We need to go."

"Go where?"

"To the mountains. No one can find us there. *Nothing* can find us there."

He got to his feet and pulled her to hers.

"But first, we will bury your Uncle Clyde."

"What about …?"

He made a snorting sound of disgust.

"The coyotes will feast tonight."

He took her hand and lead her wordlessly back to the trailer.

Day Seven

Day Seven

Chapter Sixty-One

"On this day in one year, I will go to the place where I buried your Uncle Clyde and I will collect his bones," Papa Eagle Feather told Star. "I will put them in the place of the bones of our ancestors. It is a place of honor."

"You didn't like Uncle Clyde, did you?" Star hadn't meant to ask the question aloud. Her emotions were such a wreck, she couldn't control what she said and what she thought. The pain of her grief was so staggering, sometimes she couldn't draw in a full breath.

"No, I didn't like your Uncle Clyde," he said evenly, either not offended that she'd asked such a question or able to keep all emotion out of his voice. That was the thing with Papa Eagle Feather. Star never knew if he just didn't feel anything, and that was why he was so silent and severe, or if he felt the same things she did, got mad and irritated and sad just like she did, but he was able to keep the emotion from showing on his face, in his voice or his body.

But why would you do a thing like that? Why would you keep your emotion from showing so other people couldn't see? Was there something shameful in emotion?

"He did not like me, either, so that made us even." There was just a hint of humor in the words.

She knew she would have to spend time with Papa Eagle Feather, get to know the sounds of his voice and the feel of his body and maybe then she would be able to tell what he was feeling.

Her grandfather said nothing more and she didn't feel the need for talk either. He had brought her out here to the top of a bluff, and she could see enough to know that the blue blob of sky was visible above red blobs of something which must be buttes like the ones in Sedona and the Sangre de Cristo mountains.

He had taken her into the wilderness the night after … well, after. To a campsite with more than just a teepee. Clearly, he had set up housekeeping, in the manner of the old ways and the ancient peoples, and maybe that was where he lived when he wasn't in the little box house on the reservation. Or maybe he had several places like it, tucked away in the mountains and the desert, and he traveled between them as a wandering tribe might have done two hundred years ago.

This morning, after what was probably rabbit cooked over a fire for breakfast, he had broken camp and they had traveled … somewhere. She didn't know, and didn't really care. Her heart was so filled with sorrow and loss she felt hollow, empty. He'd offered her lunch — MagnaPower bars, which seemed so very out of character for her grandfather — but she hadn't been hungry. It was early evening when they stopped. Then he had taken her hand and led her up a winding trail, steep, with switchbacks and crumbling rock. Pumpkin had raced ahead of him and she could hear the dog up ahead of them on the trail, barking at a new creature his nose had tripped over on the breeze.

When they reached the top, Papa Eagle Feather stood

beside her. She could feel the warmth on her face so they must have been facing the setting sun.

"We are looking out over the desert that has remained unchanged since the time of the ancients. The works of men come and they go, they change and they destroy and they pollute. But here, it is still pure."

"Why did you bring me here?"

"This is a special place, a sacred place. It is the place to make sacred promises."

He turned away from the scene before them and faced her.

"I have promised you here that I will bring your Uncle's bones to lie with our people for all eternity. It is a sacred promise, even death cannot break it."

She didn't know what that meant.

He took her two hands in his.

"I will look after you, my kin. I will ... let no harm come to you."

He *did* sound emotional then, a kind of zero-to-sixty emotion that certainly was excessive for a man so used to long silences and few words.

"But ... I know the gods are seeking you. You are special to them, I have seen in it dreams since you were a baby. And I must give you to them. But I will pray to the Great Spirit every day that you will be returned, and the destiny that was written for you in the stars older than the skeleton of the universe, will be fulfilled."

She stopped herself before she said, "Huh?"

"Papa Eagle Feather ...?"

"I have brought you here because this is the taking place."

Taking Place.

"When the earth was young, the gods took our people from this place. Some of them returned. Some of them ...

were never seen again. The ones who returned … had been given gifts to aid their people."

This was beginning to sound like a fairy tale, a bedtime story, but before she had a chance to ask what in the world he was talking about, he continued.

"You were named Falling Star because that was the ancient name of your ancestor who sits by the side of the white giants."

White giants!

Like the ones in her dreams?

He paused. Then spoke words in Apache that she thought meant "Go with God."

Then he let go of her hands and turned away. And he must have walked away, too, though she didn't hear him. Nobody heard Papa Eagle Feather if he didn't want to be heard. She and Pumpkin stood alone on what was obviously a high place overlooking the desert. Which meant she better keep her feet planted right where they were, not move.

She saw light. *Saw* light. Bright, golden light. It was all around her, warm. And the light had texture, as if you could reach out your fingers and rub it between them. If you did, it would be the touch of velvet.

Pumpkin snuggled up next to her leg, his body quivering. He whimpered.

The light grew so bright that it was all she could see. There was nothing in the world but golden light. The world was made of that light.

EAGLE FEATHER STOOD beside the pinyon tree, staring in gap-jawed wonder at the silver sphere that had appeared over the Taking Place. He had said the words, done the deeds, had performed the rituals assigned to him as they'd been assigned to his father and his father's father and his ancestors who first greeted the white giants.

But Eagle Feather was as much normal American as he was Mescalero Apache, as modern as he was ancient. And even after the ships were spotted seven days ago, even after his dreams summoned him to this place, even after every prophesy about their return was fulfilled, in his heart of hearts Eagle Feather had not believed.

Not until now, as he watched the golden light shine out of the bottom of the silver sphere and envelop the little girl and her dog. Watched though the light was so bright it hurt his eyes. And then it was gone. The light was gone, the silver sphere only a spot on the bright sky, growing smaller and smaller.

He went to the place where she had stood, knelt on the ground and picked up the sand that had been beneath her feet. He let it run slowly through his fingers as he watched the spot where the silver sphere had disappeared. Not into clouds. There were no clouds. Just gone.

Star was *gone*, too.

Chapter Sixty-Two

ON THE DAY the whole world was staring gap-jawed at televised images of alien space crafts, Sawyer Matheson was trying to teach two little kids how to skip flat rocks across a still pond.

It seemed like a totally appropriate thing to do — no, like a necessary thing to do.

Sawyer looked at the ground, moved a couple of rocks with the toe of his shoe, then found one reasonably small and somewhat flat. It was hard to demonstrate how to hold it, how to curl your index finger around it to put something of a spin on it, how to throw it *across* the water rather than *into* the water — all while signing the instructions rather than speaking them.

For the one billionth time, Sawyer reminded himself that it was a helluva lot harder for Noah and Gretchen Hampton.

Sawyer drew his arm back and threw the rock. It skipped three times on the surface of the water before it finally plunked to its demise halfway across the pond. Noah and Gretchen tried to do the same with the rocks in their hands.

Plunk.

Plunk.

The children picked up other rocks and kept plunking.

Sawyer turned to Ellie Hampton, who'd shown up in the middle of the afternoon driving Dr. Weiss's car, obviously as traumatized as he'd been by hours spent watching alien spaceships hang over all the major cities in the world.

"You've seen them," he said.

It wasn't a question.

"If any of the networks were doing a ratings sweep today, if there still are networks these days, these were the most-watched newscasts in the history of mankind."

He had sat glued to the screen, horrified and fascinated and scared spitless.

The big round marble that hung over Paris looked like it grazed the Eiffel Tower. The one over Shanghai was the creepiest, he thought. That one had little silver minnows or maybe minions swimming around in the air beneath it. They were already calling those spacecrafts shuttles and the big ones motherships. But maybe these were itty bitty flyspeck things compared to the real *mothership* that was the size of Venus hanging out somewhere in a black hole in space.

"The newscasters say the ships aren't *doing* anything, just hanging there motionless," he said. "Reckon it's psychological warfare?"

"If it is, it's working."

She turned her body slightly to face away from the children, so even if they looked at her they couldn't read her lips.

"Did you … ask him? What did he say?"

"I did … and he didn't. I asked him — why would he

climb up there and say he was going to jump into the grinding gears? But he wouldn't tell me."

They stood silently watching the children throw rocks into the water.

"Brother Sebastian told me that he'd had a conversation with Noah just a few days ago and they'd talked about how the door would open automatically if something gummed up the gears. That's what he was planning to do."

"But why? He's a little boy, twelve years old. *Adults* don't have that kind of courage."

"It didn't look like courage to me." Sawyer's voice was soft. "It looked like desperation, with a side order of resignation."

She didn't ask what he meant and he explained as far as he was willing to go.

"Ever since … you know there was a fire, and his mother and little sister—"

"Yes, I know."

"He was there. We found him on the back porch with a head wound where a rafter or something had fallen on him. I only asked him one time what he saw … or heard before he was knocked unconscious and he said he didn't remember anything after his mother told him to go get wood from the pile behind the barn."

Sawyer had never believed that.

"He's a different person altogether now than he was before their deaths. Four years of … depression, maybe. I think this might have offered him the opportunity to escape his pain and make that matter."

Sawyer had to resist a sudden, almost overpowering urge to go to the boy, gather him up in his arms and not let go, no matter what, just hold him there until the pain and sorrow left his eyes, no matter how long it took. Instead, he bent over and began looking for more flat rocks.

"Is there anything to drink in there?" Ellie asked, pointing to the now empty tenant house the family who'd lived on the farm for the past couple of years had vacated on Astral Day.

"I poked around, figured I'd build a fire when the sun goes down, maybe Noah and I'd cook hot dogs on sticks for supper. But all the food's gone. There are a couple cans of frozen lemonade in the freezer, though." He started toward the house but she stopped him, said she'd make it, and when he'd looked dubious she'd informed him breezily that she'd just "follow the instructions." She returned in a few minutes carrying a tray with glasses and a pitcher containing a viscous fluid that Sawyer would swear was too thick to be lemonade.

Poor little rich girl that she was, this might very well be her first attempt at culinary mastery. She set the tray down on the huge stump that served as a table. While she poured, he looked out across the pond. This was one of Sawyer's favorite places on his whole farm. He had played in this pond himself as a boy, had swung out on a grape vine over the deep end and let go to fall into the cool, fresh water.

His house had once overlooked this pond.

He turned away from the thought as a man might turn away from a snake before it bites him.

He didn't allow his eyes to stray up to the top of the nearest hillside, where a tree still stood, the one that'd been outside the kitchen window, so if you wanted to go and sit on the porch in the evenings, there was plenty of shade. There was no house there, of course. Someone, likely more than one someone, he never knew who and he never asked, had bulldozed the remainder of the burned-out shell of a house and now, four years later, the spot was bare. They'd even knocked away the foundation stones, which otherwise would have shown through the grass in a box shape, blackened, like rotted teeth.

Ellie held out a glass and he took it, turned it up, took a big gulp and spewed the mouthful of liquid out onto the grass coughing.

"What …?"

"Uh, that's a little tart, don't you think?"

Obviously, she hadn't tasted it, but she took a drink and choked.

"I don't know what … I did what the directions said."

"Did you add sugar?"

"It didn't say to add sugar."

"Most people don't need to have adding sugar printed on a can of frozen lemonade mix to know—" That was a rude thing to say. "I mean, people who make lemonade all the time—"

She picked up the lemonade pitcher and dumped the contents on the ground.

"Hope it doesn't kill the wildflowers. There's one can left. I'll give it another shot, with lots of sugar this time."

Gretchen was looking at her mother and Ellie gave her a come-with-me gesture and they headed back toward the house. Noah was still standing on the edge of the pond, methodically plunking rocks into it, one after another. Maybe he needed some alone time. Sawyer turned and followed the girls. When Gretchen got to the porch steps she turned back to grin at him, but her smile froze.

She screamed.

She was looking beyond him, back the way he'd come. He turned around and a gut-punch took his breath away.

A shiny silver ball about the size of a barn hung in the air above the pond. Noah was standing on the bank, looking up at it.

"*Noah!*" he screamed. No, whispered. He had no air to shout. He began to run, so scared, *oh dear God, no.*

A golden light shone down out of the bottom of the craft. Sawyer was sprinting as fast as he had ever run in his life and knew, *knew* he wasn't going to make it in time. He watched in horror as the light enveloped his boy, concealed him in a beam of brilliance so bright you couldn't look at it.

Sawyer wanted to dive forward, grab his son, push him out of the way, anything. But he was several steps too far away. He dived anyway, slid on the grass. Got within three or four feet of the spot where the grass was still depressed, bent down where Noah had been standing.

Had been standing.

Sawyer scrambled to his feet to …

The silver ball zipped away into the blue sky.

Sawyer sank back down on his knees, threw his head back and wailed.

"*Noah!*"

There was no answer, of course.

The bank of the pond was empty. Noah Matheson was gone.

Chapter Sixty-Three

WHEN HIS BREATHING was finally under control, Paco looked around, trying to orient himself, figure out where he was. He had run in wild-eyed panic through the shattered wall that had been vaporized by the round cylinder in the sky, had raced across a field in the pouring rain and he didn't know what then, he had just run, not to anything, just away, away from the nightmare horrors with the razor teeth.

He was leaned against the back wall of the fence around a house on the outskirts of some neighborhood, that little town the cons had talked about. As soon as he'd stopped, sagged against the wall, all the energy drained out of him and he was afraid he was going to fall down.

Nothing he had seen in fevered dreams in the midnight dark had prepared him for the reality of the creatures that issued from the silver sphere, the teeth, claws, scales ... bugs, dear holy mother of God, they were *bugs*, insects! The sucking sound. They'd made some kind of sucking sound.

He found himself heaving, dry-heaving. There was

nothing in his stomach. He'd been offered food by Spade this morning before he took the boys out into the yard, but Paco had had no stomach for food. He had none now, either, but he leaned against the rock fence violently heaving, his eyes watering. At some point he collapsed to his knees and remained on all fours, the rain pelting his back, vomiting, trying to get out of his body the horror that had been his every waking moment since.

You're mine, sweet cheeks. All mine.

He hurt then, an agony from his waist to his knees. He only just now attended to the pain, and it stabbed at him so hard he could only barely keep from collapsing into the mud, where he would have spewed the food in his stomach if there had been any.

He had to get out of the rain. He couldn't pass out here, just lying in the mud. He dragged himself to his feet holding onto the stones in the fence, then leaned against as he walked. The fence ended at a garage. There was a back door leading into the garage, but it was on the other side of the fence and Paco knew he didn't have the strength to climb it. He made his way down the side of the garage to the front and found the bay door standing open. No car in the garage. He walked inside out of rain and instantly knew how chilled he had become. He had to get dry.

Crossing the garage to the door leading into the house, he tried the knob. Unlocked. He opened it carefully. The door led to a utility laundry room. The door leading from that room into the rest of the house *was* locked.

His thoughts were brittle abrupt commands. *Out of the clothes.*

The prison orange identified him as one of the convicts who were certainly now running off in all directions, taking what they wanted ... taking *who* they wanted. He ripped off the orange shirt, kicked off his shoes and then carefully eased down the baggy, blood-soaked pants. Standing naked, he used the wet shirt to clean himself off. He was still bleeding, but not as he had been before. There were clothes hanging all around and stacks of sheets and towels. He toweled off and dug through the clothing for something to put on. Nothing but children's clothes. But a pair of black sweatpants were hanging from a hook on the back door — some dude wore them when he went to the gym. They were only about a size too big.

Standing there dry, getting warm, the full impact of everything that had happened hammered Paco and he sank down to the floor. He grabbed a pile of towels, didn't bother to spread them out, just lay down on the pile of them, used a couple of the big ones to cover himself. He'd just lie here long enough to get warm, to consider what to do. Just rest for a little while.

He awoke and sat bolt upright! He'd heard … the sounds of movement in the house. Somebody was home. He stood, woozy, in pain. He had no idea how long he had been in the windowless laundry room. When he opened the door, and stepped out into the garage, the rain had stopped and it was almost sundown. There was still no car in the garage and the voices from inside were loud and gruff. Not the family who lived here. *Escapees from the prison.*

His heart was suddenly in his chest and he eased the door behind him closed. The sounds grew louder, doors banging, like someone searching the kitchen, things falling and breaking. He heard a voice nearer than the others. One of them had gone into the laundry room.

"Hey, look at this—" a man's voice called out. He'd seen Paco's orange shirt and pants. Paco bolted out of the garage, barefoot and shirtless, racing through the damp evening air into the street.

He heard a cry behind him.

"Ain't that Spade's bitch?"

He didn't look back, just ran as fast as he could, turned up the first alley he came to and glanced over his shoulder.

Three large men in orange prison jumpsuits were charging up the street after him. He raced down the alley, straining toward the street beyond and then staggered to a stop. It was a blind alley. A dead end.

Time slowed down as Paco stepped back into a nightmare. He turned slowly around, saw the men race into the alley from the street and then they, too, stopped running.

He was trapped, his heart pulsing in his ears so loud he could barely hear what they were saying.

"Spade gonna appreciate it if we bring him back his bitch."

Spade had survived. Of course he had. He'd been on the top of the wall when the monsters attacked.

Paco understood with a calm clarity that he would die here, standing in a puddle in this alley with the stink of the nearby dumpster in his nostrils. They would have to kill him. He would never allow them to take him back.

A sudden blinding light shined down on him from above, a shroud of sparkling golden crystals. He watched the shadows around the dumpster leap back from it. A rat stopped and stared. The men coming down the alley froze with looks of horror on their faces.

Then the light burned away the images from the alley. Enveloped him. Engulfed him. It was warm on his skin, soft like velvet. It felt … good.

Chapter Sixty-Four

WHEN THE BRILLIANCE of the light faded and Paco could see again, he was no longer standing in an alley with a startled rat, three convicts and the stink of a dumpster in his nostrils.

He was standing barefoot in a small white room, the size of a walk-in closet. The floor, walls, ceiling and bench were all one thing, a single piece of molded white plastic. No doors. No windows. Just white all around. Only it didn't feel like plastic. The floor felt somehow soft, not cold but as warm as a vinyl chair where somebody had sat before you. He was looking down at his feet. They weren't wet but he had been standing in a puddle in the alley.

And he felt no pain. Wonder spread through him. The pain of the rape was *gone*. Not the memory, but the pain. *Nothing hurt anywhere.*

Where ...?

He knew but wouldn't let himself know.

It couldn't ...

But, of course, it could. It was.

The bright light shining down on him, he'd seen a light

like that before. He'd watched a light shine down out of the bottom of the shuttle on the wall of the prison. And the prison wall vanished.

Just like he had vanished out of the alley.

The wall of the prison had disintegrated in the light, but Paco hadn't. The light hadn't *destroyed* him, but clearly it had *moved* him. He wasn't in the alley anymore. So where was …?

Was …?

Nowhere on Earth looked like this because he wasn't on Earth. Dear holy mother of God he was inside …

He had been *kidnapped*. He was in one of those silver balls with the bug monsters with needle teeth. He looked frantically around for some way out but the walls were utterly smooth, as featureless as the outside of the shuttle that'd landed in the prison yard.

Then he heard, no, *sensed* a presence, like someone was with him in the room. He turned and saw a boy with blond hair who hadn't been there an eye-blink ago. The room was bigger, too, big enough now for two people.

Paco froze. This wasn't *a* boy. It was *the* boy. Him, the boy Paco had been dreaming about. The boy was staring at Paco with such a look of shock on his face, Paco wondered if he had transformed into one of the needle-toothed monsters. The boy didn't back away, though. Just stared.

"Who are you?" Paco demanded, his voice tinny in his ears.

The boy just looked at him, said nothing.

I can't hear you. I'm deaf.

The words did not come out of the boy's mouth. They had formed inside Paco's head.

∼

THE SKULL *with the spider and the snake.* It was right there on the bare chest of the boy in black sweatpants. Just like Noah had seen it a hundred times in dreams. A thousand times. And maybe this was a—

You ain't dreaming, kid. This is real.

Noah heard the words in his head as clear as if someone had spoken them.

He stared in amazement at the tattooed boy, who looked as shocked and surprised as he was.

Noah's mind went blank. He moved his eyes to … to nothing. There was nothing, just white all around, a white room. Bright, but there was no source of the light. Where—?

We're in one of them mother spaceships, said the voice in his head. *We … they musta … taken us.*

Noah remembered the golden light.

Yeah, and it felt warm. Almost soft. And then … here.

The boy with the tattoo had not said a word since "Who are you?" Not aloud, anyway.

And then the tattooed boy was looking past Noah, at something over Noah's shoulder. Noah turned and someone else was in the room. A girl and a dog. The girl from his dreams.

STAR KNEW she and Pumpkin had left the mountaintop. The sunshine in her face was gone. The light now was coming from everywhere and nowhere and she could see two shapes, two blobs in the light. Then Pumpkin barked. Not a yelp of fear or surprise or pain or alarm. That was his hello bark. That was the way he greeted people he knew.

You're her.

The words formed in her head and she instantly recognized the voice. It was ...

You're the boy with blond hair and blue eyes. I dreamed of you every night until ...

She had dreamed of him every night until—

I've seen you both, said another voice in her head and when she heard it she saw an image, a memory image from dozens of dreams. A skull, with a spider crawling out one eye socket and a snake out of the other.

Someone else was here. But where was *here*?

We're on one of the spaceships. That came from the source of the image of the spider, the skull and the snake. The words came from there, but she had not *heard* him speak.

The next words ... no, *thoughts* ... were the boy's.

We've been ... taken.

Then the whole world burst into a million tiny points of light and they were no more.

THE END

The Series Continues...

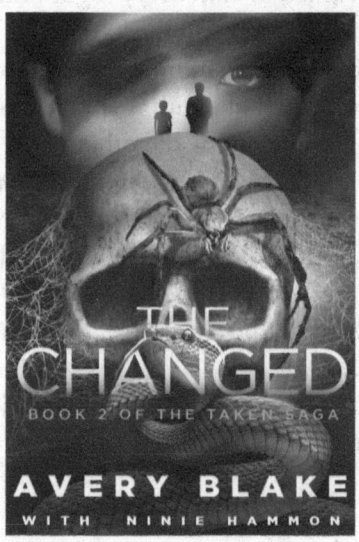

The Taken have returned changed.

Continue the adventure of Star, Noah, and Paco after the are returned from the alien ship and start to navigate across the county to try to find each other.

Pick Up Your Copy of The Changed Today!

A Note from the Author

Thank you for reading *The Taken*.

If you enjoyed this book, you please consider writing a review on your favorite bookselling site so other readers might enjoy it too. Just a couple of sentences would mean a lot to me.

Thank you!

Ninie Hammon

About the Authors

Avery Blake doesn't want you to know where she lives, or what she does. She travels the world, moving from place to place quickly to ensure she can't be tracked. It's safer that way.

When she's not looking over her shoulder, you can find her in the corner of a cafe, facing the exit, typing as fast as she can.

Ninie Hammon (rhymes with shiny, not skinny) grew up in Muleshoe, Texas, got a BA in English and theatre from Texas Tech University and snagged a job as a newspaper reporter. She didn't know a thing about journalism, but her editor said if she could write he could teach her the rest of it and if she couldn't write the rest of it didn't matter. She hung in there for a 25-year career as a journalist. As soon as she figured out that making up the facts was a whole lot more fun than reporting them, she turned to fiction and never looked back.

Ninie now writes suspense--every flavor except pista-chio: psychological suspense, inspirational suspense, suspense thrillers, paranormal suspense, suspense mysteries.

In every book she keeps this promise to her Loyal Reader: "I will tell you a story in a distinctive voice you'll always recognize, about people as ordinary as you are--

people who have been slammed by something they didn't sign on for, and now they must fight for their lives. Then smack in the middle of their everyday worlds, those people encounter the unexplainable--and it's always the game-changer."

Also By Ninie Hammon

Cornbread Mafia

Fire In The Hole

Blown' Up A Storm

Ridin' For A Fall

So Shall The Tree Grow

Nowhere, USA

The Jabberwock

Mad Dog

Trapped

The Hanging Judge

The Witch of Gideon

Blown Away

Nowhere People

Through The Canvas Series

Black Water

Red Web

Gold Promise

Blue Tears

The Taken Saga

The Taken

The Changed